I0577403

ANOTHER BODY IN BROOKLYN

A Modern Crime Story

DAVID GOLDSTEIN

PRAISE FOR
ANOTHER BODY IN BROOKLYN

"Another Body in Brooklyn is a window into life in the ranks of one of America's most dangerous jobs—the life of a police officer. I really liked Sergeant Joshua Rothchild. He works in one of the most unforgiving neighborhoods of New York City . . . and has the drive to make sure survivors of a crime receive justice that all too often slips away in an investigation. *Another Body in Brooklyn* is a dramatic distillation of police life and lore that makes you feel like you are riding in a patrol car responding to 911 calls. This book has the gritty realism of a docudrama, blending cop humor and an inside look at all the moving parts of a police precinct and how they interact. I highly recommend this book."

— Twylla Johnson, Reedsy reviewer, 5-star review

"Bed-Stuy, Brooklyn is under siege in *Another Body in Brooklyn.* The story opens in 2014. The first homicide of the New Year draws Sargeant Rothchild into a case that seems almost impossible to solve, as the victim is an ex-con no one cares much about. David Goldstein pulls together the disparate lives of the NYPD police force and the Brooklyn milieu they operate in. Readers will welcome David Goldstein's compelling, realistic examination of urban policing, racism, bullying, and bravery. An intriguing story attractive to readers of police procedurals and crime fiction."

— Diane Donovan, Senior Reviewer, *Midwest Book Review*

"*Another Body in Brooklyn* is a gritty, fast-paced dive into NYPD patrol life, told with authenticity in its raw dialogue, detail, and atmosphere. From tense street encounters to the relationships between seasoned partners, it captures the compassion officers show crime victims and the underserved—while others see only statistics—delivering a police story as real as it gets. This is a great book to read for those entering law enforcement, seasoned veterans, and anyone who wants to see what policing is really like."
—Christian Gulotta, NYPD Captain (retired),
Owner, Ten-4 Consulting, LLC

"David Goldstein, a retired NYPD lieutenant, is also a talented writer, and the result is *Another Body in Brooklyn,* an authentic and compelling real-life crime novel. Every word of dialogue is spot-on and helps bring characters to life. Joshua is an endearing, complex protagonist. His love interests are especially compelling, and his commanding officer is unforgettable as one of multiple antagonists, which include perpetrators and 'the system' in general. This book is the real deal."
—David Aretha, award-winning author

"As a retired Marine with over a quarter century of service under my belt, I appreciate how loyalty and decisiveness can mean the difference between life and death. *Another Body in Brooklyn* captured this sentiment well. It transcends military and police culture and taps into the essence of duty in a very personal way. Sergeant Rothchild's battles with burnout, lost love, and the siren call of a cushy civilian job mirror the transitions many of us face when the time to hang up the uniform approaches. What sets this book apart is its realism in depicting the brotherhood of those serving to keep our world, and our communities, safe. This isn't just another cop thriller; it's a salute to those who serve on the home front, warts and all. If you're a veteran, law enforcement

officer, or from a paramilitary background, you will appreciate the quiet heroism amid the urban chaos in this book. Great story."
—Yanni Athanasiadis, Major, USMC (retired), Iraq and Afghanistan combat veteran

"A fascinating, realistic look into the world of the NYPD, where good cops have to navigate between a broken criminal justice system and bureaucratic politics that reward coward cops. David Goldstein's writing will give readers an inside perspective of what it actually takes to police a busy urban area and still stay true to oneself."
—Noah Kaiser, educator and coach, LA Unified School District

"*Another Body in Brooklyn* is an exciting portrayal of modern-day policing. The characters are so interesting and believable that reading this book was like watching an entertaining mystery with an overarching story to keep it anchored. Note: This is not a cozy murder mystery. There *is* a murder or two, but the telling is as gritty and real as it gets, while remaining compassionate to the subjects, especially as the story winds down. I couldn't have enjoyed it more."
—Steven Berkowitz, former U.S. Navy Surface Warfare Officer, small business owner

"This is probably the most realistic cop novel I have ever read. The dialogue is sharp and witty, and the plot rolls on like a string of episodes of *Cops* with a homicide investigation to tie all the little stories together. Joshua Rothchild is a good cop who's getting hit from all fronts. Part of the fun of this book is wondering how he will emerge from everything that's being thrown at him. Detective Espinoza is a dedicated investigator whose motivation to solve a crime that isn't on the city's radar any more brings out the best in Sergeant Rothchild and his cops. Every rookie police officer should read this book."
—Joe D., Investigator and retired NYPD Detective

Copyright © 2025 by David Goldstein

All rights reserved. No part of this publication may be reproduced, stored, or transmitted in any form or by any means without written permission of the publisher or author, except in the case of brief quotations embodied in critical articles and reviews.

Another Body in Brooklyn is a work of fiction. Other than any actual historical events, people, and places referred to, all names, characters, and incidents are from the author's imagination. Any resemblances to persons, living or dead, are coincidental, and no reference to any real person is intended.

Crime in Progress Press

For more information or to contact the author, visit www.anotherbodyinbrooklyn.com.

Edited by David Aretha

Book design by Ebooklaunch.com

ISBN (paperback): 979-8-9994112-0-4

ISBN (ebook): 979-8-9994112-1-1

Library of Congress Control Number 2025921670

Printed in the United States of America

This book is dedicated, first and foremost, to my family.
And my friends
– I couldn't ask for better.

I would also like to give a shout out to all the great cops, detectives, and supervisors that I have worked with over the years in the departments I've served in. It's the people who make the organization, even one as big as the NYPD.

CHAPTER 1

HAPPY NEW YEAR

We were slowly circling the precinct boundaries, the rising sun just starting to poke through the low-hanging clouds. It was cold, like it's supposed to be this time of year, but the sun looked like it was going to be sharp and bright when it finally rose, making the outside temperature seem even crueler. My head was still groggy from the New Year's Eve party I'd reluctantly attended the night before with Melanie, my old partner and ex-girlfriend.

Eric Haynes, one of my favorite cops, was driving. He was a heavyset black guy in his mid-forties, average height, about fifteen years older than me. He'd done two tours in the Army, and he still kept his hair in a high and tight. Eric looked like he would speak in a deep, baritone voice. But he usually sounded more like a mild-mannered teacher—unless he was angry, which was rare. "How was your New Year's, Sarge?" He asked this without taking his eyes off the road.

"Well, it was the first New Year's Eve I had off in nine years," I responded neutrally. Every other year since joining the department, I'd either been scheduled to work New Year's Eve or been forced in to work to cover the myriad details, including the big one in Times Square as well as the local precinct details, like the gunfire suppression cars. These details had us driving around the precinct while we tried to stop idiots from shooting their guns into the air—with very limited success, I've got to admit.

"Me too—yeah, probably about nine years," Eric responded. "I almost forgot normal people celebrate indoors without cranking rounds in the air or waiting in pens downtown like animals. It was nice."

"Overrated holiday, you ask me," I replied, trying to keep my voice light. I must have succeeded because Eric laughed. The truth is, by eleven o'clock I'd finally realized the chances of Melanie breaking down and getting back together with me were less than I'd thought even in my most hopeless moments since we'd split up, both workwise and in the more important, Biblical sense. As I left her to ring in 2014 with the other drunken asshole cops, I finally realized that all her bullshit about my promotion and subsequent transfer to a different part of Brooklyn hadn't been the real obstacle to our continuing the thing we'd started toward the end of our partnership, when both of us knew full well that a newly promoted sergeant was going to go to a new precinct, most likely with new hours.

The obstacle was who we were. Me, a barely practicing Jew from Queens; and her, a practicing (if you discount all the swearing and premarital sex) Irish Catholic girl from Staten Island who couldn't live with the questioning looks her neighbors and big family threw her way every time they heard the name Joshua Rothchild.

Eric turned right onto Ralph Avenue for the second or third time. We passed a housing project on our right, the basketball court and surrounding areas empty. New York City at 7:45 in the morning on New Year's Day is a ghost town from the northern tip of the Bronx out to Eastern Queens. The loud music and drunken partiers, the drugs and midnight gunshots into the air, followed by the post-midnight carryings-on and gunshots into actual people, had all faded to silence. Now the streets were empty, save for the occasional trickle of cop cars, newspaper delivery trucks, ambulances, livery cabs, and Con Ed vehicles.

I pulled down the visor to check my hair in the vanity mirror. I'd been in the Army too, but I kept my hair medium-length and styled. Usually, anyway. After drinking so much last night, I'd gotten up late and had barely brushed it. At thirty-one, I hadn't started to go gray yet, and my hair was very dark, set over a decent-looking Sephardic Jewish face. I patted a few tufts down and decided it didn't look that bad. There were dark bags under my eyes that never seemed to go away, though. This was probably due to the stress of this job and the crappy hours, the two main reasons I was considering leaving for a well-paid security supervisor job in downtown Manhattan. A high school buddy of mine named William Stanton ran the security company, and he'd always been a straight shooter. So when he said it was a nine-to-five job with great perks and good upward mobility, I believed him. Besides, he assured me it would all be spelled out in my contract, things the NYPD could never promise.

We drove down Fulton Street. We passed apartment buildings, row houses, storefront churches, stretches of small businesses, many with apartments over them, not seeing a single person other than a couple of homeless male drug addicts. One of them was pushing a shopping cart loaded with copper wire and scrap metal that was definitely stolen but wasn't worth a stop on New Year's Day. Eric made a left at a big chain pharmacy. As we drove down the mostly residential street, we saw a man and his leashed pit bull exit an apartment building mid-block, both looking like they'd celebrated pretty hard the night before. Then we turned onto the normally very busy Atlantic Avenue, paralleling the elevated Long Island Railroad train tracks. Not much traffic there either. I started to tell Eric to make the loop through our trouble areas again when the call came over the radio. Our ears perked up at hearing the address, then our adrenaline got pumping when we heard the rest. "10-34: Male shot in the hallway."

Eric hit the lights and the accelerator.

3

The street number, which turned out to be wrong but in the same building complex as the one the dispatcher had read out, was a big, subsidized apartment complex with several different addresses, depending on which street the front entrance to that section of the building faced out on. To make it more confusing, there were different addresses for all the entrances on each street. The buildings were all connected, though; you could enter one address and exit out a different number or even a different street on the other side of the building. You could run through the courtyard and exit out the opposite street, or you could go in a side entrance and hide out in a friend's apartment in the six-story maze. Unless you knew the place well, you might not even be sure which building you were in.

I keyed my radio. "Central, can you verify the building address, and do we have a floor number?"

Eric drove fast on the mostly empty streets, keeping the lights on but no sirens. We were approaching the location anyway, so it was better to keep the sirens off—you usually don't want to announce your presence prematurely. After a few moments, the dispatcher responded. "Caller says the address is 220, fourth floor. Multiple shots fired. He hung up before I could get further."

I keyed my mic again, cars and street signs and buildings whizzing by me like I was in a movie. "Landline or cell?"

"Non-working cell," the dispatcher responded. "Comes back to a nearby cell tower."

This was important, because it meant that dispatch hadn't gotten the address from the closest cell tower, but rather an actual person who had called 911. Even "non-working" cell phones can dial 911. Only problem is, if it's a ghost cell phone, you have no idea who the caller is unless they provide their information. But the fact that the call came

4

back to a nearby cell tower meant the caller was at least in the area, not making a prank call from far away.

We pulled up one building shy of the address we'd been given. No one was outside; there was no one approaching us and screaming that someone had been shot. With no one to guide us, we ran past the first address and into the actual building, throwing open the outer and inner lobby doors that were supposed to be locked but weren't.

The first-floor hallway was empty. We didn't want to have to deal with the elevator, so Eric opened one of the stairway doors and we ran up.

Eric threw open the fourth-floor door and we turned and looked down the hallway. Nothing. Just the checkered linoleum floor and drab walls stretching down a hallway with, at least for New York, widely spaced apartment units on either side. We walked down the hallway and turned right, then right again, so we could see the entire rest of the floor of this building. Nothing.

Eric looked over at me. "You think it's bullshit?"

With there being only the one caller and no commotion, I was starting to hope that it was. But I'd been around long enough to know better than to give in to wishful thinking. So had Eric. We exchanged a look, then high-tailed it back past the stairway door we'd come out of till we hit a set of double swinging doors to get to the next building. Eric pushed them open, and we walked down this new hallway.

Nothing. We exchanged another look, me seeing the relief on Eric's face and I'm sure him seeing the relief on mine. We walked down the hallway, passing quiet doorways until we came to an L-shaped junction and had to make a right. That's when we saw him, lying stomach down on the floor in a pool of blood, midway between the apartments on either side. His head was turned to the side. Black guy, looked to be in his mid- to late forties. Eyes open and blank.

The hallway was deserted, and the place was so quiet that Eric and I didn't even draw our guns. Instead, Eric knelt by the guy's head and grasped his wrist, feeling for a pulse. He looked up at me and shook his head.

I already knew, having seen that look on enough dead faces. Also, there was so much blood staining the back of his jacket, which had a tight grouping of bullet holes torn into the fabric, that I could tell he'd bled out quickly. The blood was new and hadn't started to congeal; he hadn't been here more than a few minutes. So, whoever called had done so almost immediately after the bullets started flying.

The fact that there was only one call didn't surprise me much; this building complex was notorious for shootings. We took several a year in and around the place, had for as far back as anyone could recall. Most of the residents were scared, tired, or in the life themselves. All categories of folks who wouldn't dial 911 for a quick burst of shots followed by silence. I got on my radio. "One Sergeant, let me get a Level One for a confirmed male shot, likely. Make the address 224 for the mobilization point— that's the actual building—and have EMS come to the fourth floor." After a brief hesitation, I added, though it shouldn't have been necessary, "Put a rush on the bus." "Bus" meaning ambulance.

Cops don't pronounce; only EMS or a doctor can declare someone dead. I wanted them here quickly so I could set up a crime scene right after and wouldn't have to worry about any potential evidence being disturbed. While the dispatcher asked me a bunch of highly repetitive questions, I scanned the hallway, which stretched out for about half a dozen apartments before angling right at a ninety-degree angle to another set of apartments I couldn't see. Just to be safe, I walked down and glanced around the corner to make sure there wasn't anyone there or any other victims. Luckily, the hallway was empty down to the next set of double doors separating this building from the next.

I went back to the body, where Eric was standing, pointing to two shell casings lying on the checkered floor. Unlike the staircases, the hallway wasn't littered with cigarettes, condom wrappers, and empty weed baggies. Only a few random cigarette butts. So it wasn't hard to pick the shell casings out. I stepped gingerly, locating another one near the victim's right foot and another one a little further down from his head on one of the brown checkered tiles. They looked to be 9mm. This being a homicide, I didn't chance picking one up with my pen to check the markings on the back of the casing to confirm the caliber. What did it matter what caliber it was anyway? I wasn't Sherlock Holmes, and we'd know soon enough.

Though we'd only located four shell casings, it looked to me like he'd been shot at least five or six times, judging by the bloody holes in his jacket. But some of the casings could've rolled under his body or gotten caught in his or the shooter's clothing.

Two units, consisting of four cops, arrived on scene. With me and Eric, that was over half the shift. I was amazed that people hadn't started spilling out of the apartments to get a look at what was going on. I chalked it up to it being New Year's Day, coupled with the fact that no one wanted to get wrangled into giving a statement.

EMS arrived soon after and pronounced the victim dead at 0758 hours. I couldn't really rope off a crime scene, not unless I wanted to tie the yellow tape to apartment doorknobs. So I stationed cops at the staircase doors and at both sets of hallway double doors leading into this building. I told them specifically not to let anyone in, even residents, till detectives arrived.

When the remaining four cops I had to patrol the entire precinct arrived, I told them to split up and check every staircase, roof, and floor of the complex. "Mainly it's a perp search, but keep your eyes open for any evidence that might've been discarded."

"Ain't no way they're hidin' in plain sight, Sarge—they woulda' run into a friendly apartment by now," one of my saltier cops replied. He was a five-year "veteran" by the name of McCall, young and sure that after half a decade in this precinct, he'd already seen everything eight times.

I'd been a sergeant for a while now, so I'd dealt with this kind of cop shit before. I looked at the three other young cops and purposefully ignored McCall. He was a clean-cut, tough-looking, lean and muscular black guy, who at six-three towered over the other cops. "Remember that homicide on the 4-to-12 in the projects on Stuyvesant over the summer? One of the perps accidentally shot himself in the leg, and his buddies left him. He panicked, limped up to the roof, and wound up collapsing outside the elevator room. You never know."

The cops nodded and, after a few moments, peeled off and began searching. Thankfully, McCall broke off with them. More importantly, he kept his mouth shut.

I didn't want to start knocking on doors yet, even though this would've been the first logical step. If we started disturbing people, they'd likely try to leave their apartments and destroy the integrity of the crime scene. The apartment at the end of the hall by the bend was a drug location, and all I needed was those assholes getting riled up. Never mind preserving the crime scene; we could wind up having to fight it out with them. It was that kind of building. All the cops working in the entire precinct were already here, and it wasn't that many.

As if he'd read my mind, Eric came up to me. We were maybe ten feet from the victim's white sneakers. "Apartment at the end of the hall's a sale house, Sarge."

"Yeah, he might've been going there, but he definitely wasn't coming back from it." I indicated the bullet holes in his jacket. "No way they'd sneak up on him from that direction. Besides, you think they wanna draw all this attention to themselves, knowing we can get a warrant and tear their subsidized drug den apart?"

Eric nodded. "Good call, Sarge. Might as well let the Ds handle the canvass on this one."

I doubted any of our precinct's Detective Squad personnel would be in for a while, so I figured I'd be waiting on night watch detectives, who covered the hours when the precinct guys weren't working. Either that or some of our detectives would come in from home.

As I looked down at the poor guy, shot in an otherwise empty hallway on the quietest morning of the year, it didn't seem likely that anyone could've been lying in wait for him unless they'd been standing just outside the apartment he'd exited. This hallway wasn't a good meet-up location; nowhere to hide and too many people could be watching you through their peepholes. Better to meet on one of the staircases or even on the roof. So it seemed likely he'd exited an apartment that someone knew he was in. Or he'd been chased out of one and shot in the back. In that case, the shooter probably just went back inside their crib, maybe ditching the gun down the garbage chute in the hallway if they thought of it. I took out my cell and called one of the officers I'd sent searching earlier. "Dominguez."

"Yeah, Sarge?"

"Find a maintenance guy to check the garbage room."

"It's pretty dead right now, Sarge. Only person I've seen's a security guard, and he was looking like he's still celebrating the new year."

I shrugged. "Get *him* to open it, then. You don't have to go through garbage bags or anything. Just make sure there's not a gun lying on top of the trash that just came down the chute."

I hung up. Dominguez was a smart guy. He'd figure it out.

Eric was wearing a pair of good blue disposable EMS gloves and leaned over the body, gingerly patting the outside pants pockets. I started to say something but thought better of it. The guy was wearing slacks, so the pockets weren't tight to reach into. Doing as little to disturb things as possible, Eric pulled a benefit card out of the right front pants pocket. Then he half-pulled a wad of bills and a flip phone out of the left one before placing them back inside. The benefit card had a picture on it that matched the victim's face. So at least we now knew who the guy was and that this hadn't been a robbery. Lawrence Washington, forty-seven years old.

Eric called the precinct, giving the desk officer the victim's info so he could run it on the computer.

I was thinking about who I should notify next when Kevin Chan came up to me. His partner Jose Dominguez was still hopefully looking through the trash room with a hungover security guard. "This place is a ghost town, Sarge. Anything we're looking for?"

I'm five-eight on a good day, but I still had to lean down to speak softly to Chan, who was about three inches shorter. "Simple Simon— just people, weapons, and blood. Or any IDs or discarded wallets."

Chan smiled. "Bursting with hundreds. Right, Sarge?"

It wasn't a very funny line, but I allowed a small smile to show I appreciated the effort. Chan was a wiseass, but a fun one who never went too far. He shrugged, happy to have gotten the smile, his big belly rising up and down under his vest as he looked down the hallway behind me. That's when I turned around and saw a white guy in his early thirties dressed in a suit with a camera hanging from his neck kneeling about ten feet from the victim's head. He brought the camera up and started snapping pictures.

Chan, who was standing not three feet from the body and looking right at the photographer, didn't bat an eyelash. I ran at the guy and told him to get out. He snapped another couple of pics before I was in his face. "Oh, sorry," he said as he stood up, cradling the camera like it was precious gold. "I thought this was public property…"

I should've taken the camera and collared the photographer for trespassing. Instead, I just pushed him down the hallway toward the staircase door, where Jamel Harris, who was "guarding" it, stepped aside to let him pass. I told Chan to walk the guy downstairs and out of the building, then turned to Harris. "He had to've walked right past you, Jamel. What the fuck were you thinking?!"

Jamel Harris was normally one of my best cops—active, respectful, always backing his fellow cops on calls. He had a little over three years on the job, but he was young, probably twenty-four. Jamel had a lean, muscular build like his steady partner McCall, but at five-ten he was almost half a foot shorter and looked like a high school kid in comparison. While Jamel was very intelligent, his street smarts weren't where they should be at this point in his career. He shrugged, embarrassed. "He was a white guy in a suit, Sarge. I thought he was a detective."

A lot of the cops in the precinct were black and Hispanic, more or less reflecting the racial makeup of the area. And while it's true that a lot of the detectives *were* white, Jamel should've known all of them by now and challenged anyone he didn't recognize. Just as importantly, cops guarding entrances were supposed to record the names of everyone entering the crime scene. I was about to yell at him again, but his kind young face looked like it was about to crack in half. So I took a deep breath and walked away.

The guy was probably only wearing the suit because he'd been photographing an event the night before, or maybe had been to a swanky New Year's Eve party. But it had helped him walk right past at least one cop unchallenged, then get within a stone's throw of a body while another cop looked on like it was normal as he snapped picture after picture, ruining the sanctity of our crime scene and fucking over the victim's family in the process. No one should have to see their loved one like that.

This was bad. I immediately phoned the executive officer, who was second in command of the precinct. He wasn't working today, but I knew he always got up early and usually answered my calls. I'd worked for him as a cop back when he was a lieutenant, so we had a good relationship.

"I already got a text, Josh. Fuckin' shitty assed building." I agreed, then told him a reporter got a picture of the body. He was still more pissed about taking a homicide seven hours into the New Year. "I haven't checked yet, but I hope this isn't the first one of the year. I'm gonna get my ass handed to me if it is."

"I'm sure someone got blasted in East New York or the South Bronx already, sir."

"Let's hope," he said before he clicked off. Reminding me once again that we're all going to hell.

After the cops checked the garbage room and didn't find a gun, I had them go to the security office to look at the video feed from the cameras. The video surveillance in the place was horrible. There were lobby cameras that didn't even get a constant feed. They recorded for a few seconds, then stopped, then started recording again. So you missed a lot in the interruptions. There weren't nearly enough cameras in the building, and often they were vandalized by residents and visitors. They were never fixed quickly. Still, a few months before, the lobby cameras had captured the broken feed of a homicide and pointed us to a suspect. So I was hoping that something helpful had been captured. Unfortunately, the security guard in the office was having trouble pulling up the video and had to call the head security guy, who wasn't on site.

I was in the stairwell with Courtney Jones, steering the occasional person away from the hallway door. I couldn't stand to be near the body anymore after the incident with the photographer. Since Jamel Harris had screwed up by letting an unauthorized person into an active crime scene, most likely landing us in the paper, I made him stand by the body and gave Courtney his post.

Courtney usually drove me on shift, but since Eric's steady partner Shayna was on maternity leave, I'd been dividing the assignment up between them due to Eric's seniority. Courtney was a few years younger than me, and on the surface we didn't have much in common. He was a good-looking, wiry immigrant kid from Jamaica who'd grown up in Crown Heights and still lived in Brooklyn, while I'd lived in Queens my whole life and only got to know Brooklyn when I became a cop. He had more of a Brooklyn accent by this point, but you could hear his native accent if he spoke long enough. He was also smooth with the ladies in a way that I never was. We'd both been in the Army, sure, but Courtney had seen a lot of combat during his year-plus in Iraq, whereas I'd only been in a support role on my deployment, never setting foot in country. But we had a similar sense of humor and got along really well, our differences not meaning all that much.

"Even if we get to look at them, we're not gonna get shit from those crappy cameras," I complained to him.

Courtney indicated the landing we were on, with the used condoms and trash. "C'mon, Sarge. You know the cheap Jews who run this place aren't gonna spring for decent cameras. Not for a bunch of black folks."

I'd already fucked up with the photographer. Here was my chance to be the good guy, politically correct and all, even defending my religion. "C'mon, Courtney—the management of this place changes hands so much, you don't know it's Jews who run it now."

Courtney shrugged. "You're right, Sarge. I was talking out of my ass."

I nodded, glad that the matter was settled. For the next few minutes I remained by the stairway door with Courtney, chewing the shit, occasionally poking my head in to look down the hallway and make sure the body hadn't gotten up and moved, as I didn't need anything else to go wrong today. Jamel Harris was standing over the dead guy, looking more alert than Chan had been.

An Orthodox Jew wearing a yarmulke strode up the steps muttering under his breath. "Who're you?" I asked.

He stopped in the middle of the stairway and looked up at us. "I'm head of security. A cop downstairs told me to come talk to you. Sorry about the cameras, but these cheap Jews I work for won't let me get anything better!"

Courtney broke out in a huge grin. The security guy smiled too as I took a twenty out of my wallet and held it out to Courtney. "You can't ever mention this again."

"You know I can't promise that, Sarge," he said, having the nerve to reach for the bill anyway. I yanked it back before he could grab it, though.

I could tell by the way his eyes twinkled that he was going to make a "cheap Jew" joke, but for once he thought better of it. The security guy was sharp, though, and the point wasn't lost on him.

"Hey, you guys are cheap too. You think a waitress wants to serve a black guy any more than a Jew?"

Courtney shrugged. "You're right, man. A lot of black folks don't like to tip either. You guys got more money, though—less of an excuse."

The security guy laughed. "Not all of us, man."

Courtney rewarded him with a friendly smile. "Happy New Year, by the way."

Aside from the fact that it gave Courtney a never-ending stream of ammunition to use against me whenever I fucked with him in the future, the head security guy's presence didn't yield anything useful. We went downstairs to the office and reviewed the footage of people going in and out of the buildings, but there wasn't much action at any of the six or so lobby entrances in the hour before and minutes after the shooting prior to our arrival. There weren't even cameras on the courtyard and side doors that the perps might have had someone prop open or hold open for them to enter the buildings. Plus, there was a good chance the perp or perps hadn't even left the complex but rather just come from and then fled into a friend's apartment.

Once the detectives started to show up, the real ones who weren't just nicely dressed white guys with cameras, I felt comfortable having the cops go up and down the hallway, knocking on doors to check for potential witnesses. "Just be quiet about it," I admonished the four cops standing around me, the body to my back. "I know it's New Year's, but we don't need some assholes running roughshod over everything before the medical examiner gets here and crime scene processes everything."

Detective Espinoza, a middle-aged, square-shouldered former Marine with short, salt-and-pepper hair, nodded. "Sergeant's right. Try not to rile up the natives, least till the body's gone." I liked Espinoza, and I was glad it was our squad guys who'd shown up.

There were several grunts of affirmation, followed by another period of inactivity where everyone just kind of moped around. I was about to say something, but Espinoza beat me to it. "Me and Detective Williams will do the interviews; you guys just knock to see if anyone's willing to open up. We'll take it from there. For now, we'll just cover this floor, this building." He indicated around the corner.

That was an easier pill for everyone to swallow, and they hopped to it, separating so things would go faster. Detective Williams, as tall as a basketball player, positioned himself down the hall from Espinoza so that if someone opened their door, they'd be able to step in quickly to do the interview. When it was just me and Espinoza standing near the body, I asked, "Anything on the caller?"

"Male caller, non-working cell—central dispatch already triangulated it, and it comes back to *this* building, not the one he gave. So maybe he was just visiting and wasn't sure of the address. They couldn't triangulate the location any further—just to this building, not a floor or apartment."

I nodded and was about to ask, but he beat me to it.

"First homicide of the year."

"Shit."

He chuckled. "Lots of shootings after midnight, but no criticals."

The cameraman's photo was starting to look a lot worse. It was definitely going to make the front page, me and Chan standing over the victim like morons. Meanwhile, Jamel Harris, who'd let the asshole walk right by him into the hallway, wasn't even in the shot. I decided I'd give Jamel the next few hospitalized prisoners we had to sit on. He was a young go-getter; that would be a nice reminder to take a homicide scene more seriously and not be bitched out by every white guy in a suit.

The cops got answers at a couple of doors, and the detectives interviewed the tenants. Turns out the victim, Lawrence Washington, forty-seven years of age, had just been visiting an old friend by the name of Simone. She lived in the second apartment to the left if you were looking down the hallway with your back to the victim's feet. Which meant he hadn't made it more than two apartment doors down before he was murdered.

Simone had been showering when he'd let himself out. She'd heard the shots, but figured they were just late volleys of the ones that go off right after the ball drops every year. Or someone had been shot in the complex, which wasn't all that unusual. According to her, she'd finished with her shower, brushed out her hair, then lay down for a nap. It wasn't until my cops knocked on her door that she realized it was Lawrence who'd been shot.

As far as witnesses went, Simone was very cooperative. She let the cops search her entire two-bedroom apartment and provided whatever information the detectives asked of her. When Espinoza finally left, I followed him halfway down the hallway, past the body and out of earshot of the cops, and spoke with him.

"You think she set him up?"

He considered. "Could be. We ran her, she doesn't have a history, but you never know. The way she comes off, though..."

"Yeah, I don't think she had anything to do with it either."

Espinoza let out a sharp breath. "Which means someone knew where he was gonna be, or this was a case of mistaken identity. Wrong place, wrong time for Mr. Washington."

I felt Espinoza's pain. Without video footage, a homicide based on a misidentified victim was one of the harder ones to solve. If in fact the perp or perps had shot the wrong guy, and a video canvass didn't turn up anything, Espinoza would need either word of mouth from the street, positive suspect debriefings, or lots of luck.

"You want me to call K-9 out, in case they never left the buildings?"

Espinoza shrugged. "My boss is coming—I'll see what he says." He exhaled. "I doubt it, though. Only video is on those front door cameras, and it's shit. Perps could've left by a dozen different exits. Besides, doesn't look like they left anything for a dog to pick up a scent."

I looked down at Lawrence Washington. Besides the shell casings, which we'd marked with folded pieces of paper placed over them, and the blood, all of which seemed to have come from his body, the area was bare. No cigarette butts close to the body, no pieces of ripped clothing, bloody handprints on the walls, masks, wigs, etc. Unless the investigator from the ME's office turned him over and he was clutching something in his right hand, which was trapped under him, the chances of K-9 getting anything were nil. The dogs needed something of the perp to sniff. And by the way he seemed to have been shot from behind without even turning around, I doubted Mr. Washington knew he was in danger until he heard the loud report of the gunshots that struck his back and sent him face-down on the checkered floor en route to a quick death.

Usually New Year's Day is quiet. But I wasn't surprised when the dispatcher started reading out calls we had to respond to. That's the way things go. I sent two units—Courtney Jones and Keisha Jackson, and Kevin Chan and Jose Dominguez—out to pick up some of the calls. I had Jamel Harris take his old post by the stairway door, reminding him again to do a better job. He nodded, still properly ashamed. Jamel was a young go-getter; leaving him here was more of a punishment than letting him go answer calls with his partner, the wiseass McCall, who I had watching the other staircase.

I was glad to be rid of Courtney, at least for the time being. The smirk pasted on his face told me he wasn't going to let what had happened before go. Especially after the encounter we'd had with the Hassidic landlord last year, which I thought was laid to rest but would later learn otherwise. I think Courtney knew the whole time. I was glad to be rid of Chan too—how he could just smile and stare at that photographer while he snapped photos of the body was still pissing me off. Any doubts I still had about my upcoming career change were quickly draining away.

Once the Detective Squad sergeant and the medical examiner got there, I left too. I left my driver Eric Haynes to stay by the body as the ME did his examination and the detectives started a more detailed canvass of the apartments. We were holding eight radio runs, and that number would build, as I had only three units out to answer them. And one of the units, Chan and Dominguez, was now on a possible rape. The victim woke up groggy this morning outside her front doorsteps with her pants on backward and no recollection of how that had happened. I had to at least go over there and get the story before calling Special Victims, whom I was sure would be just thrilled to help us out on this one.

CHAPTER 2

ROTHCHILD:
SEXUAL ASSAULT CALL

It was a small precinct, and I got over to the rape job quickly. The victim and her mother lived in a brownstone on Monroe Street on a block of similar, attached homes. The little gate in front of the property was already swung open. I walked up the concrete stairs and entered the main floor through the unlocked security door. Chan and Dominguez were standing over a pretty young woman and her mother in the big living room with high ceilings and a staircase with an old-fashioned wooden banister. The girl, early twenties, was sitting on a couch, her head leaning on her mother's shoulder, crying. EMS hadn't arrived yet.

I was the third male in the room. Nothing a woman likes less than being surrounded by a bunch of men after being assaulted by one. We only had one female officer working today, Keisha Jackson. She and her partner for the day, Courtney, were handling a domestic dispute. It would've been too much trouble at this point to switch her out to come here. So as gently as I could, I got the gist of the story and the young woman's pedigree information so I could phone Special Victims.

I was glad to have Chan and Dominguez with me—two guys in their late twenties with nice, non-threatening faces. Dominguez was short like Chan, but much thinner. He wasn't weak or anything—just one of those guys who never put on weight. Like Chan, he was a big wiseass, and like his partner, he could play it down when he needed to, his dark, slicked-back hair set over a face that could be either handsome or infuriating, depending on whether he was fucking around or not. Neither of them were go-getters by any means. They were good with people, but they would go their whole careers without writing a ticket or making an arrest if they could get away with it.

At first, I walked toward the front entrance. But before I even opened the security door, the cold hit me. I thought better of it and instead walked back into the kitchen to speak with the detective from Special Victims.

It was a common story. Young Shawna is out in Manhattan, partying with a bunch of girlfriends. They're barhopping and by the time the ball drops, Shawna's shit-faced and separated from her friends. The next thing she remembers is her mom shaking her awake. She's lying just inside the concrete front yard of her residence. Her pants are on backward, and she's got no underwear on.

Otherwise, there were no injuries. Before I relayed the last part of the story to the detective, he already seemed put off. "So did she get raped or what, Sarge?"

"She thinks she got raped. Like I said, underwear's gone, pants are on backwards. She's in a little pain, but she can't tell if it's from sleeping on the concrete and holding her bladder for so long or—"

"All right—let me know what hospital she goes to. Your cops gotta fill out a complaint report. Somebody from our office will be there eventually to speak with her. Put my name down—Malone." He hung up before I could say okay.

Quite different from *Law & Order* on TV. In my experience, SVU detectives usually fall into two categories: highly driven go-getters or super-duper lazy ones who are put off that they would be requested to actually investigate sex crimes.

By the time I walked back into the living room, two EMS workers were speaking with the victim. She shook her head violently when they told her she would need to go to the hospital, burying her face in the crook of her mother's shoulder. Chan and Dominguez walked up to me. Dominguez leaned in and whispered, "We got this, Sarge. Mom'll convince her to go."

"Yeah, Sarge, we're good," Chan concurred. "It's getting busy— you've got other things to deal with right now."

I looked over at mom and daughter. The daughter had her mother's dark curly hair and smooth skin. If mom weren't heavier than her slender daughter, they could have been twins from a distance. "It's all right, baby. I'll go with you. It's okay…"

Chan and Dominguez went back over to them as the EMS guys waited patiently. They'd get her in the ambulance without too many more tears, I figured. Still, I lingered. The scene, mom and daughter cuddled up on a soft couch as mom comforted her, could've been for a first breakup or the loss of a prized internship. Besides for the two cops and EMTs standing over them, it didn't have to be a rape. It was so soothing for a moment in that warm living room lit only by the sunlight from the big street-facing windows that I almost closed my eyes and started crying too.

It was then I realized that Melanie, with her soft brown eyes and sarcastic smile, had turned me into a blubbering sissy. I resolved once again to quit waiting for her phone calls so desperately.

The cold air tore into me even as the sun hit my eyes. Fishing my sunglasses out of my jacket pocket, I hightailed it to my Ford Fusion, double-parked behind Chan and Dominguez's Crown Vic. After the warm living room, it was a while before the chill left me, no matter how high I cranked the heat.

The dispatcher came over the radio. "One Sergeant, be advised, you're still in backlog. Holding ten jobs. No units available."

With my left hand I fished my radio out of its holster, keeping my right hand on the wheel. "One Sergeant, any priorities?" If any of the calls were emergencies, someone would obviously have to get there quickly. But most jobs could wait on a day like this.

"No priorities, but there's a verbal domestic dispute that's almost an hour old. Only one party on scene."

Whew. Even though it came over as a verbal dispute, it could have escalated by now if both parties were still on scene. That would've been bad, and I'd have to get over there fast. But knowing the other party could always return and make it a shit show, I picked the call up. "10-4. I'll head over to that one, and you can load me up with the other calls."

"I can only give you five at a time, Sarge," the dispatcher reminded. She frequently worked our division, and she sounded cute.

I spoke as suavely as I could. "Give me the five oldest, Central."

"10-4, Sarge. You want me to read them out?"

"No, I'll call you."

I pulled over and called her, jotting the addresses down on the back page of my memo book. I figured no way I'd get to more than a few. Phone calls to the dispatcher were recorded, so I wished her a happy New Year but didn't ask how she'd spent it. She returned the nicety, but that's when the conversation got back to the jobs I was taking.

This wasn't gonna be it, but I needed something to get over Melanie. Two years is way too long to pine for a woman who's slept with at least two of your former colleagues since you split the precinct—not that I was keeping tabs. If it hadn't gone so bad with her, I'd think maybe I just needed a nice Catholic girl. Or maybe a conservative Jewish woman, cuddling on the couch with me, watching a Woody Allen movie while our six kids ran amok and filled their piggy banks. All I'd have to do is brush up on my Hebrew reading, quit eating bacon, and join a temple. And forget how Melanie's breath felt on my face as our tongues lashed each other like warm hard rain.

I thought about releasing another cop from the crime scene, but I couldn't. Given that it was in the middle of a hallway, it was being manned with a bare-bones crew already. Eric, who'd started the shift as my driver, was with the body, and Harris and McCall were watching both staircases and the hallway.

Wind and sun swirled as I passed rows of attached brownstones, multistory apartment buildings, churches, and bodegas. It was a neighborhood with its own character and lifeblood that flowed through many of its residents' hearts. Folks who could afford to live in other areas had chosen to stay here, through the '90s and the earlier part of this century, when crime raged a block or less from their front doors. Even now, with house prices rising like the crisis had never happened, parts of Bed-Stuy becoming the newest object of gentrification, many refused to leave. They were standing up to the white bullies the same way they'd stood up to the drug dealers and thugs. It was New Year's morning, though, so all the stores were closed now, and the foot traffic was light.

Born and raised in Forest Hills, Queens, I'd known little of Brooklyn before being assigned here to work. But there was something to be said for a sense of community, even if it wasn't shared by everyone. The street began to blur in front of me when I saw a shadowy figure in front and to my right, storming out of an apartment building mid-block. He made a beeline for the street, and I just managed to jam on the brakes before I was staring at his face, not two feet from my windshield. He was a solidly built black guy in his late twenties, about five-eleven with a shaved head. We were less than half a mile from the crime scene.

I was relieved to see he was still standing. I hadn't felt an impact, and his left arm was stretched out so the hand rested on the hood of my car. So I knew I hadn't hit him. Looking at his face, though, contorted in angered bemusement, challenging me to even think that I was somehow blameless, it almost seemed like I had.

Time slowed down like it tends to in tense situations. A few long moments passed, during which he continued to lean down, hand still on the hood like he'd stopped the car with his righteous strength. His lips were parted, and he bared his teeth, eyes trying to bore into mine.

At first, I couldn't move. I'd been in the middle of my musings, which he'd rudely interrupted by darting out of that building straight into the middle of the street, not even close to the crosswalk. The fact that I'd been quick enough to stop the vehicle without hitting him was nothing short of a miracle. That face should be smiling right now, silently thanking me for not laying him out on the concrete. How embarrassing to be struck by a marked police car just past eleven, with the sun shining overhead, you not even wearing a jacket, just a hoodie and jeans whose waistband rode just north of your crotch like you were a little gangbanger instead of a grown man approaching his thirties.

As my initial anxiousness drained away, I got mad. I threw open the door and got out. He stayed right where he was, but his head swiveled so that his eyes were still on mine as I stepped forward and to my left so I could see him fully but not be in his face.

His shoes were expensive Nikes, clean but untied, the laces dirty since he'd been walking on them. The hoodie and jeans weren't shabby either, in spite of the way he wore them. He was solid. I couldn't tell if he had a gut, but his shoulders and arms were strong and thick. His left hand clenched and unclenched on the hood of the car, and I realized he was trying to crush the metal. *Shit.*

At first, I'd been worried this asshole had just been angling for a lawsuit, planning to claim I'd hit him with the car. Any way it played out, he'd probably make at least a little bit of cash out of that strategy. But no, he was too far gone for that. The look in his eyes, which I'd initially mistaken for a challenge, was just blank, drug-fueled anger. Thinking he could crush metal? *Jesus.*

K2, or synthetic marijuana, was prevalent in the area. So that's where my mind leapt to. Some people got really violent after smoking it, detached from reality. Once in a while, especially around the bodegas that sold the stuff, we'd encounter one of these assholes who was just totally unreasonable and wouldn't go to the hospital or jail without a fight. K2's effects on some people were almost like PCP, giving them a resistance to pain that made them seem like they had tremendous strength.

The front bumper of a dark SUV, which hadn't slowed down in the least, almost struck me. I jumped back into my lane, closer to the police car, never taking my eyes off the guy. He turned, but toward the hood, and placed his right hand on it as well. Eyes never leaving my face, letting me know this was gonna have to get resolved the hard way. Thoughts of all the time I'd wasted brooding over Melanie and the lonely road ahead evaporated like they'd never been there at all.

I could tell he didn't have a gun in his waistband, as the jeans were too low and baggy, but his pockets were big and I didn't know what he had in them. Another car passed me from behind, going into the opposite lane to do so. Luckily, I was in my lane this time, and it didn't come that close. Impatient fucking city.

If it were any other day, at least one person with nothing better to do would've been crowding me, recording the encounter with their smartphone. But it was New Year's Day, and there wasn't much foot traffic on the street. Besides the cars passing dangerously close to me and the occasional disinterested pedestrian, it was just him and me in a mostly residential area.

"Do you need help, sir?" I asked in a neutral tone. He didn't answer and continued looking at me with those crazy, angry eyes. I moved forward a step, still keeping to my side of the car and out of his arm's reach. His head swiveled ever so slightly to my current position. Neither of us had taken our eyes off each other since the SUV almost hit me. With my left hand I unsnapped my radio holster and took it out. "One Sergeant, let me get an additional unit at Patchen and Jefferson for an EDP male in the middle of the street." EDP is cop speak for an "emotionally disturbed person." Someone who is a threat to themselves or others and requires an immediate psych evaluation at the hospital.

The dispatcher asked me to repeat the location, even though I thought I'd said it clearly. I was just about to when he shouted, "I ain't no *EDP*, motherfucker! I'm on K2, an' this is New Year's an' a new fuckin' world!"

Luckily, Courtney's partner Keisha Jackson piped up on the radio, "One Delta, we're en route to Jefferson and Patchen for the sergeant."

She stated the location so I'd know I didn't need to repeat it. I took a step back with my right leg and bladed my body, gun side to the front of my vehicle. He pushed himself off the hood of the car, turned, and charged me.

He tackled me to the ground before I could move out of the way. My back took the brunt of the impact, the accessories on my gun belt smashing into my hips. Despite the pain, I rose up into him as he tried to wrap his arms around mine in a reverse bear hug. I got my right hand out and punched him in the face. He reeled back a little, and I hit him again, right in the nose. Blood splattered, and he backed off enough that I was able to break his grip, scooch out from under him, and get on my knees. He recovered quickly, though, and hit me in the temple before I could stand up. I saw stars but came at him again. He tried to head-butt me, but I dodged it, then scooted behind him and tried to get my forearm under his chin to choke him out. I was already dizzy from the shot to the temple, and I needed to end this thing fast. Unauthorized or not, a chokehold was the best way.

Courtney's car pulled up as the guy's left arm flailed back, landing a glancing blow to my chin. I gritted my teeth and almost had my forearm in position to choke him when he bit the back of my hand, taking off a chunk of skin.

I yelled and scooted back, blood spurting out of my hand as the cops ran up. The perp grabbed Courtney's ankle and tried to take him down, but Jackson kicked him in the shoulder. He reeled back, and Courtney kicked him in the stomach. He doubled over, and the three of us piled on his back, forcing him flat onto his stomach. He kept struggling, but we managed to get his arms behind his back and avoid getting bitten again. He was strong, though, and we had to use two pairs of handcuffs because we couldn't get his hands close enough together.

By the time Courtney snapped the cuff tightly on his left wrist, completing the chain, he was already slamming his forehead against the pavement. We managed to turn him onto his side, but my head was too close to his. He spat blood in my face. "I got AIDS! Happy fucking New Year!"

As the blood and saliva dripped into my eyes and mouth, I couldn't help but repeat the statement. "Happy New Year, motherfucker!" I screamed as I drove my fist straight into the side of his jaw, sending his face crashing back on the ground.

We kept him on his side, Courtney pressing his head into the ground until he calmed down enough that we were able to roll him onto his butt and then get him on his feet. My last punch had taken some of the fight out of him, and we walked him over to the sidewalk so we could clear the street, horns blaring the whole time. And here I'd thought there was so little traffic today!

I requested an ambulance for the perp. Courtney was holding onto him on the sidewalk. He was stooped over, shaking his head, blood splaying on the ground. A middle-aged woman passed us, walking way too close to Courtney and the perp. "Be careful, miss," Courtney warned. She shook her head and shot me a look that made it clear she could see that we'd just needlessly beat on an innocent man. The perp made eye contact with her, his sad face letting her know that her impression of what had just happened was right on point. As soon as the woman was gone and the perp stopped spraying his blood all over the place, Courtney began searching him.

The only other car I had out on patrol pulled up, but I had the cops run back to the precinct to get a pair of leg shackles.

"Did he have anything on him?" I asked Courtney. He'd finished searching the perp while I was pouring a bottle of water over my face.

Courtney shook his head.

That sucked. If he'd had a weapon on him, at least, it would've made the collar stronger.

"We'll take the collar, Sarge," Courtney offered, seeing how distressed I was.

Keisha, who'd provided me with the water and some alcohol wipes, nodded in agreement, her dark, pretty face not any worse for wear after the scuffle we'd just had. She was about twenty-five, a few years younger than Courtney. She was only about five-two and had a very shapely body. She was a tough cop, though, as I'd just been reminded.

"Okay, great," I said absently, rubbing my face on my shirt to dry it off and get any of the remaining blood and spittle off. My hand was still bleeding. I applied a shitload of hand sanitizer to the wound and rubbed it in vigorously, then placed some tissues on top. They stuck easily to the blood.

An ambulance pulled up. The EMT's got out and approached Courtney and the perp.

"Are you injured, sir?" one of them asked.

"'Course I'm injured! Fuckin' cops just beat the shit out of me!"

The EMT's threw me and Keisha an amused look to let us know they didn't hold it against us. Then the perp stated, almost as an afterthought, in a much softer voice, "An' I'm still fucked up from all the K2 I smoked. Shoulda' got me a ambulance, not beat on me like an animal!"

Courtney escorted the perp to the back of the ambulance and they got in. He started to give them a hard time. Keisha got in and helped Courtney strap him to the gurney. Courtney would ride in the back with him to the hospital, and Keisha would follow in her car.

The two cops I'd sent back to the precinct for the leg shackles pulled up. They got out of their car and handed them to me. "You guys get back on patrol and pick up some of the jobs we're holding."

They both nodded vigorously, glad they didn't have to deal with this shitshow. I handed the leg shackles to Courtney in the ambulance and he put them on the perp's ankles. One of the EMT's saw the blood-soaked tissues on the back of my hand and asked if I needed an ambulance too. "No, I'm gonna drive to the hospital after."

When the EMTs were ready to transport the perp to the hospital. Keisha headed to her car to follow. As she walked by me, she asked, "Who's covering the precinct, Sarge?"

"Just those two," I responded, nodding at the officers who'd just gotten back into their vehicle. "If we're lucky, Chan and Dominguez will be free from their rape call soon and then we'll have two units."

"I'm sure they're gonna rush back, Sarg," Keisha said sarcastically. "You know how much they love to work." I just shrugged, knowing she was right.

CHAPTER 3

ROTHCHILD: OFF TO THE HOSPITAL

Even though I was the only supervisor on patrol, I needed to get my hand taken care of. Human bites are bad, especially with all the blood I'd been exposed to. If he really had HIV, I was gonna have a long couple of months of worrying.

As soon as the ambulance left, I called Eddie Johnson, the desk officer, who was the only other supervisor working in the precinct. He agreed to handle patrol while I got over to Wyckoff Hospital in neighboring Bushwick as quickly as I could. Having a cop man the precinct desk wasn't unheard of in emergencies like this and probably wouldn't bite anyone in the ass since there were no prisoners in the cells. If one was brought in, Eddie would have to head back to the precinct and monitor the radio from the desk.

The waiting room at the hospital didn't seem too busy to me. But being that I was a cop in full uniform with a giant bite on my hand, the folks at the front desk decided to make me wait while they dealt with other people who probably hadn't just contracted AIDS. After less than five minutes of this, I started to throw a hissy fit and scream until one of the nurses ushered me into the emergency room.

In a little over an hour, they administered a baseline blood test to show I didn't have AIDS or hepatitis at this point and checked my liver enzymes. A nurse provided me with an antibiotic and my first two doses of the "AIDS cocktail," as it was commonly referred to, or "needle-stick regimen." I was discharged with prescriptions for antibiotics and the AIDS cocktail, which is a thirty-day drug regimen that's supposed to significantly lower your chances of contracting HIV. Cops, EMTs, and hospital staff are all familiar with it, one of the perils of a job where you deal with a lot of sick fucks. Before I got promoted, I was guarding a prisoner at Brooklyn's infamous Kings County Hospital. He needed stitches. While the nurse was sewing him up, she accidentally stuck herself with the needle. A nice Trinidadian lady, she asked politely if he'd consent to an HIV test. But the asshole drug addict refused, and she'd had to go on the cocktail and worry for months. We couldn't make the perp take an AIDS test without a court order, which I knew would never be issued. So I was out of luck too.

I'd known plenty of cops over the years who'd gone on the cocktail, so I tried not to be too angry about it. Unfortunately, the cocktail only prevented you from getting HIV. It didn't do anything about other viruses (hence the antibiotics). My HBV vaccine was up-to-date, so I didn't need to worry about that. And apparently, HIV is very hard to get, at least according to the doctor who treated me.

I drove back over Broadway and was back in my beloved precinct by 1400 hours. It was still an hour and a half before the 4-to-12 shift got out, but Eddie Johnson called me and told me it wasn't that busy, so I could head back to the station house to get started on my overdue report on the homicide, along with my line of duty injury paperwork. The AIDS cocktail made you nauseous; some people complained of constant diarrhea. So, with any luck, I'd get a few weeks off to sit in my apartment feeling sick and worrying I'd contracted HIV.

I was standing by the precinct desk when Reggie Braggs, the patrol supervisor for the 4-to-12 shift, came up to me. He was getting ready to do roll call. So I filled him in on what I knew about the homicide, which wasn't much, and more importantly, on the crime scene, which was still up. "You just need two cops there—the body's gone already."

Reggie gave my bandaged right hand a look and then shook his head. "Your year's off to a great start, Josh." Reggie was only about five-five, but built like a tank. He was in his early forties but his smooth, unlined face and thick head of bushy hair made him look like a college kid wearing a weightlifter body suit. When he was younger he'd fought professionally, and he was the guy everyone hoped would respond to their back-up requests when they were in the shit. Our precinct's regular perps called him "Robo-Cop," and most were scared shitless of him. Nicest guy in the world, though.

Two young 4-to-12 cops, a guy and a girl, were speaking by the door leading to the parking lot. The bland precinct walls and overhead fluorescent lighting didn't do anything to help my mood, and all I could think was, *Stay away from her—she'll break your heart and stomp over it while she skips away to find a new guy, leaving you with nothing but regrets.*

An elbow poked me in the ribs through my vest, and I snapped out of my reverie.

"—Sucks, what a fuckin' savage. You gonna be all right?"

I rubbed my sore ribs, suddenly feeling very fragile. "Besides the HIV and the broken ribs?"

Reggie laughed. "You don't have HIV, bro. Trust me. You should get those ribs looked at, though. Felt a little brittle to me."

"Look at the bright side, Josh—AIDS is a great way to lose weight!" It was the 4-to-12 desk officer, Frank Cassella, a big Italian guy a few years older than me, who was in the process of doling out car keys and orders to the incoming shift. As the desk sergeant, he had a lot of responsibilities. That's why most of us younger supervisors liked to do patrol. But Frank had drawn the short end of the stick today. Nothing bothered Frank, though. And no matter how busy it got, nothing could get in the way of him ragging on people.

"I'm not in the mood, Frank." I couldn't help noting the bitchiness in my voice.

Reggie clapped me on the shoulder. "Trust Frank—he knows from experience." He met Frank's gaze, sarcastic smile and all. "You might want to get infected again, Frank. Weight's starting to come back on."

I burst out laughing and knew I'd be okay, even with the prospect of a month at home obsessing over what kind of shit Melanie was getting into with guys I knew and had worked with.

Despite my good humor, though, Frank wasn't quite done. "CO isn't gonna be happy taking a felony assault for your hand. Especially after the homicide…"

He was right, of course. All commanding officers tried to downplay as many of the seven major index crimes as they could, often bullying supervisors to take care of it for them. Our CO was worse than most— she wouldn't care that I'd been bitten and spat on, would just want us to EDP the guy as a psych patient and not record a crime. She hated taking assaults against cops and almost never did. I wasn't gonna eat this one, though.

"This guy Jenkins is a piece of shit, Frank. Seventeen felony arrests. Plus, he's got a warrant for Robbery out of the 75 precinct. They're gonna drop their own arrest number on him."

"All very good points, Josh. You know she's not gonna care about a 75 warrant, though."

"I'm sure you'll lay it out in a very reasonable manner, Frank."

For once, Frank wasn't so cocksure. "Why do I gotta tell her? It was on your tour—plus you're the one who got bit."

I shook my head sagely. "Exactly, Frank. Me having a personal stake in the matter makes it hard to be impartial. Whereas you're the union delegate and a consummate professional. The best possible messenger of bad news."

Reggie was cracking up as I walked away to let Frank know the matter had been decided.

I was working on a computer outside the cell area, not far from the front desk, doing the internal department memo on the homicide, which we called an "Unusual Occurrence Report." It was after five by that point, about nine hours after the shooting had happened. I'd asked a couple of the detectives upstairs, and so far, they didn't have any leads. So the report would be short and sweet. Since the report was already late, I'd completed my line of duty injury paperwork first. If that didn't get done, the job wouldn't pay for my medical care.

My cell phone kept buzzing in my shirt pocket as I typed. I'd check it occasionally, mostly cops I knew calling to see if I was okay. I'd just saved the summary of the homicide on the computer and was getting ready to print it when my phone buzzed for the fourth time in the last two minutes. I answered it without looking at the number.

"How you doing, Josh? I heard you got bit by an EDP."

And I heard you fucked Sanchez in the parking lot last night, Melanie.

I hadn't actually heard this, but something was definitely going on between them or was about to. I'd noticed the way their arms brushed against each other, trying to be casual, by the bar. Then how he'd slipped his hand around her waist, and she'd leaned into him. They noticed me staring and broke it up, and I left soon after.

"I'm fine," I said with finality, looking around to see if anyone was watching me. There weren't many people: Frank Cassella, the desk sergeant; Janson, the telephone dispatch operator; and Kasheem Robinson, who was processing an arrest.

I wondered how she'd found out but didn't want to ask her. Probably one of my precinct's cops, who'd been in the Academy with her and knew we used to date, called her.

She was still talking, telling me about all the guys she knew that had gotten bitten by HIV-infected skells and were fine. *All the guys she knew*. Jesus. Why was I still pining over this girl? What was so special about her that I'd let my heart leave my body and—

"—Josh, you there?"

"Yeah, just a lot's going on. You working?"

"Uh-huh. Hung over, though. You know I'm a lightweight."

It was true; Melanie was 115 pounds soaking wet. Curvy, though, for a skinny Irish girl. She usually stuck to Moscato or something fruity, but last night she'd been pounding shots like she was her alcoholic mother, doing her best to live up to the Irish stereotype.

We talked for a bit as I finally found a working printer I could send the report to. She sounded hoarse. "You gotta drink some water, kid. You sound like your mother."

It was a joke between us; her mother, a chain-smoking, alcoholic Irishwoman who was so different from her modern-seeming daughter, at least on the surface.

She laughed. "I have a cold. Anyway, that drunk bitch never sounded as cute as me."

I didn't laugh. Not only because I was still angry about the bite and the meds I'd have to take. It was everything; Melanie calling me like this, less than a day since she'd turned me down and made clear we wouldn't be starting things up again. Even worse, trying to act like she wasn't a typical girl from Staten Island, so concerned about what her conservative family thought that she'd let what we had derail before it even got going.

The artificial light and stale air in the building, combined with the pills and the fact I hadn't eaten anything all day, were making me dizzy. "You there, Josh?"

The perp who'd bit me was back from the hospital. Deon Jenkins. He told the cops and hospital staff that he'd just been fucked up on K2. This sounded reasonable, since he didn't have too much of a psych history, so he hadn't been admitted. He was screaming in the cells now, kicking the bars—*clang! clang! clang!*—reverberating throughout the room and in my head.

I didn't want to deal with him again, so I ignored the ruckus until Frank Cassella and an officer proceeded toward the cell area to handle it. The officer first put his gun in a locker behind the desk and accidentally banged the back of my chair on his way to the cells. I almost vomited right on the computer keyboard.

"Josh, you there?" I grunted something, the sounds from the cell area of Frank and the officer yelling at the asshole echoing in my ears; Frank saying, "Keep screaming and kicking the bars you're gonna get tased!"

The last thing I remember before my head hit the desk was Melanie saying something about me not sounding too good.

*****

I was only out for a couple of seconds when a cop started shaking me. Turns out I was dehydrated, most likely the result of all the drinking I'd done the night before, both at the bar and then my post-Melanie rejection at home. The only water I'd drunk during the day was the little paper cup the nurse gave me with the antivirals and antibiotics.

After my second hospital visit of the day, one of the 4-to-12 cops drove me home. At the time, I lived in a relatively nice elevator building in Kew Gardens that didn't bankrupt me. My second hospital visit of the day had been longer than the first, as they had to make sure I was hydrated before being released with a strong warning to not miss any of my antibiotic doses, even if the antivirals were too strong for my stomach.

*****

I awoke gradually, the room still dark and my mind swimming in a thick fog, while someone banged on the ceiling and walls. Eventually, I got my wits and realized it was my cell phone and not inconsiderate neighbors. I finally answered late into the second set of rings.

"Hey, Josh, you doin' okay?" It was my fellow day-tour sergeant, Eddie Johnson.

"Yeah, I'm good. Gonna call in sick today."

"Yeah, of course. Got your line of duty number already. Just make sure you call the sick desk."

I grunted something, and a brief silence ensued. Finally, Eddie broke it.

"I got in early. The newspaper was here already. Guess who's on the front cover?"

To this day, that photo, me and Chan standing over poor Lawrence Washington in that hallway, looking down on him like we're trying to piece together an incomprehensible puzzle made even more impossible due to our slow wits, is shown in crime scene classes under the banner "What Not to Do." And Jamel Harris wasn't even in the picture.

CHAPTER 4

COURTNEY JONES: MANNING A FOOT POST

It was fucking freezing. The leather gloves he normally used to search perps weren't doing much, even with his hands jammed in the pockets of his coat. Luckily, he'd invested in one of the thicker and more expensive NYPD-authorized coats, or he'd be in deep shit by now, only two hours into his tour. The black watch cap on his head probably wasn't authorized, but let Lieutenant Allen come by and say something. He could just see him, his pudgy face sticking out the passenger window of the warm Ford Explorer. "What, Jones, we don't wear our eight-point hats anymore? What's that fuckin' thing on your head?"

Fuck that. The coward rarely left the precinct. So, unless Allen was so fixated on jamming Courtney up that he'd find a sergeant to relieve him at the desk, find a driver since he was scared shitless to drive alone, then come out here to fuck with him, he figured he'd be okay.

The lieutenant might not have given him this shitty post if he'd had two sergeants working and wasn't much involved with the roll call assignments. But since Sergeant Rothchild was home on the cocktail, Allen didn't have an extra sergeant, so he had to either be the patrol supervisor or work the front desk. A bitch like Allen, of course he'd choose the desk. But the desk was still a big hassle, dealing with prisoners, walk-ins, and phone calls. So he was angrier than usual.

He'd given Courtney this post four days in a row, and it didn't look like that was going to change anytime soon.

Cars passed regularly down Howard Avenue, and there was a decent amount of pedestrian traffic. But everybody was huddled up in their coats, and the girls passing by barely gave him a glance. Despite being a violent and crime-plagued intersection, it was actually quite boring in the daylight hours, with not much going on a lot of the time. The perps in the barbershop across the street weren't out due to the weather, instead huddling inside behind the windows, not even hiding their plastic cups filled with liquor or smoking weed and cigarettes while the barbers serviced the occasional customer. At least it wasn't one of those hot summer days when they'd be outside the shop, trying to stare him down while smoking weed and drinking, knowing that as soon as he walked toward them, they'd go inside, shutting and locking the door behind them. It had happened to him before, with other shops. And he'd taken it to the extreme on more than one occasion, either calling for backup and breaking in or getting in some other way. Once he got a bunch of crack for his troubles. The other time, a different barbershop, not much, just weed and alcohol. He got the conditions unit to come by, and they wrote a bunch of summonses for unsanitary conditions and the like. The shop didn't even get shut down, though.

In the end, it wasn't worth the trouble and inevitable Civilian Complaint Review Board investigation unless they were trying to dump a gun, or someone was fleeing from a serious crime. The CCRB from that last all-hands-on-deck call he'd put out, yielding only the weed and booze, had gotten him bounced from four-bys to day tours about nine months before. The owner of that shop had known the commanding officer. As soon as she took command of the precinct, she found a reason to kick him off his shift. Besides, the owner of this barbershop across the street, despite being a major perp, was on the community council and also buddies with the commanding officer. She would flip her lid if he fucked with them.

Two young guys reeking of weed walked past him and went into the corner bodega that was his de facto post. He'd seen them coming and moved out of the doorway, where he'd been huddling, the temperature a few degrees warmer than standing on the corner. It wasn't that busy now, with school in session, just the locals getting their snacks, beer, and juice. Courtney didn't drink or smoke, but he didn't judge those who did. He liked to tag the troublemakers with summonses, though.

He spat on the concrete, breath billowing out behind the saliva. Looking at the wet spot on the pocked concrete, he figured it would freeze quickly, maybe causing a mouse to slip. For some reason, this struck him as funny, and he chuckled to himself like a crazy person, relieved to be expelling some of the marijuana smell from his nostrils. Unfortunately, a pretty young woman with a fat ass that couldn't be hidden by her winter coat turned the corner and saw him laughing to himself like a weirdo. She rolled her eyes and gave him a wide berth as she walked around him, swaying hips mocking him with something he knew he'd never get after this debacle. *Shit.* The one good thing about a foot post was that sometimes you'd meet a nice-looking neighborhood girl. He shook his head. Thus far, 2014 wasn't shaping up to be his year.

His gaze fell on the plate glass window of the barbershop across the street. Not surprising, since there wasn't much around here to look at, just the bodega behind him, the barbershop and the small laundromat next to it, nondescript multistory apartment buildings, and what looked to be attached townhouses, but which probably housed three or four different sets of unconnected people.

A medium-skinned, medium-height brother, who was thick across the shoulders like he'd been locked up a long time, was staring straight at him from the other side of the barbershop window, like he'd been expecting him to look that way. Or had been eye-fucking him since before that, while a few of his friends were smoking and gesticulating grandly behind him, there apparently being no customers at the moment.

Courtney focused his gaze and made a point of not looking away. Sure, the guy was warm and satisfied from drinking the "juice" from the plastic cup he held loosely at his side. Sure, Courtney was freezing his ass off, alone. Sure, a cop car hadn't passed in over a half hour, and the Arab guys who ran the bodega were currently pissed at him and all the other cops on account of one of their "brothers" in blue who'd made a scene about tripping on a loose cardboard strip inside the store by the drink cooler. The cop had been pissed about getting the foot post that day and had threatened to sue over an alleged ankle injury, even going "line of duty" like a pussy. Unlike Courtney, or any of the other cops who'd had the post since it had been re-established as a continual fixer six months prior due to numerous shootings at the intersection, that cop had taken his anger out on the poor shits who ran the establishment, guys who worked twelve-plus-hour days and rarely had a day off or got to see their families, even if they were in the U.S. So any time he popped inside the store to warm up, the clerk would be staring daggers at him. It almost wasn't even worth it.

He tore his gaze from the asshole in the barbershop and re-oriented himself to his surroundings. Almost no foot traffic; that's how cold it was, in these days when winters weren't always such anymore. *Heck, tomorrow it could be sixty degrees and no one would bat an eye.*

The cars passed regularly, none of them slowing down to take in the meager surroundings or the lone cop manning this bullshit post. When he looked back through the window across the street, the dickhead was gone, his friends still acting fools in the background.

He turned away from the depressing sight of healthy, mostly jobless grown men wasting their lives in a weed- and alcohol-induced haze, and paced a few strides in either direction to get the blood flowing in his feet. He removed one of the gloves from his mostly numb hand, leaned against the side wall of the bodega, and checked his phone. A few messages, nothing crazy. His daughter's mom said he could still pick Kara up next weekend and bring her to New York for a few weeks. His mother would watch her when he's at work. At four years old, she was well behaved and could miss a few weeks of the preschool she was in down south, which was more or less daycare. She could already read better than half the cops he worked with.

He chuckled as he wrote back, "K, talk to you later," and froze the phone. He and Mia still got along well despite the circumstances that led to their breakup: distance and cheating on his part, then hers, being the main contributing factors. The fact that she'd refused to leave North Carolina, where he'd met her when he'd been activated in the National Guard, and come up to New York had always upset him and provided a rationalization for the cheating. She was no dummy, though, and figured it out, getting back at him by sleeping with one of the guys he'd served overseas with. He'd of taken a bullet for that motherfucker back in Iraq. Funny thing is, he probably would've taken one for Courtney too. But once you're back stateside, all bets are off. Especially when women are concerned.

He looked up from the phone and saw the guy who'd been staring at him through the window. He was looking right at Courtney as he exited the barbershop and crossed the street, like he was trying to make his body an arrow. Thick arms bobbed up and down, fists clenched, bouncing lightly on his feet like he was a boxer charging an opponent. Courtney put the phone safely in his pocket. He could put out a "10-85" over the radio, have backup come. It was a small precinct, and even with the low patrol manpower, it wouldn't be too long before a car got here. But the guy's friends were still inside the shop, standing by the window, drinking, smoking, and giggling as they looked out onto what was about to happen.

If this was a calculated thing, at least one or two of them would've come out to help their buddy. The guy slowed down when he was halfway across the street, hands relaxing but still with that look of menace on his face. A car passed behind him and he looked back, annoyed, as if the driver should know that it was *his* street. Courtney looked behind the guy, at his buddies standing behind the barbershop window. They were taking out their phones, one of them now walking out the door to record the encounter. So it was probably gonna just be this asshole trying to bait him into doing something that looked bad on camera, something that had been happening more and more lately, with cell phone video getting better and better. He didn't want to call for backup yet and risk looking like a punk before he had anything he could charge this guy with.

Courtney stood by the side of the bodega, knees slightly bent and hands at his sides, as the guy cleared the street and stepped onto the sidewalk. His friend was almost at the middle of the street, cell phone held high and pointing at them.

The asshole sauntered down the sidewalk toward him, eight feet away and closing slowly. Courtney stood his ground and watched his hands. His right hand now sat just over his holstered gun, ready to draw it if the shithead reached into his clothing for a weapon.

He stopped a few feet away, just out of kicking distance, spreading his feet slightly and holding one hand over the other by his waistband. He was wearing a thick hoodie, though, and Courtney couldn't tell if there was a gun under it.

"You gotta be a cold bitch, bro—" Before he finished the sentence, the guy's right hand darted under the hoodie to the front waistband of his baggy jeans. Courtney almost had his gun out of the holster before he saw the skin of the dude's stomach under his shirt, just over his drawers. It was bare, no gun. Amazingly, he was even wearing a belt. The guy let the front of his hoodie fall back down and took another step, smiling cruelly. He leaned in; even from a foot away, Courtney could smell his rank breath.

"You a pussy, nigga. Almost shot me for adjustin' my drawers."

His friend, who was standing a few feet behind him in the street, howled with laughter, still recording them with his phone. "Pigs be jumpy these days, even the black ones. They seein' we ain't gonna take their bullshit no more."

The aggressor shifted, hands in front of him and a little under his chest. He threw a quick glance back at his friend, then turned back to Courtney and made a show of looking at his name tag. "Hope you got this shit, yo. Officer Jones was ready ta' shoot me for 'walkin' while black.' Guess he forgot his roots, workin' with them white pigs."

Courtney's body was still tense, ready to react quickly if he needed to. But he hadn't taken the bait and drawn his gun, hadn't given the assholes an embarrassing shot of him backing away from them. They saw this, and after a little more chiding, they turned and walked into the bodega. The aggressor looked back over his shoulder as he threw open the door, the friend no longer recording. "Cold as shit out here, yo. Glad I don't gotta be standin' out here like a chump!" They both laughed as the door closed behind them.

He didn't even feel cold anymore. Realizing how hard his heart was beating, he slowed his breathing, taking longer, deeper breaths so he'd look calm and composed when the assholes came out of the store. When he exhaled, his breath looked like thick cigarette smoke. *Shit.* In the cold, you can't even hide how hard you're breathing, even from a distance. And just like that he was cold again, thinking he still had five more hours before this crappy day ended.

* * *

Was anyone going to relieve him for a meal? That was the question. The sergeant had said in roll call that they were really short today, running only four patrol cars to cover the whole precinct. Once you factor in arrests, prisoner transports, DOAs, and the like (all handled by patrol personnel), the chances were pretty slim. In a little bit, he could call a unit over to stay here while he sat in the back of their car and warmed up, maybe have them bring him something to eat. But later, with school dismissals, it would get busy. There were several big high schools in the area, and some even crazier middle schools, and it was always hectic. So a meal was probably a no-go. And if he complained? That asshole Lieutenant Allen would make sure he was here every day, at least till Sergeant Rothchild got back. And he'd just gone on the cocktail, so that was what—almost a month on this corner, the toilet bowl of this shithole precinct?

The thing was, Courtney could've ended this thing with the lieutenant before it even began. That day Allen had walked in on him in the "124 Room," which was the place where all the walk-in victims made their reports. Courtney had been working on an arrest report at one of the computers, but he'd taken a break to speak with Keisha Jackson, his partner for the day. When Allen walked in he'd seen Courtney with his arm around young, pretty Jackson, whispering something stupid in her ear. She'd giggled and leaned her head into the crook of his neck. Nothing crazy or sexual; he wasn't even sure if Jackson liked him like that. But they'd always had this semi-flirty thing going on since he'd come to the day shift, and sometimes that could lead to more. Or not. Looking at Allen's pudgy face, Courtney started to question why it even mattered to him. He did all right with women without dipping into the company trough. Besides, Jackson was a good cop. He didn't want things to get weird.

The lieutenant practically screamed at him. "What're you doin' in the station house, Jones?" The look he was giving him was pure poison.

"I got a collar, Lieu. Jackson was helping me out."

This answer did not seem to temper Allen's anger. "Yeah, I bet she was. She got other stuff to do, though, don't you, Keisha?"

"Yeah, Lieutenant. I was just leavin' to go out and write some summonses."

Allen had wanted to fuck Jackson since she arrived at the precinct fresh out of the Academy, standing foot posts on bad blocks as a part of Operation Impact, a mess of an idea that further alienated the communities the cops were supposed to serve. Keisha had played along, like every cop had, white or black or Asian or Hispanic, doing what she had to ticket-wise without being a total asshole. But for a pretty young cop, that included putting up with horndog supervisors like Lieutenant Allen, giving them cute smiles and laughing at their stupid jokes so they didn't start being a dick.

Courtney watched Keisha as she walked away. Allen didn't like it. He strode up to him aggressively. "You processing your collar or what, Jones?"

Courtney tried to play it off, giving a smile that was occasionally endearing to women but that seemed to piss most men off. "C'mon, Lieu, just enjoyin' the sights. I'm almost done anyway."

Allen fixed him with another hard look, then turned away to go do whatever the fuck he did with his day. But after that, any time he was at or by the desk, or in roll call, or just passing Courtney in the hall, he'd find something to harass him about. And now a fourth straight day on this foot post, no end in sight.

He couldn't wait till Rothchild got back. If the sergeant took him as a driver, Allen wouldn't say anything. He shook his head. When were women going to stop getting him into trouble? Come to think of it, the only time in his Army and police career he'd actually stayed out of the doghouse with the higher-ups was during his fourteen months in Iraq. The fighting had been intense, and his unit was in the thick of things. But everyone had gotten along, more or less. And there were the NCOs to form a bridge between the officers, so he didn't have to deal directly with them that much.

Maybe because he was getting older and wiser, he was starting to think that maybe *he* was the problem, not the girls. Jackson hadn't done anything but be herself, friendly and a little flirty. And he couldn't blame her for playing the game with the lieutenant; this job was hard enough that you had to take every opportunity you could get. He respected that she hadn't hooked up with him, was playing him just enough to keep in his good graces. That's a dance he'd never learned, and probably never would. Guys like Sergeant Rothchild were cool because as long as you were straight with them and more or less did what they told you, they'd look past the petty bullshit. That was the difference, Courtney figured, between actual patrol guys like them and admin guys like the lieutenant, who'd worked mostly non-enforcement duties his whole career.

Rothchild was cool, all right. He just needed to stop pining over that cop he used to date. Based only on the stories Rothchild had related, Courtney knew she was trouble. Not the kind of girl for a nice, straight-up guy like him.

The only other thing with Rothchild was that he couldn't quite grasp that the rabbi they'd collared last spring was still a problem. Sure, it was a good collar—guy's license was heavily suspended, plus he had a hooker in the front seat and a baggie of cocaine in the glove compartment. Sure, things had been quiet on that front since the CO (an attractive black female in her forties named Inspector Ruth who never would've given a shit about some Jew unless he knew people)

48

initially blew her lid. But she'd actually called Courtney into her office a few weeks earlier, just before Christmas. Maybe she was in a good mood—she seemed a little drunk. She'd leaned over the desk and said, "Jones, why do you think the Jews do so much better than black folks?"

Courtney knew better than to say anything, so he'd just smiled. "'Cause they stick together." She said it like it was a decree straight from Jesus. He tried his hardest not to look at her cleavage, tits practically bursting out of her low-cut dress, forcing himself to look her in the eyes, which, though nice, were among the least interesting parts of her body.

She went on to chastise him for collaring the barbershop guy she knew for the hundredth time. But that had been an epiphany for him. He'd always considered himself street-smart, worldly—being a young immigrant kid growing up with a single mother in Crown Heights. But the black woman sitting before him wasn't where she was because of the Jews. Sure, maybe she worked with them, but it was their fellow black people who'd gotten her there. Just like pretty much every police commissioner's Irish buddies had gotten them to where they were. It wasn't race or religion, no—it was power. Knowing who buttered your bread and sticking with those folks, no matter what kind of shit they spewed.

CHAPTER 5

ROTHCHILD:
MONTH OFF WORK

There was no way of knowing if the shithead who bit me was actually HIV positive; we'd gone to different hospitals, but it wouldn't have mattered anyway. Hospital staff aren't allowed to forcibly draw blood from a perp, or even let us know their status if they are aware of it due to HIPAA laws. So I had to take the whole thirty-day cycle of antiviral meds.

Even with the nausea and weakness brought on by the meds, I started to get bored after that first week. I guess that's why I called Melanie. The whole week, I'd been fuming at her, how she'd let Sanchez touch her like that when she knew I was watching. So I didn't pick up any of her calls or answer the texts she sent until I was so tired of being with myself and my morbid thoughts that I just gave up.

The main thing to quash was hope. That was the thing I kept telling myself as I walked out of my apartment. She'd insisted on driving out from Staten Island and picking me up. "You're on the cocktail, Josh. I'm not gonna make you drive all the way out to me."

We'd decided on a movie, since I wasn't supposed to drink when taking the meds and probably couldn't even if I wanted to. I saw that she'd gotten a new car, a Honda Civic, which would've looked like a square car if not for the almost blacked-out windows and darkened windshield. It was night, but even if it was twelve noon I wouldn't have been able to see her until she rolled down the driver's side window. As soon as I saw her face, though, all the feelings came rushing back.

Her auburn hair was tied back in a ponytail, her face all cuteness—little nose, little ears, big dark eyes, and surprisingly thick, full lips on a smooth face that was darker than her Irish roots would lead you to expect—almost Mediterranean. She was wearing a low-cut shirt under her jacket, and the tops of her breasts were poking out.

She got out of the car as I approached, her waist-length jacket doing nothing to hide her curves.

"How do you see out of this thing at night?" I asked as I leaned down, avoiding her kiss on the cheek and instead giving her a hug like an old pal.

"It's hard," she admitted as we both got in the car, happy to be out of the cold. "But there's a few perp houses cropping up in my neighborhood, and I got recognized at McDonald's a couple of weeks ago. Guy we locked up together, as a matter of fact."

"Who?" I asked as she pulled out, realizing I could see out the windshield okay, but barely out the side windows.

"Rayshawn Simmons—it was about two years ago, I think. We collared him for 511 (Suspended License), and he had a couple of decks of heroin in the glove compartment. You took the collar. He was on probation already, but I'm not sure what happened with the case."

"Yeah, I remember him. What'd he say to you?"

She pulled onto Queens Boulevard and drove about half a block before hitting a red light behind a line of cars. Typical cop, she darted into the other lane to gain no more than two car lengths, tops, before grinding to a halt. Without missing a beat she said, "Called me a whore cop. Pussy whispered it under his breath as he passed me, telling his friends I'd locked him up for bullshit. Luckily, I remembered his face and looked up your arrest the next day to get his name. I got an IAB log and everything, but the CO said it wasn't enough to collar him on."

I nodded. It wasn't a threat, so there really wasn't anything to be done other than get a log number from Internal Affairs, something that's worth as much as it sounds like. "You say anything to him?"

She turned to me, a big, pretty smile on her face. Big dark eyes glistened in the backlight shining through the windshield. "You know me, Josh. I told him to go fuck himself."

"Sounds about right," I agreed, getting a little weak-kneed. Her hand brushed the back of mine as she reached down to adjust the radio, and my cheeks flushed. Hope began to spring forth, as it always did when I had any physical contact with her.

"Sorry," she said as she tuned to Z100 and changed lanes. I muttered something under my breath, and we drove without speaking for a while, the nonsense songs on the radio saying everything there was to say.

After battling traffic on the Grand Central for a bit, we were finally nearing the theater. "Anyway, so I saw him again a few days later—little shit is staying in this perp house with like twenty squatters not two blocks from my place. Staten Island's becoming Brooklyn."

"Brooklyn if it was built on landfill, mobsters, and dirty money," I chided.

She laughed. "Exactly." Then, out of left field, she asked, "Are you still thinking about taking that job?"

Melanie was the only person on the department other than my brother who I'd told about the opportunity.

Unconsciously rubbing the back of my hand, where the bite marks had faded away but not the wound they caused, I said, "Yeah, I'm leaning towards it." I almost said "heavily leaning."

She chewed her lower lip for a moment before speaking. "It's just...I can't see you being happy working in an office. You always loved being a cop."

"Loved" being the operative word.

She continued. "I mean, I know you have a bitch CO, but they only stay so long—"

"It's not just her," I said, my voice low but confident in a way I didn't know I felt. "It's everything. I'm just tired of all the bullshit and the uncertainty—I've been either in the Army or a cop since I was seventeen. I wanna see how normal people live."

Melanie giggled. "Good luck finding some of those."

The movie was uneventful and unremarkable. I lost interest almost immediately and started munching on popcorn even though my stomach was queasy. Melanie didn't mind splitting it with me despite my current predicament, even offering me a sip of her soda. I whispered, "You know I just got bit by an AIDS-infected whack job."

She leaned over and whispered in my ear. Her breath was warm and tickled me. "You're fine, Josh. Anyway, I didn't say you could kiss me. Or anything beyond that." The way she rubbed the back of my neck afterward and kept it just under my collar left me with the impression that I could have done such things if it weren't for my current predicament. And once again, I was head over heels, hoping and totally gone for her.

We started petting each other as the movie wound to a close, innocently at first, then in inappropriate places considering the things we couldn't do at the moment. I'd been planning to ask her about Sanchez. This didn't seem like the time, though, and by the time we got to the car, holding hands the whole time like high school sweethearts, I resolved to wait a few days on that one. When we got in the car, she embraced me, kissing the crook of my neck and under my ear. I wanted to ask her why she was so affectionate now when I'd been throwing myself at her a week earlier, and for months before that, like a forty-year-old townie at a hockey game. Instead, I kissed the nape of her neck, her earlobes, and her breasts, which she'd pulled out at some point. I sucked her nipples like a man dying of thirst in the desert. What little gallantry I had wouldn't let me go further, though, and she seemed to also realize this was a mistake.

She smiled shyly as she pulled her shirt back over her exposed breasts and wriggled back into her jacket. "After you're done with the cocktail," she said softly.

Why was she being like this now, when I'd been trying for so long? I didn't care. I was hooked again.

CHAPTER 6

CHAN AND DOMINGUEZ: ROUTINE DAY ON PATROL

They were driving a Nissan Altima Hybrid today, an odd vehicle for police use. It might have been a good civilian car, but as a hybrid it wasn't meant to be driven as a police car and was always breaking down—the useless car guy told Dominguez that the NYPD had already phased it out for that reason. This was the only one the precinct had left, in addition to the assorted Fusions, Impalas, Ford Edges and Explorers, the remaining Crown Victorias, which for some reason had halted production, and even a Taurus or two. Not like in the old days when you'd know what you were getting: the Crown Vic, which was fast and big enough to hold a perp in the back even with the cage, or the much inferior Impala, which handled okay but was slow and more cramped.

As usual, Chan drove and Dominguez leaned back in his seat, his uniform hanging loosely over his thin, wiry frame. He smelled like he'd drunk too much the night before. This didn't bother Chan—he was used to it. "Right at the next block," Dominguez said softly. Chan made a right onto Howard Avenue. Since Dominguez didn't say anything, he kept driving straight. "We gonna visit Jones?" Chan asked.

"Wow, you actually know what street you're on. After only four years in the precinct."

Chan laughed. "Poor fucker's been on that post for two weeks straight. What d'you think he did to the lieutenant?"

"Probably fucked Jackson," Dominguez guessed. "You know how the lieutenant's been sniffing around her ass. She's not gonna fuck that sweaty pig, though. Wants a young, good-looking guy."

Chan laughed again. "You sound like *you* wanna fuck Jones."

Dominguez snorted. Chan pulled up to the curb where Jones was standing without being prompted. He wasn't slow or out of it; just didn't know his way around the precinct that well and hadn't driven much before taking the job. He'd worked with Dominguez since they came off Operation Impact in the neighboring 73rd Precinct in Brownsville, where they'd stood on street corners at night and written as many summonses as they thought would keep them out of trouble. Once they got here, they were paired up, and he'd always driven while Dominguez had navigated. Dominguez had an almost uncanny sense of direction and had figured out the small precinct within a few weeks. When Dominguez wasn't here, Chan worked with someone else, and they usually drove. If not, they didn't get to jobs as fast as they maybe could've. He didn't like to drive fast anyway. "Slow and steady wins the race" was his motto for operating a vehicle, as well as going through life.

Jones walked up to their car and opened the back door. He sat down, rubbing his hands. Dominguez turned to talk to him; he could see him well since there was no cage partition in the car. "It's not that cold, Jones. Why you acting like a bitch?"

Chan laughed. "C'mon, give him a break. He's still freezing from last week." Chan turned in his seat. "Dominguez told me you were good-looking." He winked. "*Young* and good-looking, just like he likes."

Jones laughed. "You're just realizing he's gay, after all these years?"

Chan shrugged. "I'm naïve."

Dominguez snorted. "That's true—he doesn't know anything he didn't read in a fortune cookie."

This time, it was only Jones laughing. "Hey, Dominguez, point the heat back here."

Dominguez played with the vents. "Not gonna do you much good. Not much coming out of this little shit box."

Courtney responded, "These Altimas got some nice pickup, though."

Dominguez turned to him again. "How would *you* know? You're stuck here every day."

Chan piped in. "A golf cart would be fast for him."

Courtney ignored him, instead looking over at the dirtbags in the barbershop. It was a little warmer today, and a few of them had been sitting on chairs in front, not even bothering to hide their beers. But once they saw the car pulling up, they'd gone inside. As soon as Chan and Dominguez left, they'd come back out. Same as for the dirtbags in the apartment building diagonally across from the barbershop. They'd drink and smoke in the doorway, then run back inside as soon as Jones got to the middle of the street. When he got bored he'd fuck with them, but it was embarrassing how easy it was for them to just get away and make him look stupid.

Dominguez noticed him staring at the barbershop. "Those assholes been out today?"

Courtney considered. "They been out a bit, drinking. Not acting up or anything, though."

Chan piped in: "The crime team grabbed a guy with a gun coming out of there the other night. He got into a livery cab, and they pulled it over at the next block. Gun was shoved in the back seat cushion."

Courtney looked away from the shop. "If only you cared as much about doing police work yourself as talkin' about what others did…"

Dominguez: "He'd be fuckin' Columbo."

"You would too, Jose," Courtney reminded. "Didn't you go six months without collaring last year? How you manage that in Bed-Stuy?"

"At least I don't have a girl's name," Dominguez retorted.

"Yeah, just a girl's body."

The dispatcher was saying something they hadn't heard at first with all the noise they were making. "—One Charlie, copy?"

Dominguez keyed his radio. "10-5, Central. Say again."

"10-34 Assault in Progress at Stuyvesant and Pulaski, unknown weapons, female caller screaming on the line then hung up."

"Roll down the window, Chan," Courtney said. Chan did, and he reached outside to open the door since the child safety locks were engaged. He got out, giving a wave as they pulled off, Chan driving like an old woman as usual.

"Turn left on Broadway," Dominguez said calmly as he switched on the turret lights. Chan did, slowly, going under the elevated J train tracks that paralleled the busy street. There wasn't much traffic, but Dominguez told him to pass a car at the next light as he activated the siren. Chan went into the other lane, and Dominguez looked to his right and cleared him to run the light and proceed through the intersection. He did, several seconds after most cops with a police car with lights and sirens activated would've.

"The way you drive, she's gonna be raped and murdered by the time we get there."

"Slow and steady wins the race," Chan replied good-naturedly.

As they pulled up to the location, going the wrong way down Pulaski, they saw Harris and McCall's car parked in front of a bodega on the corner, across the street from a group of towering housing project apartments. Harris and McCall were speaking to a young black woman wearing pajama bottoms, a cut-off T-shirt, and slippers. She was crying and waving her hands frantically, intermittently wiping her bloody lips and nose, the two cops backing up a bit so her jerky movements wouldn't spray blood in their faces while they tried to calm her down. Dominguez turned to Chan as he put the car in park across the street. "Never fails. You got here so slow that our backup beat us."

Chan ignored him. "She's not dressed for the weather, buddy. Bet she ran out of the projects."

"You should be a detective," Dominguez hissed as he threw his door open and stepped out into the cold air. Chan turned off the ignition and followed his partner as they crossed Pulaski to join the other cops and the victim.

As Chan had suspected, the victim, early twenties and very good-looking for a ghetto rat dating a perp, by his estimation, was clearly outside as a matter of necessity. She was too upset and scared to be cold yet, still gesticulating, cussing, and telling Harris and McCall everything but where the perp currently was. "He's my baby's daddy!" She screamed at Harris in response to his question, "Who is he to you?" Chan missed the next thing she said, then caught "...stupid nigga never does nothin' for his babies, 'cept if his mama makes him, an' even then she don't care what he does to me or any of the bitches he's fuckin'..." Chan drifted off, observing the scene with a clarity that none of the others could've possibly attained at that moment, as they were trying to get the story out of her. Even Dominguez, who knew that Harris and McCall, two hungry young cops in a way they'd never been, would take the collar in a minute. That would let him and Chan get back to job-hopping and ragging on each other and any other cops that crossed their paths.

Her nipples were definitely feeling the cold, even if she wasn't, their darkness pushing against the tight white T-shirt, almost a wife-beater. A tear and some streaks of blood marked up her unadorned face, pretty without any effort. Chan would've fallen in love if he didn't know the deal, which was that, after this guy was arrested, she'd be back with him at some point. Maybe days, maybe weeks—if not him, another savage who beat on her and maybe the kids too. Behind her, the natives were still going in and out of the bodega. Over the bodega was a multistory apartment building that Chan had been in many times. She was saying, "Eleventh, no *twelfth* floor—"

Harris again, his cool, confident black man's voice filled with intelligence and patience, so unlike McCall, who, despite his intelligence, had none of the understanding and patience of his partner: "What apartment number?"

So Chan had been right that she'd run out of one of the high-rise project buildings, and not the apartment they were standing in front of. Score another one for the Chinese guy! Something he *hadn't* read in a fortune cookie, ha-ha. He was listening enough to gather that she didn't remember the apartment, but that she could show them. Chan was looking over Dominguez's shoulder, not hard, since they were around the same height, five-foot-five or so, Chan rounder than his sometimes emaciated-looking partner, who seemed to like cards and drinking more than food. A girl-guy couple was walking into the bodega, his arm around her shoulder in a manner that seemed forced. The look on her face seemed forced too, and Chan knew she'd probably be calling 911 soon. He stared at her until she caught his eye, but the look she gave him—annoyance that he was staring—told him that she didn't need or want help yet. Served him right for trying to be chivalrous.

Before Harris said anything else, Chan motioned to the victim. "C'mon, show us. It's getting cold."

"True that," she agreed, sniffing in some mucus and blood that had been trickling out. They walked across the street, with shorter him and Dominguez in the lead since they wanted to get out of the cold, and taller Harris and even taller McCall walking behind them with the girl. This project consisted of a bunch of towering, at least for Brooklyn, stand-alone buildings. Luckily, though, this chick had run out of the nearest one, so the walk wasn't too bad. They passed three older gentlemen who looked to be in their mid-sixties sitting on a bench in the courtyard. One of the old men gave the cops a dirty look while the others studiously ignored them. Chan and the other cops did the same.

Luckily, someone exited the lobby door as they walked up, so they didn't have to wait to be buzzed in. There was a door leading to the staircase in front of them. To their right were two elevators, both of which happened to be working. Fuck if Chan was gonna walk his fat ass up eleven, or twelve, depending on which apartment the asshole actually lived in, flights of stairs. Luckily, Harris and McCall, both workout buffs, had the same idea as him. Harris pressed both elevator buttons. If the perp happened to walk down the stairs and out the rear or front doors while they rode up, then so be it. The two wannabe studs had better be able to snatch up a better collar than a misdemeanor domestic assault, Chan figured. Otherwise, they were just dreaming that one day they'd be working side by side in the Anti-Crime unit. Suckers, even if they made it.

They got to the eleventh floor, and she stepped out, looking. Harris held the elevator doors open. She turned around, shaking her head. "It's the next floor."

"You sure?" asked McCall, his eyebrows raised.

She raised her own eyebrows, like he was asking a stupid question. But to Chan, it looked a little like flirting. It must've to McCall too, because he smiled kindly as she replied. "I know where he lives, been there enough. I mostly take the stairs so I don't have to smell—" She waved her arm, indicating the invisible smell of urine that hung in the air of the elevator. "I know what the door looks like where I get off the stairs—I'm just not sure of the floor."

"Or the apartment," Dominguez piped in. She threw him a dirty look, as did McCall. Harris pressed 12, and they went on up.

When the elevator doors opened she stepped out, looked around, then pointed to a door on the left, halfway down the hallway. She was sure, that was evident; the weed sticker on the door confirmed her confidence. They ushered her to the side of the door, everyone standing away from the peephole so whoever was looking out was seeing an empty hallway.

Harris knocked softly at first. When no one answered, he knocked louder. He motioned for the girl to stand in front, so her boyfriend would think it was just her, but McCall shook his head and kept her back. He'd grown soft on her, apparently.

Chan knew that when she got back with the dirtbag, he'd forgive her even if she had set him up. At least until the next time he got angry. After a minute and a half, Harris stopped knocking and looked over at McCall. McCall left the girl, strode up and started kicking the bottom hard enough that the thick metal door rattled. They could hear people talking inside, and so they knew that the perp was probably still there, no doubt fully aware of what was going on, having just beaten his girl. Now strong knocks on the door and no one in sight through the peephole. He was just being a cowardly dick, as was in his nature, no doubt.

There was a lot of noise on the other side of the door, the idiot and his mother yelling at each other once it became evident that the cops weren't planning on leaving anytime soon. That was the trick of a lot of these arrests: keep knocking, knocking, maybe kicking the door till the perp realized you weren't going away. This being the twelfth floor, it was not like he had any other options, especially if his mother wasn't willing to wait it out with him.

McCall, still standing to the side with his hand on the wall for support, kept kicking the bottom of the door, the loud metallic crashes echoing down the hallway. It had been several minutes already.

Dominguez and Chan would've left by now, taken a report, and left it open for the Detective Squad. He'd be arrested eventually, whether or not the girl wanted to press charges. After that, most likely it would be nothing, as she would refuse to cooperate with the DA's office, and he would skate. Harris and McCall didn't play, though. They liked to slap the bracelets on, regardless of whether anyone cared in the end or not.

The loud report of McCall's boot kicks eventually had the desired effect. The mother, clad only in a bathrobe even though it was only an hour till noon, opened the door a few inches. "Watchoo want with my son?"

McCall put his hand on the door, foot too, so she couldn't close it on them. He didn't bother asking how she knew it was her son they wanted; it would've been par for the course in her life. "We need to talk to him, ma'am. We can't leave until we do."

She shook her head, then threw open the door, turned away, and walked into the living room, throwing her arms out and stating, "*You* deal with his shit!"

They walked inside; Dominguez stayed outside in the hallway with the girl, on account of his proximity to her and the fact that Harris and McCall really wanted the collar. Chan was right behind as they stepped into the living room. On the left was a kitchen. The perp, Rashawn, wasn't in either. To their right, a hallway led to two bedrooms and a bathroom. The bathroom door was open, as was the first bedroom door. The room at the end of the hallway was closed.

Harris and McCall checked the bathroom and the first bedroom as Chan watched the mother. When they were sure it was clear, they all proceeded down the hallway to the last bedroom door. Harris turned the knob—it wasn't locked. He looked back at McCall and Chan to let them know he was going in, and they both nodded. He threw open the door and stepped inside, McCall following on his heels.

By the time Chan got in, Harris had his expandable baton out and McCall had unsnapped the holster on his gun. Rashawn was six-foot-one, with a lean, strong build. Chan could see this even though he was fully clothed, even had a puffy jacket on, but he was barefoot with his hands in his pockets and facing the window. Harris was telling him to show his hands, but Rashawn wasn't having it. Then he turned quickly, flailing his hands out of his pockets so quickly that McCall drew down on him. Luckily the hands were empty, and McCall wasn't the shaky type.

"Get your fuckin' hands up!" McCall implored. But young Rashawn acted like he didn't hear, instead jamming his hands back in the pockets of his jacket again.

He stomped his foot like a child and screamed/whined: "Y'all need to get the fuck outta here! You ain't got no warrant! Mom, get in here!"

Chan's own hand went to the butt of his gun. Rashawn stared straight ahead, his angry gaze telling them all they needed to know about his mindset. Harris and McCall darted in. McCall holstered his gun as Harris dropped his expandable baton. They each grabbed one of Rashawn's hands, pinning them to his side so he couldn't take a weapon out. "Give us your hands!" McCall and Harris shouted, over and over, in one form or another.

Dominguez ran into the room. Chan snapped his holster shut and rushed in to help them as McCall punched Rashawn in the side of the head, using his other hand to keep the one in the pocket pinned. Rashawn screamed, then threw his body into Harris, sending them both reeling sideways into a dresser. Harris took the brunt of the hit, losing his grip on the hand. As they fell sideways, McCall lost his grip too. Chan, worried about what he was reaching for in the jacket, went for his right hand.

Before he could do anything, McCall wrapped his forearm under Rashawn's neck and threw him down to the floor, landing on his side. Like lightning, McCall rolled him onto his stomach, putting his knee in the center of his back to pin him to the floor. Rashawn lashed his head backward, trying to catch McCall on the chin, but he was pinned to the floor and he never got close. Harris bounced off the dresser, dropped down, and kneeled by his left side, yanking on that hand. Chan helped him, and eventually they got it out of the pocket. McCall and Dominguez managed to yank his other hand out of the pocket as Harris and Chan got the other hand behind his back. Harris pushed up the jacket sleeves, and they were able to complete the cuffing. Chan felt like he'd just run a marathon. Even workout junkies Harris and McCall were breathing heavily.

They kept him on his stomach, something that a year from now would basically be grounds for termination. McCall ran his hands over Rashawn's clothing, then checked the jacket pockets he'd kept reaching into. He shook his head as he removed a large box cutter with an orange plastic handle from the right jacket pocket. The blade was deployed, ready to cut. McCall looked back at Chan and Dominguez as if to justify why they'd come at him so hard. He didn't have to. Chan sometimes thought they were too aggressive, but in this case—shit, if he'd have taken that out, he'd have probably slashed at least one of them before getting shot and causing this thing to become a huge shitstorm.

Nothing they could charge him with, but something that could've made things very ugly. Chan would never forget what a razor like that had done to a teenage girl's face a couple of years back in Brownsville. She was still pretty, but she'd have to live with a scar running down half her face for the rest of her life.

McCall finished the search, half-turning him over on each side to check his front waistband and pockets. He found a few baggies of weed, which he held out to Chan.

"I don't have gloves," Chan said quickly.

Dominguez nodded. "Never know if it's laced with anything."

McCall shook his head. Harris jumped up, fished in his pocket, and took a plastic glove out. He opened it, and McCall put the baggies in there. He finished the search but didn't find any other weapons.

Once the search was complete, they rolled him onto his side, then sat him up. He was bitching and cussing, but the fight had taken a lot of the venom out. His mother poked her head in the door as they sat him up.

"Why you be doin' my son like that?! Four of you against one? You some pussy-assed bitches! I'ma call Internal Affairs!" She showed them her phone—she probably had the number for Internal Affairs and the CCRB on speed dial. Before she left the room, she shouted, "Don't say nothin', Rashawn! They can use it against you—we both know you didn't lay hands on that stupid girl!"

"Thank you, ma'am," Harris stated firmly but politely, catching his breath.

"We'll keep it in mind," Dominguez agreed.

She turned and left the room in a huff. Once she was gone and they could divert their attention back to Rashawn, Harris and McCall stood him up. He didn't give any trouble as Harris took him tightly by the elbow and led him toward the door. *Strange*, Chan thought.

As soon as Harris got him out of the room, McCall expanded his baton and lifted up the stinky blanket and sheets. There wasn't anything there. He lifted the mattress by the corner—nothing.

Dominguez picked up the expandable baton that Harris had dropped on the floor. He depressed the button and collapsed it against the floor. "What do you think he's got, McCall?"

"Don't know," he answered as he got down on his knees and looked under the bed. "This dude's a Robinson boy, though. He got picked up for a shooting last year."

Dominguez arched his eyebrows sarcastically; McCall always thought there was a gun somewhere, and he'd tear the place up 'til he found something. Chan smiled; he'd never heard of this guy Rashawn. Then again, he and Dominguez didn't keep up on the perps like Harris and McCall did.

McCall reached for something; Chan saw it was a boot. He turned it upside down. Nothing fell out. He grabbed some more footwear from under the bed, including some nice sneakers. A red Air Jordan, which probably cost more than Rashawn had ever earned honestly in his life, was the jackpot. McCall whistled, picking the sneaker up and showing it to Chan and Dominguez. A silver 9mm semi-auto was tucked inside.

Nice job, Chan had to admit. But the look of utter triumph on McCall's face, like he'd just slain a dragon, was a little much. Chan didn't return his boastful smile.

Dominguez said, "Nice," though Chan could tell he felt a little stupid after his initial sarcasm. McCall yelled for Harris to come back to the room, then started muttering about the New Year's Day homicide and how this gun might be related. As if they'd ever have that kind of luck! Guns were a dime a dozen in Bed-Stuy, especially nine-millimeters. But McCall was so proud of himself for grabbing one he was thinking he was a detective now.

Dominguez and Chan headed out to watch the perp in the living room while the two partners completed the search of the room. No way they were gonna waste time applying for a warrant at this point. It would take all day, and they'd have to deal with the crazy mom, who was already screaming and accusing them of things that weren't actually crimes, like "comin' in here without no warrant" when, in fact, she'd let them in.

Chan got on the radio and called for one unit to meet them so they could take Rashawn down to their car, and he and Dominguez could still watch the mom, who was smoking a cigarette and pacing across the cluttered living room. "Fuckin' whore lyin' on my son like that! These little bitches are ruining all our young men!" she howled at the ceiling, a plume of smoke drifting out of her mouth.

Chan and Dominguez realized at the same time: the girl! Shit, she hadn't even signed a domestic incident report, nothing. They didn't even have her full name or phone number.

Dominguez yelled, "Harris—get out here!"

Harris and McCall ran into the living room, and Dominguez shoved Rashawn into Harris's arms. "We gotta get the girl!" he shouted as he and Chan ran out the door, almost colliding.

The hallway was empty, but the closer of the two stairway doors was just swinging shut. They ran to it. Chan stopped at the closer staircase, and Dominguez ran down the hallway to take the other one in case she was using that. As soon as Chan threw the door open, he heard hasty footsteps banging on plaster, getting lower and lower, farther and farther away.

He caught up to her about five flights down. He was out of breath already and couldn't say much. "Wait," he huffed, reaching for her arm. She twisted out of it and continued walking down. Chan took out his radio and yelled, "Dominguez, my staircase!" and got in front of her on the landing before she could get to the next flight.

He managed to hold her there until Dominguez arrived. "You're sweating like a pig," he said to Chan as he descended the final half flight of stairs to join them on the landing. At least the girl didn't giggle at that. Also, she seemed to have accepted the fact that they weren't going to let her just walk away. She was leaning with her shoulder against the wall, a look of resignation on her face.

Chan unzipped his coat and shirt and pulled out a somewhat crumpled and sweaty domestic incident report. Eventually they got her to sign it, using the wall to write on. It wasn't great, and there were a few little holes in the paper due to the wall's roughness, but she managed. They also got her sister's phone number since her phone was shut off, and a brief story as to what had happened and how she had suffered her injuries. Dominguez also managed to get the sister's address. Chan knew his partner would go all out for an arrest he didn't have to take.

Chan snapped photos of her injuries with his cell, and she walked away. "You need to answer when the DA calls later," Dominguez yelled after her. "It's gonna be a blocked number."

She didn't answer, and Chan figured Harris or McCall would have to go by the sister's house and try to hunt her down later. Even if they couldn't find her, the DA would probably charge the assault that led to the gun, since they had the pictures of her injuries and the signed domestic incident report. He was sure glad he didn't have to deal with this messy shit, though. Dominguez said, "Let's go back up—it smells like shit in here."

Chan got off the staircase on the next floor. "I got enough exercise for today," he explained to his partner, who snorted. Still, Dominguez got off too and waited for the elevator with him.

Harris and McCall found a bunch of baggies of weed in Rashawn's room, but no more guns. They left the apartment with the mom screaming bloody murder, already on the phone with the Internal Affairs Bureau.

After the tour ended, as Chan was signing out at the front desk, Harris came up to him. "Hey, thanks for grabbing the victim. That would've been bad—I don't know what we were thinking."

Chan shrugged. "It was cold."

Harris laughed. "Still. Anyway, you know Espinoza up in the squad?"

"Yeah." Chan was getting impatient. He was still in the process of binge-watching *Breaking Bad* and had to get as much in as he could before the weekend, when he'd have his nephew with him.

"He caught the homicide on New Year's Day—that guy shot in the hallway?"

Dominguez walked up behind them. He'd also changed into plain clothes already. "You mean the one you made Chan and Sergeant Rothchild famous on?" Chan laughed. Harris had been the one guarding the door, who'd let the photographer in. He winced.

"Yeah, I fucked up on that. Anyway—"

Dominguez again: "First, you get Sergeant Rothchild on the front page of the paper looking like an idiot, then the poor guy gets AIDS. Hope you feel good about that."

"He doesn't have *AIDS*, asshole."

Chan liked Harris, despite how he was currently wasting his time with nonsense. "Dominguez is just hoping he'll have someone to go to the gay bars with."

Harris laughed. "Anyway, the detectives said this perp, Rashawn, might've been involved. Plus, the caliber used was nine-millimeter—six shots fired. The gun we got today, Rashawn's—had a fifteen-round magazine, only two bullets in it, and one in the chamber. So that means a lot of rounds have been fired out of—"

"We both went to college, Harris. We can add," Dominguez retorted as he signed out on the roll call. Chan shrugged; he really didn't care either way. Harris was left with hours of paperwork ahead of him while he and Dominguez could get on with their lives. Chan counted his blessings.

CHAPTER 7

JAMEL HARRIS: PROCESSING THE ARREST

The collar was a bitch and a half. McCall stayed for a few hours to help him, but he had to pick up his kids from the babysitter and bailed around six, already pressing the overtime with the desk sergeant. Jamel had to wait for the Evidence Collection Team to come and swab the gun for DNA, then steam it for prints. Prints, obviously, came up negative like always on a gun. Hopefully, the DNA would match Rashawn.

Sure, the gun was found in his room—in his shoe, presumably. But Jamel had seen this kind of thing go south before. A few months earlier, he and McCall collared a guy in a private apartment building for beating up his girlfriend. They'd heard that this prick liked to fire rounds out his window. Sure enough, Harris found a loaded six-shot revolver under the mattress, with five live rounds and one spent shell casing. Unfortunately, they hadn't done a good enough job of proving that this room belonged to the perp, since multiple people lived in the apartment.

The ADA declined to proceed with the gun charges. Slouching back in his chair at the Brooklyn DA's offices on Jay Street, he'd shrugged. "Maybe if DNA comes back, ties him to the gun, we talk." Thus far, Harris had heard nothing and wasn't holding his breath that he ever would.

So, this time he'd taken pictures of anything in plain view in the room with Rashawn's name on it—mail, the first page of a notepad with gang doodles and idiot rap rhymes on it, even a tattered GED certificate that was lying under marijuana dregs on the dresser. Let them try and say this wasn't Rashawn's room now.

There *was* the search, though. He knew they should've applied for a warrant once they found the gun, but the sergeant might not have gone for it. They were already short-staffed. *Fuck it. They wanna throw out the weed, so be it.* The gun had been within arm's reach of where Rashawn had been standing by the window; all he had to do was squat and grab it. According to the Penal Law, you could search within a suspect's grabbable area without a warrant pursuant to an arrest. Especially when the guy keeps playing games with his hands and resists arrest. *Let's just hope the ADA sees it that way*, he thought.

This was a bigger grab than usual, though, since Detective Espinoza initially thought they might tie this gun to the homicide on New Year's Day. The only problem was, when the detective began probing further after Harris brought him in, it turned out that Rashawn had been locked up for credit card fraud in Westchester County on New Year's Eve and didn't get out till two days later. Espinoza had reassured Harris, "Still might be the gun, though. And it doesn't mean he's not involved in the homicide. He's just got a very good alibi. I still think someone in the Jackie Boys did it, but he's not talking."

"They had a beef with the old guy?"

Espinoza laughed. "Old to you, young man. The victim was only a few years older than me."

Jamel winced. He didn't want to offend the detectives, especially Espinoza. But Espinoza just smiled and continued. "Victim—Lawrence Washington—did a bid upstate a few years back, was mostly clean since. So I think the beef was personal. He has a niece who lives in Brownsville. She had her baby daddy, goes by Big Boy—he's a big player in the Jackie Boys—locked up for busting up her face a few weeks before the homicide. He's still in Rikers on a parole violation, and since he made a lot of money for the Jackie Boys—even ran his own crew—they're hurting. Unfortunately, after her uncle gets killed, the niece isn't talking; refusing to cooperate with the DA's office on the domestic violence charge. Only thing they've got on him now is the parole violation—I gotta talk to the arresting officer and make sure he's got his shit together at the hearing. He gets out, we're likely to have more problems."

Parole hearings were usually easier than those presided over by a judge at a criminal hearing. The standard of proof wasn't as high to send the guy back to prison, since he owed time anyway on whatever charges he'd been convicted of. Harris had only done two parole hearings so far. Both had gone well, the perps sent back upstate to serve out their time. He shook his head. "I don't know how you keep track of all this shit, Espinoza. I'm still just prayin' they're not gonna throw the gun charge out."

Espinoza patted him on the shoulder. "Have to be up on 'all this shit' when you're in the squad. Most of the shootings we've taken lately have involved either the Jackie Boys or the Jenkins family. Gotta know all the ins and outs, otherwise you're lost in the sauce, and no homicides would ever get solved after the first few days. You'll get there eventually. Be up here (he indicated the Detective Squad room) in a couple of years if you keep working hard."

Now *that* was nice to hear. Harris glanced at the fish swimming in the well-kept tank near the door. With no prisoners in the detectives' single holding cell, the room was actually very relaxing, a few DTs typing away or going through paperwork at their desks. So different from his last three and a half years of chasing the radio, dealing with violent crazy people, domestics, shooting scenes, even just stupid disputes over petty shit that spiraled way further than they would have if even one person involved had a lick of sense.

"Yo! Harris!"

It was Espinoza, waving his hand back and forth near his eyes like he was administering a field sobriety test. "You still there?"

"Yeah, uhh...I gotta get downstairs, finish the paperwork."

Espinoza patted him on the shoulder softly. "I get what you're doing—I did it too, when I was coming up. You're living at the station, practically, maxing out on OT."

Harris smiled proudly. "I got seven collars this month already. Mostly off the radio, but a couple on observation. All good shit, nothing petty."

Espinoza sighed. "I know you're a worker. But you gotta be smart. This department doesn't like go-getters." He exhaled. "I mean, they like 'em until they don't. You look at the crime guys, especially Smith..."

Smith had been an Anti-Crime cop in the precinct, working the evening shift. He probably bagged more guns than some entire precincts did in a year. Seven years on the streets—four of them in Anti-Crime. He was active, decent, and humble. But tough as shit too. He studied like a motherfucker and did really well on the sergeant's test. But before he got made, he had to see the Borough chiefs because of all the complaints he'd accrued over the years—not one of them substantiated. But they all stayed on your record.

They allowed the promotion to go through. But then they sent him to Queens Central Booking. This was only a desired assignment if you were a sergeant who didn't want to do anything and still get easy overtime. For a guy like Smith, it was a death sentence. He couldn't help but get involved, break up fights, and charge assholes that smuggled shit in. He wouldn't last long there. Everyone knew that.

"Yeah," Harris admitted. "Smith got a raw deal. But I'm not gonna get like that. I'm a college graduate. I write *well*. Even these three-line reports we do, I get things in. And I record everything else in my memo book. I'm always ready at court."

One of the detectives, a white guy in his fifties, piped up. "But you'll let any random asshole walk into a crime scene and click away!"

Harris was stung by the laughter. It was coming from everyone—the three white detectives, sitting at their desks, the two black ones. Even Espinoza couldn't help but smile.

"It's gonna take a while to live that one down, bro."

Jamel's face got as red as it could get, and he should have just walked away then. But he was curious. "Did they get any DNA or prints off the shell casings from the homicide?"

The same detective who'd just insulted him spoke up again. "They don't swipe for DNA or prints on fired shell casings. Tell that to your photographer friend." A few chuckles ensued.

Espinoza felt bad for him and explained. "OCME (Office of the Chief Medical Examiner) says the heat from the bullet firing would burn off DNA and prints. But other departments do it, and I've heard they sometimes get a hit."

Jamel knew better than to ask why the NYPD didn't swab ejected shell casings if other departments did—he was already properly ashamed, and it was probably obvious to anyone with half a lick of common sense.

Espinoza read the confusion on his face. "Then again, those departments don't police a population of almost nine million people and investigate thousands of shootings a year. I doubt it would hold up in a New York City court, anyway."

That Jamel could understand.

CHAPTER 8

ROTHCHILD: ON THE COCKTAIL

The "AIDS cocktail" didn't sound so bad, disregarding the *AIDS* part, anyway. But the series of pills made you feel like shit. Some people got horrible stomach issues; for me, it was just a general sense of nausea and fatigue.

"Wow, that cocktail's really kicking your ass," my brother Jason remarked once it was clear I wasn't going to be of much use babysitting, at least for the next few weeks. We were at their house on Long Island. Jason, me, his wife Ellen, and their two-year-old son Jonathan were all seated in the cozy living room. The little tyke was busying himself tearing pages out of a magazine Ellen had left on the coffee table. I knew it wasn't Jason's magazine since I'd never once seen him read anything after his high school graduation. Luckily, the Army hadn't been too judgmental over his lack of intellectual curiosity, which is how he'd managed to get hired by the NYPD with no college. Not that I was a lauded scholar myself. I graduated from high school a year early, at seventeen (New York City public schools—you can keep the applause to yourself). Instead of college, I enlisted in the Army too, following my older brother's footsteps. Jason had combat experience, though, and I didn't. My unit had deployed to the Middle East, but we were a support unit and didn't see any action. Jason insisted that that was just as well.

Jason was three years older and looked like me, only a little more handsome, I'll grudgingly admit. He still lifted regularly and didn't have a dad-bod yet. Ellen was a blonde, Waspy beauty-queen type we'd known since high school. One of the nicest people you'll ever meet, and a real trooper—she'd converted to Judaism after they got married, religion apparently being so important to Jason suddenly, though he still rarely went to synagogue and kept about as Kosher as I did.

All cops knew about the AIDS cocktail. So, while Jay had never had to take it, he could empathize. He sat back on the couch across from me, his arm around his pretty, pregnant wife as he assessed me like only an older brother could. "I mean it, Josh, you really look like shit. You sure that perp didn't butt-fuck you too?"

Ellen slapped him on the arm so hard that little Jonathan jumped. "It's okay, baby," Ellen cooed, shooting off the couch like a bullet to cuddle her son in her arms. "Daddy just said something stupid." She turned to me, standing with him in her arms. The little guy didn't seem any the worse for the bad language or the spousal abuse he'd just witnessed. "Your brother's a real—" She thought better of it. "Silly goose, Josh. Sorry you're going through such a rough time. We all hope you feel better soon."

Now I felt bad for Ellen. Jay seemed over the slap, though, lounging back on the couch again with that smirk on his face like he was still king of the castle and hadn't just been put in his place by his wife. "It's just hard for me to express my feelings, babe. So I joke."

"Actually, Ellen, I've only got two more weeks and I'll be back at work."

"It's sad when the best part of your life is looking forward to going back to patrol in Bed-Stuy," Jay mused. There wasn't much to it, though, since he was the Anti-Crime sergeant in the 75th Precinct in East New York. I was about to point this out when I looked over at

Ellen and Jonathan, her bouncing him in her arms as he scrunched another magazine page in his hands and giggled. No sense reminding her of the dangerous area her husband worked in.

I responded in a tone that I hoped came off as cool rather than bitchy. "We can't all be you, Jay."

"Yeah, I got it made," he said sarcastically. Ellen looked at him sharply. "I meant in terms of my current work assignment, babe."

She ignored him and carried little Jonathan out of the room. "You're really good at pissing off your wife, Jay."

He took a large sip of beer and shrugged. "I learned from the master."

He meant our father, who spurred such contempt in my mother that once they got divorced, they did the handovers of me and Jay inside the 112th Precinct station house. Once I became a cop, I saw this was a pretty common thing: every Sunday loads of parents doing the "exchanges" inside the precinct so there wouldn't be any trouble. Though I have to say I never saw my father lay a hand on my mother or get out of line. I think she just really didn't like him.

A few minutes went by, the two of us sharing a comfortable silence. We'd both gotten a few jabs at each other as was our custom, and now he was content to drink his beer while I took baby sips of ginger ale. I couldn't wait to drink again.

"So, what're they charging him with?"

"I didn't tell you? Since the bite was so bad and I needed stitches, plus him telling me he just gave me AIDS—his record's really bad too. So the ADA charged him with felony assault, and we did a grand jury."

Jay could tell by the way I was talking that the story was gonna get worse. "So what happened?" he asked, like he didn't really want to know. For all my older brother's bluster, he had always been an optimist at heart and hated that his bubble was always burst.

"So…the dickhead testified."

Jay whistled. In a grand jury in New York, the defendant has the right to testify, but rarely does. This asshole opted to, not being able to make bail and refusing to waive his right to the grand jury being held within a reasonable time after the arrest. "The ADA told me he started crying, talking about how he just bit me because I was beating on him so bad."

Jay shook his head; he knew where this was going. Brooklyn juries, Brooklyn grand juries…they were often pretty anti-cop. "So they wind up charging him, but with attempted assault three."

"What the fuck? How's it *attempted*?!"

I shrugged. "Who the fuck knows? Afterward, the ADA's like, 'Yeah, we should've just hit him up with the misdemeanor assault initially, so we didn't have to deal with the grand jury. With his record, he would've gotten at least something.' But now—attempted assault three's only a Class B misdemeanor. We'll be lucky if he pleads guilty to disorderly conduct. Plus, he's already sued our crime unit once and some cops in the 73, so you know I've probably got a lawsuit coming down the pike."

"Fuckin' assholes," Jay said, probably meaning both the jurors and the ADA who'd screwed things up for his brother. "Why didn't you tell me?"

"Honestly, I was so pissed about the whole thing, having to go to court feeling like shit and testifying—twice, since they had all these questions. I just couldn't, Jay. I didn't wanna ruin your day."

Jay shook his head sadly. "Little brother, you just ruined my whole week."

Jay was always my rock, ambitious but easygoing. I didn't like it when he was depressed.

"Look at the bright side, Jay. I was having doubts about taking the security job, but this bullshit really puts things in perspective."

Jay smiled. He wanted me to take the job, not only for the salary potential but also so his little brother would be in a safer environment, able to live a more normal life. "I'm sad it had to happen this way, but Billy's a solid guy, and he likes you a lot. You're too smart to be a cop, Josh. You'll make more money working for him right off the bat. And he sees your potential. I mean, fuck, you're almost done with your bachelor's, working full-time as a cop all these years. I barely got through my associate's degree."

"That's because you have to read for college."

Jay put his hands up in a hopeless gesture. "I don't know-it's like I look at a book, and there's all these weird symbols on the pages, and I'm supposed to make sense of all that shit? It's fucking gibberish!" We both laughed.

For some reason, Jay decided to talk shop. "I heard it was the Jackie Boys who did that homicide you made the paper on."

"No witnesses, no video footage-they're probably never gonna solve that one. How do you know about the Jackie Boys, anyway?"

"They're a bad crew-they dropped two bodies in my precinct last year."

The Jackie Boys were the biggest gang in my precinct. I hadn't realized they were well-known in other precincts as well. "Why do you give a shit about one of our homicides, anyway?"

Jay shrugged. "I'm the Anti-Crime Sergeant in a neighboring precinct. And it's still my city."

"Not anymore, bro. You live on Long Island now. At least till Ellen comes to her senses and sends you packing. But I'm sure mom will let you sleep on her couch when you move back to Queens."

Jay laughed, then decided to change the subject. "Don't worry about that perp who bit you- he'll piss the wrong person off and get what's coming to him."

"Let's hope," I said half-heartedly.

***

Overall, Melanie, the only other person I'd talked to about the Grand Jury other than Courtney Jones and Keisha Jackson, who'd also testified, had been much more positive about the whole thing. I called her the night I'd found out the grand jury's indictment, in a huff.

She sighed. "What're you gonna do, Josh? This city sucks. At least you get some time off work, tax-free."

This had calmed me down a bit, but she declined my offer to hang out that night. The whole mess was starting again with me and her. Melanie was twenty-six, having just hit five years on the job. I'd just turned thirty-one and knew I should be over these games at this stage in my life. Easier said than done.

CHAPTER 9

ERIC HANES:
BACK WITH THE PARTNER

Eric turned onto Reid, or "Malcolm X Boulevard," as it was officially titled, passing the big Utica Avenue Train Station "esplanade." A few bus stops and then a big concrete area, with the stairs leading down to the express A and local C subway trains; beyond that, a handful of businesses, including a small grocery store, a bodega, and a chicken place. Rising behind the stores was one of the main cruxes of Eric's existence, a series of connected six-story buildings that were very fucking confusing if you happened to be chasing a perp through them. You could enter one building, run through the hallway, and wind up in another, then have to chase the perp out a rear exit onto the opposite street you came in from or into a big, wide-open concrete courtyard that was more like an ambusher's dream, the windows of the buildings looking down on you from above.

Eric had been in a bunch of these pursuits over the years, and he liked to think he was past the point in his career where he'd chase a perp into those buildings for anything even remotely minor. Of course, he'd been driving Sergeant Rothchild on New Year's Day when they took the homicide there, one of several that would likely occur in these buildings throughout the year. He'd had to man the crime scene for hours, dealing with assholes jaw-jacking him the whole time.

All for a homicide that would probably never be solved, a career perp who'd finally pissed off the wrong guy or had just been in the wrong place at the wrong time.

Luckily, they were just passing through the area; this wasn't part of their assigned sector. They were assigned the northwest part of the precinct, their usual beat before Shayna popped out the baby and went on child-care leave. Eric had been floating since then, usually driving the patrol sergeant, sometimes working his preferred sector, or filling in a car when someone's partner wasn't working. It wasn't bad, but he was glad Shayna was back. After sixteen years on patrol in this crazy place, Eric liked structure more than anything. While Shayna could be a bit much sometimes, they'd worked together for so long that there wasn't anything she could throw at him or he at her that would cause more than a slight ripple in their relationship.

Shayna looked good, as always. Sure, she still had a few pounds of baby weight to lose, but her smooth, dark complexion still didn't have even the slightest line or wrinkle that a lot of thirty-five-year old faces did. He was about ten years older, but he'd started to notice small wrinkles even in his early thirties on his jet-black face, making him question the wiseness of the expression "black don't crack." He was only about five-eight, but thick across the shoulders and heavy in the belly so that, even sitting, he seemed to tower over her five-four, curvy but athletic frame.

Shayna was looking out her window at the myriad of folks standing at the bus stop on the corner of Reid and Utica. It was mostly working folks at this hour; women wearing heavy coats over scrubs or orderly uniforms, commuting to their jobs as home health aides or nurses, guys working construction gigs, men and women dressed nicely for office work, even some white faces, mostly younger men and women. Eric noticed one of the said white guys waiting for the bus.

He had a long coat that covered down past his socks and worn-but expensive-looking shoes. "White guys are probably doctors, going to Kings County Hospital or Brookdale."

"Why they gotta be doctors?" Shayna asked, though there wasn't any real challenge in the statement.

"It's too late for teachers to be going to work, and what else would non-weirdo white guys be doing taking that bus?"

"You know there's more white folks moving in around here—it's not like the old days. 'Sides, was he wearing scrubs?"

"I couldn't see," Eric admitted. "He was standing near the back of the crowd, opposite of the old days."

Shayna appreciated that one and laughed. "Bed-Stuy's becoming like Birmingham in reverse."

Eric snorted. "That'll change. Once enough of 'em move in, they'll chase all the black folk out like they always do. Now they're still all polite and cowed, smokin' their weed and not making eye contact with the natives. Once enough of 'em get in here, our peeps will all be kicked out to Long Island."

Shayna shrugged. "Long Island's not so bad. Me and Hank got a nice place."

Eric snorted. "They wouldn't have sold you that house twenty years ago."

"I was in middle school twenty years ago, not like your old ass— probably already thirty by then."

They drove in a comfortable silence after that, Eric making passes down Stuyvesant, Lewis, circling around the projects, then over to Marcus Garvey, where there was another set of Section 8 buildings. He didn't feel like getting out and strolling through the courtyard between the big apartments and row houses, knowing Shayna was still getting back into the swing of things after six months out. Last thing he wanted was to be chasing some shitheads for rolling dice or drinking. No one, least of all him, was thinking about such things on a cold day in late January. Heck, even in July it would've been a tough sell to most of the guys on the tour, Harris and McCall excepted. But those two would go overboard like they always did, thinking they were in Crime already and not just barely off-probation rookie patrol cops. Heaven forbid one of the perps slipped past them and ran inside one of the courtyard apartments. Giant-ass McCall would kick the door in and they'd wind up fighting three assholes just to get the one, after which the two young dumb cops would tear the place apart looking for guns. Even if they found one, a complaint or lawsuit was a likely possibility.

Folks in Bed-Stuy loved to sue the cops. The more wrong they were, the more serious their crime and criminal history, the angrier they got over even the slightest perceived trespass on their rights. And the more money they'd usually get once the city settled, to put the case to rest. Eric had been around long enough to know that the bloodsucking suing kind of lawyers and the public defenders loved the bad guys more than anything in the world and considered it their sacred duty to ensure they got whatever they could get on any technicality. An innocent person who'd never committed a crime but got caught up in something, though, like a young brother hanging out at a relative's house that got raided for guns or drugs that were then found inside, or a young brother whose only crime was to accept a ride from a shady dude who then got pulled over, didn't rate the same level of sympathy or sense of purpose for these kinds of lawyers. So used to perverting the law in service of the city's worst offenders, they just went through the motions with the innocent ones.

He made another loop and came up Vernon Avenue, checking the big public housing building across the street. This building was actually in the neighboring precinct. Still, a lot of shit popped off there that couldn't be discarded due to the artificial borders set up to delineate the precinct boundaries. It wasn't like there was a force field preventing those shitheads from crossing the street and becoming his problem. So he liked to push them back away from the borders when he could.

"Why you so quiet, dark-man?"

She called him that sometimes, when they were alone in the car. Though in truth, she wasn't much lighter than he was. Point that out to her, though, and she wouldn't talk to him for a week. Sometimes he thought it would be better to have a male partner.

There wasn't anyone hanging out in front of the projects, so he drove past and turned back onto Garvey, figuring they'd check out the men's shelter housed in a big armory a couple of blocks up. "Just thinkin'," he answered after a few moments.

"Didn't the doctor tell you not to be doing that anymore?"

He pointed to his shaved head. "Nope. What he actually said was that the mechanics of this fine brain are what've kept our team afloat on this ocean of sewage all these years."

She snorted. "*Ocean*? You couldn't swim if a mound of bacon was waiting for you on the other side."

"It would be." He patted his ample belly. "Stacked right next to a gaggle of naked ladies, all the colors of the rainbow ready to please me. Mostly nice little white girls who don't even know there's such a thing as talking back to a man."

She snorted again. "You wish."

"Oh, it would happen." He smiled. "Or maybe I'd just flop around in the water for a while, checking out the sights on the other side until I finally drowned and kissed this hellhole of a life behind." He pulled up in front of the shelter.

"*Their* lives are hell," Shayna remarked sagely, indicating two gentlemen walking out the shelter doors into the cold air. One of them, wearing a beat-up old camouflage coat, had a bad limp and took every step gingerly as if he might fall face-down on the concrete like he was seventy instead of forty.

Eric snorted. "Why, 'cause they have to leave the shelter and pretend to look for work for a few hours? Then drink all day and come back and have their meals on us."

Shayna laughed. "You're right about that—the guys in this shelter are all deadbeats. But they aren't all like that."

"I know that." He was looking at the two perps, guys who'd gotten kicked out of other shelters and wound up in this one, an all-men's shelter with a lot of security. Even with the security, though, the cops were called here several times a day. They walked down the stairs and then crossed in the middle of the street, not even glancing at the cop car, and headed to the corner bodega. Probably buying booze, Eric figured.

Shayna read the look of disgust on his face. "Then again, your life was that depressing you'd probably be boxed all day too." She sniggered, then did quotation marks with her fingers. "*If* your life was that depressing."

"Ha-ha. Matter of fact, I got some last night."

"Some what?"

Even though he knew she was being coy he looked at her suggestively. "Some you-know-what."

She shook her head. "Bragging about getting Popeyes? Pretty sad…"

"I almost did pop her eye out."

"Please. The girls you mess with are all beat up. You know what, big man? Why don't we drive by one of the women's shelters in East New York and you can take your pick."

"You think every woman's ugly."

"Just the ugly ones."

The two guys came out of the bodega, paper bags in their hands. The one without the limp was a lot younger than Eric had originally thought—late twenties, early thirties. He glanced in the direction of the cop car, probably feeling their stare on some level, before the odd couple headed up Jefferson Street. It had been too much to hope that they were gonna open the drinks right in front of them so they could get an easy summons. Shitbags couldn't even do that right.

Eric pulled out onto the street. They passed the "Bed-Stuy Volleys" on their left, an all-volunteer ambulance gig. He was gonna remark to Shayna how he hadn't stopped in there in a while when the dispatcher raised them to respond to a landlord/tenant dispute on Lewis Avenue. Shayna acknowledged the transmission over her radio and Eric headed over there. He knew the address; they'd been there before, though he couldn't remember what the last job had been. Over the years, radio runs blended together until only a few stuck out in his mind. Sure, if someone reminded him, he'd remember. Otherwise, it was the complete opposite of when he'd been a rookie, back when he remembered every job crystal clear. Now he only remembered when there was a reason to. Call it getting seasoned; call it getting older.

He drove casually since it wasn't a priority call. Even though they regularly texted, and he'd been out to the house a few times during her maternity leave, Shayna asked the question. "Anything interesting happen while I was out?"

He thought about it. "You remember that rabbi Sergeant Rothchild and Jones collared last year?"

"The Hassidic one. You know they send lawyers to the public assistance office to get benefits for them, right?"

"This one had a benefit card on him. Owns a few houses in the precinct."

"Renting them out to poor black folk. I'm so glad I was on limited duty that day," Shayna said. It hadn't been long after she'd started the limited duty for her pregnancy.

"Yeah, if I wasn't on the other end of the precinct, I'd have been the one who transported him back to the station. They'd hate me too."

"So what happened?"

"Some of his friends—a city councilman, a few other bigwigs—they staged a little protest in the front lobby once the CCRB complaint was thrown out. They wanted blood."

Shayna shook her head. "That's ridiculous. He was with a prostitute."

"And his license was suspended. But you know, politics."

"I hope you stayed away from that protest."

"I did. I guess they spoke with the CO and she calmed them down or whatever."

Shayna shook her head. "I can't see her calming anybody down. She's probably gonna sell Rothchild down the river."

Eric nodded.

It took them less than four minutes to get to the landlord/tenant dispute. He pulled up in front of the location, a three-story brownstone. It was in a row of similar attached homes, all with waist-high metal gates over a concrete patio before a set of steps that led up to the first floor. There was no angry tenant standing in front of the location, so he and Shayna got out of their car and approached. As he got to the gate, his eyes scanned the building, top to bottom, finally settling on the basement window that looked out onto the street. He didn't see any shades parted or faces staring out at them. So he reached over the gate, unlatched it, and swung it open. He and Shayna then walked through the small courtyard and padded up the steps.

Two minutes of banging on the metal security door with his collapsible baton. The last minute and forty seconds only because

Shayna had asked the dispatcher to call back the complainant before he'd even knocked and the dispatcher responded, "Call back goes to voice mail." He heard yelling inside and knew they'd have to come back one way or another, so he kept at it. As was often the case in this line of work, pure persistence, not blinding intelligence or charm or skill, yielded the desired result. The front door was finally opened by a fortyish woman wearing a too-tight tank top for her wide body, sweats, and a do-rag for her hair. Before they said anything, "Y'all need to tell this bitch downstairs to stop complainin' about some bullshit noise! She don't even pay rent!"

"Are you the owner?" Eric asked as they stepped into the living room. It was messy, and there were holes in the plaster walls.

"No, an' neither is she! Bank owns this place, and the more problems she causes, the more they're gonna try an' get us out!"

"So you're not paying rent either," Shayna pointed out.

"That's not the fucking point!" she screamed. "I got rights against harassment!"

Eric asked, "What noise is she complaining about?"

"Bullshit noise—my room's back there." She motioned down the hallway. "Just 'cause I don't go to bed at eleven like her don't mean I got to walk on eggshells! This is fuckin' New York City—there's *gonna* be noise." She shook her head angrily. "I don't even gotta be talkin' to y'all—she's the idiot who called 911 for this nonsense! Then she goes and runs downstairs 'cause she can't handle the shit *she* started!"

"All right, we'll talk to her," Eric said, knowing this was in fact nonsense but that the downstairs tenant would call back if they didn't.

He walked toward the basement. There was no door, so he poked his head down. He could hear a TV playing. He tapped a few times on the wall, hoping to get her attention. "Miss—it's the police. Can you come up?"

90

She padded up the stairs, muttering under her breath. She was just as bad as the first one. Loud, obnoxious—no shame that she was living rent-free until the bank got off their lazy asses and finally kicked them out. That could take years, Eric knew—a lot of times the banks just let these places go to shit until they were ready to sell. All the while, the neighbors had to deal with a house on their block with ten different people living there basically illegally. The kind of folks who liked to cause problems.

Eric got the gist of it—the downstairs lady, the one who'd called 911, was mad that the one who answered the door made too much noise when she walked around at night. She concluded by saying, "I go to bed at ten—that's not so early I should be disturbed all night by this bitch" before finally shutting up. Across the room, the other woman was sucking her teeth. Shayna gave her a look that said she better not get into it with the other one right now. She turned away, muttering obscenities.

"What time you start work?" Shayna asked Eric's downstairs lady from across the room. She didn't say anything. The other lady said, "She don't work—she a fuckin' bum! An' you could sleep ten hours and still look like shit, bitch!"

The downstairs lady started walking toward her angrily. Eric got between them.

"Settle down, miss. We're not trying to mess with anyone's situation." He motioned with his head to indicate a man coming down the stairs. He didn't seem to be involved in the dispute or care either way. Shayna asked him to leave, and he did without protest.

The women started to yell again, and Eric put up his hand and raised his voice. "Quiet!" Amazingly, they both shut up. "Look, everyone in this place is squatting. That's cool. We're not the squatting police, and the bank doesn't seem to give a shit."

Both of the women nodded.

Shayna said, "But if we have to keep coming back here, I'll call the bank myself and get them to press charges for trespassing."

For a second Eric thought they might lose it—but they didn't want to fight with the cops too, and it seemed to have the desired effect. Both women agreed to stay away from each other.

"And no more calls unless it's a real emergency," Eric reminded. They waited till the downstairs lady went back down to the basement so they wouldn't get into it again, then left.

As they walked outside, Shayna asked, low, "How long before we're back here?"

"I give it a day, tops," he replied without missing a beat. He'd really missed Shayna. Not that he'd ever tell her that, or she him.

CHAPTER 10

ROTHCHILD: BACK AT WORK

I returned to work on January 29, exactly four weeks after I got bit. I still had a few days left of the cocktail, but the NYPD Department doctor sent me back. I was going stir crazy anyway. That one night I went to the movies with Melanie and the night at my brother's house were pretty much the highlights of the month. Pretty sad. Even sadder, I hadn't seen Melanie since that night, though we had been texting and even spoken on the phone a few times.

Roll call was uneventful. Dominguez, standing in the second row of the cops lined up before me, eleven in all, gave me a shout-out. "Welcome back, Sarge!"

"Thanks, Dominguez. Maybe you could make a collar to celebrate the occasion. You haven't had one in four months."

Jones piped in happily, "Sarge has been doing his homework!"

His mood brightened even more when I told him he was driving me for the day. Since Shayna had gotten back from maternity leave in my absence, I wasn't going to take Eric again.

Courtney was driving down Ralph Avenue, a straight shot from the precinct to a Dunkin' Donuts on Atlantic Avenue. It was a little before eight. "So, what've you been doing lately?" I asked the question innocently enough, though I kind of knew the answer I was going to get. Courtney didn't have a steady partner, so every day was a crapshoot on assignments for him. Add to that Lieutenant Allen wasn't exactly his biggest fan.

"Oh, it's been a blast, Sarge. Fixed post every day."

I whistled.

"To tell the truth, I'm kind of exaggerating. One day I got to hang out at Central Booking all day in this little room guarding a perp with TB. Kept pulling off his mask and coughing. Not that I'm trying to *brag…*"

I laughed. "Well at least you had that mini vacation."

He shrugged. "A couple days the weather wasn't too bad. There's that, anyway." He held his non-driving hand in front of his face and looked down at it. "Arthritis from the frostbite hasn't set in yet, so I'm doing pretty well."

I looked at him proudly. "Wow, Courtney. You're usually not that much of a glass-is-half-full kind of guy."

"I'm gonna be twenty-eight in a few weeks, Sarge. Trying to be more Zen about shit."

"Well, I just hit thirty-one, and it still hasn't happened for me yet," I informed him.

We made it to Dunkin' Donuts without any priority calls coming over the air. There were only a few people ahead of us in line, but the cute girl I was kind of crushing on wasn't there today. Was she still working here? I turned to Courtney, and he read my mind.

"She was here the other day, Sarge. Asked about you."

I nodded casually. I wasn't sure if this was actually true. Courtney was always trying to get me dates.

"You need to ask her out, Sarge. I guarantee she'll say yes."

I shrugged and went up to the register to order my coffee. Before I even handed over the money, the dispatcher's voice echoed loudly over my radio. "One Sergeant, be advised, holding a violent EDP with a knife on Monroe and Garvey."

I was still holding my money, not sure if we should just run out. From behind me Courtney asked, "You think it's Linda?"

Linda was an older crackhead who sat on a wooden box by a liquor store near that corner. She was batshit crazy and often waved knives around at passers-by but never actually assaulted them. Local dealers often hid their stash under her box, so to speak, as Linda was so nasty and dirty no cops wanted to arrest her or even send her to the psych ward as long as she calmed down. Anyway, fishing under that box might wind up with you literally holding a steaming pile of Linda's shit. So if it was Linda I was just gonna pay and wait for the coffee.

I keyed my mic. "Central, is the EDP male or female?"

"Says…male, mid-twenties, violent with a knife." Would've been nice to know that originally.

I nodded to Courtney and we left, apologizing to the cashier on our way out.

Courtney was a skilled driver, though not the most considerate. As we turned back onto Ralph Avenue, our lights not yet activated, a woman pushing a stroller had just stepped into the crosswalk. Courtney bleeped the siren at her and went ahead, forcing her to stop.

"She had the right of way, Courtney."

"We always got the right of way, Sarge."

I switched on the lights. "Now we do."

Courtney nodded. "Sorry about that, Sarge."

Boy, Lieutenant Allen must've really done a number on him while I was gone. I mused as he kept driving, "You're like a willing little Boy Scout now. So well mannered."

Courtney laughed as he made a wide turn. "I learned my lesson. You could grab my dick now and I wouldn't say a thing."

"I'll try to resist."

"Good luck with that, Sarge."

I laughed. "Let's see how long this new attitude lasts. I give it two weeks."

Eric and Shayna were already there as we pulled up. As they stepped out of their car, I observed a young male standing in front of the liquor store holding a folding knife at his side, the blade deployed. There weren't any other people around. He backed up against the glass pane of the liquor store as they approached, keeping their distance due to the knife. Thankfully, Linda was nowhere to be seen.

As they approached, hands on the butts of their guns, Eric yelled, "Drop the knife!"

I'd just gotten out of the car at this point. The guy was clearly crazy—you could see it in his eyes. Thankfully, he looked down at the knife, then slipped it, blade first, into his pants pocket. He then kept his hands at his sides, though they were balled into fists.

Shayna: "We're here to help, sir. What's going on?"

"Nothin goin' on!" He was a thin young man in his early twenties who looked like he'd been living on the street for a while. He glanced behind him, seeing only the posted-over windows of the liquor store. Nowhere to go but toward us if he didn't want to get all cut up crashing through the glass.

Shayna again. "We're here because someone was concerned about you. You're not in any trouble."

The kid muttered something unintelligible, still clearly distressed.

The four of us were in a semicircle facing him. Shayna had her hands out at chest level in a neutral gesture, trying to calm him down and let him see we weren't here to hurt him. She kept the kid's attention.

Eric still had his hand on the butt of his gun. Only supervisors carried Tasers back then. I had mine out, hid behind my left leg in case he reached inside the pocket with the knife.

Since it was a quiet, wintery weekday morning, EMS wasn't that busy and had made it over here fast. I could hear the sirens from a few blocks out. When they pulled up it might amp the guy up even more, knowing he was going to have to go to the hospital. I made eye contact with Eric and Courtney and gestured with my head, signaling for them to move in.

Eric moved in on the guy's right side, and Courtney on the left. While Shayna continued making eye contact and talking calmly, Courtney grabbed the guy's left hand as Eric grabbed the right. He struggled, but Courtney and Eric were able to pull him away from the window and cuff his thin wrists up without much trouble. I keyed my radio and told the dispatcher that the EDP was in custody and to cancel the response of any further units. "Any complainant who wants to talk?"

"No," the dispatcher stated. "Callers were all passers-by."

"Straight up EDP," I told them. "No crime." This meant he would just go to the hospital and not be arrested.

Courtney patted the guy on the shoulder and spoke calmly as the ambulance pulled up, seeing the alarm in his eyes. "You'll be okay, man. They're gonna help you."

He tried to throw his body down but Eric and Courtney held him up, then dragged him to the ambulance. Eric searched him, first removing the knife and slipping it in the back pocket of his pants. He then found a picture ID Benefit Card, a toothbrush, a plastic shaving razor, toothpaste, and a couple of other items that confirmed my suspicion that he was homeless.

One of the EMS workers opened the back door of the ambulance. Eric and Courtney got him in without too much trouble, but they had to then help EMS strap him down on the gurney since he was too hyped up to ride in the bench seat, even handcuffed. Courtney was leaning over the guy when Eric said, "Make sure the cuffs are on good, Jones. He's got thin wrists."

Courtney snapped to mock attention. "Aye, aye, Sergeant!"

Eric said, "Just pointing it out, bro."

"Jeez," I said, looking at Courtney. And to think I gave you two weeks."

Courtney smiled and patted Eric on the shoulder. "You know I love you, man. I was just fucking around."

Eric shook his head. "All those cold days on the corner are catchin' up with you."

Shayna said, from outside the ambulance, "What're you talkin' about? He's always been a dick."

Courtney shrugged, then leaned down to make sure the cuffs were on snug enough.

* * * * *

That morning turned out to be pretty busy. While we were dealing with the guy at the liquor store, a couple of domestic disputes came out. Out of the three calls, one resulted in an arrest, which Jamel Harris readily volunteered to take. Since we didn't have any cops to send McCall back out on patrol with, I resigned myself and Courtney to essentially being the third patrol car while he helped his partner with the arrest. At around noon, things got quiet and I headed back to the precinct to see if Harris wanted me to sign the arrest paperwork so he wouldn't have to bother Eddie at the desk.

Harris was grateful for the gesture, looking up from his computer in the arrest processing area, which was just outside the door to the cells. He handed me the handwritten arrest report and the complaint report to go with it and I signed both. As usual, both of his reports were neatly written and thorough. I decided to try to forgive him without reservation for the fuck-up back at the crime scene that made me look like an idiot.

I left him to put the reports into the computer while McCall dealt with the perp's incessant demands for cigarettes and snacks to keep him from insisting he be taken to the hospital for some imagined medical concern. Then I walked behind the front desk to talk to Eddie. He looked up from the computer, where he seemed to be surfing the Internet.

"Just make sure you're not downloading child porn, Eddie. I'm pretty sure that's against regulations."

"You sure? I never read that in the department manual." We laughed. "Nah, I'm looking at colleges for my kid."

I leaned down and whistled. "MIT, huh?"

Eddie shrugged. "He's only a sophomore now, but he's rocking the grades and doing wrestling and football. I can always hope. How you feeling, anyway?"

"Well, I've got a few more days of the meds left. The antibiotics were done in ten days, but the infectious disease specialist said I should take the whole lot of the antivirals to be safe. Then HIV tests for the next six months." I shrugged. "She said I'm probably good—it's not that easy to get AIDS. But it's better to be safe."

Eddie nodded. "Yeah, definitely."

I looked up and saw Detective Espinoza exit the stairway door and stride up to the desk. "Hey, Sarge, welcome back. How you feeling?"

"I'm good, thanks. Back in the swing of things."

"Mind if I talk to you a minute? It's about that homicide on New Year's Day."

I gulped, thinking he was going to tell me about all the negative feedback he'd received from the picture in the paper. As a detective he couldn't scold me or anything, but he could let me know if his bosses were still pissed. I glanced back at Harris to see if he was properly ashamed, but he apparently hadn't heard our conversation as he continued typing on the computer.

Espinoza and I walked into the property room behind the front desk so we could have some privacy.

As soon as he closed the door I turned to him. "This about the picture?"

"The pic...oh. No, Sarge, nothing's come from that. I mean, my lieutenant was pissed, but you know...shit happens. I haven't heard anything about that since the day after."

"So what's up?"

"That guy who bit you—Deon Jenkins. He did a bid upstate with a high-ranking member of the Jackie Boys: Dante King, a.k.a. 'Big Boy.' Apparently, they were really close—got busted on a few things together while they were up there."

As I said, the Jackie Boys were the biggest gang in our precinct. They were local, but apparently caused issues in other precincts too, as Jay had informed me. They had dropped a lot of bodies in our precinct, at any rate. They ran drugs and sometimes girls, in addition to committing drug-related robberies and burglaries. The Jackie Boys originally formed in the block of buildings where Lawrence Washington was murdered. But I wasn't sure how many of them still lived there. That building had a high turnover rate of residents, many of whom were paying the owners off the books or participating with them in whatever Section 8 scam they were running. The Jackie Boys were Bloods-affiliated, but that didn't mean they coordinated with other Bloods gangs.

Espinoza continued. "Big Boy got collared a few weeks before New Year's for breaking his girlfriend's jaw. His girlfriend was Lawrence Washington's niece. She's no longer cooperating with the DA's office, but Big Boy's being held at Rikers on a parole violation for that assault. He could go back in if the parole hearing goes badly for him. Very bad for business."

"I see the connection," I said skeptically. "But this guy Jenkins—he was high as a fucking rocket ship. The state he was in, no way he could've pulled off a homicide without a dozen people knowing about it. Anyway, I ran into him like a half mile away from the shooting scene. Pretty much literally. And he didn't have a gun on him—not even a knife."

"Yeah, Sarge, I know it's a stretch. But I got video of a guy, similar build, looks kind of like him, though it's not great clarity—going in the front door of one of the buildings the night before the homicide. I was wondering if you could take a look at the footage, let me know what you think."

"Of course. You didn't see any footage of a guy like that leaving any of the exits?"

He chuckled bitterly. "You know how bad those cameras are, Sarge. Only get those three seconds, then a delay before they come on again. And the mutts in that building are always breaking the cameras anyway—he could've gone out a couple of exits after the homicide and not been picked up on any video. Like I said, I know it's a longshot. But he could've gotten high after—a lot of them do that. Sometimes they smoke to get up their nerve too. Maybe it didn't hit him till after the deed was done."

I shrugged. "Let's go."

Espinoza and I walked upstairs to the Detective Squad. It took him only a few minutes to key up the video on his computer, me sitting down so I could get a good look. Taken from the overhead inside front door camera, it was brief: Four young people, three men and a woman, all came through the door around the same time, as someone had just exited. They looked like they were together, happy to get out of the cold. As they entered, a guy who looked to be about the same height as the asshole who bit me, and wearing a thick jacket with a black hoody pulled over a baseball cap, cut in between them and walked into the lobby with them. His head was tilted down, and the hoody and cap blocked most of his face from the camera. They all went through the inner lobby door and then all you could see was their backs as they walked toward the elevator.

I shook my head. "No way I could say with this video."

Espinoza nodded. He'd obviously figured as much, but he had to try. "What about the pants?"

Once again, the pants looked to be darker jeans, same as Deon had been wearing. I couldn't even tell what color the shoes were from the video. "The hoody is similar, at least at the top," I said cautiously. "But he wasn't wearing a jacket or baseball cap when I ran into him. And I can't tell from the little I see of his face. Jenkins is five-eleven—this guy looks about the same height, but I can't even tell his build with all the layers he's wearing." I added, "Sorry," not really sure why.

"Every little bit helps, Sarge. We'll see how this shapes up." He shook my hand. "Thanks again. You know how it is—after the first two weeks they expect you to move on with your other cases unless it's a really high-profile one. Homicide continues working it, but they've got such a big caseload they're not doing much on it at this point. I hate to let things go cold, though."

I respected him for that. The squad room was mostly empty today, only one other detective seated at a desk. I walked by the fish tank that seemed to be customary in every Detective Squad and almost opened the door before I turned back to Espinoza, who had sat back down in front of his computer. "You know," I said, "you could've called me at home."

He looked up. "I didn't wanna bother you. I already had Jackson and Jones look at the video—they didn't see any more than the rest of us did. Besides, I know how that cocktail is. Got stuck by a needle about ten years ago. I was shitting for a month straight."

I shrugged. "They say it hits people in different ways. I just felt weak a lot of the time." In fact, as I spoke, I realized I was feeling dizzy and lightheaded. Like I said, I still had a few more doses left to take, and I wasn't looking forward to it.

"—Even though we don't have any documented 'hits' that he's done…"

Shit. Espinoza was talking about Jenkins again. I really didn't want to have to think about that guy right now and was kind of regretting not just walking out the door. Espinoza continued, "But he's shot at least two people over the years—one of them was his girl's ex-boyfriend, but the *other* one—it happened in East Flatbush, but they were never able to figure out why. The victim had enemies, but Jenkins didn't seem to be one of them. The detectives never even figured out how, or even if, Jenkins knew the guy. Helped him beat the case."

Maybe because he saw I'd kind of zoned out, he fixed me with a look that had probably worked on a lot of the suspects he'd gotten into the box over the years. "I know he bit you and spat at you and shit—I'd be fucked up about it too. But Jenkins is more than just an EDP. Big Boy is being held at Rikers—all calls and correspondence are recorded. But I think one of his associates on the outside asked Jenkins to take out Lawrence Washington as a warning to his niece to stop cooperating. A warning, given out to a man no one was gonna care about, by a guy with no obvious connection to the gang."

I was skeptical. "Look, I'd love to pin a murder on that piece of shit. But I just don't see it."

Espinoza fixed me with another of those knowing looks. Then he shrugged. "I hate these kinds of cases. After two weeks—and *that's* even a stretch on this one—no one gives a shit." He shook his head. "I know he wasn't a good guy, but he still had people that care about him. They deserve answers, same as anyone else." Despite my skepticism and the sneaking suspicion that I was being subtly played by an expert, I realized why I'd always liked Espinoza so much.

"I'll keep it in mind," I promised, not really intending to do anything but not wanting to hurt his feelings. If I didn't have to deal with Deon Jenkins again before I called it quits and changed careers, that would be just fine.

Espinoza nodded thanks, and I walked out. He had a lot of cases on his plate; as one of the senior detectives this included robberies and shootings and other serious felonies. He didn't have the time to cruise the streets looking for Deon or roust him when he looked like he might be holding a gun or drugs. Those are things that the Anti-Crime cops and uniforms like me could do. And I certainly wasn't planning to.

Midway through my first week back at work, I got a call from Melanie. We hadn't spoken in a few days, hadn't seen each other since that night we went to the movies. I had just gotten in my car in the precinct lot, about to head home. There was one cop smoking a cigarette outside the rear door; other than that, just a few personal cars belonging to supervisors, marked police cars, and civilian vehicles being held for evidence. The 4-to-12 shift had started almost an hour before, so the sector cars were all out on the street. It wasn't pitch-black yet, but it was getting there.

"How's it feel to be back?"

"Same old, same old. I take my last dose of the cocktail tonight. How you doing?"

"That department doctor's such an asshole. He should've kept you out another week."

I shrugged, realizing this was a useless gesture since she couldn't see. "Josh, you there?"

"Yeah. Anyway—" I was caught somewhere between *I have to go now; I'll call you later* and *I need to see you; finish what we restarted a few weeks ago.* So I just trailed off.

"Well, just seeing how you're doing."

"You working today?"

She responded too quickly, anticipating a question I hadn't asked. "No, but I'm helping my sister out with some things."

Don't ask what about tomorrow. "What about tomorrow?" She was a 4-to-12 cop and I knew her squad, so she couldn't lie. All patrol squads had rotating days off, and it was uniform throughout the department. "Uh, no, I'm not. You wanna do something?"

I wasn't sure if she wanted to, or if I'd just trapped her. Since I hadn't really pressed her to hang out since the movies, she might've gotten lulled into a false sense of security, a good-friend kind of thing. "Uh, I wanna wait a few days after I'm done with the meds before I go out again."

"Probably a smart move, buddy." She didn't sound disappointed. I was beginning to get the impression that if anything had happened that night it would've been a one-off. Or just a recurring booty call, which was not what I was looking for with her. With anyone, at this point in my life. "So call me later, okay?"

I said I would and pulled out of the lot. Then I went home, had my first drink in almost a month, and fell asleep on the couch.

* * * * *

I spoke with Espinoza again about a week later, after I swung back in from three days off, stopping by the Detective Squad after my shift was over. He nodded to me as I walked up to his desk.

"Any luck on that thing?"

In response, he rummaged through a stack of papers and pulled out a sheet with Deon Jenkins' mug shot. It was an I-Card, something detectives issue when they're working on a case. I-Cards come in three types, including "Witness," which means the person might have pertinent information regarding an active case. They cannot be forcibly detained or made to speak with anyone. However, if cops arrest them, then the detectives can take a shot, though they don't have to talk. The "Suspect—No Probable Cause to Arrest" I-Card is pretty similar: The detectives want to speak with someone they suspect may have committed a crime, but there's not enough evidence for an arrest. Then there's a "PC" I-Card, which means the suspect can be arrested without any issues, as there's already probable cause to believe they committed the crime. The PC I-Cards weren't warrants—they didn't allow cops to enter buildings or any of the other options a warrant did. A PC I-Card was basically like we were looking for someone off a completed complaint report.

Espinoza had a Witness I-Card put out for Jenkins. "Witness?"

He shrugged. "This way if he gets collared for something else, I'll get notified. See if he'll talk, 'cause right now there's no way. I went by his girl's place last week and she laughed in my face."

"I could've told you that. Why 'Witness,' though?"

He fixed me with one of those seasoned detective looks. "I like to play it close, Sarge. No sense letting him or anyone else know we're looking at him like that. Just seeing if he has any information." He pantomimed with his hands. "Plant a seed; might grow into a great big tree." He shrugged. "Or just a pain in patrol's ass any time they stop him."

I laughed. Not all detectives seemed to realize the trouble these non-arrest I-Cards sometimes cause us. Especially back then, when many of our cars didn't even have working computers. We often had to call someone at the precinct to run the name of a person we'd stopped. Or run them over the air. Sometimes we would get wrong information. A lot of cops had at one time fought with a guy to get him into custody, only to find out when they brought him back to the precinct that there was no "Probable Cause to Arrest" on the I-Card. Or even worse, that the detective had forgotten or been too lazy to cancel the I-Card when the case was closed, leaving it open in the system.

"Does he live at that apartment I saw him come out of?" I'd been sure that Courtney included the address in his arrest report.

Espinoza shook his head. "I don't think so. I checked the lobby door—it doesn't lock well, and you can shove it in pretty easily. He might've just ducked in to get out of the cold, since he wasn't wearing much at that point."

I nodded, feeling kind of guilty about not wanting to help Espinoza out if it meant dealing with Deon Jenkins again. Even though I was planning to leave the profession soon for greener pastures, it would feel better to go knowing I'd done something good on my way out the door.

A week or two passed. I kept an eye out for Deon, hoping I'd catch him doing something we could bring him in on, even if it was just smoking a blunt or even littering. He'd most likely fight again, especially if we told him he was getting collared for something petty. This time I'd be ready, though, and put him down fast and hard. I still got queasy thinking about that month on the cocktail.

CHAPTER 11

ROTHCHILD:
BACK TO THE GRIND

I was the patrol supervisor again, Eddie Johnson graciously agreeing to take the desk for the second day in a row. Eddie had a lot of time in rank and didn't really mind the desk. He usually let me go out.

As usual, we had only four units to cover the whole precinct. It was supposed to be five, but Harris and McCall had just received a "short notification" to go to court for a grand jury on a robbery arrest from the week before. I was standing behind the desk, making the necessary adjustments to the roll call, such as changing officers to court like Harris and McCall, and in another case to the pistol range, a not unforeseen change that should've already been reflected on the roll call. Eddie was scribbling his entries in the command log as I divided my attention between the roll call and handing out car keys to my cops. Some of the cars were such pieces of shit that they barely drove. I figured we had maybe six good cars on hand to assign the four sectors, knowing we had to save one of those cars for the youth officer, who would complain to the Patrol Borough command if we didn't have a car waiting for him. I picked up the keys to a car that none of the midnight cops had taken, as it had no heat and the sirens didn't work. I put them in my mailbox.

Eddie looked up. "Saving that one for the youth officer, I see."

I shrugged. "Fuck that guy. He's gonna call the Borough and rat us out if we don't have something waiting for him—might as well be a piece of shit."

Eddie laughed. "I'm with you on that one—I do the same. By the way, we're gonna have to do a prisoner transport. Walk-through. Central Booking's already calling for him."

A "walk-through" meant that a prisoner, due to medical, psychological, or just general behavioral issues, had to be escorted by a police officer through the entire process at Central Booking, from when they first walked in to be searched and photographed through the arraignment with the judge.

The typewritten roll call already looked like a child had scribbled all over it with the tons of changes Eddie and I had made in our sloppy writing. Luckily, a "cop" who was usually assigned as the precinct cleaner was actually around, and I'd put him out with Keisha Jackson to get that fourth sector car. Most of the "house mice," as we referred to the cops who worked inside jobs, were pretty much untouchable and hard to put out on the streets even if we were really short on people. But this guy, Jacobson, wasn't in anyone's good graces. He just had the cleaner position because he'd been one of the guys who drove around in little scooters writing parking tickets for years, rarely interacting with the public in any way other than when they got upset about a ticket, which wasn't that common since the parking sneaks tended to be very stealthy. The NYPD doesn't even have that position anymore; now only civilian traffic agents to do that kind of thing. But back then we still did. Only thing was, Jacobson had finally been thrown out of the position after almost twenty years. He'd been caught stealing overtime and writing tickets that probably shouldn't have been written. Not wanting to deal with double-parkers, who often came out of wherever they were and argued, sometimes aggressively, or unregistered vehicles

—same thing—Jacobson concentrated on issues like alternate-side parking and failure to obey posted signs. Spurred by a bunch of complaints, it was discovered that he often falsified data on the tickets, things like how long the car had been parked and distances from posted signs, fire hydrants, etc. Add to that the fact that he had towed a bunch of cars—always at the end of his tour, so he'd get overtime—that turned out shouldn't have been towed.

There'd been an investigation, interviews. Jacobson pulled every white-cop grievance card he could, shit like uttered sayings in the locker room, perceived slights—shit that didn't add up to anything. But coupled with race—a white cop working in a precinct of mostly black and brown, claiming reverse racism—he'd managed to not only avoid being forcibly retired but also to land an inside gig that fit his gruff but cowardly personality. "Bitchy white guy" is how Frank Cassella had described him.

Like most house mice, Jacobson had been taken care of even after he got caught fudging things. They made him the station house "cleaner," even though the department already employed two civilians to clean the station. He didn't actually do much, just like the "plant manager" and other jobs that were created due to civil-service bullshit. Still, he was a body that we could use pretty much whenever we wanted. So I didn't hate him.

I said, "I'll send Jackson and Jacobson with the walk-through prisoner." They were assigned to what was probably the most violent sector in the precinct, but I figured Keisha Jackson wasn't gonna be doing much other than babysitting Jacobson anyway. "I'll make Chan and Dominguez IJ and change the other units." Though this meant having the other three sectors phone in and be told they were each gaining a letter or two for their responsibilities, this was a pretty common occurrence and wouldn't cause much confusion.

Eddie nodded. "Good choice. I don't trust Jacobson down there with the perp by himself anyway—guy's a space cadet."

McCall and Harris came up to the desk to check in. Eddie said, "It's 7:05. You're doing a court tour. Supposed to start at 8:00. If you go over 1535, you'll have to eat the time."

McCall smiled. "We know that, Sarge. Just wonderin' if we could get a car to go to court. You know we'll hurry back as quick as we can."

Eddie had resumed making his entries in the command log and didn't look up. "No cars. You gotta take the iron horse." By this he meant the subway.

McCall shirked off his easygoing demeanor and seemed to grow taller than his six-foot-three frame. Something mean got in his face, like it had that day at the crime scene when he pulled that shit on me. "Sarge, we're the hardest workers you got. Takin' the train, it's gonna take longer—plus, what if something happens?"

Eddie didn't look up. "Then you take police action, like I've done a million times, like Josh has." Now he looked at me. "Josh, you always take the train to court, don't you? And if I'm not mistaken, you're a whole rank higher than McCall here. You managed to survive, right?"

"I did." Harris was embarrassed for his partner, probably wishing he could just walk away instead of standing behind him and trying to act like he wasn't hearing this conversation. Knowing his partner was about to say something he'd regret.

"Can we get a ride to Utica?"

Utica Avenue had the A express train. A few stops and you were at Jay Street, right at the courts.

Eddie still wouldn't look at him. He hated McCall. "If I wanted to be a day-planner, I wouldn't have taken two civil service tests. Ask one of your fellow cops."

McCall was getting angry. "This is—"

Harris walked up and put his hand on his shoulder, knowing this was about to get out of hand. "It's good, bro. Just walk down to Gates and take the J' to Broadway Junction. We'll get the 'A' there."

McCall shrugged off his partner's hand. "I grew up in Brooklyn. I know how to take the fuckin' train, Jamel."

"Great. It's settled then." Eddie again, still not looking at them. I held my hand up in a conciliatory gesture. McCall and Harris were in my squad, not Eddie's, and I depended on their high arrest activity to keep us looking okay, what with slackers like Chan and Dominguez.

"Just take the train, guys. I do it all the time."

McCall couldn't really say anything to that and he walked off, still in a huff. Harris gave an apologetic nod that Eddie didn't see and walked off after his partner.

"I hate that fuckin' guy," Eddie said.

"Well at least he's not in your squad. Harris is a nice kid, though."

"Yeah," Eddie agreed. "But that shithead McCall is gonna get him in trouble one of these days."

CHAPTER 12

CHAN AND DOMINGUEZ: BRINGING UP THE REAR

It was a little past nine, and Chan was hungry. They were holding a residential alarm (bullshit—just the homeowner leaving for work), a call of a "past threats made" (bullshit—but might require the preparation of a meaningless complaint report if he and Dominguez weren't their usual charming selves today), and a domestic dispute, no weapons, no injuries (report definitely required but also bullshit). He made a right onto Monroe Street.

"Where you going?" Dominguez asked.

"We got three non-priority calls holding. I'm hungry."

"I know you're hungry, fatty. You're always hungry. But you're going the wrong way. You like that spot on Fulton."

Chan didn't take his eyes off the road. "I'm going to the Dominican place on Ralph today, genius. You think I don't know how to get around?"

Dominguez scoffed. "Only to get food. A shooting on the other side of the precinct, you'd be lost."

Chan laughed. "You wouldn't wanna go anyway, bitch. First on scene gets stuck with all the paperwork and bullshit." That shut him up.

He pulled up to the corner in front of a hydrant and turned to his partner. "You coming in?"

"Yeah, I'll get a coffee."

Dominguez liked that Bustelo coffee, all dark and flavorful. Drank it black. Chan got enough caffeine from soda—he didn't need more.

There wasn't much of a line. Chan didn't bother perusing the hot food lining the counter behind the glass; it wouldn't be anything he'd eat till lunchtime. So he ordered a BLT and a Pepsi. Unfortunately, Dominguez noticed him eyeing the cute counter girl as he handed her the money. He said something in Spanish to her and she smiled.

Chan turned to him. "What'd you say?"

"How'd you grow up in Bushwick and don't speak any Spanish?"

"I speak enough languages, buddy." The girl gave him back his change. She was too young anyway, not much more than nineteen.

Dominguez paid the girl for his coffee. "Like what?"

"Some Chinese and *lots* of English."

"Which Chinese you speak again—Mandarin or Cantonese?"

He turned to Dominguez, cheeky. "Fortune cookie."

They walked toward the back of the store by the couple of tables lining the wall to wait for Chan's food. The short-order cook was good; he'd have the sandwich done in no time.

Dominguez wasn't done with the fuck-fuck games, though. "What's my lucky number?"

Chan was trying to think of a response when the dispatcher's voice came over the radio, her tone indicating it was a priority job. But unless it was a woman being butchered in the middle of the street or a cop screaming for help, Chan was not leaving without his sandwich. Never know when you're gonna get another chance to eat.

Dominguez seemed to have the same idea, removing the lid on his Styrofoam cup and blowing on the hot coffee. Chan gave the cook a laser stare, hoping he would speed up on the sandwich as the dispatcher's voice droned on in the background, indicating a domestic assault in progress. Nothing that justified her loud voice ruining the tranquility of his food hunting, and it wasn't even in their sector. However, the sector in question, manned competently all these years by Eric and Shayna, wasn't picking up the job, meaning they were currently stuck on something else. Those two were the last people who'd ever neglect a call in their sector.

After the dispatcher read the job out for a second time, Chan accepted that he would probably have to leave and pick up the food later. Sergeant Rothchild came over the air. "One Sergeant, who do you have available for that job?"

Chan looked at Dominguez. "How many cars we got today?"

"Four."

The dispatcher came over the air again. "Uhhh...One Sergeant, all units on priorities. Except..."

Chan and Dominguez started to walk out as the dispatcher assigned them the job. Before Chan got to the door, though, the cook called to him. The sandwich was ready, wrapped in white paper, feeling hot and greasy underneath. Chan told him he didn't need a bag, then ran out behind Dominguez, storing the BLT safely inside his patrol bag in the back seat.

As Chan sat down in the driver's seat and turned on the ignition, Dominguez laughed. "Your lucky day."

Chan wasn't convinced. "Let's see how this call goes first."

Dominguez told him to turn around and take Reid down, since Lafayette was a one-way. Chan made a U-turn when he could, and they made it there quickly, at least in his opinion. "Turn right."

That he knew. He made the turn and saw Courtney Jones and Sergeant Rothchild already getting out of their car, which was parked half a block up, across from a playground. Chan hadn't associated the address with this building, since it wasn't his regular area. But once he saw the four-story building they were going into he remembered.

"This place is a shithole."

"Yep," Dominguez agreed as Chan pulled up behind the other car. They got out and walked toward the building, Jones considerately holding the front lobby door open for them. "Don't want you guys to miss the party. I know how much you love to collar." He sniggered, knowing that if there was an arrest, they'd have to take it. Harris and McCall had court today, and no one else would want it. As Chan walked past Jones, making sure to ignore him completely, and walked into the dark hallway, he wished those two didn't have court today. Even worse, rumor was that they were going to the night crime team soon. Fuck that. Who was gonna take all the collars now?

CHAPTER 13

ROTHCHILD: JOB STRESS

I was a little peeved but trying not to show it. Granted, the grand sum total of the three units I had on patrol were all loaded up with calls, everyone on priorities except Chan and Dominguez. They handled the other side of the precinct and had three jobs in their que anyway, so I hadn't expected them to jump on this call. And they *had* answered up immediately when assigned, so I couldn't really say anything to them. I was just mad in general, how our low manpower was made even worse by lots of cops trying to do as little as possible.

The building would've been nice if it was well maintained. As it was, it was awful. Garbage strewn about the dimly lit hallway and lobby, if you could call it that. Gang graffiti written all over the walls. There was no elevator, so we walked up to the third floor, the same type of graffiti following us, scrawled in marker and paint or etched into the plaster.

I'd been in the lead the entire time, as Jones had stood back and held the front door for Chan and Dominguez. So I got to the apartment first. I stood to the side of the door and listened for a second. Not hearing anything but our radios, I knocked.

After a few seconds the door opened partially. A young woman, black, mid-twenties, a little heavy, with tears streaming down her bruised face looked out. I started to push the door gently, but she had her shoulder and feet planted and wasn't letting it open further. "Miss, we need to come in."

She flicked a tear from her eye with one hand but didn't move her shoulder or feet so I could push in without hurting her. "It's good—he left. I'm okay."

"We need to see for ourselves, miss. Then if you want us to leave we will." She settled back a little and eased up the pressure on the door. I was able to push it in without hurting her, and she stepped back as I walked inside.

We wound up finding her boyfriend hiding in a bedroom closet. We literally had to pull him out, kicking and screaming as we cuffed him up. I had Dominguez take the collar.

CHAPTER 14

ERIC AND SHAYNA

Eric was driving again. They tended to split this job, but since she'd gotten back Shayna had wanted him to drive every day. He'd never been off patrol for eight months and then had to swing right back into things after giving birth to and caring for a baby, so he couldn't judge. Anyway, he liked driving better than taking reports.

They both knew the addresses of their sector better than a lover. Not that their sector was that big, changing depending on if they were covering only Charlie (very rare), Charlie-David (sometimes), Charlie-David-Eddie (more often), and Charlie-David-Eddie-Frank, when manpower was particularly low. But if you gave them an address, they usually could picture the place, or at least the surrounding properties, especially anything in Charlie and David. This job was not in their sector, though.

The precinct was not big. So Eric could pinpoint the location they were going to within a block or two, even if the dispatcher hadn't read out the cross streets. Addresses were weird around here, though. It wasn't like Manhattan, where everything ran in a grid. Many a time over the years he'd made the mistake of listening to the numbers only without regard for the cross streets.

"Home invasion robbery," but in the past. The dispatcher stated two hours.

"It's probably drugs," Shayna said matter-of-factly.

"Yeah, probably," he agreed. "Or just bullshit." She nodded. Two hours was a long time in the past to report a home invasion robbery.

CHAPTER 15

ROTHCHILD: JOBS THAT STICK

Eric and Shayna were assigned to the home invasion robbery. As the supervisor, I had to respond to the call as well. "Two hours in the past means it's either a drug thing or total bullshit," I informed Courtney. He apparently agreed, because he wasn't driving that fast. Even let a woman and her kid cross in front of us before putting his foot on the gas. "Good job, Courtney."

He nodded. Then he turned and hit me with a sly grin to let me know the praise wasn't a big thing to him either way. "Driving the sergeant ain't a game for the reckless."

"Or the inconsiderate," I added, feeling like a schoolmarm. A comfortable silence ensued during which Courtney drove and I tried to catch up on my memo book. Obviously my writing wasn't great, what with the car moving and potholes and all, but I did the best I could. At least put the domestic violence arrest Chan and Dominguez had just made: Mr. Closet. I hated to come up empty-handed if a case went to court and the ADA wanted my notes. Unfortunately, oftentimes this did indeed happen on routine arrests such as that.

Anyway, after a few minutes we got to the robbery location. The residence was a block or two from Fulton Street, somewhere between the building the New Year's Day homicide occurred in and a relatively large housing development. It was a two-family house. The victim lived on the first floor, the basement also having an apartment but one that couldn't be accessed through his floor due to renovations carried out to split the place into separate living quarters.

The victim was a Hispanic male in his late twenties. The precinct was still ninety-six percent black at that time. Mostly American, West Indian, and even some recent African immigrants. But there were Hispanics, both white and black, spread across the precinct.

We walked inside the apartment with the victim, having to step over random food items spilled from two paper grocery bags. I saw electrical wire strewn about the floor. A flatscreen TV that had rested on a stand was lying face-down on the floor. A few other items were strewn about the place, but it didn't look that bad overall. The victim was clean-cut, well-dressed and put together, but he looked like he'd been tuned up a bit, bruises and swelling to his face and neck. As we entered, Eric and Shayna pulled up and walked in behind us. I made sure that no one touched anything.

I got the guy's ID and called someone in the precinct to run him; he had no record and didn't strike me as a perp, not even a minor weed dealer.

In sum and substance, he stated that as he was coming in with a bag of groceries, two masked black guys came up from behind and pushed him inside at gunpoint. They roughed him up a little, then bound his wrists and ankles with the electrical wire we saw on the floor and took his cell phone, duct-taped his mouth, and left him face-down on the carpet as they rummaged through the apartment. Before they left they told him to count to a thousand before even thinking about getting up. He counted to two thousand, then spent a long time freeing his wrists, after which point he freed his feet and stood up. Then he knocked on a couple of neighbors' doors before someone let him use their phone to call 911.

Courtney asked him what we all were thinking. "So, why'd they pick you?"

I could see the red marks on his wrists where the electrical wire had bitten into. Along with his injuries and lack of a record, I felt that it had definitely happened.

"I don't know." He saw the skepticism in Courtney's eyes. "I don't hang out, no drugs or nothin'." Seeing we weren't completely satisfied with this answer, he said, "My wife's a nurse practitioner. Makes good money—she has lots of jewelry, some her mom gave her."

Once we started itemizing the jewelry that was stolen, a rough estimate that required him to use my phone to call his wife and break the news to her so that she could give some idea of the value, it became apparent that what had been taken amounted to a lot of money.

"She wear the jewelry out a lot?" Eric asked as Shayna was filling out the report.

"Yeah, sometimes, I guess." He sounded like he felt guilty about this. None of us dissuaded this notion. You flaunt expensive shit in this area, quite possibly your boyfriend is gonna wind up lying on his belly on the living room carpet, mouth duct-taped and wires biting into his wrists till he's finally able to squirm out of them. For us, it's like two plus two equals four.

At least one of the cops was gonna have to stay in the apartment until someone from the Evidence Collection Team came and dusted for prints and swabbed for DNA. That was going to take a while. One of them could go back to the precinct and put the report in the system, a move that was required for the Evidence Collection Team and then the detectives to assign a case number. So, with Jackson still out at the bookings with the station cleaner, Chan and Dominguez with their collar, and now this, I was down to one sector car working the entire precinct. Eric said he'd stay in the apartment and make sure the victim didn't mess with anything while Shayna went back to the station house and put the report in the computer.

This was a much busier winter weekday than we usually experienced. But I doubted things would miraculously calm down at this noontime hour. I don't have that kind of luck.

Courtney drove us back to the precinct so he could pick up Chan and they could go out as a sector in Chan's car while Dominguez processed the domestic violence arrest. As Courtney took his stuff out of our car, he said what I was thinking. "Last time you drove yourself you got bit by Mr. AIDS, Sarge."

"Yeah, I remember. You still gotta work with Chan."

Courtney laughed. "I'll make sure he knows who's boss. Very easy with him."

So now I had two sectors for the whole precinct. And we were holding eight jobs. What the fuck was going on today? I had to get another car out.

I walked into the precinct to check in with Eddie Johnson. He looked up. "Bad news, Josh. Jackson and what's his name had to bring the perp to LIU Hospital. Guess he started bugging out in the cells—they wouldn't let him see the judge. And the admin lieutenant sent Chan to pick up something from Headquarters downtown."

There went my plan to get another car out. I stepped behind the desk, took a deep breath, and picked up the roll call, which already looked like it had been scribbled on by a hyper three-year-old. "We can still put Dominguez out with Jones to get a second car; he can finish processing the arrest later. I'll call Jackson and tell her to leave Jacobson with the perp—" I locked eyes with Eddie, whom I knew was trying to keep me from making a mistake that would bite me in the ass. As the patrol supervisor, I was responsible for the security of our prisoners until they were lodged into downtown Central Booking, whether they were in a hospital in the confines of our precinct or not. If Jacobson fucked up and let the perp escape, I'd be on the hook too. "The perp's got leg shackles on?"

Eddie nodded. "Bookings won't let the perps go to the hospital without shackles." Then he stated, kind of to himself, "If they don't get them back quickly, though, they're gonna be calling me and bitching. Like they belong to them and not the city." He chuckled. "Gotta love this fuckin' job."

You had to. I decided I'd call Keisha and tell her to make sure she handcuffed the perp to the gurney at the hospital, snugly, before leaving. After that it would be on Jacobson. Escapes are rare, but they do happen. Usually when the cop isn't paying enough attention and taking proper precautions.

I picked up the roll call again and shuffled through it. I was looking for a house mouse I could take from inside to put out with Shayna once she was done putting the home invasion robbery into the computer so we could have someone from the Evidence Collection Team come out. That shouldn't take long—Shayna walked in through the rear hallway door as I was thumbing through the roll call, so many names but few that actually did patrol. "Just reserve a report number for now, Shayna. I'm gonna find someone to sit at the apartment so you can pick up Eric and answer some of the jobs." This made more sense—put the house mouse in the apartment so Shayna and Eric could go back out on patrol. She nodded and headed to the report writing room. Before I could resume leafing through the roll call, Dominguez walked up. This was only surprising since I'd imagined I'd have to hunt him down to get him to go out with Courtney.

I was about to break the news to Dominguez that he was going to have to leave his arrestee in the cells and go out on patrol, meaning he'd finish the arrest later and definitely get overtime today. But he walked up to the desk, shaking his head sadly. "My perp wants to go to the hospital." He shrugged. "You know me, Sarge. I tried to talk him out of it. He's not having it, though."

I knew Dominguez would have used all his charm and guile to convince the prisoner not to go to the hospital. It was natural for most cops to try to avoid this needless hassle, which was almost always unnecessary. The guys who got arrested frequently, our regulars, so to speak, often played this game. Claim they have some kind of medical issue, one that didn't prevent them from robbing someone or beating their girlfriend, running half a mile while jumping fences as they fled from the cops—but that, at this particular moment, needed immediate attention. They'd go to the hospital, come back after hospital staff basically told them they were full of shit, sometimes repeat this procedure once or twice more before they were finally accepted into Central Booking with one of our cops sitting on them the whole time, on through their arraignment in front of the judge. A needless waste of time and resources and something a regular citizen who got arrested would never pull, since most normal people's goal is to get out of police custody as quickly as they can.

"What's he complaining of?"

"Psych issues. Said he's bipolar and schizophrenic and hasn't taken his meds."

I was skeptical. "Dominguez, you of all people—" I always counted on Chan and Dominguez to keep things running smoothly. Not because they were really active cops, but because they were smart, good with people, and could almost always avoid this kind of needless bullshit.

Dominguez shrugged. "Started pretending to hyperventilate, then smashed his head against the wall. Hard. He's playing the game."

When they started hurting themselves…it meant they were serious about delaying the process. So serious we couldn't ignore them till they calmed down. They had to go to the hospital like they wanted, if only to cause just a little more drama in their otherwise chaotic lives. The fact that he'd beaten his girlfriend just a few hours earlier was the furthest thing from his mind at this point. He was the only victim in the world right now.

Over the radio, I requested Emergency Medical Services to respond to the station house for a prisoner complaining of psych issues. This was another routine call for EMS, a pain in the ass, and would be answered fairly quickly, but not super-quick like a shooting or heart attack.

Since Dominguez would have to accompany the perp to the hospital, I started thumbing through the roll call again, looking for a house mouse I could put out with Jones to get another car out there. The first name I stumbled upon was the RMP coordinator—a fancy way of saying "cop who is supposed to make sure the police vehicles get their scheduled maintenance and keep the cars in good working order." As we had only about twelve patrol cars currently operating at anything near full capacity in a busy precinct in the biggest and richest police department in the history of the world, that tells you how hard he was working.

"Where's Mann?"

Something in Eddie's languid brown eyes told me I'd just asked the dumbest question in the world. "You're never gonna find him. He hides downstairs or at one of the shops."

He was right, of course. He could be crouching behind a boiler in the basement or smoking cigarettes at one of the repair shops with the guys who were supposed to be fixing the cars. So I kept looking. There were three full-duty cops who worked upstairs in Crime Analysis, along with a civilian employee. Everyone up there should've been a civilian, but that's the way this job is. Then there was the assistant training officer, the Traffic Safety officer, the "plant manager" (whatever that meant), the assistant operations officer, the CO's secretary, and the crime prevention officer. All full-duty cops.

Before I got promoted, I didn't have much of a problem with the house mice. Sure, I didn't respect them—most of them did little to no patrol time because they were scared, then worked inside the rest of their careers. But as a sergeant, responsible for making sure that I had at least some cops to answer radio calls and back each other up, I'd grown to hate them.

Since there were three candidates in the Crime Analysis office, I went up there. I walked in and saw all three cops. The sergeant, another one who had spent his whole career inside, wasn't there. Maybe he was in the gym or getting something to eat. One of the cops, Rodgers, had his back to me. I could see that he was surfing the Internet. The other two were on my left and I couldn't see what they were doing. So I figured Rogers was the least busy of them and informed him that he needed to suit up to do patrol. Admin guys wear a uniform but no bulletproof vest, only their gun on a regular belt.

It seemed like he was about to say something in protest, but the look on my face must've made him think better of it. "Sure, Sarge."

"I need you to hurry too. I've only got one car out covering the whole precinct."

He nodded and I walked out. I walked down the stairs and headed to the front desk to tell Eddie to indicate the change in the roll call. But as I walked up to him, I could see the look of resignation on his face. Pressing his hands into the arms of the soft-backed chair like he was going to break them, he informed me that the commanding officer had called and said that under no circumstances would anyone from Crime Analysis be used to backfill patrol. I should've figured—fuckin' rat had called his sergeant as soon as I'd left. And his sergeant had called the

CO. Meanwhile, if I'd have told him that he had to attend a brunch at One Police Plaza or some fancy restaurant, he'd have found time for that and his boss never would've been notified.

Since the youth officer was out at a school (allegedly), I figured I'd take the Traffic Safety officer. She always seemed to have time to watch TV, work out, and eat, so I figured it wouldn't be a big deal. I walked back to her office, where a real-life cop show was playing on the overhead TV. She looked up at me with eyes that said I must be smoking something I'd taken off a perp. But I was in no mood to argue, and she could see that.

But same thing, before I made it back to my car Eddie called me on my cell and told me to go see the admin lieutenant in his office.

Before I went back there, I called the Conditions sergeant, Sean Bryant. I told him how short we were and asked if his guys could pick up some of the slack. "No problem, Josh. But I've only got three cops today, and we're all riding around in one car. I got you, though."

I thanked him and hung up. The Conditions Unit was basically a summons and arrest unit, enforcing quality of life and other crime conditions. But Bryant was always good at backing us on jobs and picking up priority calls when we were getting killed. Even so, that was still only one and a half cars out if I couldn't get the Traffic Safety officer.

As I walked into his office and saw the look on his face, I knew that I wasn't getting the Traffic Safety officer. Lieutenant Francis was a long-term admin guy. He didn't have much street experience and therefore had a hard time understanding that at the very least, when someone calls 911 for an actual emergency in a big city, they expect a speedy response. While a lot of our calls are nonsense, there's a bunch on every shift that aren't. But guys like him didn't get it and never would.

He looked up from a stack of paperwork as I walked in. Middle-aged white guy with wire-rimmed glasses. He was a workout buff, big arms stretching his long-sleeve uniform shirt. But he was growing a belly.

Gesturing to an office-issue chair at the foot of the desk, he said, "Josh. Have a seat."

I declined, the seat not looking too comfortable to sit in with a vest and gun belt on your waist. Besides, I was anxious to get this over with and pick up some of the jobs we were holding.

"All right." He took a deep breath, drawing the moment out. On his desk there were pictures of his wife and kids, a clock stand with two fancy pen holders on either end, and the caption "World's Greatest Cop-Dad" engraved on a little plaque. If they only knew their dad hadn't put his hands on a perp in fifteen years, and even back then not much.

"You can't take the Traffic Safety officer. Not to mention I'm hearing you tried to take Crime Analysis? The CO would've lost her mind. You should know better, Josh."

"We're short, sir. I've only got one unit out. And we're holding a bunch of jobs. I need people to answer them."

He already had a copy of the roll call on his desk and made a show of leafing through it. "What about Mann?" The aforementioned RMP coordinator.

"I've got no idea where he is, sir. Have you ever tried to track him down?"

He chuckled. "Mann is a slippery one. He's got an important job, though. We all do. I think sometimes you lose sight of that, Josh."

I didn't answer. There was no point. He turned a few more pages before looking up at me again. "We gave you five sector cars to start with. What happened?"

I relayed how Harris and McCall had grand jury, Jackson and Jacobson were on a combative EDP prisoner at LIU, Eric and Shayna had a home invasion robbery with a crime scene, and Dominguez had a collar, which the lieutenant already knew about since he'd sent his partner Chan to One Police Plaza.

"What about the crime guys?"

There were two sets of Anti-Crime guys in the precincts, working a sort of modified day shift and then a modified night shift. Even on a good day there probably might be four working with a sergeant on day shift, since they go to court a lot. The crime guys are the gun guys—they work in unmarked cars, in plain clothes, everyone knowing who they are as soon as they exit the vehicle, usually before. You see two white guys and two black guys driving around in a car wearing baseball jerseys, it doesn't take a genius to figure it out. But the unmarked cars give them an advantage, even if it's short-lived, the element of surprise that you can't achieve with a marked police vehicle, which perps see two blocks out.

The crime guys are very good at what they do, which is getting guns off the streets by doing proactive stops, usually targeting career perps and known gang members. They go through the crime reports and see who's wanted, where the robberies are happening, who's beefing with who and therefore likely carrying a gun for protection. They work in a gray area, no doubt, but are highly effective. That said, even if they were working today, the best I could hope was that they'd rush over to any robberies or shootings. They would do that, on their own, anyway. But domestics, accidents, shoplifters, disputes? No way. The Special Operations lieutenant would have had my ass if I'd even tried to get them to go to those calls. Lieutenant Francis knew that— he was just trying to act like I had all these options I wasn't using.

As it was, though, the day shift crime guys had done a search warrant earlier. They'd gotten a gun and five arrests out of it. Two of them were still in the precinct processing the arrests, and the others had already gone home. No way could I have them help out. Warrants are generally executed early, around sunrise. And the process of writing them up sometimes requires a cop to work around the clock to get it done, while other cops have to watch, or "freeze" the house, if that's the kind of warrant they're doing. The lieutenant, who probably knew about the warrant, made me explain this to him anyway. "They did a warrant this morning, sir. Not working."

He shrugged. "Well, seems like you're doing all you can. But I have to look out for my people. I can't lose them to patrol every time things get a little hectic. I'm sure you'll manage."

I walked out of the admin office, passing the Traffic Safety officer who was doing her nails now and watching an episode of *Judge Judy*, apparently having had enough of the cop show. At least she was getting a rounded criminal justice education.

Shayna would have preferred to keep working with her partner, so I let her finish up inside, figuring it didn't make much of a difference at this point. I decided to just go back out with Courtney.

He was shooting the shit with Nick Haskel, the only cop who was working by the desk. Technically there was supposed to be two, a cell attendant to watch the prisoners and a T/S operator to deal with all the walk-in complainants, answer the phones, and assign 311 jobs to the sectors. Having the T/S operator also be the cell attendant was something we did almost every day. It was against regulations, but there was nothing we could do about it. So it sucked for Nick, who in addition to his responsibilities at the front window also had to go back into the cell area every thirty minutes and check on the prisoners. When it got busy at the window he couldn't, and the desk officer or someone else would do it once someone realized. Basically, it was a big gaggle-fuck. So Nick was probably glad for the light conversation with Courtney, as Eddie Johnson wasn't usually known for his small talk.

I gestured to Jones to get his ass moving. Then, not sure if he saw me since he didn't exactly hop-to, I yelled across the room, "Jones, let's go. Holding jobs!"

If we were holding a shots-fired or man with a gun, Courtney would've been the first one to run to his car and race over there. But he had what I will kindly describe as a laissez-fare attitude to much of the other police work, especially the bullshit jobs that we had to rush to all day if I didn't want to get shit from my superiors. As a police officer, Courtney didn't have as much skin in the game as I did, being a sergeant. So as usual, his carefree attitude took hold. He would've kept jawing for another minute if I didn't fix him with a look that required no effort to be angry and mean. Still, the wiseass made a show of bowing out to Nick. "Sorry, Nick. The mastuh beckons me. Gotta help him round up trespassers on the plantation."

Dick.

Sergeant Bryant and his Conditions cops had picked up a bunch of the calls that wouldn't require much more than going there and being the police. I appreciated it, knowing that his personnel had to get a certain amount of activity, namely summonses and arrests. The fact is that, in this precinct at least, patrol was not the commanding officer's priority. She wouldn't want to hear that they came in low on activity because they were helping patrol answer jobs. I'd been in this department a little less than a decade, but I'd seen enough to know that the kiss-ass admin types like her got promoted by talking a big game, showing numbers, and kissing the rings of the powers that be in the community; i.e., the big churches, businesses, and community organizations. They couldn't give a shit if some mother with three kids got beat bloody by her ex because there weren't enough cops to get there on time, or a vehicle accident with serious injuries where the cops didn't even make it there until well after the person had been transported to the hospital.

As it happens, that's what the cops in my only other sector car were currently doing—speaking with a motorist who'd already been transported to the hospital after a collision. There was a fairly serious accident on Atlantic Avenue, and they didn't make it over there for a while, due to no fault of their own.

Anyway, this being a ridiculously busy winter weekday, I was just happy that Sergeant Bryant was out there to respond to an assault in progress on Myrtle and Broadway under the "J" and "M" subway lines, a busy intersection with a lot of businesses, a drug-rehab clinic, the above-ground subway, and a shit-ton of K2 users, because me and Jones, the only other available car, had just picked up a "10-31, Burglary in Progress, Suspect Still at Scene." After a minute or two we were able to get a better perp description: "Male, black, fifties, black jacket and blue jeans, wearing a Mets cap."

Courtney turned onto a street consisting of attached multi-story brownstones. As we approached the location, I saw the suspect the caller described in the middle of the street, swaying and stumbling like he was drunk or high. He did look older, but a lot of the crackheads from the '80s and '90s still did burglaries and car break-ins to make dough, so it wasn't all that surprising. As we rolled up, I saw he wasn't dressed like a street person, but he was even older than the caller had described—probably mid-sixties.

An attractive black woman of average height, in her early thirties, was standing just inside a waist-high black iron fence delineating the house's front patio from the street. She was pointing at the man as we got out of the car. "That's him! He tried to break into the house and attacked me!"

Most of my attention was focused on the suspect, still swaying in the middle of the street. But on a quick glance the young woman didn't look hurt, at least from this distance. She was dressed only in a shirt and pants. It would've been way too cold for her to be out in that in this weather.

Courtney got to the guy first. Definitely mid-sixties. Huge welt on his forehead. I'd seen this before on older people who had been assaulted, or in this case who had gotten into a fight—they tended to bruise easier, and their wounds would swell up more than on a younger person. He was still in the middle of the street, his hands completely empty. "What's going on today, sir?" Courtney asked, keeping a safe distance.

"—was tryin' to get in that house," he said, pointing to the door. "It looked like mine."

The woman came out of the gate and approached us angrily. "Bullshit! He don't live anywhere around here—this house has been in my family for twenty years!" The door the man had pointed to was set in from the street, on the side of the house, so you'd have to open the gate and then walk through the patio to get to the door.

I turned back to the guy. "Where do you live, sir?"

He thought for a second. He seemed a little out of it; whether it was due to drugs or the beating he'd just gotten, I wasn't sure. He pointed and gave the nearest street intersection to his supposed residence. "Livin' with my daughter and her husband."

He was pointing in the wrong direction, and the location he gave was several blocks away. That neighborhood probably didn't look too much different, though—similar architecture to this one. Had he just gotten confused? The woman was adamant, though. She walked out onto the street. "He tried opening the door, then banged on the window. When I came to the door he tried to push in—" Now she held up her right wrist, showing a small cut over a larger patch of redness to the skin. "An' I defended myself. He's a fuckin' crackhead—why aren't you arresting him?!"

A couple of cars had stopped since we were taking up a good patch of the right side of the street. I indicated for them to go around us, and they did.

Courtney went up to her and gently backed her away, out of the street, to get some distance between them. "Please, miss, let's talk up on the sidewalk. We're just tryin' to figure out what's going on."

She did back up onto the sidewalk but then shrugged her shoulder away from his hand. "This is fuckin' bullshit! I never saw this man in my life till just now. I want him arrested!" Her hands were balled into fists, not in a threatening way but just highly frustrated. She drove them into her upper thighs. "Why the fuck is he lookin' at me?!"

The old guy *was* looking at her, but not in a threatening way. "I didn't mean no harm, young lady. Just got confused is all."

I asked him for ID and he gave an older Georgia driver's license. "I thought you said you lived in Brooklyn, Mr. Woods."

"I did, but I've been living down south for a few years. My daughter still lives at the house and I'm stayin' there now while we sell the place in Georgia."

"What's the address?"

His hand went to the big bruise on his forehead. "I can't remember just now."

I sighed. "Do you have keys for your daughter's house?"

He patted his pants pockets. "I think I might've dropped them back there when the lady came out."

Courtney moved past her and found the keys near the door, where the scuffle had started. Then he walked back, making sure to stay between her and Mr. Woods. We looked at each other—this poor guy was just confused. The woman was probably scared and they scuffled, but I didn't see a crime here. No way we were arresting this man for burglary like she wanted.

We had the woman go inside to get her ID to prove that she actually lived here while I requested an ambulance for the man. She was not happy, returning after a minute or two with the ID held high.

She practically shoved it in Courtney's face. "That's right—I live here. Never been arrested, college-educated, and I work full-time. Not like that fuckin' crackhead! What kinda shit is that—Georgia ID—he don't even live in New York! Probably just got outta jail."

"All right, Miss," Courtney said with just the right touch of sincerity and dismissiveness that comes easier to some cops than others. The radio was still busy, and I wanted to get going, but we had to document this situation. At the very least an "aided" card for the old man, maybe even take a report against the woman for misdemeanor assault but close it to patrol, meaning she wouldn't be arrested on it. Or just cross-complainant harassment reports, which likewise would go nowhere. As long as this encounter was documented, and we got this guy seen by EMS.

He didn't have a cell phone, so we couldn't call his daughter to verify where she lived, or at least notify her of what had happened. Of course, he didn't remember the home number either. We ran him to make sure he wasn't reported as missing or, like this woman was insisting, was in fact a criminal. But the search yielded little; he hadn't been reported missing, had no warrants, and only had one minor arrest in New York City back in the early '80s. Though we only got New York City arrests on our system and couldn't check outside jurisdictions for anything other than warrants, I didn't think we'd find anything major if we got someone to run him on Triple I, which would be a major pain in the ass but would show a criminal history outside of New York City. It appeared this was just an unfortunate misunderstanding and maybe this chick overreacted a bit. In fairness to her, folks in Bed-Stuy aren't known for their acquiescence to home intruders, this being a tough neighborhood and all.

The dispatcher said that the EMS unit was just a few minutes out, an estimation always to be taken with a grain of salt. I had the old man sit down on the curb while Courtney distracted the woman, acting like we were taking the report of the century to calm her down. I didn't hear the ambulance's sirens yet. Sergeant Bryant's voice came over the air; the assault job on Myrtle and Broadway had resulted in an arrest. They'd have to bring the perp back to the precinct. If I was lucky he'd head right back out with his other cops, leaving the one to process the arrest. Meaning we were still up shit's creek either way. I had to get out of here. An assault in progress call, a trespassing call, a past robbery call, several domestic disputes and traffic collisions, and a 911 call where screams were heard in the background then the line clicked off were holding. That last one is more common than you'd think—it's usually a domestic. Rarely is the person actually in the process of being murdered. Beaten up, though? Fairly common. So it obviously had to be answered quickly. However, I had no one to get to any of the calls quickly. What the fuck was going on today? I had to get out of here, but I couldn't till EMS came and took this guy to the hospital.

The woman's voice yammered through my thoughts, combining to make a mess of confusion. I heard most of it—"Your boss is a racist motherfucker, and you're a sell-out Uncle Tom faggot!" Though his back was to me, I knew Courtney was grinning and still trying to charm her. This kind of talk didn't get to us. The thing is, people get upset when the cops don't do exactly what they want. Sometimes they're right; more often they aren't. Courtney and I both knew this was a case of the latter.

I was about to leave Courtney with them and respond to the 911 hang-up call when I saw that there was a guy sitting in a work van a few houses down. The van was off, which is probably why I hadn't noticed him before. After a second or two we made eye contact.

I got Courtney's attention and indicated I was walking over there. He nodded, repositioning so he was between the woman and the old man.

The van driver rolled down the window manually—it was an old work truck. "You're not cold sitting there, sir?"

He laughed. "Just giving the engine a rest. Got a busy day today."

"You have a job in one of these houses?"

"I did a little while ago." Before I could ask the question, he answered it. "I saw a little of what happened. That girl's full of shit—I heard her calling 911, sayin' she fought off an intruder. It wasn't like that."

"He didn't try to break in?" I was already pretty sure he hadn't, but I wanted to keep him talking.

"That I don't know. I did see him by the door, but look at him. He's an old man. Not small, though—you think she coulda tuned him up like that by herself?"

"Chicks in Bed-Stuy are tough."

He laughed. "Yeah, but not this time. He was standing in front of the door—maybe had his hand on the knob, I don't know—when she came out, yellin' at him. He backed up, though. She was angry as shit and I didn't get the same feeling from him, by his body language. Then a guy—black, early thirties, maybe—comes out of a car parked across the street—I'm not sure how long he'd been there—runs across the street and jumps over that little fence like he's training for the Olympics, then tunes that old man up and throws him out of the yard. Even after he got him off their property, he hit him a few more times. Poor guy fell on the street, looking helpless and scared. It happened so fast. I started to walk over there but the guy runs back to his car and tears off. That's when she calls 911, screamin' like she'd just gone ten rounds with Tyson."

"I heard her 'cause I was trying to help the old guy. I helped him up and asked him if he needed help, but he said no." He considered. "I should've done more. It's just...the guy looked so confused, so beaten. Like he had lost the last of his pride. I felt so bad for him I didn't want him to think he was a pity case or anything." He shrugged. "So I waited here to make sure the police came and he got help. At the end of the day, I don't know if he was trying to break in or not. I just know that young man beat him like a savage."

I got the van driver's name and phone number before asking any questions that might spook or offend him. "Can you describe the guy and the car?"

After I got a halfway decent description of the suspect and his car (newer model white Dodge Charger, but no license plate), I had to ask the asshole question. "You weren't gonna tell us any of this?"

He looked me in the eye, not angrily but with a no-nonsense pride and honesty I respected despite the circumstances. "Yes, Officer, I was. But I didn't wanna say it in front of her. That's why I stayed— you think I don't have better things to do?"

Wow. Guy was willing to sit in a cold car so he didn't burn gas just so he could be a good citizen. What a rare treat. I felt like a real asshole. I thanked him, copied down his license plate number just in case, and walked back to the old man. Courtney was filling out a complaint report and I let him. I wanted to get her entire statement on record. Then we'd write the actual story below it as provided by the witness. Due to this man's age and the young age of his attacker, this was going to be a felony assault.

EMS finally got there, a male and female I knew from a bunch of previous calls. "How bad is the head?" I asked the male as the female tended to him in the ambulance.

"Not bad. It's because of his age: Swells up bad when they're older. Looks worse than it is."

"He seems a little out of it. We thought he might've been senile or even on something."

"A lot of times diabetics get confused when their blood sugar's low. He missed a dose of insulin—probably would account for the behavior. We'll take him to Interfaith. He'll be okay."

I would've sent a cop with the guy until we got in contact with a family member, but I literally had no one. Me and Courtney were gonna be working hard the rest of the day like we were just another sector car. The guy seemed okay, though—he had to be convinced to lay on the gurney and answered their questions to satisfaction.

The woman was standing just inside her gate with her hands on her hips. "So what happens now?" she asked me.

"Well, my officer took a report. The detectives will be in touch." I thought this might cause her to get nervous, but I didn't even see her lip tremble. And her eyes were glass.

"I'll let 'em know you didn't arrest him 'cause you're a scared little bitch and they gotta do it."

No point letting on that we knew her charade, so I just nodded and walked off. After we'd spoken, the witness had left, so there was nothing more to be done right now. We drove away, her not giving the slightest tell that she was worried. Some people are really good at that kind of thing. Comes with years of living a dishonest life, I guess.

As Jones drove to the 911 hang-up (which did turn out to be a domestic), I caught him up on what I'd learned from the guy in the van. "It's gonna be a felony assault," I informed him. "That guy in the work truck I was talking to—said her boyfriend ran across the street and beat the shit out of the poor guy. He's young like her, so it's a felony assault. I'll give you all his info. Make sure you write down her statement word for word on the complaint report, then we'll put his statement down."

"I figured she was full of shit. Whenever they're that angry they usually are."

"Yeah. As soon as we clear out some of these jobs we'll go back to the precinct and you can finish the report. I'll sign it, then bring it right up to the squad so they can interview the victim."

He looked at me like I was crazy. "You know they're not gonna go over to the hospital and interview him, not unless he's likely to die."

I shrugged. "Well, it's on them, then."

As it was, we didn't get back to the precinct till the shift was over. Courtney finished up the report and I signed it. Right before I was about to go upstairs to change out of my uniform, I saw Courtney, already dressed in his well-cut civilian clothes, walking out. I called to him.

"You showed the report to someone from the Detective Squad?"

Courtney nodded. "What do you think they said, Sarge?"

"What?"

"They'll try an' get to it. Hope you're not holding your breath." I wasn't, but I should've been.

CHAPTER 16

ROTHCHILD: JOBS THAT REALLY STICK

The next day I had the front desk. I kept Jones inside with me, since he was now my steady driver and that was the custom. He was the T/S operator. This meant he had to assign the 311 jobs to the few cars we had out, talk to all the walk-in complainants, answer questions, and keep the peace in the lobby, *and* monitor the precinct cells, meaning he couldn't really do a thorough job on anything. The T/S operator basically served as the desk sergeant's front line. Seated behind a countertop and wall partition that divided the inner part of the precinct from the public area, they took reports, referred people to outside services, and served as a filter for the desk officer, who was responsible for running the inner workings of the precinct and keeping track of the arrests and prisoners coming in and out.

If an issue warranted a complaint report, the T/S operator could refer some of the people at the window to a civilian employee in the neighboring room if it fit the criteria. Or they could refer a report to one of the precinct's sector cars, if the situation was ongoing or an immediate follow-up was warranted. Either way, if they were doing their job right, they'd usually wind up taking at least a few reports themselves each day. This, coupled with the constant stream of people coming by for help or advice, could be a real pain. Especially if you actually cared about the people you were supposed to be helping, which Courtney sort of did. Add to that you were also the de-facto "cell attendant," a position that I've rarely in my career actually had assigned despite it being a major priority in our Patrol Guide. You were also responsible for checking on the prisoners lodged in the command. The job could be a big hassle.

The morning passed in a blur, prisoners sent to the bookings, lodged in our cells, talked to in a nice, soft way so they calmed down and stopped banging on the bars, which had this horrible reverberating effect that drove even the calmest desk officer mad after a while. I might've spent a couple of bucks buying soda or candy bars for the perps whose arresting officers were either too cheap to do so themselves or had long since left.

Around twelve in the afternoon, the commanding officer came in. I rose from my chair and gave her a salute, then handed her my pen so she could sign in the command log. If our relationship hadn't been so cold, I could've gotten a glimpse of some very nice cleavage, but I wasn't looking. She stood back up and held my pen straight up, her eyes big like she was trying to remember something.

"Oh, yeah. Rothchild, that Complaint Report for Felony Assault yesterday—the Crime Analysis sergeant called me. Told me you took a report for a drug addict who tried to get into some woman's house...and made it felony assault *against* the homeowner? I told him there was no way you'd do something like that." She sighed. "Then he says, 'No, ma'am, that's actually what he did.' I couldn't believe it. I even had him call back the homeowner—she laughed as hard as I did when he told her you thought the man was just "confused."

I took a breath before responding. It was bad enough she was trying to downgrade this crime. Even worse, now the homeowner was privy to the fact that we knew there was more to it. She should never have been called. Who knows how much that idiot Crime Analysis sergeant said to her over the phone?

"Ma'am, the homeowner was lying. The victim was an old guy, a diabetic who got confused—he wasn't a drug addict. Her boyfriend or some guy she knew beat him up; I don't know, maybe to show off to her. But that was not a burglary."

She shook her head like I'd just disappointed her in ways that couldn't be conveyed in words. She tried, though. "Burglary?! It's a trespass, that's all. Nothing to even be investigated. Just send him to the hospital and move on. I can't think of anyone who would believe that horseshit other than..." She trailed off, her eyes looking at the only fool capable of such naivete. Burglaries and felony assaults were two of the seven index crimes that had to be reported to the department and then the FBI at the end of the year. It was how an area's crime rate was measured. Misdemeanors like trespass, and even some felonies, didn't count against a commanding officer.

I held my ground, though. "Not a trespass, ma'am. A felony assault, due to the victim's age. We had a witness."

She shook her head again. "Witness? How come when I go out there, no one sees anything. A male shot in broad daylight? No witnesses. But you, Rothchild, you have some special gift that just finds these 'witnesses.' Of course I'll take a felony assault if that's actually what it is. I'd never say anything about a legit crime. But it seems like you've got some personal agenda...like when that EDP bit you. That man wasn't a perp. He was sick and needed help. He shouldn't have been charged with felony assault on a police officer." She shook her head. "I thought Brooklyn North cops were supposed to be tough."

If I'd told her that Deon Jenkins' criminal history said otherwise, or that he was a person of interest in the homicide on New Year's Day, she'd have screamed at me. So I just said nothing, the only other alternative being pointing out all the flaws in her logic, which I'd tried before and had gotten me to this point with her. Never mind that he was wanted for robbery at the time of the arrest...

I didn't even hear whatever she said after that. Eventually she went into her office, shaking her head and saying, "Sergeants I had as a cop wouldn't have pulled this kind of shit." *No*, I thought, *because you were the commanding officer's secretary and any sergeant you dealt with either worked inside or was trying to talk to you.* I resolved to call Billy as soon as I got home and tell him I wanted to begin the hiring process. The job wouldn't start until the end of August, but I didn't want to lose the opportunity because I was dilly-dallying.

Being a cop, you learn that happenstance, for lack of a better word, drives a lot of the human condition. And since your career basically revolves around other people's lives, it stands to reason that happenstance plays a big role in many of your work experiences. Call it coincidence, fate, destiny—who can say? All I know is that at that point, I worked the desk one or two tours a week, given that Eddie usually took it, and Chen, the other one of three day shift squad sergeants, didn't mind it either. So the fact that I was working the desk that particular day, with only Courtney to keep the hordes away, was a bit of a coincidence. Not too much, but a bit.

I think I was writing something in the Command Log—maybe we'd just lodged a prisoner or sent one to the bookings, or maybe it was just one of the required entries I hadn't gotten to yet since it had been so busy. I just remember Courtney's hand on my shoulder, leaning in close.

"Remember that old guy from yesterday?"

For a second I didn't know what he was talking about. Then it came back. "Oh, yeah." I didn't see anyone through the lobby window, but that could've been because they were standing to the side or seated on one of the benches. "Is he here?"

Courtney shook his head. "No, his daughter is. You gotta talk to her."

The fact that Courtney hadn't just directed her to the hospital we sent him to and sent her on her way told me this was serious.

I went up to the window, looked to the side, and saw her, talking on her cell phone. Once she turned and saw me, though, she ended the call and stepped in front of the window. She was a very attractive woman, short and shapely under her conservative dress, looked to be in her mid-twenties. Her dark, smooth face was kind but very stressed and worried.

"I'm Sergeant Rothchild. Can I help you, miss?"

She took a breath to compose herself. "Yes, Sergeant. My father was…assaulted yesterday."

"Yes, ma'am. I was there—after, I mean. The guy who did it wasn't at the scene, but we took a report and sent your father to the hospital. How's he doing?"

Given the look on her face, I should've known this was a stupid question. I'm amazed she didn't bite my head off.

"He's in a coma."

I felt like I'd been hit by a truck. What the fuck? He'd been walking around, talking…two experienced EMTs hadn't been concerned in the least.

She could see the shock on my face. "He's diabetic and has high blood pressure and epilepsy. But he's on medication for all of that and is usually okay. But after he was admitted to the hospital, he lost consciousness…" She started crying softly. "And he hasn't come out of it yet."

Jesus. This case just got very serious. We could even be talking about a homicide. And while the commanding officer had obviously seen the report, or at least heard about it, I doubted the detectives had seen it yet. We took a lot of reports that were left open for further investigation. And Courtney hadn't had much luck yesterday trying to bypass the middleman and give it directly to them.

"I'm so sorry, Miss. We didn't think…he didn't seem…" I almost said not badly hurt but thought better of it. "I'm going to speak with the detectives right now and see what we can do to find the guy. Can you wait here a few minutes?"

She nodded. I was surprised she wasn't angry. Most people in that situation would've been screaming all sorts of insults at me. And in this case, I'd have them coming.

Courtney walked out of the report-writing room and handed the report to me.

The computer-generated report was stapled to the handwritten one Courtney had taken the day before. Which meant the detectives might not have seen it yet.

Courtney spoke as I was going through the paperwork. He'd written a good report, mentioning the inconsistent statements the woman had made versus the statements of the witness, coupled with our observations. A very thorough report by the standards of our department at the time. Most crime reports were only a few lines, really bare-bones.

"You can have a seat while you wait, miss," Courtney offered kindly. His eyes then drifted to a line forming behind her—just a few people, but I could tell by his expression he was wondering what the fuck *they* wanted? It was one of those days.

I went upstairs to the Detective Squad. Walking past the detectives seated at their desks, I went straight into the rear office, where the squad lieutenant sat. Neither of the sergeants were there— they could've been off or out in the streets.

Lieutenant Mulcahy didn't look up when I walked into his office. He was a tall, lean white guy in his late forties or early fifties with a full head of graying, well-styled hair. Not the friendly type. In all my time in the precinct, I'd never seen him on the street, even at crime scenes. He'd been a squad lieutenant forever and probably hadn't had an aggressive encounter with a suspect in twenty years or more. But he'd been a supervisor of detectives in a high-crime precinct so long that he was able to ride the mystique and pretend that his practiced cynicism was a byproduct of competence.

I waited until he finally looked up. His blue Irish eyes didn't offer any greeting, just appraised me with a look of tempered disdain. So I spoke first. "Sir, yesterday we took a report for an Assault 2…"

His eyes didn't get any friendlier, and I knew it was going to get worse when he found out what we were dealing with now. I tried to get to the point quickly. "He was an older guy, sixty-five. It came out as an attempted burglary, but we found a witness who told us the homeowner's—boyfriend, probably—beat the guy up. He's a diabetic and has some other health problems."

He didn't say anything, just looked at me like I was a piece of shit.

"His daughter came into the precinct just now," I continued, stammering, feeling like I was a private in the Army again talking to a colonel. "He was conscious and alert when he was transported to the hospital, but he lapsed into a coma soon after."

Still, he said nothing. Just kept looking at me like I was one of the perps his detectives brought in, guys who had already been interrogated and were sitting locked up in a cell, already drained and presenting not the slightest bit of danger to him. Only someone with that kind of power, safety, and detachment can look at another man like that.

Still confronted with his angry silence, I mentioned that Crime Analysis had fucked up by calling the homeowner who was, in essence, the perp's accomplice, and that they'd then changed the report to a misdemeanor trespass based on her false statements. Used to the shady shit they always did, he waved that last part off. He was not happy.

"Why weren't we notified about this yesterday?"

I explained to him that Officer Jones personally brought the report up to the Detective Squad when we got back in at the end of tour, still thinking at that point we were just dealing with a felony assault where the victim should make a full recovery and not an incident that might turn into a homicide.

"Who'd he talk to?" I admitted I wasn't sure. Now he smelled blood in the water and attacked. "How do you not send a cop to the hospital with an elderly victim?"

"We had nobody on patrol, sir."

"We look out for our elderly. That's disgraceful. And the squad should've been notified immediately. We would've gone to the hospital and interviewed him."

I knew this was wishful thinking on his part. Whatever detective Courtney had spoken to was told that it was a felony assault due to the victim's age. With a witness and a good victim, there's no way the Detective Squad would've taken the time to interview the old guy at the hospital, not unless they were psychics who could predict the future. I thought back to a couple of months prior. An old lady pushing ninety was found dead, lying face-down in her bed in the bedroom of her second-floor apartment by her niece. No signs of forced entry and she had a ton of medical issues. It appeared so cut and dry that her personal physician was willing to sign off on the death certificate. The medical examiner's office was notified by the cops at scene of her physician's name and that he was willing to sign off due to all her health issues. Since the private doctor was willing to sign off on the death certificate and there didn't appear to be anything amiss, the ME didn't need to come out. So the family was able to call a private mortician to come pick up the body, always the preferred scenario. No one wants their loved one going to the city morgue unless it's absolutely necessary.

Precinct detectives are supposed to respond to all deaths in residences, regardless of the person's age or if the death appears suspicious. But given the circumstances of this death, our Detective Squad guys opted not to. They gave the cop a detective's name to put on the report and hung up. This was SOP for them; if it didn't appear suspicious at first glance, they had no desire to leave their office and their caseloads and come out to the scene. Granted, they were busy— there were multiple unsolved shootings, homicides, robberies...no one was looking for extra work that didn't appear to be necessary. Luckily, I wasn't on patrol that day.

When the private mortician arrived, he signed the toe tag receipt for the body as per procedure. Then he turned the old lady over. Her throat was slashed. Now the open bedroom window, which the cops had figured was because the heat was cranked up so high and she'd gotten hot, looked suspicious, it being off a fire escape.

So, I'd figured the detective squad wouldn't interview the victim at the hospital even before Jones told me their answer. I'd at least tried, though. But there was no point in arguing. I stood there and took the ass-chewing. I didn't bother to point out that a lot of cops would've just collared the poor guy for burglary based on the lady's statements and his odd behavior. Or the fact that our commanding officer, despite being aware of the witness, had tried to downgrade the report to avoid taking a felony. He was a lieutenant, and she was a deputy inspector and commanding officer. Even if he'd been willing to challenge her, it wouldn't have gone anywhere.

The lieutenant called a senior detective into the office and had me explain the whole thing again. He took it better than the lieutenant had, not only due to the fact that I outranked him. He knew the way it would've gone.

The lieutenant started speaking with the detective, not including me in the conversation. After a few minutes of being ignored, I walked out of the lieutenant's office and into the Detective Squad room. A couple of the detectives were already doing a workup on the woman so they'd have something to go on. Like me, they figured the perp was the lady's boyfriend, so they ran her domestic violence history. Sure enough, after a few minutes it was determined that she had a boyfriend who'd been collared for hitting her previously. He drove a white Dodge Charger and was a black male in his late twenties, average build but tall, like the description I'd gotten from the witness in the van.

The lieutenant was standing in the doorway of his office, glowering at me like I'd fucked his puppy in front of his kids. I asked him if he wanted me to bring the daughter upstairs to speak with the squad. He shook his head no, not even trying to hide his contempt for me.

As I was walking out someone yelled behind me, "Don't let her leave, Sarge."

She was seated on a bench in the lobby by the T/S window. She gave a sad smile as I walked up to her. Jesus. This lady was so nice I couldn't believe it. "I spoke to the detectives. They're already working on figuring out who did this. Like I told you before, there was a witness who can probably identify him."

She nodded. "I appreciate it, Officer. I know you're really busy. I grew up a few blocks from here and my uncle—my dad's brother—was a cop for a long time."

She wasn't looking for an apology, but I couldn't stop myself. "Ma'am, I'm really sorry this happened. Like I told you, this lady whose house he was trying to get in—mistakenly—she called it in as a burglary and was insistent that he fought with her while trying to get inside. It was only after we located the witness that we found out what actually happened."

She nodded again, not really looking at me.

"He didn't look that bad. Like he'd been hit, yeah, a welt growing on his forehead. But he was talking and everything. He got in the ambulance on his own—the EMTs just thought he was a little out of it because his blood sugar was low."

Still seated, she looked me in the eye. "The hospital said the same thing. He didn't lapse into the coma for a few hours. Before that he seemed okay." She choked up but held in the tears. "At least we know what happened now—the hospital had no idea about any of this." Her eyes were red and a little watery, but she was obviously a strong woman. "I'm going to go back to see him. Can I leave my number?"

"The detectives want to speak with you, so I'll ask you to wait here a little bit. They'll probably want to go to the hospital with you so they can get whatever releases they need signed." This last part wasn't really true; in criminal cases it wasn't hard to get pertinent medical information concerning an incident and a victim's prognosis from the doctor who was treating them. But I didn't want her to feel like she was waiting here needlessly.

She agreed. I got her ID and asked for her phone number, just in case she had a change of heart and just walked out, something that frequently happens. I was writing her ID information on a piece of paper when she spoke, for the first time with a trace of humor in her voice.

"It was a bad hair day when I took that picture."

I looked up from the paper. "What—no. I was just...you're thirty-one. You don't look it." I stumbled. "I mean, I would've thought ...you look really young."

"Thanks, I get that a lot. Thirty-one's not *that* old, though."

My face was as red as a tomato. "No, I didn't mean…I'm thirty-one too." Jesus. Not only did this woman have to come in and tell us how we'd dropped the ball, but now I was stumbling like an idiot.

She saved me. "Well, you don't look it either."

I gave her back the driver's license, my finger inadvertently brushing her palm. It was smooth and a little moist. Her eyes were large and brown. She was even prettier than I'd thought when I first saw her. I started to feel like a man talking to a woman and I put it out of my mind. I should have just appreciated the fact that she wasn't screaming and calling me an incompetent idiot like the lieutenant upstairs had.

It appeared my initial assessment of this year, made on the first day of it, was shaping up to be dead-on.

At around 3:20 I got relieved at the desk by the 4-to-12 sergeant. We conducted the handover, so to speak, while his shift was in roll call. I filled him in on the prisoners in the cells and whatever else was going on. Then I went back to the crime scene with a couple of the detectives to go over what had happened. At this point there was no homicide; the victim was in a coma and we didn't know if he would wake—if he would stay like that for a long time or die. Even if he did die, it would be up to the medical examiner to determine if his death was caused by the assault he'd endured. Given his age and serious health issues, this determination was by no means guaranteed.

To their credit, though, the Detective Squad ran with it as if we were looking at a potential homicide. They took pictures of the area and canvassed the block for potential witnesses, as well as video cameras. I didn't stay that long. Once I'd walked them through what had happened, both from my perspective and from what I'd learned, I went back to the precinct.

By the time I changed and made it to my car, I was in a slightly better place. Granted, being belittled by that cocky Irish dickhead hadn't been fun. Nor had finding out that the commanding officer and her Crime Analysis bozo had tried to reclassify the crime, re-interviewing a potential suspect and using her words as truth, something that would most likely come up during the evidence hearings and trial if this case made it that far. Nor had my own actions. Sure, I had no one to send to the hospital with the old man. The CO and admin lieutenant had made damn sure that none of their precious house mice could be used to do the actual job they were being paid to do. But in the end, I bore some responsibility. What could I have done differently? Several things, based on what I now knew.

What I'm trying to say is, yeah, I had plenty of reasonable rationales for my actions at the time. But that didn't change the fact that the poor guy had gone to the hospital without any notification to his family, and that he could die without having gotten to say goodbye to them.

Before I knew it, I turned west onto Atlantic Avenue and was headed to Interfaith Hospital.

I parked in a free spot on Herkimer Street on the rear side of the hospital. Then I badged my way in and found out which room the victim was in, not giving myself time to wonder if this was the right thing to be doing, if it could come back to bite me in the ass. I only knew that I needed to do it.

He was in the ICU. By the time I peeked into the room, my palms were slick with sweat. His head was bandaged, and he was intubated. Lisa was seated in a chair by his bed, and an older gentleman stood with his back to me.

She noticed me standing in the doorway, but it took a moment for her to recognize me, being that I wasn't in uniform. Luckily, she smiled when she remembered as she stood up. "Officer Rothchild, thank you for coming by. But I thought the detectives were investigating this."

Her brief smile is the only thing that saved me from stammering. "They are. I just came by to make sure you're okay. And apologize again for the way you had to find out what happened."

The older guy was tall and looked like he'd cracked a couple of heads in his day. He looked me up and down in a quick glance, his eyes pausing on the bulge in the waistband on the right side of my jacket. *Must be the uncle*, I figured.

"Aren't you a sergeant?" He turned to Lisa. "Thought you said he was a sergeant."

She put her hand up to her mouth. "Oh, I'm so sorry. That's what I meant." She looked at me but indicated to her uncle. "I don't have the whole cop thing down like my uncle. He still acts like one too."

He chuckled. "Only when you and the other girls were little." He walked around the foot of the bed and strode up to me. He'd definitely been a tough nut when he was on the job. He extended his hand and I shook it, embarrassed of the sweat on my hands. But he acted like he didn't notice. "Harry Woods. I worked patrol and crime in the 73, then retired from the 75 Detective Squad. Twenty-six years." His eyes locked on mine. "Don't ask me when I retired."

"What—two, three months ago?"

He smiled and looked at Lisa. "I like this guy."

I hadn't expected this. Lisa, yeah, she hadn't seemed to be harboring any grudges. But the family? I'd been ready to be chased out of the room, their screams following me down the hallway to the elevator.

He must've seen something in my face. Like I said, he was a sharp guy. Probably a great detective back in the day. He'd certainly seen more than most. "No one here's mad. The squad guys told me the story. Lady calls sayin' he was trying to break in, then he's all loopy you're thinking he's drunk or on drugs. I told Lisa, back in the day he would've been locked up in a second."

"Yeah, well…at least there was a witness." I looked down at the comatose man, about to ask how he was doing. Glad I stopped myself in time.

We chatted for a few minutes, the two of them telling me that Harry's adult girls were coming by later and that Lisa's older sister had been here for several hours earlier in the day. "She's got two young kids, though, so she had to get home to them," Lisa offered by way of explanation. "I don't have any, so I'm taking lead on this, I guess you'd say. Not that there's much we can do now, except be here for him."

"He knows we're here," Harry said with the confidence of a cop who'd told the same thing to so many families in the past that he had to believe it.

"Either of you want a coffee? There's a cafeteria downstairs."

Harry shook his head. "I drink two cups of black in the morning. That's it for me these days." He turned to Lisa. "You need some coffee. And a break."

Lisa hesitated.

Harry patted his comatose brother on the shoulder. "Go. I'll be here."

We sat at a table in the cafeteria and people-watched for a bit, both thinking our own thoughts. Her eyes wandered even more than mine did.

"You should've been a cop, the way you watch people," I noted lightly.

She blushed. "I'm too little. Besides, I don't like confrontation."

"No one does."

She looked at me earnestly. "Lots of people do."

157

We lapsed back into a comfortable silence, me knowing that, like most cops, I was probably one of those people who did in fact enjoy a little bit of confrontation from time to time. After that we spoke casually, and I almost forgot why I was there.

I walked Lisa back to her father's room after we finished. Before stepping in, I noticed a young woman was seated by the bed where Lisa had been earlier. I hesitated.

Lisa looked up at me. "You can come in if you want. It's just my cousin."

"I should get going. I have a lot of stuff to do."

She considered. "You have kids?"

"No, I have to get a wife first," I said.

She tried her best to smile. "Well, thank you so much for coming, Josh. We really appreciate it."

I said good night, waving to Harry through the open door, then walked to the elevators, a gnawing feeling itching at my back. Thinking I should've maybe said more, explained my actions better. Then thinking that it would all sound like excuses. Which they were. But aren't some excuses excusable? I forgot to call Billy about the job and barely slept that night.

CHAPTER 17

ROTHCHILD: THE RECKONING

The next day I was out on the streets. Courtney was driving, just making the rounds of the precinct when my cell phone started buzzing. I looked at the clock on the radio; it was 12:15. I knew it was the CO. She always got in around this time.

I was pretty sure the phone only buzzed once, twice at most. But it stopped as I took it out of my jacket pocket. The missed call indicated that I was in fact correct. Before I could call her back, the dispatcher came over the radio. "One Sergeant, 10-2 the station and see the CO." "10-2" is just a fancy way the NYPD has of saying to go somewhere. Exactly as many syllables as "go to" or "come to." The radios weren't encrypted back then, but any outside person monitoring them would know what all the codes meant. Silliness.

Courtney drove back to the precinct and I stepped into the CO's office. She was seated at her desk, wearing a sleeveless black dress. She rarely wore a uniform.

I walked toward her desk and stopped a few feet away. She didn't tell me to sit down, so I didn't. She did not look happy.

"Rothchild, what's this I hear about you messing up some DOA?"

DOA means "dead on arrival." We use the term to indicate anyone who has died either before or just after our discovery of them. I knew who she was talking about but decided to play dumb. He hadn't died yet, and we both knew full well that she had tried to fuck with the complaint report, making him the perp and the perp/accomplice the victim. Not to mention weakening the current investigation in the process and possibly providing fuel for the perp's defense attorney by having the idiots in Crime Analysis changing the report.

Obviously, someone had said something to her and she was doing damage control, making sure nothing fell back on her.

"DOA?"

She grew angrier. "You know what I mean—the elderly man who was beaten. Why wasn't I notified about that?"

"I thought you were notified yesterday, ma'am, after we found out he was in a coma."

She leaned forward, forearms on the desk. "I mean the day it happened. That was a serious crime that should've had an immediate investigation. We look out for our senior citizens, Rothchild. It's just something we do."

I couldn't believe what I was hearing. At the same time, it didn't really surprise me. "I made it a felony assault—we talked about this yesterday. Crime analysis re-interviewed the woman and then changed the report."

She shook her head. "I don't know why Kevin's people did that. I assume it's because it was so poorly written."

I would've lost my mind if this was the first time she'd pulled this kind of thing. But it wasn't.

I took a breath and responded calmly. "I checked it over before I signed it—it was well written."

"This isn't a creative writing class. You should've come to me and I would've told you how to phrase it."

I didn't say anything. It was well known that she had been the commanding officer's secretary as a young cop. When she got promoted to sergeant she quickly went inside as administrative. Then she'd gone on to Inspections, a sort of junior Internal Affairs that mostly just concentrated on minor things, like officers not wearing their hats or having facial hair. She had no real street or detective experience.

"Something needs to be done about this," she mused after I didn't respond to her last statement. "A man is in the hospital now. Hopefully he won't die—we're already up in homicides for the year—but he very well could. I'm moving you to 4-to-12."

This wasn't exactly a punishment for me. I'd worked midnights and 4-bys as a cop, so I liked the hours better than waking up at 5:00 in the morning like I had to now. "Okay, ma'am."

"You know, I'd put you on midnights, but I think you need more supervision. You're still on probation, right?"

A sergeant was on probation for a year after they got their rank. She'd been here about nine months and might have assumed that I'd gotten to the precinct just before her, around the time Courtney and I arrested the Hassidic guy and everyone lost their minds. "No, ma'am."

She shrugged. "Well, that's good for you, at least. Anyway, the Operations lieutenant will let you know when you're starting. I assume it'll be after your days off. If you need to take care of anything before, I'd suggest you let him know. Maybe he can work with you."

I didn't need any favors. "I'll be okay, ma'am."

She didn't tell me to leave. Maybe she was expecting me to apologize. That was not going to happen. Sure, I might've owed the apology to Lisa and her family. But what the CO and Crime Analysis had tried to do when they thought they could get away with it was disgraceful. And they had no remorse about it, trying to paint me as the bad guy. I wouldn't play along with the charade.

After a minute of her shuffling papers on the desk she looked up, apparently realizing I wasn't going to say anything. "You can get back on patrol. You're supposed to be out there supervising—at least that's what I'm told."

I kept my face neutral and thanked her before turning to walk out. Show a sign of weakness with these kinds of people, they'll tear you up like a starving pit bull.

*****

Back in the car, I told Jones what had happened. He was livid. "She's batshit crazy. We were trying to help that old man. Gave the detectives the witness and the story on a silver platter. How does she get away with this shit?"

"You can get away with a lot when you're in a position of power and have no conscience," I replied neutrally.

"Plus, the fat ass doesn't hurt," Courtney added sagely. We were stopped at a light and he turned to me. "You think she's still mad about that Jewish guy we collared?"

I shook my head. "Nah. We were exonerated on the complaint. Then some of his friends came into the precinct a few months ago and tried to pull some shit, but there was nothing they could do. It was a legit collar. I talked to the union guys, and they told me I was good."

Coutney's face was doubtful. I asked, a little too loudly, "What?"

"I grew up in Crown Heights, Sarge. Those people don't forgive shit."

I decided to let the matter drop. There wasn't anything they could do to me at this point, I figured.

Neither of us said anything for the next several minutes. Courtney finally broke the silence. "You know what the worst part of you getting kicked off the tour is, Sarge?"

"I'd say being humiliated in the eyes of the entire precinct."

"Yeah," he conceded. "That's bad. But you know where Lieutenant Allen's gonna have me standing the next few weeks?"

"You're right, Courtney. I guess I was being selfish for not seeing that sooner."

He smiled broadly. "That's okay, Sarge. You've got a lot on your mind."

CHAPTER 18

HARRIS AND MCCALL: CAR TROUBLES

"It's cold as shit," Harris complained, chin nestled into the neck of his coat and black watch cap pulled tight over his ears. McCall was driving down Broadway, bustling at 1100 hours with cars, workers, shoppers, subway riders, bus riders, people doing their laundry or getting something to eat, patients of the urgent care clinics, street guys, and addicts.

McCall wasn't having it. "You're the one who agreed to take this piece of shit. No heat. A fuckin' rookie wouldn't be so stupid."

Harris shook his head but didn't answer. There was nothing he could say that wouldn't make him sound stupid and elicit an angry, condescending response from his partner. And, while both of these were probably justified, he was too cold to fight right now.

McCall finally turned off Broadway, a little sun shining in their car since they were out of the shadow of the J train. It didn't help much.

Dominguez and Chan had done him dirty, that was for sure. They'd come out two Academy classes before him, but McCall was senior to them by a year and a half. If there was a car with working heat to be had on a cold winter's day, it should go to them. But McCall was running late and didn't make roll call. Then after roll call, Harris spent ten minutes or so getting his testimony ready for traffic court

164

later that day. He didn't feel like losing again, especially since they'd started getting so anal down in traffic court, with those IAB asshole sergeants grilling them on why they hadn't won the case. "The judge was a liberal cocksucker" was not a valid excuse anymore. Chan and Dominguez had grabbed the keys from the desk and run out while he was prepping. He'd caught up with them as Chan was gassing up the car in the lot.

Dominguez looked down at the keys Harris was holding in his hand, the ones to #3004, the car with no heat. "Why you showing me the keys to your car?" Dominguez asked before he could say anything.

"Because McCall's senior to both of you, so we're taking your car."

Dominguez was such a natural liar that he didn't bat an eyelash. "Sarge said we could take this car, since McCall didn't show up for roll call."

Chan piped in sagely, "Early bird gets the worm."

Harris knew better than to get into it with those two assholes, especially since he was outnumbered and there were a couple of other cops around who'd be watching the show like vultures. So he went back inside and found Sergeant Rothchild, who'd just informed them that tomorrow was his last day before getting switched to the 4-bys.

Sarge was seated at a desk in the report writing room, doing the roll call changes. He looked up as Jamel entered. "You got your car?"

"I have 3004, the one with no heat and a fucked-up passenger door that's hard to close. Dominguez said you let him and Chan take 2597 since McCall was late."

Rothchild couldn't suppress his smile. "McCall's the senior cop. I thought I assigned 2597 to you in roll call…" He turned a page and checked by their names. "Yeah, I did."

Harris hadn't been paying attention during roll call, bummed out that Rothchild was getting moved and he'd have to get used to a new sergeant. More importantly, he'd have to get that new sergeant used to McCall.

Fuck. Those two sneaks must've seen him busy with his testimony and decided to grab his car. Rothchild was a little amused, but he didn't seem likely to get involved in the spat. So Jamel turned around and ran back to the gas pumps, ready to use a very limited amount of physical force if necessary to get the keys. But they'd already pulled out of the lot.

When McCall came in, he'd relayed the story to him by the desk, the desk sergeant sniggering. Surprisingly, McCall didn't take it as badly as he'd expected. No flare-ups, threats, or insults. Instead, he just shook his head sadly. "I'm driving."

It had been Harris's turn to drive, but he didn't argue.

"For the rest of the week," McCall stated in no uncertain terms.

Jamel bit his tongue, knowing this was better than his partner's usual temper pissing off the bosses. He didn't really mind taking reports, but, at least in their partnership, the driver was the one who got to kind of plan the day, apart from the radio calls and other things they had to address as directed or that just popped up.

In fact, McCall didn't even criticize him until they were seated in the cold car. But once he turned on the ignition, knowing whatever air was blowing was never going to warm them up, he turned and looked at him in that way he had. Like he was his older brother and was too disappointed to be angry. "I expected better from you, Jamel. You gotta grow up and start acting like a man."

Ouch. But he knew that his partner was at least partly right.

They drove in silence for a while, Jamel feeling every bit his twenty-five years to his partner's twenty-eight. It was more than the years, though. McCall already had two kids—same woman—and really did a good job with them. He was a concerned and highly involved father. Even though he wasn't still with their mom, he gave her and the kids whatever they needed. He also cooked and drove them to daycare and school and all that stuff.

Jamel knew Tanesha pretty well—she was really nice. Not to mention super-hot. But McCall had, at least by his own recounting and Jamel's understanding, left her instead of getting married. One day Jamel had straight-up asked him why.

"She's too ghetto. I'll be there for her, on account of the kids, 'cause that's what's important. But I can't let myself settle. I have to be more than a leader in a relationship. It's better if I have someone who's my equal. I've already got enough stress dealing with your naïve ass."

That had saddened him. Though McCall had a temper—and an attitude he displayed whenever he thought he was being screwed—he was, in some ways, one of the most self-possessed people Jamel had ever met. He'd never known his father, and his mother was really bad. Jamel didn't know the specifics, but for a boy to be taken from his mother in Brooklyn permanently, not to be temporarily placed with relatives but to straight-up go into the foster care system, she had to have been a total mess. McCall once told him she'd probably OD'd on a street corner with a load of cum in her mouth. For him to not even be curious about what had happened to her…she'd been very bad.

So McCall drifted through the foster care system, a smart but angry boy who had no one in the world who really gave a shit about him. Luckily, he finally landed in a good home at fourteen. He was able to complete high school and then go on to college on a football scholarship, the foster parents professionals who'd helped a bunch of kids like him. But the damage had already been done. The anger, the loneliness—it would always be there. Even those parents, they'd stopped taking in kids by now, but there were so many successes who wanted to see them. McCall could call them, maybe get dinner. But it wasn't the same as it was for Jamel, who had two parents who would jump in front of a bus for him. As much as they annoyed him, he knew this was true. Befriending McCall had really made him understand how lucky he was.

Jamel had grown up in a rough neighborhood, but they were basically middle class. They owned their own home, and Jamel and his two older sisters were always loved. Though they'd both surpassed him educationally and professionally, a point that his mother brought up frequently, he knew his father was proud of him. "A cop," he said on the night Jamel graduated the Academy. "It's a tough job, but an honorable one." They clicked beer bottles—the first they'd ever shared together—and Jamel felt like a man for the first time in his life. Maybe he would again once this car incident was forgotten and he finally moved out of his parents' house.

McCall convinced himself that Tanesha brought him down, because she wasn't educated and came from only a slightly better background than he did. It was sad, because she really was a good person, and Jamel could tell she still loved him. But he'd never walked a day in his partners' shoes. Who was he to give advice, still living with his parents and having to fuck his girlfriend in his car on shady side streets and vacant lots? Maybe one day…

McCall's Zen-like-attitude started to erode as the cold bit into his skin. "Fuckin' bullshit department—what the fuck does that bitch RMP coordinator do?"

"Coordinates," Harris said lightly.

"Coordinates away from any work or responsibility. What a fuckin' coward."

Again, Harris couldn't argue with that one. The "Radio Motor Patrol," which no one ever said, or "RMP" coordinator was responsible for ensuring the cop cars got repaired in the shop, ensuring basic maintenance was done on them, figuring out when a car was too fucked up to be driven, even by a couple of no-name patrol guys in a precinct few people could name. That should include things like having no heat and, even more importantly from a safety standpoint, a passenger-side door that you could throw open without having to put your shoulder into it—and even then having to worry. Not to mention three of the windows didn't roll down. And it wasn't like this was new—everyone had known how bad this car was for months. Even among all the other piece-of-shit cars, this one stood out.

They were going to a domestic dispute on Howard Avenue, a few blocks down from where Courtney Jones would be freezing his ass off in a few days once Rothchild was gone from the shift. McCall slowed down as they passed a park, not too many folks in there today due to the weather. One mother was pushing a kid in a stroller in the little playground, then one walker and one old man sitting on a bench under a bare tree. Nothing to lift the mood Jamel was in, at any rate. Detective Espinoza had let him know the day before that the gun they'd found in the sneaker at that domestic assault a month ago didn't match the shell casings from the homicide on New Year's. For some reason he'd just assumed it would, maybe as a way of making up for letting that reporter snap that picture and cause problems for Sergeant Rothchild. He wondered if that was why he was getting transferred off the tour.

They were a half a block away from the domestic, a woman screaming on an open 911 line that she wanted her husband out of the house. Nothing crazy or out of the ordinary. Harris was still focused on the disappointment at the stupid bullet not matching when McCall interrupted his sullen mood.

"Whoa—look at that. Walkin' like he's the king of the Stuy."

Harris looked up and saw the asshole who'd bit Sergeant Rothchild, strolling down the street toward Howard Avenue with a blunt in his right hand like he didn't have a care in the world. McCall slowed the car to a crawl so they were slowly passing the intersection as Deon Jenkins casually dropped the blunt behind his right leg and kept walking. McCall's face was calm, only his eyes and the small smirk he threw Jamel indicating what he was planning to do. This was why, despite his temper and habit of pissing off the bosses, Jamel still loved his partner.

McCall's left hand, the one holding the wheel, slid downward in a quick but smooth motion as the car turned around on the one-way street, nearly fishtailing despite the slow speed before arcing to the left at an angle headed straight toward Jenkins.

Jenkins tensed as he saw the car turning before stopping with the front bumper pointed at him. His head swiveled left and right—only attached apartments and multi-story residential buildings; no alleys he could duck into. So he just stopped and stared at the two black cops exiting their vehicle, a look on his face that had probably intimidated a bunch of pussy cops in the past. But this was the wrong duo for that tactic.

Harris threw open his car door before the vehicle stopped and stepped out as it did, watching Jenkins' hands like a hawk. McCall wasn't far behind, putting the car in park and approaching so that they wound up in a triangle formation with Jenkins at the top. Harris's right hand rested on the butt of his gun as he approached. "Don't reach for anything, Deon."

Deon either didn't have anything worth reaching for or didn't think it was worth it in this situation. His hands remained at his sides as he spoke. "I ain't doin' shit, bro—nothin' for you to stop me on."

Harris walked up and grabbed his left wrist as McCall closed in and grabbed the right. Jenkins tensed, and they both thought he was going to fight. Instead, he remained rigid so that after McCall got the cuff on his right wrist, he couldn't bring it behind his back to get the left wrist cuffed. Knowing this was often a precursor to fighting, McCall spoke loudly, in a voice that tended to scare people. "Relax your hand, bro." Jamel tensed, ready to throw him to the ground if need be.

Jenkins just laughed and shook his head. "Whachoo got me for, a spliff? Y'all some petty-assed niggers." He relaxed his arms, and they got the other wrist cuffed without a problem.

While McCall held onto Jenkins, Harris retraced his footsteps back to the area they'd first seen him, just a little further up the block on the sidewalk, and found the blunt. It wasn't burning anymore, but the smell of weed was strong. McCall shouted to him.

Harris turned to see his partner holding up a big bag of weed. "Was in his pocket. Enough for CPM" (Criminal Possession of Marijuana, a misdemeanor). It made the case better than just the smoked blunt.

Jenkins looked at Harris. He screamed, "He planted that on me. You *seen* that shit!"

Perps always seemed to zero in on him as the easy mark, maybe because he looked younger and more naïve than he was. They never tried that kind of shit with McCall. McCall was just the asshole black cop who was out to fuck over his own peeps. Standing in the cold freezing, probably high as a kite, Deon had come to the same conclusion as many of the others. That naïve little Harris was gonna save them from the big asshole Uncle Tom cop.

Harris ignored him and walked back over to them. He grabbed control of the cuffs as McCall stepped away and wagged the baggie in front of the perp's face—probably four or five ounces of little zips of weed inside the bigger Ziploc, easily enough for misdemeanor weight. "Yeah, we drive around with this stinky shit in our car. Just lookin' for the one innocent man we can stick it to."

Jenkins looked around for an audience. But it was cold and there was no one. He couldn't play for a crowd, so he gave up on the charade and looked down at his feet.

"Smokin' the natural stuff now, huh? No more K2?" McCall chided.

Jenkins looked up. For a second Harris thought he was gonna spit in McCall's face and set off a whole other fight, mostly him trying to keep his partner from beating this asshole to a bloody pulp. He didn't, though. "Nah, that K2 fuck your head up."

McCall chuckled. "Not like the weed, right? Keeps you running like a fine-tuned sports car."

Jenkins looked at him meanly. "Ain't nothin' wrong with the weed. Should be legal like Jamaica."

"It's not legal in Jamaica," Harris piped in.

Jenkins piped back. "How you know?"

"'Cause I got people there."

Deon Jenkins assessed the younger man. "Yeah, you look like you be wavin' the flag at the West Indian parade, jus' hopin' you don't get shot 'cause folks know you too pussy to do somethin' about it."

McCall chuckled as he guided Jenkins to the car. They stopped at the rear passenger door and McCall got in his face. "Yeah? How *I* look?"

"You look like one a' them niggers be doin' the shootin'."

The ride back to the precinct was uneventful, Harris sitting in back with Jenkins since there wasn't a plastic partition, or "cage," in this Ford Fusion. Not enough room for one anyway, Harris figured. But the whole short ride to the precinct was even colder than before since he'd asked McCall to crack the window on account of Jenkins smelling like ass mixed with body odor and foot fungus. McCall would take the collar, he figured, since it was early. He didn't like unscheduled overtime that much these days on account of childcare issues. Harris figured maybe sitting back here with this asshole and helping his partner with the arrest as much as he could before he got sent back out on patrol would go a long way toward the whole car fiasco being forgotten. At least till the next time they got into an argument, anyway.

After McCall pulled into the precinct lot, Harris took the perp out of the car and walked him into the station and up to the front desk, where a seated Sergeant Johnson was looking down on them like a disapproving judge. "What you got this guy for?"

"CPM."

The frown on his face deepened. "You know we only got three cars out, Jamel."

Unlike McCall, Jamel got along well with all the supervisors. He smiled. "This is the guy who bit Sergeant Rothchild," he offered by way of explanation.

Sergeant Johnson shrugged, the frown dissipating slightly. "All right, but—"

"That bitch?! Faggot damn near broke my fuckin' jaw! He shoulda got locked up."

"We'll keep that under advisement," Sergeant Johnson answered neutrally.

Harris found a few more baggies of weed in the perp's socks—always make them take the socks off and turn them inside out, then check the shoes thoroughly—when he lodged him in the cells. He saw McCall already seated at a computer, trying to get the paperwork done as fast as he could so he wouldn't be stuck too long after the shift ended.

"I'm gonna go tell the squad. You know he's got an I-Card for the homicide on New Year's Day."

McCall looked up, giving him that big brother smile. "Look at you, all excited. It's a 'Witness' I-Card, though. He's not gonna talk to them, not to get out of a weed beef. He's not *that* stupid."

Harris shrugged. "He doesn't know about the I-Card. He might talk to them."

McCall, still looking doubtful, went back to his paperwork. Harris walked upstairs to the Detective Squad. One of the DT's informed him that Espinoza wasn't in. "He's working 4-bys this week."

Harris told the detective that he'd just collared Deon Jenkins. "All right, bring him up. We'll talk to him."

Harris went back downstairs. He took the cell keys out from a drawer behind the front desk. Then he opened the door to the cell area, which was always unlocked, and approached the first cell, where Jenkins sat on the bench, alone.

He eyed the big cell keys in Jamel's hand suspiciously. "Where we goin'?"

"Upstairs. Might be able to get out right now if you're willing to talk—tell us if you know about anything going on in the neighborhood."

He didn't miss a beat. "I want a lawyer."

As soon as Jamel stepped out of the cell area, McCall, not even looking up from the computer, said, "Told you he wasn't that stupid." Still typing, he added, "A stupid asshole, but not *that* stupid."

"You think he knows they're looking at him for the homicide?"

McCall kept typing and didn't look up. "Naah, probably not. But he's been collared enough to know to ask for a lawyer so the DTs can't question him. 'Cause once they get you in that box, all bets are off. And that crazy brother—even if he ain't the shooter for New Year's, he's always up to so much shit in his time between jail stints that he can probably clear a few open cases."

Harris shook his head. "How crazy do you think he is?"

McCall leaned back in the chair and looked his partner straight in the eye. "He's not insane—he knows what's up. That's why he's not biting on the bullshit you're trying to feed him. Also why he didn't fight us like he did your boyfriend." Harris knew he meant Rothchild. "He thought about it for a minute, but then he saw two hardcore brothers who would pound the shit out of him if he tried to bite or spit."

Harris almost blushed—it was rare that he got these kinds of compliments from his partner, especially concerning anything mas-

174

culine. McCall went on. "He's just an asshole, evil, fucked-up, crazy piece of shit. Same as most of the folks we got to deal with." He leaned back and considered, going into the teaching mode Jamel valued so much, despite his knowledge of his partner's weaknesses with tact and chain of command. "Like the deadbeat fathers we're always dealin' with, the ones who got ten kids and are still gonna make more. They're not raising any of 'em, don't give a shit about them. But one of them gets smoked on a street corner or beat to death by the mother's piece of shit boyfriend—all of a sudden they're Father of the Year. They know; they just don't care. They can act different; they just don't want to bad enough. That's Deon."

Jamel wondered if his partner was, at least in some way, referencing his own father, an unknown presence that had still managed to haunt his life in his absence.

He just nodded, though. McCall wasn't ready for that kind of a conversation.

CHAPTER 19

ROTHCHILD:
MAKING CONNECTIONS

Courtney and I were super busy and didn't get back to the station until our shift was almost over. Eddie Johnson was seated behind the front desk, looking down at me with a broad smile. "Check the cells, Josh. Got a friend who wants to say hi."

I walked around the arrest processing area and headed to the cell door, which was metal with a wired glass window set into it about eye-level. Before I opened the door Eddie called out to me. "Better if you don't go in, Josh. We finally calmed him down." I looked through the window and saw Deon Jenkins, the asshole who'd bit me. He was seated on the bench in the first of the two cells, twiddling his thumbs like he was waiting at the post office. I was a little surprised that he was behaving this well. Still, seeing him brought back to mind what I'd been trying to forget; I had months of testing ahead before I could be sure I was okay.

Eddie read my mind. "I don't think he has the HIV, Josh. Before EMS came I asked if he's on any meds and he said no. And he didn't have any on him. Said his medical issue was he's got shrapnel in his leg from a shooting a few years back. EMS wouldn't even take him to the hospital. Of course, as soon as they left he started wiling out for an hour straight."

"So how'd you calm him down?"

Eddie smiled. "I let him smoke a couple cigarettes and got him a sandwich. I figure it'll give us a half hour, so you better get him transported right out of roll call."

Eddie knew I was doing a double to cover for one of the 4-by sergeants I'd soon be working with anyway, and that I was going to take the desk for the shift.

I wasn't too worried about asshole Jenkins flipping out on me, though. And I wasn't particularly keen on letting him get to the bookings as quickly as possible so he could see the judge and get out tonight. "Glad you're treating him so harshly, Eddie. You really showed him not to bite a cop."

Eddie laughed. "C'mon, Josh, I still got a desk to run. What do you want me to do, go in there and hype him up?"

"No, Eddie, maybe just not give him the royal treatment. You know it won't matter anyway—he'll start wiling out again no matter what we give him."

Eddie patted my shoulder. "Them's the breaks, Josh. You should thank Harris anyway. I think he collared him just for you—smoking a blunt, pick-up. Like a going-away present."

I noticed he didn't mention Harris's partner McCall, who was seated at the arrest processing area. I nodded to him. "Good job, Shawn. He's a real prick."

Shawn smiled. "Thanks, Sarge."

"Did he fight with you guys?" I figured he had.

McCall shook his head. "Nope. He might've thought about it for a minute—he's probably still feeling that shot you gave him to the jaw."

I shuddered. I wasn't sure if he was talking about one of the punches I'd thrown while we were fighting or the one I'd given him after he spat in my face, when he was already in handcuffs. That one could have landed me in a lot of shit—maybe even arrested. I was once again very thankful that no one had recorded it, and that it was Jones and Jackson who'd been with me. Neither of them had seemed concerned about that punch—he'd just spat blood in my face and told me he had HIV. If it had been a cop who didn't like me, though, it might have caused problems, even with the extenuating circumstances.

Cops talk, though. I studied McCall's face—neither his tone nor his expression gave any indication that he was speaking as if he had something on me. And although McCall wasn't one of my favorite cops to deal with, I'd never had any big issues with him. I'd always supported him and only put my foot down when he tried to be a know-it-all like that day at the crime scene.

McCall noticed me looking at him. "He was bitchin' about that for fifteen minutes—'fuckin' white sergeant tried to break my jaw!'" He chuckled. "Definitely well deserved."

I relaxed. "Yeah, he's a dick all right. Still have to get tested the next few months."

"You'll be all right, Sarge. I don't think he has it. Anyway, that shit is hard to get. I knew people growin' up should've gotten AIDS ten times over. Healthy as Magic Johson now."

I laughed. "Fuck you."

He laughed too. It was nice to finally break the ice with him a little. Then he kind of ruined the moment.

"Hey, mind if I cut out soon? The DA's office has my cell." Even though his shift was ending, he was supposed to stay at the precinct until he finished up all the charging paperwork with the ADA downtown by phone and fax and they released him. He also might be required to sign a supporting deposition. Almost as importantly, if he was here he could help with the prisoners, including his, to take some of the pressure off the desk sergeant and shift officers.

McCall's sharp eyes looked like they were reading my mind. "I've got a fax at home—I can sign the supporting dep and send it back to them. Just my kids get out of daycare soon. I'll get my perp something to eat before I leave."

What could I say? They'd collared this asshole on their own initiative, knowing he was likely to fight and possibly even bite. Lots of cops wouldn't even bother with someone like that, especially for a minor collar. And even though I didn't have kids, I was sympathetic. "You got a ready time yet?" A ready time meant that all his paperwork had been received by the DA's office.

"Yep, 1310."

"Okay, no problem," I said, feeling like I'd been duped a little. "Don't get him anything to eat, though. We'll do a meal run later, but I'm not giving him anything extra." McCall nodded.

Now me and the 4-by guys were gonna have to deal with this asshole without any help from the cops who'd brought him in. Sure, it was nice that they'd locked him up—these arrests just take them off the streets for a day or two tops, but it's an inconvenience for them and gives them yet another case they've got to fight. A battle of attrition. But we were tight on personnel tonight, as usual, and now I'd have to assign a cop to the cells to watch him and then walk him through Central Booking till his arraignment with the judge, since there was no way they would accept him on a regular transport.

After the roll call was done and I'd handed out whatever car keys there were behind the desk to the cops taking the shift, I peeked in the cell area again. There were a few arrestees in the cell further from the door. Jenkins was all alone in the closer cell, gripping the bars, gyrating his body backward and forward, breaths coming out in short, quick bursts. Hyping himself up to start throwing a fit. I looked back—McCall was already gone.

Normally I'd try and calm the perp down, see if he wanted a phone call, some chips or soda. No way he was getting any of those things from me, though, especially after Eddie had spoiled him so much. I went back behind the desk and put my gun in a locker, then glanced at the small black and white video feed of the cell. It wasn't a great view, but I could see that he was still gyrating.

Before I even had the cell door open the screaming started, followed by the loud metallic thumping of him kicking the bars. I walked in.

He stopped kicking the bars and looked at me. "Fuck you! You the bitch that hit me! I already beat that case an' I'm gonna sue your ass!"

"You bit me," I reminded him. "Then told me you have HIV."

He shook his head. "I don't have no fuckin' HIV—I was *fucked up*! You didn't have no right hittin' me like that!" He stepped away from the bars and screamed at the pale plaster walls. "I NEED TO GO TO THE FUCKIN' HOSPITAL OR I'M GONNA BREAK THIS BITCH DOWN!!!"

Two cops walked in, having heard the screaming and banging on the bars. One of them started to speak, but I waved him off as I tried to get Jenkins' attention again. "You serious? You don't have it?"

His look went from batshit crazy to cunning in a half a second as he approached the bars and put his face up to them. "I don't know. Maybe if you give me a DAT I can tell you…"

Someone who's been arrested as much as him knows our language—DAT meant "Desk Appearance Ticket." Meaning you were photographed, printed, then released from the precinct with a notice to appear in court at a future date. No having to go to court downtown and then wait in a cell until your appearance before the judge. A Desk Appearance Ticket was basically the Diet Coke of arrests.

Fuck this guy—no way was I giving him a DAT. He wouldn't qualify for one, and I'd have to be creative to get it done. Then risk something happening and being second-guessed as to why I did it. No way would I do that kind of a favor for him just so he could lie to me. It wouldn't settle anything.

I motioned to the cops to follow, and we walked out of the cells. For the next thirty minutes the sound of Deon Jenkins kicking the steel bars reverberated in my brain and I got a major case of déjà vu. As I'd figured, the crazy shtick, at least in this case when he hadn't just smoked K2, was a show. He'd briefly ditched it as soon as he thought he could get something he wanted, like a lot of perps. I'm not saying there's not some underlying condition, but most criminals aren't actually insane. They're just very selfish, don't deal well with things they don't like, and have poor impulse control. To me, that's just being an immature baby and not really a medical condition. I mean, I've met crazy people—insane people—ones not even on drugs who had legit hallucinations and intricate alternate worlds they dwelled in. They really weren't responsible for their actions and belonged in a hospital. But most of the perps we call "crazy" don't truly fit into that category.

As I tried to get back to my desk duties, Deon's banging on the bars already giving me a headache, I started to wonder if Detective Espinoza might not be right about this asshole. Previously I'd figured he was too crazy to commit a planned homicide. At any rate, I was going to lose a cop for the whole tour when we finally sent this asshole downtown to the bookings. No way they were putting him in a pen with the rest of the perps waiting to see the judge. Instead, in a process called a "walk-through," a cop from the arresting precinct stayed with the prisoner for the whole process, up to and including his arraignment before the judge. After that, the perp was either remanded to Rikers, in which case the cop took him upstairs and lodged him with corrections personnel, or he was released. I'd done my fair share of walk-throughs at Kings County Central Booking (KCB) as a cop and didn't envy whomever we picked to take this guy down. Central Booking probably wouldn't even take him if he continued screaming and carrying on. In that case, EMS would be called. The cop would accompany him to the hospital in an ambulance, and the whole process would start over again. That's how some of these perps wound up in custody for two or three days before seeing a judge, even though it was supposed to be within twenty-four hours.

The banging on the cell bars ebbed and flowed for a few hours, but he must've gotten tired around 9:00 and it finally stopped. We had two more prisoners come in that shift, one from patrol and one the detectives brought in. Both were males, and they were put in the second cell with the other perps whom I still hadn't found someone to transport to the bookings. Luckily, they all stayed quiet.

It was a little after 10:00 when a sergeant from Central Booking called. "Deon Jenkins is ready. You can bring him down now." This was a little surprising, as the tour shifts, which took effect about 11:30, usually meant a delay in almost everything. But maybe the bookings had different hours for tour changes; I never really understood it. All I knew was that sometimes court would run past midnight and sometimes it wouldn't. Same as everything else on this job, there was no rhyme or reason.

Since this collar was at least partly due to me, I asked one of the midnight sergeants to give me two cops who could take the perp to the bookings before roll call was conducted. They walked Jenkins out of the cell area, rear handcuffed and leg shackled due to his uncooperative demeanor. Before they even tried to turn him so that they could stand in front of the desk and check out with me, I stopped them.

"It's okay—I logged him out already. I'll walk out with you."

I walked behind them as we went through the back door and into the parking lot, where their car was parked. Jenkins was breathing hard, not as a result of a medical condition—he was either trying to psych himself up to do something crazy or make himself hyperventilate. I yelled to the cop on his right. "Hold onto him—don't let him fall."

The cop, who'd previously barely been holding his left arm, now straightened up and tightened the grip. Jenkins' head swiveled in my direction. He laughed. "You all scared of a nigga in handcuffs. How 'bout you take these off an' we see what happens?"

I wasn't in the mood. "You already had your chance to be a tough guy, Jenkins. Save it for next time."

He scoffed. "Fuck you Roth-*child*. I be seein' you next time. Ain't gonna be like on the first, when I was all fucked up from—" He suddenly went silent and put his head down as the cop guided him into the back seat of the car. He didn't resist or cause a scene, which I figured was a result of him regretting running his mouth off. He stayed silent for over half a minute, just staring at his feet. I stared at his regretful face and felt a flutter—I'd have to let Espinoza know about this. Maybe he noticed something in my face, because he looked up at me and smirked again. "It was K2—THAT'S IT. But next time ain't gonn' be no li'l love bite. Next time I'm gonna rip that piggy throat out."

"Shut the fuck up," a cop named McCarthy hissed.

If Jenkins was looking to intimidate me, this was not the way. I'm no hero, but I will fight any man, any time. Win or lose, I'm not going to bitch out. The only thing I was worried about was what that bite and the blood-riddled spit had maybe put in me. So I held his stare as McCarthy closed the back door. Then I went back inside to conduct the hand-off of the desk to the midnight sergeant. Though he wasn't happy we still had five prisoners in the cell, he understood. Tomorrow morning, when the day shift started, he might be giving us those same perps and maybe even a few more. Since he was already losing a car for this prisoner walk-through, it was doubtful he'd be able to do another transport with the low manpower. Once you accept that everyone gets screwed, especially with prisoners, it makes things a lot easier. Better for your mental health too.

I couldn't stop thinking about that last interaction with Jenkins, though. Not the threat, but the way he started running his mouth off about our fight on January 1st, then thought better of it and went dead silent for half a minute. I'd seen in his face that he'd regretted saying so much. While this didn't even qualify as an admission—it wasn't something that could be used in a criminal case—maybe Espinoza had been right about this guy. I told him as soon as I could.

CHAPTER 20

ROTHCHILD: LAST DAY SHIFT

It was my last shift on the day tour. I'd gotten less than three hours of sleep after coming off my double, tossing and turning in bed, debating if Jenkins' behavior meant anything or if I was just looking too deeply into it.

Courtney was off, and Eric's steady partner Shayna had returned from maternity leave. The only other cop I'd worked with more than a handful of times was Ronnie, a British-born but mostly Brooklyn-grown redhead whose accent was so off the wall that even a lot of the angrier folks we dealt with got a kick out of it. Due to the accent and his relatively high-pitched voice, one of the more creative cops had dubbed him "The British Nanny" before I got to the precinct. The nickname had stuck, obviously, as it was too good not to. Ronnie went along with it, which everyone appreciated. But he was off today also.

I was going to go out by myself, as I usually did when one of my regulars wasn't around. However, after manning four sector cars, I had an extra body, Keisha Jackson.

I normally didn't take female drivers. This wasn't a sexist thing—Keisha was a very good cop. It's just optics. A male sergeant takes a young female cop as his driver one time, that's just things. But if he takes her the next day…people are going to talk. Plus, Keisha, through no fault of her own, was very attractive. I'd already fucked up well and good working with Melanie all those years, only to let it become romantic toward the end. Even though Melanie and I had been the same rank, it could look like a pattern if I started taking a pretty young driver now. But it was my last day on the shift, so fuck it.

We'd just cleared a domestic dispute. Keisha was driving slowly as we passed a big armory that now served as a homeless shelter for men who'd been kicked out of other shelters. She eyed a guy sitting on the steps, but he didn't touch the brown bag by his feet and she cruised on by.

"You should've let him drink it, Keisha. His life is shitty enough already."

She laughed. "Wow, Sarge, you're getting jaded already!" Her right hand reached down and patted my arm. "Don't worry—you'll be back with us soon as that bitch CO gets transferred."

I tried not to flinch or tense up. I might have succeeded. Even though her hand left my arm quickly, she didn't give any indication that I'd been weird.

"So, who you gonna take as your driver on 4-by?"

"I don't know…I guess I'll figure it out."

Keisha smiled as she took a looping left off Marcus Garvey. "You should take Samantha Adams."

"Yeah," I replied neutrally. "She's cool. She doesn't have a partner?"

Keisha slowed down so she could look at me. "I don't even know, Sarge. But she said you're cute."

Samanta was a pretty blonde girl who'd been in the precinct a few years. She was probably twenty-four or twenty-five.

"I don't want to be one of those supervisors who tries to get with all the pretty female cops," I responded neutrally.

"Well, that puts you in the minority, Sarge. But I respect it. There should be more guys like you."

We drove in silence for a bit. "Look, Keisha, I'm not saying I'd never date a cop that worked in my precinct. Just not one that worked for me. It's creepy."

She looked at me. "Again, that puts you in the minority."

Her smile was like a pleasant dream. I don't know if I was staring or being creepy, but she responded quickly.

"I'm dating someone—practically engaged. Nice guy, not a cop. So I don't have to deal with all that shit."

My face felt hot; it was probably beat-red even though the car was still warming up from being parked a while on our last job. Luckily, she didn't look over.

"That's smart, Keisha. Stay away from cops." I paused. "Someone should've told *me* that a couple years ago."

"You're dating someone, Sarge?"

Jeez. She didn't have to sound so surprised. "I was. It didn't work out."

She laughed. "Buncha hos."

A few minutes later the dispatcher piped over the radio, "Shots fired at Stuyvesant and Pulaski. Multiple calls."

I keyed my radio. "One Sergeant, show me going. Any perp description?"

"Negative, Sergeant," the dispatcher responded. "Can I have anyone back the sergeant?"

Keisha got there fast, and I didn't even need to tell her to turn the siren off as we got closer.

The intersection was in the shadow of a towering housing project on our right. On the opposite corner, there was a small group of people of varying ages standing on the curb by a bodega, looking at something on the sidewalk. The parked cars blocked my view of what it was, but I already knew. It was just to be seen how bad it was.

Since everyone was so comfortable standing around, it was clear that the shooter had already fled. That or he'd been super slick and blended in with the crowd. Very hard to do in daylight, though—especially when there couldn't have been much of a crowd prior to it at 11 a.m. on a chilly weekday.

Keisha pulled up a couple of car lengths from the group and we hoofed it over there. Eric and Shayna pulled up from the other direction and came over too.

It wasn't as bad as it could've been. A young man in his late teens to early twenties sat on the sidewalk holding his left shin. Blood had already stained through his pants and was leaking on the concrete. Looked like the bullet had hit the front of his shin. Judging by the bleeding, it hadn't hit anything that important.

Thank goodness. The last thing I needed was to take another broad-daylight homicide on my last shift on this tour.

Keisha and Eric ushered the onlookers back as Shayna ran back to her car to get crime scene tape. Hopefully they had some. I could hear Keisha and Eric asking if anyone had seen the shooter so we could put out a description.

I stood over the victim as I called for EMS. "One Sergeant, send a bus for a male in his early twenties, shot in the left shin, not likely to die, conscious and alert." The dispatcher acknowledged.

The kid seemed to be taking getting shot pretty well, so I had hope I might get something from him. "What happened?"

He looked up at me with an expression I'd already seen too many times. "I dunno," he stated with just a hint of annoyance. "I heard a shot an' my ankle gave out."

"Was the shooter in a car or on foot?"

"I don't fuckin' know! I'm shot, man! Get me a fuckin' ambulance!"
I didn't see any shell casings on the sidewalk. There were enough
people around that they could have been kicked away by accident. Or
the shooter could've used a revolver. But this guy's demeanor, coupled
with him giving me the stock answer (in essence: "I heard a shot and
felt pain") told me that he knew more than he was saying. I hoped
Eric and Keisha could get someone in the crowd to give us something.

The vic didn't want to give his name. I could see the outline of a
wallet in his right front pants pocket: *Nix robbery as a motive, "Sherlock
Holmes-child."* He stated that he didn't have ID on him, though.
Eventually I just reached down and pried the wallet out of his pocket. He
was too busy trying to keep the blood inside his leg to offer any resistance.

Keisha came up to me after a few seconds, holding her memo
book open. "All we got right now is a guy saying it was a dark four-
door sedan, possible older-model Maxima with tinted windows, fled
toward Marcus Garvey. No plate number or shooter description."

Even though it wasn't much, I put it out over the air. You could
probably close your eyes, count to ten on any busy street in Brooklyn.
When you opened them, you'd see a Maxima with tinted windows roll
by.

"Good job, Keisha. You get the witness's info?"

"Just a first name and phone number. He was real casual about
it—didn't wanna be seen talkin' to the cops. He walked off already."

"That's fine," I said, meaning it. With this many people out, you
can't be seen having a long conversation with a potential witness. It
could put a target on their back.

I had Keisha phone the front desk with the victim's information.
Before the ambulance even arrived, we knew this twenty-year-old had
a long rap sheet and was affiliated with a gang from the Bronx, where
he lived. I asked if he still lived there, and he said that he did. What
he was doing here was anyone's guess—he wasn't forthcoming.

I had Eric and Shayna check under the cars and on top of the tires to make sure this guy hadn't stashed a gun or drugs. The wound did not look self-inflicted, but he could have been carrying and dumped the gun after getting shot.

Just to be sure, I gave him a quick pat-down as the EMTs walked up. No weapons, only a little bit of weed that I left in his pocket. They would remove his pants at the hospital and give it to the cop who escorted him to voucher as evidence. They'd get the weed then. Better than setting him off now over something minor—he was uncooperative enough as it was.

The CO was calling me before the victim was wheeled into the ambulance on his stretcher. I had told Eric to ride in the back with him while Shayna followed in their car; Keisha and I could handle this thing until my other sector car got here. Right now, she was directing traffic.

"What do we have, Rothchild?!" the CO demanded as soon as I answered the phone.

I ignored how she made my last name sound like a cuss word and told her what we had. She was not happy. "A Bronx perp?! What the fuck are you doing out there, Rothchild?! It's not enough we got Brooklyn perps shootin' each other—now we got the Bronx' problems too?!"

Two old-timers from the Detective Squad pulled up down the street in an unmarked Crown Vic and made their way over to the relatively small crime scene. Eric and Shayna had quickly taped off from a fence behind the victim and wrapped it around a car, using the sideview mirror for support, and then ran the tape across the street before looping back to the victim's side to encompass the two shell casings they'd found. Not bad for how quickly they did it on a busy street.

One of the detectives glanced at the rocks Eric had placed by the shell casings; paper would've blown away and we didn't have any cones. He laughed and said to his partner, "You think he walks around with those rocks?" The partner laughed. As they passed, the detectives both glanced down at the victim, who was on the gurney being placed into the ambulance. They had a quick conversation—I didn't hear it due to the CO yelling in my ear—but it didn't look very productive.

They walked up to the edge of the tape near where the Vic's blood stained the concrete. They saw I was on the phone so one of them grabbed Eric, who was waiting with EMS as they raised the gurney into the ambulance.

I answered a couple of the Commanding Officer's questions to the best of my ability, things like, "How come the Bronx comes down here for shootouts when you're on patrol?" (I don't know, ma'am). "Guess you don't scare 'em like I used to when I held the streets down as a patrol sergeant."

"I guess not," I conceded, knowing she'd never actually been a patrol sergeant.

Finally, she sighed. "Oh well. I'm still down one homicide for the year. Despite everything you're tryin' to do to change that." Then she hung up.

I gave the detectives the victim's name, since they hadn't gotten it from the front desk and Keisha was busy directing traffic, along with Dominguez. Chan was standing just outside the crime scene tape near where the DTs had walked up. He had a pen and memo book out, so I was hoping he'd gotten their names while I was on the phone. I only knew one of them; the other had been out on medical leave for a long time when I got to the precinct. Something 9/11 related.

The detective whose name I didn't know motioned to the back of the ambulance, which was just pulling off. "I gather Mr. James was as helpful with you as he was with us?"

I shook my head. "Probably even less. I only got his ID by stealing his wallet."

The 9/11 detective laughed. "Long as you give it back at some point."

"It's already back in his pocket," I assured him. "Had some weed in his pocket too but I didn't wanna set him off."

The detective looked around at the crowd, which was increasing. Not in a bad way—no one was yelling or causing a disturbance. Just folks being curious. "I'd say that was a good call, Sarge."

The detectives hung around a few minutes, interviewing potential witnesses and checking in with a few nearby businesses before heading to Interfaith Hospital to see if they could get something from the victim. Unfortunately, he didn't have any warrants to hold him on, and that little bit of weed in his pocket was going to scare him about as much as the thin piece of paper the summons would be written on. Not even enough to wipe your ass with, much less get him to help with the investigation.

Chan did in fact manage to get the names of the two detectives and their sergeant who showed up as I was leaving. And I appreciated him handing me a scrap paper with those names along with all the other cops who were at the scene scrawled in neat writing.

* * * * *

We were in the precinct parking lot. He and Dominguez had just gotten off an end-of-shift burglary report and were already twenty minutes into overtime, so I appreciated the fact that he'd remembered to give it to me.

"Your going-away present," he stated with a smile as I took it from him.

"Just what I wanted. You're a sweetheart."

Dominguez was walking past us to go into the precinct and laughed. "He's gonna get a big head, Sarge. Usually guys just call him easy."

Chan put his nose in the air. "At least they call me!"

I was gonna miss these guys.

CHAPTER 21

ROTHCHILD: DATE NIGHT

It had been a few weeks since my forced shift change. Things were going okay; 4-by was busier, with more violent crimes and shootings. But I was used to that already and didn't mind.

I'd talked to Lisa on the phone a couple of times. Her father was still in a coma, and things weren't looking too promising. The perp had already been arrested, after the witness in the van IDed him in a six-pack, or "photo array," and then again in a lineup. As we'd thought, he was the boyfriend of the woman who'd called and given us the bullshit story. She still wasn't cooperating, but that might change with time. If not, she could very well wind up being collared too. Making a false police report, possibly as an accessory to manslaughter if he died, something it seemed everyone was expecting.

Turns out the perp worked for Sanitation. He had a criminal history, a few assaults and domestic incidents, a burglary, plus a gun charge a few years back. He'd probably never done any state time, though, given he'd managed to land the sanitation job.

Lisa was focused on her father, her family, and her own job. Although I'd felt a connection at the hospital, it didn't seem like this was the time to ask her out or even inquire if she was dating anyone. While she was very friendly and seemingly welcoming of my concern, it didn't appear she wanted anything more than friendship right now.

I'd dated a girl about six months before. It didn't last long—two months, tops. But she was the only person I'd slept with since the last time with Melanie, almost a year before. And that time was just a re-kindling, at least in my hoping, of what we'd had prior. And I still hadn't seen her since that night we fooled around a little after the movies.

At thirty-one, I was starting to think that I was on my way to becoming a lifelong bachelor. Nights were easy now, as I normally got home after midnight and went to sleep an hour or two later. The mornings were a little harder, sitting around with my thoughts till I worked up the energy to go to the gym.

I've never needed that much sleep—six hours is my standard—but I'm okay with a little less. So, with a tour of about nine hours, and let's say a little over an hour of commuting, then twenty minutes to change into and out of my uniform—then six hours of sleep—that's still about eight hours I needed to fill. And those hours were getting harder and harder lately.

I was on my "RDO," or "Regular Day Off." It was a little after 11 p.m. The 4-by-12 shift would be getting off soon. I was sitting in my apartment, nursing my second beer. Thinking about Lisa was getting me kind of down. Even if I managed to get a date with her, and this was seeming less and less likely, I'd have to mention the fact that I'd been bitten by a possibly HIV-infected individual, his latest statements aside, who'd also spat blood in my eyes and mouth. Not exactly a great starter for a relationship. I remembered Melanie that night two months ago, her breasts tasting like sweat and salt, insisting that I didn't have anything and seemingly inviting me to push things further.

I picked up the phone. She answered on the first ring, like she'd been expecting my call. Like she could sense the desperation.

I'd taken two tests since the biting, and all the bloodwork was good so far. My Hep-B vax was good, and all the other readings were normal. I let Melanie know this over the phone that night. She didn't seem surprised.

"You're so *Jewish* sometimes, Josh. You took the cocktail—you're fine."

"I'm just trying to be straight with you."

She sighed. "You're always straight. That's why I—that's why we always worked so well together. I mean…you took me, rookie chick….(she didn't say "that every guy in the precinct was trying to fuck," but it was understood) and you taught me to be a cop."

I had about four years on the job when I started working with Melanie. It was just after she got off "Operation Impact," a crime strategy developed by statistic-obsessed leaders that put rookie cops on every corner of higher-crime precincts and made them write tons of petty tickets and also make arrests that could've been handled with either a warning or a ticket. But she'd thought of me back then, and maybe even now, as a mentor. In the beginning I'd appreciated it. It's always good, when you even *kind* of know what you're doing, to have someone who will back you up and not ask questions unless they're actually warranted. To nod to that person and they instantly get that they have to grab one of the guy's hands while you grab the other because he has to get arrested. Someone who won't pipe in "I don't think that's true" when you're laying it on thick to a suspect, trying to get an admission or even just making the arrest process go more easily. Someone to stand beside you no matter what kind of shit comes down the pike.

"You wanna hang?" I asked this like I used to, back when I thought she was cute but I was dating other women and still saw her as just a partner (most of the time).

"Yeah," she said. "I'm leaving work in a little bit. You wanna pick me up?"

We skipped the movie this time and headed straight to this bar in Forest Hills we used to go to when we worked together. It was a relaxed place; good drinks and decent food if you wanted it. Melanie was on her third cocktail; I was nursing my second since I was the driver tonight. Now that I was doing the 4-by shift again, 2 a.m. didn't seem so late.

A Jimmy Buffett song was playing on the radio as we sat at one of the tables in the bar area. On the other side of the place was a sit-down area mostly used for big parties. Something was definitely going on tonight behind the curtains, but most of the noise was from the bar-sitters.

Her face was a little flushed, the redness flowing softly down her tanned skin to her upper chest and the top of her bra, which was visible due to the low-cut shirt. She noticed my eyes wandering. "I see where your mind's at tonight, Josh."

"It's always there, in one way or another. You think any man is different like that?"

She laughed. "Only the gay ones. They'd be trying to claw that shirt off you, though. Very sexy."

While she *was* right—my shirt clung to my body like a glove and didn't leave much to the imagination—I was too far gone in this thing to be distracted by the compliment. My hopes had gone up and down for so long that the ebbs and flows in her mostly vague interest didn't get to me as much anymore. "What's going on with us, Melanie?"

"We're having a good time. Like we used to."

I put my drink down. "Look, what happened last time after the movies—I wanted it to go further. And I think you did too."

She took another sip, doe eyes giving me nothing I could read. "The bite—" I stopped when she shook her head. Melanie didn't think it was a big deal. She'd been bit by a heroin addict/prostitute a few years back when she'd been asked to search her in front of the desk by Vice officers. I was working with her at the time, but not dating yet. From what I could tell, though, the month on the cocktail didn't have much of an effect on her dating life. Back then she was seeing a sergeant who worked in the precinct. Obviously he knew about the bite, but it didn't seem to bother him much either. During the four weeks she was off, they definitely saw a lot of each other. I'm guessing he wasn't hanging out with her to watch TV and play Scrabble.

I kept talking, knowing I shouldn't. "Look, on New Year's—before—" I could tell I was losing her. A lot of weird stuff had happened to me since that night that it was almost like I was looking at my life as a before and after. But it only meant something to *me*, this delineation. "You made clear we weren't getting back together. Then all of a sudden we're messing around in your car, talking again like we used to…hanging out tonight…"

She was definitely pretty buzzed. "Whatever happens *happens*, Josh. I don't think we need to call it anything."

My heart sank in my chest. I took a huge gulp of my drink, suddenly feeling very alone.

*****

The place was hopping; music playing, the bar and the small tables behind it packed. We spoke, but I don't remember much of the conversation. All this time I was thinking it was either one thing or another—we'd be together or we wouldn't. But this casual, on-again off-again thing, with no hope that there was a future to it all…I was finally getting what she'd gotten all along.

I didn't order another drink, afraid I would get wasted and she'd have to take a cab home. I remember looking at her, the pretty way her head would cock to the side, her thin eyebrows rising when I said something that got her, thin wrists flitting this way and that. When she got up to go to the bathroom her round ass poking out of the jeans, her hands a little damp with perspiration when we started to fool around. If this is all she was willing to give me, it would be enough. But just for tonight.

She stayed over at my place. We fucked three times over the course of that evening and the following morning, and I can honestly say it was the best sex we'd ever had. Probably because we both knew it was the last sex we would ever have. My feelings for her were too deep for an on-again, off-again kind of thing. She didn't want to hurt me, but I think she now realized that was all that could happen if we kept going like this.

I needed what she was willing to give, anyway. The drive back to her precinct, where she'd left her car, was almost blissful, the two of us so tired we barely spoke but didn't mind. The energy we'd expended over the last eight or nine hours, the pent-up frustrations we released—it made it so things weren't awkward like they usually are when both parties know that it's come to an end. We just listened to music and enjoyed the ride, the way I should've been enjoying it all along.

CHAPTER 22

ERIC AND SHAYNA: SCHOOL FIGHT

School dismissals had just started, so the call was no surprise. "10-34, large group of students, late teens, fighting in the street." The address was at the end of a mostly residential block that intersected with Broadway, not too far from some of the area schools.

The fight was already breaking up by the time they got there. What looked to be a late-teens group of males, six or seven participants, scattered in different directions down Broadway in the shadow of the "J" train. Eric hadn't seen anyone looking toward the police car; they might've heard the sirens that Shayna turned off a block out, or they might've just gotten spooked from something else. Good news: No victim was lying on the street bleeding. Just a bunch of assholes fucking around.

One guy was standing on the periphery of the group and didn't look like he'd actually been fighting. Good thing, since he looked to be at least twenty-five. He stood stiffly, though, and Eric's eyes fell on his face. As soon as he noticed Eric looking, he turned and ran. When he turned, Eric saw the gun in his right hand. He was running toward the propped-open front door of an apartment building just in from the corner of Broadway.

Eric and Shayna burst out of their car and ran toward him, guns held down at their sides, hoping to head him off before he made it into the building. But he was closer, disappearing inside as a previously unseen male popped out of the lobby and kicked the brick that was holding the door open, then pushing it closed as Eric practically crashed into it. He could see through the glass window set high into the door that the brick-kicker was sprinting up the staircase just off the tiny front lobby, probably close behind his friend with the gun.

Eric tried the door but it was locked. Shayna started pressing buttons, hoping someone would buzz them in as she spoke into her mic. "One Charlie, 10-85 at our location, male with a gun."

Eric pounded on the door so hard he thought it might break. It didn't—not that he was a pussy or anything. It was thick wood. He took a few steps back, aiming to run up and kick it, hopefully not making a fool of himself in the process, when an older woman walked up and peered out through the glass. Eric motioned for her to open it, and she did. He thanked her as he rushed past, Shayna right behind.

There were two apartments on the first floor—one with the door open. The lady must've seen him peering in. "That's mine. I heard 'em run upstairs." Before he could ask for more she said, "Third floor. Last apartment at the end of the hall, behind the stairs. Either that or they're on the roof."

He ran up the stairs, glancing up and around as he hit the second-floor landing. It was deserted, the doors all shut. The building was only three floors. Up above, he heard a loud crash. He motioned to Shayna that the perps were upstairs. Then, with his gun drawn and pointing up, he quickly made his way to the third floor. All of the doors were closed, but as he pivoted and walked down the hallway to the last apartment he heard more loud movement. As soon as Shayna tapped him on the shoulder to let him know she was there, he tried the door with his left hand. It was locked. He looked back at her and she nodded.

It was a wood panel door, not as thick as the one downstairs. It took him only two kicks to send it flying open.

The living room was a mess but empty. He heard noises coming from one of the bedrooms down the hall, on the street side of the building. They ran into the room. The guy who'd shut the door for the one with the gun was standing at the open window, one foot out. There was no fire escape.

He looked back as they entered the bedroom, torn. Couldn't get up the nerve to jump. Eric pulled him out of the window and they cuffed him up without much struggle, the weight of the decision having taken all the fight out of him.

Shayna held onto the perp while Eric looked out the window onto the street. He could see their car, a couple of pedestrians, and the J train tracks over Broadway. Two floors below the window, there was a metal awning over the entrance to the neighboring bodega. The orange-red metal looked caved in, but had that been from the perp with the gun jumping?

Down on the street, Courtney Jones, the perennial fixed-post guy, jumped out of the back of a livery cab. Eric called down to him. "You see anyone jump out the window?"

Jones looked up and shouted back, "No! You want me to look around?"

By yourself, in your stolen cab? No. "Nah, come up! We got one of 'em."

***

While Shayna held onto the perp, Eric and Courtney searched the rest of the apartment better. More cops arrived and joined them as they checked under the beds, in the closets, in the crawlspace over one of the closets, even in the big plastic storage moving bin that turned out to just be filled with clothing. Shit. Fucker had jumped out the window. Probably still had the gun too. What could they charge his friend with now? OGA—Obstructing Governmental Administration, a.k.a. "Fucking with the cops during a legitimate police encounter." Not much. And it would get plead down to a nothing violation very quickly.

They were able to check a few of the apartments with the owners' consent. But Eric was pretty sure the perp had more nerve than his friend and made the jump. Something like that had happened to him a few years back.

After a while they gave up. At least they had the friend—maybe the detectives could squeeze him. Unfortunately, there was no evidence of forced entry into the apartment, and the perp they had said he didn't know who actually lived there. And he wasn't giving up his friend's name.

*****

Shayna was processing the arrest downstairs. Eric was with Espinoza and Williams in the squad, looking at pictures of likely suspects. He remembered the guy's face crystal clear but hadn't recognized him from any previous encounters. As they scrolled through the pictures, Espinoza spoke in his ear. "Getting old, bro. You used to know all the players."

Eric looked at him, still pissed about the whole situation. "Older and wiser. By the way, I didn't see you guys out there backing me. Whole precinct came. But none of you suits." They didn't like that one.

Not that he really cared about gun arrests anymore—his hero days were behind him. But it really stung to lose one like that. Who the fuck jumps out a third-story window and can still run away? Fucking awning must've been like one of those movie props.

He was getting tired of Espinoza and Williams breathing over him when he saw the guy. "That's him."

Espinoza read the guy's stats. "Eddie Davis, six feet, one-eighty, twenty-six years old."

Eric nodded. "Yep. Go get 'im, boys. We'll bang out the report for Criminal Possession of a Weapon, which I believe is a felony of some sort or other." Then he walked out before Espinoza could say anything further.

CHAPTER 23

ROTHCHILD:
WHEN SHIT HITS THE FAN

Lisa's father died after a few weeks in the coma. I called as soon as I heard about it. It had been a few days since we'd last texted—nothing much more than saying hi.

She seemed to be holding up well, the length of the coma kind of preparing her a little, I guess. We spoke for a few minutes; mostly I listened. Eventually she asked, "How are you doing, Josh?"

I considered. "I know you're running on empty now, but…"

"Yes?"

"Maybe we can get a cup of coffee or something, after the funeral and everything?"

She said yes.

* * * * *

Paul Hastings was in the patrol squad I inherited upon my transfer to the evening shift. Although he was at least a decade older, he'd worked in the department only a few years more than I had, as he'd come on the job later in life. Paul had a good head on his shoulders and was active. More importantly, he drove well and made good conversation. Luckily, he didn't have a steady partner, so I made him my driver.

There was a good pizza place just over the border of our precinct. We both got a couple of slices, eating them quickly at a table. I was the only supervisor on patrol, so getting food and eating it at our leisure in the station house wasn't an option. The 4-by was usually very busy, considerably more so than the day tour. And tonight wasn't any exception.

We left the pizza joint and were driving eastbound on Gates Avenue. It was after 8:00 and full-on dark. Up ahead, on my side, a young man was walking past one of the buildings of a private housing development. He wasn't wearing a hat or hoody, just a black puffy jacket, head down against the cold. Hastings slowed down as we got nearer.

Paul spoke up. "That's Eddie Davis, the one who jumped out the window on Broadway. He's got a warrant for possession of a firearm. Also on parole."

I'd heard about Eric and Shayna's crazy caper but wasn't aware they'd identified a suspect. I didn't have the chance to praise Paul for being so up on current events, or his eagle eyes, though, because we were now almost upon Davis.

He probably hadn't realized he was wanted for that stunt, maybe thinking that if a gun hadn't been recovered that he couldn't be charged with one (although the case falling apart in the months after the initial filing was a given). If he was on parole, though, it would be enough to violate him.

So he didn't run until we were very close. A lot of perps aren't scared of the uniforms in marked cars, figuring we'll only stop them for crimes in progress, not investigative stops like the plain-clothes units.

At any rate, the change happened quickly. One moment he was casually walking, hands in his jacket pockets; the next moment his right hand came out holding a semi-automatic pistol. Before Hastings even stopped the car, Davis turned and started running in the direction from whence he came, paralleling the buildings. Unfortunately for him, the doors of these buildings were usually locked. It was a long block, and there were no alleys he could duck into.

I was the passenger officer, who's always first out of the car while the driver throws it in park and hopefully remembers to pull out the keys. So I was way ahead of Paul. I wasn't too far behind Davis as his head swiveled this way and that, looking for an escape that wasn't forthcoming unless he wanted to try one of the building entrances, which were probably locked.

I'll say this: Whatever damage he'd done to his legs when he jumped out a third-story window and landed on a metal awning en route to another landing on the concrete below hadn't seemed to affect him much. He had a decent lead, and I could barely keep pace with him. Then he came to a black metal fence between the buildings. It was tall and not easy to climb—by necessity, as a covered parking structure was behind it.

But like a ninja, he grasped the bar at the top of a locked service door, jumped up, then launched himself over the curved metal at the top and landed on the other side. I made it to the gate as he turned left and ran into the dimly lit parking lot.

I scaled the fence and landed on the concrete soundly, reaching for my radio. But then I heard Hastings from the other side of the fence behind me, broadcasting our location and the suspect description. So I left my radio in its holder, drew my gun, and fast-walked into the dimly lit parking structure.

I circled around a parked car and saw a flash of movement up ahead and to my left, a head bobbing under a mid-sized SUV. Pointing my firearm in that direction, I tight-walked over there, hearing Hastings come up behind me. He tapped me on the shoulder lightly to let me know he was there, whispering, "You see him?"

I nodded and pointed with my gun, also whispering. "I think he's behind that car."

I wasn't even sure where the exit was, or if he could get to it from what I thought was his current position. Knowing backup would have to figure out how to get in here, we had to move. Hastings and I spread out, trying to keep either a car or one of the thick beams that held up the concrete roof between us and the perp as we approached, guns out at the ready.

I was coming in from the perp's left and Hastings from his right. But it got too tight for Paul with the parked cars so he had to drift more toward me as I started to angle to my right, seeing more and more of the far side of the front bumper the perp was hiding behind. That's when the sirens began blaring in the not-so-far distance, our backup racing here.

Paul and I continued to pan in a semicircle so we would see the perp before he had a good shot at us. A few more steps to my right and I would see him, if he was still there.

Whether it was the sirens or our impending approach that spooked him, we'll never know. As we continued to move, Davis popped up over the hood of the SUV and began firing.

The sound and muzzle flashes were both blinding and deafening. The shots went wild, striking the roof and metal girders. Paul and I returned fire, even though I could barely see him between the muzzle flashes and his cover behind the car. I squinted and squeezed off two more rounds, thinking I was going to hit him in the head. But I missed, both times—I knew as soon as he ducked back behind the hood.

Paul and I were in the open—we'd both drifted from the cover of the parked cars and steel beams into the main walkway. We couldn't retreat—he could cut us down if he popped back up.

ANOTHER BODY IN BROOKLYN

We kept firing, trying to keep him pinned down behind the car. The vehicle's windows shattered and the doors and hood were pockmarked with holes as we both reloaded and kept shooting.

I finally cleared the bumper where I had a good shot at his left side when he popped up and began firing again. Paul yelled and his gun clattered to the pavement as he fell. I pumped three rounds into Davis' head and neck, then went to slide-lock. I quickly reloaded my last magazine.

Davis fell on his side, blood everywhere, his gun landing on the pavement a few feet away. His eyes rolled back in his head, and I figured he was already on his way to dead. So I ran back around the front of the car to Paul. He was holding his right arm just below the shoulder, his gun having fallen somewhere in the darkness. "I'm okay!" he yelled. "You got 'im?"

I told him I did, then broadcast that we had an officer shot. I took some rubber gloves out of my back pocket and stuffed them into the wound on Paul's arm, which was bleeding badly, pressing down as hard as I could, pressing till he screamed.

In less than a minute, cops started showing up on the other side of the garage, flashlights arcing toward us.

The first guys to get to us started screaming questions, but I waved them off and pointed to the other side of the car. "The perp's behind the car! Be careful—he's still gotta be cuffed!"

A few of them ran around the car. "He's dead!" I heard one of them shout. Before I could yell back that only EMS can pronounce someone dead, I heard the distinct sound of metallic cuffs clinking, probably done hard and quick by cops with adrenaline coursing through them. Must've been, for me to hear with my ears messed up from all the gunshots.

Eventually the cops ushered me away, a couple of them taking my place alongside Paul. One of them had ripped his shirt and was using that as a makeshift dressing for Paul's arm. EMS got there soon after and put Paul on a gurney. I'd seen my fair share of gunshots and didn't think it was that bad. Paul agreed, apparently, giving me a thumbs-up and a grin as he was wheeled out of there. "Good shooting, Sarge!"

More and more people of all ranks began showing up: detectives, captains, chiefs. Frank Cassella, who'd run out from the desk, only his off-duty gun in a holster, and Reggie Braggs, whose squad I'd taken over since he was now the Anti-Crime sergeant, ushered me through the gate we'd climbed, hanging open now since the lock was cut. A captain, wearing his hat like all the brass and none of the street cops did, approached us, but Reggie held up his hand. "Sergeant Rothchild can't hear anything, Cap. Ears are shot. We're gonna bring him to the hospital." The Captain nodded and said something back, but I couldn't hear what it was because he wasn't shouting.

I handed my gun to Reggie, who handed it over to the captain. Then he and Frank accompanied me to Wyckoff Hospital in one of our marked cars. As we pulled up to the front ER entrance, I experienced a weird sense of déjà vu. Then I remembered: Last time I'd been here, a little over two months prior, I'd just had one of the worst days of my life after one of the worst nights. This year just kept getting better and better.

***

Frank walked me into the hospital while Reggie looked for an out-of-the-way place to park, not wanting to take up a spot that another police car or ambulance might need. Even with the ringing in my ears, Frank's loud Italian voice sounded like a megaphone. Everything was big with Frank—his size, his voice, his personality. Even with my mind preoccupied, I couldn't help noticing that he managed to snag a nurse's number during our ordeal. At least someone had a social life.

I was sitting on a bed in the ER when my brother Jay burst through the curtain. Before I could say anything, he ran up and hugged me tight, then planted a big kiss on my cheek. Frank walked out to give us some privacy.

I wiped my cheek. "I'm flattered, Jay, truly. You're a handsome guy. But you're a married man. Plus, you're my biological brother. I just don't think it would work out."

I expected him to tell me to go fuck myself, but he didn't say anything. Just stood there, tears in his eyes. I hadn't seen him cry since we were kids.

"I'm really proud of you, bro. And I can't wait till you get the fuck off this job."

I nodded, feeling the same way. But I guess Jay felt it more. He was my big brother, after all.

"Mom and Dad are coming," he mumbled, wiping his cheek.

"At least I'm already in the hospital," I mused. "Because the two of them in the same room—they're gonna give me a heart attack."

* * * * *

The next day I spoke with the shooting team, then walked the incident scene with them. Davis' body was gone, but it was daylight and I could see the blood staining the floor of the garage where he fell. There was also a smaller, dried pool of blood where Paul had fallen, and random spatters here and there. I wanted to go see Paul—he'd gone to Kings County and was scheduled to be released later that day, the bullet having been removed cleanly.

Seeing all the blood on the ground was jarring, reminding me of what had just happened to us, to Davis. It wasn't a pleasant experience.

211

Usually, in shootings on the street or in parks and such, the firefighters will be called after the body has been removed and all the evidence has been processed. They'll hose down the street to get the blood out. I guess they couldn't fit a truck in the lot, or maybe nobody had called them yet. The crime scene tape was still up on both entrances, at any rate, and cops were stationed by both. Even the shot-up Honda CRV had been removed, probably for further processing at the lab. I guessed the detectives were just waiting on me to conduct the walk-through, Paul Hastings obviously not being up to it now.

There wasn't much to it—it was a good shooting, and no one seemed to be disputing that. Davis was a major perp, and he'd made a very bad decision to shoot a cop. Sure, his mother was all over the news talking about what a good boy and father he had been. And his friends insisted his criminal past was behind him. Now an aspiring rapper, Davis was apparently swiped from this earth just before he made it big.

"You shot the next Jay-Z," one of the detectives said sarcastically before shaking my hand. "You'll be fine, Sarge. Not gonna get your gun back for a while, though. It has to be processed."

I was going to be weaponless now since I didn't own a backup gun. I'd always carried my service Glock off-duty, never seeing the need for a second weapon until now. I'd adjusted to the regular-sized Glock, wearing hoodies most of the year to conceal the weapon when I carried it. On hot summer days I left it at home or in my locker.

For the first time, though, I felt naked walking around without the gun.

CHAPTER 24

ROLL CALL:
THE MORNING AFTER

The mood in the precinct was somber. Roll call was conducted by Sergeant Johnson in front of the desk instead of in the muster room. Courtney looked around; only nine cops total for the day tour.

At least Hastings was gonna be okay. Courtney had worked with Paul when he was on the 4-to-12 shift. A stand-up guy if there ever was one. And Sergeant Rothchild? What a fucking stud. Killed a perp with cover and a good gun with three well-placed shots. Courtney knew Rothchild was an experienced street cop who'd also served in the Army, and figured all that had probably helped in this situation. Courtney, who'd seen his fair share of combat overseas, knew that a lot of times in these shootings, some guys couldn't hit a wall five feet away no matter how well they shot at the range.

They had four sector cars working, but one would be tied up with a prisoner transport. Sergeant Johnson had finished up the assignments and was now speaking about Paul and Rothchild's shooting. Courtney looked over at Eric, who'd gotten there late and stood in the back next to Shayna, both looking somber. Eric shrugged with a "What can you do?" Both of them knew it was gonna be a long day.

CHAPTER 25

ROTHCHILD: RESTLESS NIGHTS

I hadn't slept in a day and a half. It was 11 p.m. and I was tossing and turning, my sheets soaked with sweat. Spring had just hit, but my building hadn't turned the heat off yet because it was still cold. I thought about turning down the knobs on the old radiators, but I was too lazy. Instead, I opened a window, looking down on Union Turnpike and the cars rushing by. The cool air helped, but I wasn't going to be sleeping anytime soon. Despite the late hour, I called Lisa.

She answered on the first ring. "Josh, how are you?" She'd texted me in the morning, then tried calling later. But I'd been so busy with the shooting team and everything that I hadn't responded, having to speak with concerned friends as well as field at least half a dozen calls from Jay and my parents.

"I'm good. A little jittery, but okay."

"Okay, good. My uncle heard it was you. He said you were all right and the other cop was going to be okay too, but I was worried. I'm glad you called."

"Yeah, sorry it wasn't sooner. How did everything go?"

"The funeral was—you know, it was okay. Given the circumstances and everything, knowing it wasn't a natural thing…." She started to choke up. "That's still hard, you know? I hope the asshole that hurt him…. The DA hasn't been returning my calls."

"It's gonna take a little bit. He was collared by the detectives for felony assault, but since he made bail they haven't done a grand jury yet. Now we have to wait till the autopsy results come back. If the medical examiner determines he died from the beating, then it will be re-classified as a homicide. I'm not sure if they'll charge murder or manslaughter or..."

I could hear she was crying. "It's gonna be okay, Lisa. I know how mad you are—I am too. That guy's a piece of shit. We just have to hope he pays for what he did."

Her voice was a little shaky, but it seemed she had stopped crying. "I don't want to think about him now. I'm sorry I'm so all over the place—I called to see how you were doing, not vice versa."

I took a deep breath. "I'm good, Lisa. You want to get coffee tomorrow?"

"That would be nice. Call me in the morning."

I called her around 7:00. She said she didn't need to be at work till 9:00, so we could meet up before. I offered to pick her up and drive her to work, but she said she'd rather just meet. I suggested a diner that wasn't too far from either of us, on Atlantic Avenue in East New York.

She was already there when I arrived, seated at a two-person booth. She was dressed for work, wearing a gray blouse and a conservative dress, hair pulled back in a ponytail. Her smooth, round face looked well rested despite what she was going through. I sat opposite her. "Wow, you look really pretty," were the words that came out of my mouth. It was true.

She smiled. " How are you doing?"

"I'm good," I said as off-handedly as I could, picking up a menu. "You eaten here before?"

She smiled. "Yes. And breakfast is on me. I'm really thankful for everything you've done."

I smiled back. "That's okay—I'll get it."

She shifted in her seat, uncomfortable. "It's just…I think you're a great guy. Good-looking, nice… But I've been seeing someone. When we met—I know it was a bad situation, obviously, but I…I didn't think it was going anywhere with him. But he's been really great through all of this, sat with my father and my sister when I couldn't be there."

She must have seen my face drop. "I just don't want to… I appreciate your friendship."

I was too tired to put on airs. And she saw it.

"Josh, I'm sorry. My uncle loves you, wants me to dump Michael and go with you. He's probably right. But I have to give it a chance." Her eyes got serious then, so I knew there wasn't any misunderstanding. "I hope you understand."

I did understand. And while it wasn't fair to her, having met me in these shitty circumstances that I'd at least in part created, I was still not happy about it.

We both ordered coffee and tried to make small talk until we could get out of there. I know she honestly liked me and wanted to remain friends. But at this point in my life, I couldn't deal with that kind of hassle. Even if she hadn't seen it as anything more than "friends with benefits," at least Melanie slept with me occasionally. A proper friendship with a woman I'd developed feelings for wasn't really in the cards right now.

CHAPTER 26

ROTHCHILD: MORE BAD NEWS

I awakened early the next morning. This wasn't exactly unwelcome—I'd been in the middle of a dream where I was being shot at by a shadowy perpetrator—he didn't look like Davis, but he didn't *not* look like Davis. As soon as the shots started, I shakily unholstered my gun and tried to return fire. But nothing happened. NYPD guns don't have safeties—the Glock and other guns we're authorized have heavy trigger pulls to hopefully avoid accidental discharges. But the guns I'd trained with in the Army did have them. So I tried to thumb the safety off before realizing that the gun didn't have one. The muzzle flashes were blinding, the noise was deafening—I don't know how it ended because my phone started buzzing and I shot up in my bed. Turns out it was the fourth call I'd received in the last few minutes.

"You see the paper?" It was Frank Cassella, my fellow sergeant and union rep. Before I could say anything else he hissed, "That fucking bitch."

Obviously, I didn't have a paper on my doorstep to thumb through. So while Frank broke it down for me, I went online and found the article, billed as an exclusive in a mid-sized, mostly anti-cop newspaper. Headline: "ONE OF COPS INVOLVED IN DEADLY BED-STUY SHOOTING UNDER INVESTIGATION FOR DEPRIVATION OF RIGHTS."

As Frank, who'd set me off in the first place by waking me up and not preparing me for what I was about to see, now tried to calm me down, I skimmed the article. It was full of lies and omissions, as many single-source articles are. It was obvious it was my commanding officer who had been the source, though.

Even on my quick first read it was clear that there were no allegations regarding the legality of the shooting, other than trying to malign my character to the point that it might be looked at more closely. The article centered around the powerful Hassidic man whom Courtney Jones and I had collared the year prior. The author of the article was quick to point out that he had beaten the drug charges—though this wasn't exactly true. Due to the large amount of drugs in his possession, we had charged him with Possession for Sales. However, before we even did a grand jury, the ADA dropped the charges down to personal use, a misdemeanor. I think he might have completed a drug program or something, because then the drug charges were dropped to a violation, and the judge issued an ACD—basically suppressing the charges if he managed not to get in trouble for a while. Same with the operating with a suspended license charge. What the article didn't mention, though, is that even though this guy had a good lawyer and all the connections, he still got found guilty of two charges, however minor they now appeared after the legalese got sorted out. And our CCRB was unsubstantiated, meaning they didn't find that we'd done anything wrong, but couldn't say for sure that we hadn't—this is a typical finding of the CCRB. The article didn't even mention the young prostitute who was in the car with him. Those child endangerment charges were likewise dropped, anyway.

"It's a hatchet job," Frank said as I reread the article, muttering under my breath the whole time. I think Frank had read too many '50s detective novels. "She did it so the department shuts up about a textbook good shooting and two hero cops and moves onto something else. Doesn't want you to get the good press and kudos from the brass."

For some reason, maybe my naivete—whatever—it hadn't dawned on me till just this second that the commanding officer of my precinct actually hated me. Not disliked, was overly critical of—actually *hated* me. The unease and nervousness in the pit of my stomach that had been there most of the year returned with a vengeance. And it wouldn't leave for months.

CHAPTER 27

ROTHCHILD: PICKING UP THE PIECES

Paul Hastings and I hadn't been allowed to speak to each other until we'd both given our official statements on the shooting. Paul was going to be out "line of duty" a while for his arm—luckily, the bullet was removed intact and didn't cause any major damage. But the wound still required stitches and clean dressings. I was going to be assigned to the Patrol Borough with all the higher-ups and their suck-up underlings for a week, after which time I'd be able to return to patrol. It was the first officer-involved shooting either of us had been involved in, so even though the perp was dead, it wasn't being held against us. At twenty-six, he was already a career criminal who'd just come home from a three-year stint for a robbery/shooting and seemed to always have a gun on him.

I ran into his parole officer after I gave my official statement to the shooting team. They were going to interview him too.

I walked out of the room with my sergeant union rep and an attorney, both telling me I'd done well. The parole officer saw us coming out of the room and nodded to me. "No loss. That one was gonna be a lifer. If he didn't shoot a cop, he would've shot one of his girlfriends or some young brother who pissed him off."

I nodded, while the sergeant rep and the attorney acted like they didn't hear. In my experience, most parole officers weren't that negative on their clients, so that told me something about the guy's character. Not that I'd had much doubt to begin with, after all the shots he'd fired at me and Paul.

But while the shooting wasn't being held against us, the article the CO leaked to that paper served to make the NYPD public relations people move on quickly from it. So instead of us being given some nice nods or shout-outs in the papers, the cop beat folks in the press were encouraged to move on to other things. The good news was that no one else picked up on the negative story she'd mostly fabricated.

Due to the stress of the shooting and finding out about the article, I hadn't even thought about the fact that Eric and Shayna could've wound up getting in a shoot-out with Davis the week before. They would've been less prepared than Paul and I were—we kind of knew what we were potentially getting into when we went to stop him, whereas they just rolled up on a group fight. There hadn't even been a gun mentioned in the 911 call. So they would've been caught completely flat-footed if he'd started shooting. Also, the fact that he'd pulled a gun out during a high school fight gave some insight into just how crazy he was.

Of course, there was his mother and one of his baby mamas, both insisting he'd been getting his act together and was now an "aspiring rapper," a vocation many of the career criminals who are killed in shootings seem to have.

The press didn't bite on that line of thought, other than mentioning it briefly in their articles. But his criminal history, which dated back to when he was twelve and included two prior documented shootings, was bad enough that shooting a cop that was just trying to arrest him seemed pretty unreasonable, even to the more liberal press types. So even though we didn't get many kudos, there wasn't much negative pushback.

Paul and I met up for lunch in a diner about two weeks after the shooting. It was the same place I'd had what might be my last conversation with Lisa. That was okay, though—the food was good, and it was convenient for both of us.

I was going back to work in two days after my weeklong stint in the Borough headquarters, where I'd been dodging chiefs and inspectors and ignoring all the cowardly cops and sergeants who roamed the halls.

I walked in and saw Paul seated with his back against a wall, facing the front door. He waved to me and I came over and sat down, my back to the door. Despite the bit of unease this caused me, I had to admit that Paul looked good. He was wearing a sweater, since it was morning and still cool outside, but I could see the shape of the bandages and dressings bulging out the right shoulder area.

"Wow," I said after we shook hands. "Not even in a sling."

He laughed. "The PBA trustee tried to convince me to wear one—said I'd be out for longer. But I've got too many kids to be playing it up like that. A month or two tax-free family time is plenty—trust me."

"I don't know how you do it," I marveled, briefly remembering the conversation I'd had here with Lisa not too long before. At least Paul wasn't going to break my heart. Hopefully not, anyway.

"Do what?" he asked as he grabbed a menu.

"Work 4-to-12 with three kids and a wife. You ever sleep?"

He laughed. "Not since before Obama got elected." He meant the first time. "Nah, it's not that bad. I get up and drive 'em to school in the morning, then go to the gym if the wife hasn't laid out a big to-do list before I go into work. Being home, though, that's a whole different animal. She's been cutting me a lot of slack, but I think her sympathy for my arm's starting to wear out."

"Nothing lasts forever," I mused.

He put down his menu, apparently having decided what he wanted while we were talking. "I shoulda gone with the sling."

I laughed. "You can always get one."

He shook his head and smiled wryly. I kind of got where he was coming from.

The waitress came by, and we both ordered. But once the food arrived, neither of us was particularly hungry. Paul noticed me half-picking at my fries.

"I haven't been eating much." He said it like it was a confession. "You?"

"I don't know, I guess not. Lotta shit going on."

He looked at me sincerely. "We both shot a lot of rounds downrange. I got hit—" He indicated his right arm. "—and you had to kill a guy. It takes something out of you, I think."

He wasn't trying to make me feel bad—just the opposite. I think, since I'd been the one who'd killed the guy, I thought the whole thing kind of fell on me. What's worse, I didn't feel the least bit bad. Not good either—just a kind of numbness.

I shrugged. "I don't know, Paul. The guy was gonna kill us—he almost did."

"I know—we did the right thing. And I'm glad it was you that was there with me. I just….he was so young. Twenty-six. I had a cousin get killed who was only a few years younger. Ronnie Parker." He paused. "You know, we grew up in Brownsville, he got involved with the gangs …it still hurt, though. He lived in the PJs with his mother, my aunt." He laughed kind of sadly. "I still remember playing hide and go seek and running through the roofs of the buildings. Amazing we didn't get killed.... I was wilder than he was back then, stupid kid, but I had a better support structure. Plus, we lived in a house on a decent block. When I was eleven or twelve my father told me to stop going over there. I'd still see Ronnie at family events, but less and less. When you're with someone all the time and then suddenly you aren't, you see the changes in them. He wasn't always what he grew into. I just had better role models, more involved parents."

If Paul's intention was to make me feel like eating my gun, he was doing a wonderful job. He must've seen something in my face.

"I don't mean...look, Davis was a piece of shit. If he hadn't shot at us, it would've been someone else, maybe someone who wasn't even in the life. He was bad news, all the way. I just...I don't know. Fourteen years of this shit, you start to wonder what it's all for. I mean, most of the folks we see shot, murdered—no one gives a shit about them. Not the press, not the community, not the department—except for being pissed they're taking another statistic. But they all had someone who loved them." He wiped a tear from his eye. "My aunt never got over Ronnie. The grief fuckin' killed her. My cousin Tara...she had a hard time too. She's got a family now, kids...but she's never been the same. It hurts everyone, I think, even worse because there's no sympathy for guys like Ronnie. Folks just figure it was bound to happen sooner or later."

I thought about Lawrence Washington, lying dead in that hallway on New Year's. The only reason his death had even been a story was because he'd been the city's first homicide victim of the year. Only the friend he'd been visiting and a very small family to mourn his passing. All I'd cared about at the time was managing the scene and the fallout from the photographer sneaking in. Did Paul and his family see the indifference on the faces of the cops when his cousin was killed? Did they hear the cops making stupid jokes and laughing on what was the worst day of their lives? I suddenly felt very ashamed.

CHAPTER 28

ROTHCHILD: TRYING TO CHANGE

I was in the middle of my first week back at the precinct. The Borough hadn't been that bad—I'd mostly been left alone. Unfortunately, Paul Hastings' plan to come back to work in a month didn't pan out for him. The PBA got involved, convincing him to stay out for longer. We spoke on the phone just after I was cleared for full duty. "They said I should milk it at least another few months," he said to me on the phone. "All these high-ranking trustees, even the PBA president. I told him three weeks, tops. But they kept pushing."

"I guess they were really concerned about you," I responded.

He could hear the sarcasm in my voice and laughed. "They want to play the injury up as much as they can, gets them attention and gives 'em something to complain about. I know the deal. Figured I'd give in so they stopped calling me. Those union guys haven't seen the streets in years, if ever. I don't like talking to 'em." That I understood.

"Well, Paul, next year when you file your taxes you can thank them." He laughed—line-of-duty injuries were tax-free days off. But you couldn't work overtime, which I know Paul did a lot of.

"Yeah, tax-free with no OT," he lamented as if he'd read my mind.

So, I was driving solo. The 4-by-12 shift had more cops than the day shift, but not nearly enough. Once you factored in all the other stuff—

225

prisoner transports, hospitalized prisoners, permanent and temporary fixed posts, crime scenes, new arrests, priority calls that tied a sector up for an extended period of time, sick days, etc.—we were running at just as low manpower as on my previous shift.

The dispatcher's voice came over the radio. "10-10, shots fired."

She read out the address, then the cross streets. I keyed my mic as I made a U-turn. "One Sergeant, how many calls on this?"

She replied, "One call. Landline—comes back to an apartment in the building." Back then, some people still had landlines.

Since the call had originated in the building, there was a higher chance it was legit than a reported street shooting, where it was just one anonymous caller on a cell or pay phone. I switched on my lights and sirens and sped over there. A couple of seconds later, the dispatcher announced that there were two more callers regarding it. "Multiple shots fired inside the apartment." This was almost one hundred percent likely to be legit.

I was passing cars, then weaving back into my lane quickly since nobody yielded to cops in New York, slowing down and clearing intersections before passing through, the red lights bouncing off the street, cars, and buildings—I realized how much I'd missed working at night. Not so much in the winter, but even now, in the early spring, and especially in the summer, there was always a crackle of excitement in the air once the sun went down. Strobe lights and sirens seemed more serious than they did in the daytime. The element of surprise and danger was lurking around every shadowy corner until the headlights or searchlights cleared it. And the later it was, the fewer working folks and kids. There were just more folks up to no good at night.

One of our patrol cars was already in front of the building when I arrived, and another one came up right behind me. I got out of my car and raced to the well-lit lobby, which I could see through the glass door. The cops who arrived first had placed a pen between the door and the jamb to keep it open. Since it was only a minute at most before I arrived, the pen was still there.

The pair of cops who parked behind me—McCall (no relation to the day-shift guy) and Stevens—followed me inside. I handed the pen to Stevens, and he let the door close on it at eye level. McCall might have been too pissed off to do that, especially if it was me requesting it. He was a grumpy young white guy from out in eastern Suffolk County, big and tough but also lacking in any kind of empathy or awareness of how his poor attitude rubbed the residents of this almost one-hundred-percent black precinct the wrong way. The kind of guy who thought anyone who voted for Obama was a leftist communist. Stevens was a little better, though, quiet and not as jaded.

As we walked through the lobby, the cops upstairs indicated, over the radio, that they had two males shot inside the apartment. The officer broadcasting this information was shouting, so I figured it was a shitshow.

Since it was on the third floor and we had no idea how well the elevator would work, we found the first staircase and sprinted up the stairs. The cops hadn't put out any suspect description, probably not having one yet. The dispatcher didn't have one either. So, if we had run into anyone coming down the stairs, it might have been awkward.

I opened the third-floor stairway door, glancing left and right as I walked through. I saw an apartment door propped open further down the hallway, the light from inside spilling out. We ran toward it.

The yelling coming from inside grew louder as we got closer, but we could tell it was either one of the victims or another resident, so we didn't draw our guns. It seemed that the perps were already gone.

Stevens got in first, moving to the right so I could follow him in. Officer James was standing over a young man who was sitting in a chair against the wall in the dining room. The guy was screaming, on and off, a little over the top. He was holding his left arm; there was a dark stain around the area, his light blue shirt not hiding the blood. But the amount of blood, coupled with his posture, told me that his injury was very far from life-threatening. Just being a bitch, like a lot of the perps who try to make everyone believe they're so tough just because they're in the life.

"What do we have, James?"

He turned to me, pointing down the hallway to a bedroom. He had to speak over the seated victim's periodic screams. "We got a male shot in that room, looks DOA. Richardson's with him—we already cleared the place. No one else here besides her," he said, pointing to the kitchen. An older woman I hadn't noticed was crumpled in the corner, crying. "No description yet on the shooters."

He said "shooters" and I agreed. I saw at least seven shell casings scattered around the floor of the area we were in—the guy in the chair should have been counting his lucky stars he was not dead like the guy in the back room. Who knows how many shots were fired back there, but whatever this was, there was clearly some questioning going on, judging by the holes in the wall over and to the side of where the living victim was seated. Like they'd been asking questions and he'd kept getting the answers wrong.

The victim sitting in the chair was still screaming pitifully. "I'm gonna die…ahhh!"

"You're not going to die," I assured him as I reached into my back pocket and found two latex gloves. I put them on as I spoke. "Who's the guy in the back room?"

"I don't—that's my cousin. They killt him, yo! Now I'm gonna die too…"

"We have EMS coming. They're gonna take you to the hospital and the doctors will patch you up."

He perked up a little. "They gonna give me somethin' for the pain? It hurts *so bad…*"

I nodded. "Sorry about your cousin."

"I just wanna get some meds and get fixed up. I'll be good…" He said this like he was trying to convince himself. Then his eyes darted to a cell phone on the floor beneath his chair. He started to reach for it.

Before he could get it, I reached down and picked the phone up with my gloved hand. His eyes shot to mine, alarmed.

"That's my phone, yo! I need it!"

Given this guy wasn't the bravest of souls, or the most caring, considering he didn't seem to give a shit about his cousin being shot and whatever was going on with that older woman in the corner, I figured he was going to call someone and tell them what had just happened. Someone with whom he was involved criminally. The phone was evidence, and he wasn't going to get it back, at least not until the detectives had gone through it.

Once I took the phone, any cooperation I was going to get from this asshole was minimal. I told "White McCall" to keep an eye on him. "See if you can get an ID," I said as I made my way down the hallway toward the back bedroom where Officer Richardson, James' partner, was standing. As soon as I walked in the door, I saw the body on my right, between the foot of the bed and the wall. A young guy, shot a couple of times in the torso. A shot to his neck is what sealed the deal, though, the blood having come out hard and fast. He probably died in a couple of seconds after that. There was a wooden baseball bat lying on the floor a few feet away from him.

Richardson looked over at me. "He probably came at them with the bat."

That seemed like a pretty good assessment. I saw a clear spot on the dresser and gently placed the cell phone down there. I told Richardson, "I'm putting this here. It's the other vic's phone. He was trying to call someone. Don't let anyone touch it." He nodded.

I made my way back to the living room as more sirens approached. Officer James had left Stevens and White McCall, who were trying to get info from the victim seated in the chair, and he was now standing over the woman, trying to get something out of her. Chances are, the young man in the chair was never going to give us anything, so the woman was the best bet at this point. But she was still shaking and crying. She looked to be in her early fifties and was thin but strong, judging by her sinewy arms. But her back was bent and she looked broken.

I remembered what Paul had said to me in the diner, about how, even if a shooting victim was in the life, the family was still shattered. Right here, this poor woman, crying and shaking, was *shattered*. And I felt something I hadn't felt at one of these kinds of shootings, where it looked like the people were targeted for illicit drugs or money: real compassion.

I knelt down beside her and gently put my hand on her shoulder. She didn't flinch or move away, but she didn't look at me either. I said, as softly as I could, with all the sirens and now the noise of cops running down the hallway and radios crackling, "I'm so sorry, ma'am. Can you tell us what happened? We really want to help."

She looked up at me. Her eyes were wet and unfocused. I figured she probably knew the young man in the back bedroom was dead.

"We want to catch whoever did this," I assured her softly.

James, taking my lead, knelt down too. "Miss, we're just here to help."

She stuttered. "H-Michael's dead."

James and I exchanged a look; better not to tell her that EMS was coming and would work on him. She already knew. Plus, it wouldn't be right.

"I'm sorry," I said, meaning it. "Can you tell us—?"

The look she threw at the young guy sitting in the chair was pure poison. Still, family was family. "I don't..." She looked like she was considering. But if these were the only two young family members in her life, and she'd just lost one of them, she couldn't be blamed for not wanting to lose another. "I don't know why. But there was three of them—black, around the same ages as my son and nephew."

"So early twenties?" I asked. I didn't want to ask her if the body in the other room was her son or nephew. I'd try to get her to it.

"Yes, but they were wearing ski masks, knit ones like you wear in the winter if it's really cold. I couldn't see enough of their faces to identify them."

I believed this. "What were their builds? Is there anything that would distinguish them?"

Two fire department guys walked in, carrying their gear, followed by a few EMS workers. It was rare that they arrived at the same time. Since EMS was better at the EMS stuff than the firefighters, they took the lead.

I scooted on the floor so I was in between the woman and the folks who were going to confirm what she already knew. I could tell she was intelligent and knew what was up, because she didn't seem that concerned about the victim in the chair. Which meant she knew he was gonna be okay. I figured he must be the nephew.

Her eyes locked on mine, and she came back to the conversation. "Th-one of them was tall, like a basketball player. Six...five at least. The other two were medium height or even a little short. It was hard to tell..."

"No, that's fine. The tall one, was he thin, medium build?"

"Thin," she said. Like in good shape. The other two…average, I guess. All of them were wearing dark clothes. I think they all had hoodies."

"Thank you," I said. Normally I would have gotten up, stepped away, and transmitted this information over the radio immediately. Chances are the hoodies were gone, but if they had fled on foot or on bikes and were dumb enough to stay together, then the description could possibly lead to a stop.

But I wanted her to know that I really did feel for her. I motioned to the young man sitting in the chair. EMS was already working on him. "Your—he's going to be all right. I've seen much worse."

She smiled sadly. "That's my son. He's…he means well. Michael, though, was such a *good* young man…"

She leaned in and I hugged her, feeling her thin chest on mine. I nodded to James, and he stepped away to broadcast the description we'd gotten over the radio.

The sad thing was, I could tell by the way that she'd accepted things so quickly that she had been through horrible things before. This was a woman who had lost dearly. Yet she was still trying to help.

She grabbed my jacket, trying to bring me close. I let her. She whispered in my ear, "Michael had nothing to do with this. My son…. Those boys came here to rob him. Michael was just trying to protect us."

I had to ask. "What were they after?"

A horrible sound escaped her, something I could only describe as a tragic laugh. "Weed, money. That's it. Weed and money."

* * * * * *

The detectives got there a few minutes later, both the precinct squad and homicide. While they were interviewing the mother/aunt, I retrieved the cell phone from the bedroom and gave it to our detective squad sergeant. "The guy who got shot in the chair was very eager to call someone on this phone," I told him softly. He nodded and took the phone.

I wound up leaving Stevens and "White McCall" inside the apartment, as the whole place was a crime scene. The mother/aunt was transported back to the precinct so she could be properly interviewed, and the Crime Scene Unit was already en route to process the scene.

I was standing outside the building, talking with James and Richardson. They were getting ready to go back on patrol, as we were holding a bunch of jobs. I had another cop, I don't remember his name, some cowardly house mouse we'd made suit up, watching the front door of the building.

Two women—one middle-aged, the other in her early thirties— approached. Richardson and James were already walking to their car, which had been re-parked half a block away so the ambulances and fire trucks could get through. I approached the women before the house mouse guarding the door had to.

"How are you ladies doing tonight?"

"Not good," the older one said. "We're cousins of Michael. The dead guy?"

Shit. "I'm sorry." I didn't ask how they'd already heard.

"How's Tyrone doing?" It was the younger one.

"He's at the hospital. He'll be fine."

She exhaled. "I'm glad, but he's gotta make this right. Michael was a good guy. He worked at the airport, never got in trouble. He never even went out. We were always trying to get him to be more social. But he was a really nice young man. Hardworking, loyal."

I already knew Michael had almost no record. Basically, a Boy Scout. And they knew that Tyrone's illegal business was the reason behind this whole mess. So we were all on the same page.

"I'm sorry, but you can't go in there now. The crime scene has to be processed. Is there anything we can do, though?"

Both of them seemed kind of taken aback at my overture. A couple of seconds of silence ensued.

"No," the younger one said. "We figured…how's Mabel?"

"She's fine—she's at the station, talking to the detectives. Tyrone is going to be fine, so she's just trying to help them figure this out."

The younger one scoffed. "Ain't nothing to figure out. Tyrone is slinging weed all around the neighborhood, and people know he's got lots of dough and product that he keeps in his mother's apartment. This shit is all on him."

The older one gave her a stern look.

But the younger woman was not to be deterred. "It's fuckin' true! Michael was a *good* kid. He didn't deserve this shit."

I'd already made notifications to the Patrol Borough, and the chief of patrol's office, speaking with the same cops and detectives who had been there since I'd been promoted and would still be there until they retired, answering phones and relaying information, hobnobbing with chiefs and inspectors their whole careers.

The CO had called me, of course, even though I'd already notified the executive officer, a guy named Captain Owens. The old one I'd worked for as a cop was gone; she hadn't liked him, nor he her, so he'd been willingly transferred. She hadn't been happy about taking another homicide. Not once did she mention it was a shame that this kid, with no criminal record and a job, had gotten caught up in his cousin's bullshit. She was no more upset than if he'd been a forty-five-year-old career criminal. He was just a negative statistic that she'd have to explain at the next COMPSTAT meeting.

Both women were crying softly. I found myself telling them again how sorry I was. The night air was getting cooler, especially after being in that hot apartment. And while I felt it, the sorrow, I also wondered if it was just because of what Paul had said about losing his cousin to gun violence. If so, I was just as bad as the CO and all the others. And, speaking of forty-five-year-old homicide victims, had I even given a second thought to the poor schlub, who had aged out of violent crime and how he'd died alone in a hallway outside his friends' house on New Year's? All I'd been worried about since was my health, which still appeared to be just fine, my pending career change and how events at work affected it, Melanie, and other women—all about me.

One of the detectives from Brooklyn North Homicide was conferring with our precinct guys just outside the front door to the building. They were talking low, as they were used to discretion, so the women couldn't hear what they were saying. Still, I gently walked them away, not wanting them to be wondering.

* * * * *

Either our detective squad guys or the homicide guys wound up locating a potential witness, an older lady who lived on the first floor and had seen the males walk into the building behind her after she unlocked the door, meaning they had probably been waiting. Since the scene was still fresh, the two detectives on scene couldn't leave yet. Two of our precinct detective squad guys were interviewing Mabel at the precinct. The only other two working were interviewing the surviving victim, Tyrone, at Woodhull Hospital. So I had to come up with somebody to drive the witness to the precinct so she could be properly interviewed in a private setting where no one would see her speaking with the po-po.

It's always better to use an unmarked car to drive the person, and even then, you don't want the car to pull up in front of their building. Luckily, we had the Anti-Crime guys working; they pulled up in a civilian-looking vehicle two blocks up and around the corner, and she walked over to them, getting in the back seat without anyone the wiser.

Since the radio had calmed down, I hung around the scene for a while. Because no one was allowed into the building, I had the two women I'd spoken to and a few other family friends and relatives who'd come by when they heard what had happened standing a little farther down the block, where they could still see the entrance and the police personnel coming and going.

I stayed nearby, answering what questions I could and generally trying to be a sympathetic ear. Through their conversations, I learned that Michael had been basically orphaned in his early teens, at which point his Aunt Mabel had taken him in to live with her and her son Tyrone.

Michael was a good kid, shy and hardworking. He was currently holding down a full-time job at the airport and also cut hair on the side. He'd always been close to Tyrone, but he'd stayed away from his cousins' hustling and drug dealing.

Everyone was mad—Tyrone's poor decisions had led to Michael's death. An older male relative shook his head. "Ty's gonna have to live with this for the rest of his life."

A couple of the others agreed. It didn't seem to me that Tyrone was as racked with guilt as they thought he should be, judging by how he hadn't given a shit about Michael or his mother, just about his bullshit gunshot wound and his cell phone. I kept my mouth shut.

After a while, I got a cop to babysit the family. They were all really nice, and I felt super bad for them. But it was better for them to hang around, just in case the detectives wanted to talk to them, see if anyone knew anything.

I walked past a couple of the crime scene techs as they exited their van and walked toward the building. The sergeant nodded to me as they passed. I whistled; a sergeant had come out with the two cops—they must have been taking this one seriously. I think they were all detectives, actually. Unlike in the TV shows, they just process crime scenes; they don't do any other police work. No investigations, no arrests—just process crime scenes and testify. A job that's done by civilians in many departments.

I got back to my car with a bad taste in my mouth. Just seeing the smug look of that sergeant who hadn't done any police work his whole career and now coasted like he was Columbo—those kinds of things were pissing me off more and more.

I drove away, passing the crime scene van, the detectives' cars, and my own guys' marked vehicles. But as I passed the seven or eight relatives of the victim, Michael, I remembered what I'd just finally realized. That life is precious, and it's too much of a drain to worry about things you can't change. To stay sane and give yourself a shot at happiness, you have to concentrate on what you can.

The rest of the night passed in a blur of headlights and shadows and faces, people screaming at me, my cops, and each other. Those things I couldn't change. But maybe I could make a difference in a way I hadn't considered.

The next morning, after fifteen minutes of twisting and turning, I came to the conclusion that the four hours of sleep I'd had were enough. I rolled out of bed at 5:45, got dressed, and hit the gym. Then I showered and headed to the precinct.

CHAPTER 29

ROTHCHILD: DUE DILLIGENCE

I pulled into the lot around 9:45 a.m. I was headed to one of the staircase doors when the desk officer, Eddie Kozlov (a.k.a. the "White Russian"), shouted, "What, you forgot you had court?"

I froze, believing that I had forgotten to come in for a court date, which usually started at 8:00 at the precinct. Even if I rushed, I wouldn't get to court till about 10:30, which would make me very late.

I must have looked shocked, because he immediately stated, "You're not on the roll call, Josh. So you're good."

It *would've* been funny if he knew I didn't have court and was just fucking with me for coming in five hours before my shift started. Cops always pull that kind of shit with each other. But humor wasn't Eddie's strong suit. He'd spent a good part of his childhood in a former Soviet Bloc country—I can't remember which—before immigrating with his family to the US.

In truth, there had been at least a couple of times over the years when I'd missed court after being properly notified. It was a scary feeling. Although many times you just waited around, there were plenty of times when you were needed there. No one wanted an assistant district attorney calling the precinct to say you were MIA for a court hearing or trial.

So my heart was just settling back into my chest when Eddie yelled again, despite the fact that I was not even ten feet from him: "The Borough didn't get your 49 on the homicide last night." He shrugged. "I sent it to them. But they were very mad it got there so late."

Meaning a "cop" at the Patrol Borough headquarters, whose job it was to answer the phones and pass information along, hadn't gotten my report on the double shooting/homicide from the night before. A report that I'd also faxed to the Operations Division, the chief of patrol's office, and the chief of detectives' office. A report that I'd left a copy of hanging on a clipboard behind the front desk. Quite an easy fix.

I shrugged. He didn't want to let it go, though. "I told him, this guy—Josh—he's just been in a shooting, so you have to cut him some slack. The cop was very pissed, though. I think maybe I smoothed it over..."

Why a sergeant thought he had to explain an easily fixable situation to a coward who'd spent his whole career at a desk, not to mention a coward who was subordinate to him—

I realized he was still going on about it. Saying, "Gotta look out now—you know I got your spot on days since you were moved to the 4-by. I've always got your back, bro. I smoothed it over with him, and I don't think it's gonna go anywhere else."

I was done listening to the White Russian. Without a word, I turned and headed upstairs to get dressed. He very well might still have been talking. Working with him had been a real eye-opener as to why communism doesn't work.

By putting on my uniform, I would bypass just about all questions as to why I was here already when my tour didn't start for five hours. Full gun belt, vest...the CO was in today, and I didn't want to have to explain myself to her or her secretary, a sneaky little full-duty cop whom she'd always kept inside as her assistant, in one way or another, as she climbed the ranks. This dude knew exactly who buttered his toast and was always looking for anything he could use to ingratiate himself with her. Which was usually intel on someone she didn't like.

I wasn't going to submit an overtime slip for this time, and I wasn't going to go out on the street unless a cop was calling for help. I just wanted to use a computer and access information in relative privacy.

I used a computer that was stowed at a small desk in a corner of the Special Operations office on the second floor. The Anti-Crime guys were out on the streets, and the conditions and other units weren't milling around. Hopefully, they wouldn't bother me when they came back in—I'd only been back from the shooting for a week, and everyone still wanted to ask me if I was okay, probably hoping I'd provide some details on the fallout in case they were ever in that situation. I always did, because I'd never really been told what happened after. But I just wanted some peace and quiet now.

First, I ran Deon Jenkins through a database that showed pretty much every documented interaction he'd ever had with the NYPD. This included juvenile arrests and complaint reports, regardless of whether he was listed as the suspect or the victim. It was the same program the precinct detectives had used to figure out who the woman's boyfriend was when Lisa's father had been beaten.

The system also included aided reports, where the person had been taken to the hospital on account of mental illness, drugs, or an injury; domestic incident reports, whether they'd been a suspect or a victim; arrest reports; and even tickets they'd been given. It was all there.

As I clicked on the dozens of documented interactions Deon had had with the NYPD, I thought about Detective Espinoza telling me, after I'd just gotten back to work and was still so fixated on what had already happened, versus what *could* happen, if everyone were on the same page:

"I know he bit you and spat at you and shit—I'd be fucked up about it too. But Jenkins is more than just an EDP. Big Boy is being held at Rikers—all calls and correspondence are recorded. But I think one of his associates on the outside asked Jenkins to take out Lawrence Washington as a warning to his niece to stop cooperating. A warning, given out to a man no one was gonna care about, by a guy with no obvious connection to the gang."

A man no one was gonna care about. Except Espinoza, I guess. And now maybe me too.

* * * * *

Scrolling and clicking through Deon's records, the first thing that struck me was that the only aided cards I saw on him were for the time he'd been shot and one for a high school fight. Usually, crazy people will have at least a few documented times when the department does aided cards for sending them to the hospital for a psych evaluation. Granted, a lot of times those aided cards don't actually get done. But usually, frequent EDPs will have at least a few aided cards in the system. So, it was possible that he'd never been taken in on a straight psych hold.

Another thing I saw: Deon had grown up in the building complex where the New Year's homicide had taken place. Granted, a lot of folks had, but it meant that he knew the buildings well.

A bunch of Deon's arrests were sealed, but the complaint reports associated with them could still be accessed. He'd been arrested for shooting a young man in the courtyard of a housing project when he himself was only eighteen. Since the arrest was sealed, I assumed he'd beaten the case. He'd also been arrested for murder at twenty. Again, that arrest was sealed, since he had obviously beaten that case too. Then he got arrested for a home invasion robbery and did a five-year bid upstate. He was twenty-nine now, and apparently off parole for that, despite the eight arrests he had amassed since coming home.

Of those arrests, three were already sealed, meaning the cases were done, and I couldn't view the arrest reports. This included the robbery he was wanted for when I collared him—looks like he beat the case. Then there was the recent one for weed that my day shift cops had made, plus the one when he'd assaulted me on New Year's Day. The other arrests were for mostly minor shit like weed and petit larceny. But when I clicked on the complaint reports for the two sealed cases, I saw that they were both misdemeanor assaults.

One of them had him punching a guy twice in the face and laying him out inside a Crown Fried Chicken about a year and a half earlier. It was apparently unprovoked. I ran the victim's name and didn't see anything on him to indicate he was anything other than an upstanding citizen.

The other sealed assault arrest was fairly similar in nature: Deon approaches the guy at a bus stop, says, "Wachoo doin' in this hood?", and punches him in the temple. In both cases, he was arrested by cops immediately after. Like he really didn't care about getting away, since the crimes were relatively minor. The only times besides the New Year's arrest that he'd either run or had resisted arrest were when he'd been pinched with a gun at nineteen, when he'd gotten caught for the home invasion robbery that wound up sending him to prison, and a more recent arrest when he'd been one of several occupants of a car where a gun was found; that case seemed to have gone nowhere. But in all these serious instances, when he either had something bad on him or had just done something really serious, he'd run or fought the cops. Not for the minor stuff, though. Same for the recent arrest by Smith and McCall: minor weed charge; no running or fighting.

Another thing I noticed—there were no property invoices associated with the arrest on New Year's Day. Courtney had processed Jenkins and done the reports, which meant he had no drugs on him. It also meant no cell phone. Perps can keep their wallets in the cells after they're searched, but not cell phones or anything like that.

Courtney wasn't working that day, so I called his cell. He picked up after a few rings. "Sarge, what's up?"

"The perp who bit me—he didn't have *anything* on him?"

Courtney thought for a moment. "Nah, no drugs, no weapons..."

"What about a phone?" It was possible that Courtney had called a family member and given them the cell phone.

"Nah, Sarge, easiest collar I ever made. No vouchers—just had a few bucks on him and his Benefit Card. Only thing that sucked was he kept complaining about the fucked-up K2 he'd been smoking. Wouldn't shut up about it—kept saying he should've just stuck to the natural weed."

K2 wasn't actually illegal—they kept changing the ingredients to throw the state legislature off. "Any K2 or even wrappers?"

"Nah, I would've charged him with anything after he bit you. I was looking too."

"Thanks," I said sincerely and hung up.

I went back through the arrests. Almost every time he was arrested, he had a cell phone that was vouchered. And the other times, the cops could've given the phone to a family member or friend instead of putting it into property—it happened all the time. Cops had recently been required to list the phone's serial number of any person arrested—usually an IMEI number. Interestingly, Jenkins had the same phone when he was arrested by Smith and McCall as he had during the arrest just prior to mine on New Year's Day. So it's not like he lost his cell phone when he was high that day. No, he'd left it somewhere and had gotten it back when he was released from the bookings.

Which begged the other question: Why had he been so hyped up that day with me? He had nothing illegal on him, not even any personal property he'd be worried about losing. No warrants. Sure, he told everyone who'd listen that he was high on K2, but he had none on him, not even empty wrappers. So there was no way to prove or disprove that he'd actually smoked some. And he basically got arrested on purpose.

Maybe because he wasn't crazy at all. Maybe he was trying to make it look that way. You get arrested not even two hours after a homicide, a half mile from the location, acting like a crazy asshole but knowing you're carrying no weapons—a fact that will be documented in the ensuing police report—maybe he was smarter than he looked. And if he ever got asked about his whereabouts at the time of the murder—easy. "I was so fuckin' high, I don't remember. You can ask the cops who arrested me!" No way to track his movements by his cell phone pinging off towers, because he didn't have one on him.

He'd beat a bunch of high-stakes cases and somehow managed not to get sent back to prison despite his penchant for getting into trouble. Maybe what happened that day was even worse than I'd thought— maybe Jenkins had *planned* to get arrested. If so, I'd fallen for it hook, line, and sinker, thinking Espinoza was so off base for suspecting a clearly insane person of carrying out a very well-executed homicide.

Over the next few days, I tracked down every go-getter cop and sergeant in the precinct and told them that Jenkins might be carrying. "Not personal," I'd answer when asked if this was because he'd bitten me. "Just trust me—anything you can stop him on, do it. Just remember, he likes to fight..." I'd hold up my hand, where the scar was still visible. "And watch his fucking hands," I'd remind the younger cops.

Luckily, I had a good reputation among the cops and sergeants, and they knew I wouldn't ask them to stop him if I didn't have somewhat reliable intel. I spoke to everyone privately, as I didn't want this getting back to the commanding officer, or even the lieutenants, who worked more closely with her.

For the next two weeks, I kept expecting to see Jenkins locked up on something. But no one saw him. I was looking hard too—and came up with nothing. Everything was quiet on his front—he didn't even get collared in another precinct.

CHAPTER 30

HARRIS AND MCCALL: IMPACT OVERTIME

It was spring, but there was a chill in the air that made it seem like winter had never quite left. Jamel chalked it up to maybe being tired; he'd gotten up at 4:30 to work out before his tour, then remembered, after he'd gotten in, that he and McCall were working the Impact Overtime tonight.

Jamel loved overtime, especially when it didn't involve him being stationed on a fixed post for eight hours, standing around like an asshole with no one to talk to and very few prospects for a decent collar or anything exciting. But he and McCall had been given a car by Sergeant Johnson, who was running things tonight, with more senior cops given foot posts. Because the Sarge knew that they'd deliver. No petty bullshit either. For all McCall's faults, Jamel knew that he hated rousting their fellow black men just to get another statistic for the fucks who ran this incomprehensibly big and confusing department. That ethos had rubbed off on him. Unlike some young cops who'd sell their own mothers down the river to get to into Anti-Crime, gangs, or narcotics, Jamel would never try to roust a man for drinking a beer on his own stoop or do a guy dirty for smoking a cigarette coming off the subway steps or a young couple making out in the park after dark. Not unless he knew they were wanted for something serious or were on the precinct bad-boy list—known perps responsible for a large amount of the violent crime in the area. You couldn't pass up on guys like that—there were few enough opportunities to get them on something they couldn't argue.

It was 8:15, and the sun had set already. But as they drove through the dark streets, there was an electric feeling in the air. Like something could happen at any moment.

It hadn't yet, though. They'd been driving around for four hours already. They'd backed a unit on a "domestic" and another on an assault job. Besides that, there hadn't been anything except some old-assed drinkers on the corner by a bodega whom they'd told to pack up and leave before one of the other impact units took notice.

"It's a nice night—pretty. A little cold, but you can feel summer in the air," Jamel commented lightly.

"Your boyfriend tell you that line?"

Jamel was not going to be bullied tonight by his friend. As he drove, he threw him a look.

"Yes, he did. He also told me you're a dick that can't let anyone get close to you."

As soon as the words poured out, Jamel knew they were a mistake.

McCall straightened in his seat. "You get that one from Oprah or the ladies on *The View*?"

Jamel, chastened and regretting his words already, fell silent.

He drove down the dark streets, remembering things that they'd experienced in their years-long partnership—while McCall was probably sitting there regretting that he'd tied the fate of his career to a drama queen.

It seemed like several minutes passed before McCall broke the silence, Jamel driving down streets and forgetting them as soon as he turned onto another. "You know I love you, man, but you gotta stop being such a chick."

Jamel, stuck on "I love you man," almost slammed on the brakes. It was a good thing he didn't, as there was a Hum-V straddling their ass.

"Fuckin' asshole," Jamel hissed as the Hummer's lights hit his rearview mirror and then his eyes. "I think he's got his brights on!"

McCall turned and glanced at it. When he swiveled back, he was squinting too. "Let him pass and then light him up. Shithead's gotta be drunk off his ass to be doin' this."

Jamel was already on it, pulling over to the curb as soon as he saw an open space so the Hummer could pass them on the one-way road.

He stopped behind a Chrysler that was at least a foot off the curb and tensed, seeing in his sideview the blinding lights of the Hummer passing by. If it was some EDP who just wanted to shoot a cop, they were toast.

But the big monstrosity passed by, the lights finally not blinding them anymore. Jamel's night vision was shot, but he wouldn't have been able to see who was inside anyway with the heavily tinted windows.

Jamel waited a beat, then pulled out and sped up so he was right on the Hummer's ass. He switched on the turret lights and beeped the siren, half-expecting them not to stop.

After a second blare of the horn-siren, though, the driver actually pulled over. McCall got on the speaker mic. "Take your foot off the brake and roll down the windows."

Jamel didn't take his eyes off the car. "I don't think it works."

McCall clicked it a few times, realizing his partner was right. "Shit." He threw the mic down in frustration.

They threw open their doors, seeing only the rear headlights (luckily the shithead had taken his foot off the brake and put the car in park, at least) and blacked-out rear window, the gray Hummer sitting way up high.

Both had their hands on their guns as they approached. Jamel took out his flashlight and shined it into the driver's sideview mirror. McCall did the same on the passenger side. They cleared the rear compartment; no idea if there was anyone back there, as the blacked-out windows were still up.

McCall stopped just short of the front passenger's side window—it was up too. He shined his flashlight in, hoping he'd at least startle the passenger, if there was one. This was the kind of stop you'd see on police training videos, gunmen jumping out both sides of the rear passenger compartment and lighting up the two naïve cops. Then some career coward at the shooting range or in the Academy who had never done anything on the streets would criticize the shit out of their tactics. Like if they called out for additional units on this stop and it turned out to be nothing, they wouldn't be torn apart in the locker room for the next six months. McCall had had that happen before. Taking his chances on a shady car had become his preferred option.

He couldn't see Jamel over the roof of the big car. This wasn't a good way to do a traffic stop, but what the fuck did they have? A shitty microphone that didn't work and nothing more than a couple of traffic violations to pull this vehicle over for. His adrenaline was definitely elevated, not to a crazy level but he was aware of it. To die like an idiot, no commonsense asshole was something he just couldn't do. Not after everything he'd been through. The front passenger window was still rolled up—Jamel would've told them to lower it by now. He'd already cleared his gun halfway from the holster. Now he took it out and held it at his side.

"We're good, bro!" Jamel shouted from the other side.

He trusted Jamel, probably more than he'd ever trusted another man. But in many ways, Jamel was still just a boy. He shouted back, "How's that?!"

"Hey—" It was Jamel, talking from behind him, having walked around to McCall's side of the car. He turned toward him. "Female driver—she knows you, bro. Just her and her boyfriend in the car. He's teaching her to drive."

"You tell him he's doing a shitty job?"

Jamel smiled shyly. Looking at him—perfect teeth and cheekbones, dimples visible in the glow of their headlights—McCall wanted to punch his pretty face. "Whachoo mean, she knows me?" In all honesty, this line had worked on Jamel about a year ago. At which point they'd wound up throwing down with a piece of shit McCall had gone to school with in Brownsville, before the crazy fuck had been expelled for stabbing a teacher. Jamel had eaten that asshole's lies until the fight started.

Jamel was twenty-five. Very smart, at least IQ-wise. But still naïve in a way McCall hadn't been since he was a child.

Jamel's face faltered a little when he saw McCall's look. "Tell her to roll the windows down," he said, annoyed. Jamel nodded and hopped to.

McCall scanned the back seat and floor as the windows rolled down, his flashlight illuminating the dark spaces. Like Jamel had said, the rear passenger compartment was empty. As his eyes focused on the driver, she smiled. "Knew that was you, Mac! How you been?"

Stacey. They'd been friendly in high school during McCall's junior and senior years, after he'd been taken in by the Hendersons and had started to get his shit together. Nice girl, pretty, down to earth. Didn't act out like some of the other ghetto girls did. He'd always liked her.

"Stace, good to see you. How you been?" Jamel was standing directly opposite him so McCall could see him pretty well, even in the dark. He didn't like the smile, like a kid who'd done good and hadn't been able to convince his dad that he had things under control.

He caught up with Stacey for a few minutes. She was dating the passenger—unfortunately, because McCall had always wanted to bang her. But the car didn't reek of weed and he figured maybe the boyfriend wasn't so bad. He didn't look threatening—he wasn't even showing any jealousy that his girl was chewing the shit with a stud cop. Just an asshole about his car choices. Who'd let a five-foot-one girl like Stacey drive this monstrosity? She'd probably be pulled over three more times tonight. No tickets for that pretty face, though, unless the cop was a racist faggot.

So it was now almost 2100 hours and they hadn't written a single "C" Summons. Sergeant Johnson wanted at least one of those from each of them, unless they got an arrest. This was Impact Overtime, supplementing the rookies dotting the street corners of the trouble-prone intersections, harassing enough black people with petty stops that they eventually did wind up lowering the crime rate, as some bad folks were inevitably caught when you cast the net so wide. McCall didn't like that shit, and neither did Jamel. But they could drive around this area with their eyes half-closed and easily find two or three dirtbags smoking weed, pissing, or carrying open containers that deserved to be stopped, frisked, summonsed, and/or arrested. You just had to pick the right ones, not some old guy drinking a beer on a stoop.

They drove around for a while. Jamel spotted a guy taking a piss in a dark playground—good eye. Disgusting. He was in his fifties and was drunk as could be, so they wrote him a "C" summons and sent him on his way without running him for warrants.

They had the Criminal Court Summons, so that was something. And it was after 2200 now, an hour and a half before they could leave. McCall figured it would be enough for Sergeant Johnson. He wasn't a hard-ass about this kind of stuff. Some of the sergeants—the young ones and guys who needed the overtime badly—were really hard-asses about the activity you got on these overtime details. Which was ironic, since a lot of the cops had to be forced to do them.

McCall had to take a piss. There weren't many places to do that at this time, at least not legally, so Jamel was driving back to the precinct. They were coming up on a bus stop followed by a bodega on Jamel's side, so he slowed down to see if anyone was hanging out—he knew his partner would rather hold his piss than miss a decent stop. But all was clear.

They were just passing the bodega when McCall yelled, "Hold up!"

Jamel slammed on his brakes for what felt like the tenth time tonight. "On the right—saw us and he's tryin' to duck into that building!"

The building was a little in from the corner on McCall's side, but Jamel couldn't see anything yet. Luckily, he'd been going slowly so he was able to turn onto the street without backing up first. That's when he saw—in the well-lit area outside the apartment building—Deon Jenkins looking right at them while he tried to push the glass lobby door in with his right shoulder. He was wearing a black hoody. His left arm and hand were visible, but his right hand was tucked away on the other side of his body around his waistband.

"That's Jenkins!" McCall shouted as Jamel stopped the car and they both threw open their car doors. Jamel didn't have the chance to let his partner know he'd recognized him too because Jenkins turned like a spinning top and sprinted in the direction they'd just come from, keeping the right side of his body bladed away from them. Jamel and McCall had to pivot and turn to run after him, then lost sight of him as he made a looping right onto the next street.

Jamel was a little ahead of his partner as he turned right and saw Jenkins still running, holding what looked like a black plastic bag in his right hand. Drugs? Gun? He didn't have any warrants—Jamel had just run him earlier that day after speaking with Sergeant Rothchild. So he definitely had something in the bag.

Jenkins was fast as shit, wearing only sneakers and the hoody versus the gun belts, vests, and boots the two cops wore. They tore down the mostly commercial street so fast that Jamel, a good sprinter, was already feeling pain in his thighs. He could hear McCall, a few steps behind him, putting out their location and then the foot pursuit—it sounded garbled, and Jamel wasn't sure if it transmitted clearly over the radio, if at all.

They ran past a school building. Jenkins, still holding the bag, cut left sharply and turned down the next street.

Jamel had to slow down to turn, losing sight of Jenkins on the dark, mostly residential street.

He completed the turn, his eyes adjusting to the darker street and the houses on his right, which were all connected. No alleys. He didn't see him. Where the fuck did he go? His eyes darted up ahead, scanning the parked cars. McCall had turned into the middle of the street, though, not too far behind him. He would've seen if Jenkins had ducked behind a car.

Then he spotted it up on his right—a tall metal fence covering a break between buildings. The fence had a "No Parking" sign meant for people on the street. There was an SUV snugly parked a few feet in, but there was space on the driver's side for someone to walk through. Jamel tried the fence—locked with a chain. He hoisted himself up and over, landing on the other side and immediately taking out his gun and flashlight. McCall came up behind him a second or two later, hissing, "You see him?"

No—they had to go single file through the gap between the car's driver's side door and the wall of the building since there was no room on the passenger side. Jamel shone his flashlight into the vehicle, looking into the windows to see if Jenkins had gotten lucky and found an open door. But it was empty. He ducked to check under the car—nothing.

When they cleared the SUV there was a smaller car. Also empty. They jogged across the yard to a fence that led to the backyards of the houses on the next block. They didn't see any movement there or hear anything. They shone their flashlights across the yard, into the brush over the fence line, and under both cars again. Nothing. Not a sound. Approaching sirens cut through the silence as their backup got closer.

McCall got on his radio and put out where they'd lost Jenkins and his description as they climbed back over the fence and turned right. A few buildings down they found another gap, this one much bigger. They hopped a small fence and then a larger one and were in a bushy area when they realized they were being hailed over the radio. McCall took it.

"Impact 3, we're good. In the rear of…" He hadn't checked the address so he said, "Mid-block Monroe, Ralph to Patchen." A rough estimate to say the least. Again, they shone their flashlights over the dark area but didn't see any movement. Jamel checked behind a clump of bushes while McCall checked behind a tree. "Shit!" McCall exclaimed. "He must've cut down here."

Jamel didn't think so—he felt like Jenkins hadn't had enough time to make it over here before he turned onto the block. He was pretty sure he'd climbed that first fence and fled that way. Either way, though, he appeared to be gone in the wind.

Four units, including Sergeant Rothchild, who was the patrol supervisor, came by. Most of the cops were cool, helping them search under cars, in garbage cans, doorways. A few of the cops grumbled, complaining that they were searching for a guy who hadn't even done anything. They searched for a while longer, though, a few other officers assisting them checking the alley and the second yard again, while some drove around looking. But they didn't find him or anything he might have thrown. Then a "shots fired" call came over the radio, and everyone took off. Before he left, Sergeant Rothchild walked up to them.

"You sure he went down this one?" He indicated the second alley.

McCall, who thought he had, looked to Jamel. Jamel shrugged. "Not sure, Sarge."

"You think he was strapped?"

McCall and Harris answered in unison. "Definitely."

Rothchild seemed to believe them, unlike a lot of the cops. But he had to get over to the shots fired call.

Soon they were standing alone on the dark street. McCall asked, "You got the keys?"

Jamel's eyes shot up in his head—he didn't remember if he had taken them out of the ignition or not. But he felt around in his pockets and found them, taking them out for McCall to see.

"Thank fucking goodness," McCall said. The last thing they needed was to have to report their car had been stolen. They'd never live that one down.

They were walking past a string of dark storefronts, still about a block away from their car, when headlights came up behind them. They glanced back and saw one of the two Ford Explorers the precinct had slowing down. Probably a supervisor driving it.

The driver's side window rolled down and they saw it was "White McCall," smirking like he'd just caught them stealing from the cookie jar. Beside him, in shadow but still recognizable with the white uniform short, was the 4-to-12 lieutenant, a white middle-aged dickhead with a balding head of red hair named Landers.

White McCall smirked. "How come you two always get the ninjas? Fuckin' vanishing acts. No gun, no body…" he teased, that snide grin on his face letting them know he didn't believe for a second the perp had a gun. "You harassing teenage drinkers again, McCall? Thought you'd know better, bein' from around here an' all."

Lieutenant Landers snorted, then White McCall drove off without offering them a ride back to their car. McCall again counted their blessings that Jamel had taken the keys. He could only take so much humiliation tonight, and the walk back seemed like it was taking forever, though it couldn't have been more than two and a half blocks, tops.

After clearing from the shots-fired call, which turned out to be nonsense, Sergeant Rothchild called Jamel. "Where you guys at?"

"Just getting back to our car, Sarge." Rothchild was silent and Jamel realized he didn't know where they were parked. He gave him the intersection.

"Stay there—we'll walk the route, see if he threw anything. I'll be there in two minutes."

When Sergeant Rothchild got there, they walked the route of the chase to see if Jenkins had thrown a gun or drugs. It was dark, though. McCall had seen the bag too—it was black, probably plastic, the kind you get in a bodega. In any case, any black plastic bags they encountered during the search were empty or just holding empty bottles. They opened all the garbage cans and recycling bins in the area where Jenkins had disappeared but didn't find anything. Before they could even discuss climbing over the fences again to check the backyards and brush, a domestic assault call involving a firearm came out over the radio. They all ran back to their cars to go to it.

The sector cops assigned the call already had the perp in handcuffs by the time McCall and Harris rolled up. No gun was actually involved—knife displayed only.

McCall and Harris drove around for a while after that, checking every alley and shadowy nook they could find without any success.

"He was definitely strapped," McCall was muttering as Jamel drove around, trying to kill the last forty minutes till they could turn in the car and go home.

McCall thought everyone who got away from them was carrying a gun. But he might have been right in this case. They'd never know now.

CHAPTER 31

ROTHCHILD:
TURNING OVER EVERY ROCK

After checking the area of the foot pursuit with Harris and McCall, I responded to a bunch of calls in a row, two of them domestics that resulted in arrests. By the time I got back into the precinct, Harris and McCall had already left. They had to be back in seven hours, so I didn't blame them for hurrying out.

I went upstairs to the Detective Squad, hoping Espinoza was still working. He actually walked out the door as I was walking toward it. "I was just gonna come talk to you, Sarge."

"We didn't find anything, but I figured I'd let you know."

"One of the Field Intelligence officer's snitches said Jenkins sometimes carries a gun around in a plastic bag, like you get in the bodega."

I perked up. "They think he had a bag like that. Couldn't see what was in it, though."

He shrugged. "I'm all set to leave, but I'll walk the area with you if you want."

I nodded. "Like I said, I respect that you still care about the case even with all the other shit we've got going on." We had taken five homicides since that one on New Year's, and it wasn't even summer yet, when things really heat up. Not to mention over a dozen shooting victims that had dropped since then.

We took an unmarked detective car, since I had to give mine to the midnight patrol sergeant.

The Crown Vic was spacious. Ford had phased the vehicle out a few years prior, and we were still going through replacements like Fusions and Nissan Hybrids and even a couple of Tauruses, Ford Edges, and more recently the Explorers to go with the remaining Crown Vics and Impalas. I'd been driving a Fusion tonight, so the extra room was nice. The lieutenant got to take the Explorer when he was in.

Espinoza glanced over at me after he pulled out onto the street. "These cars are all gonna be gone soon."

I nodded. Police cars don't last long in the NYPD. Two, three years tops, the way we use them 24/7 and basically treat them like shit, driving over sidewalks and leaving them running for long periods of time. Then there's accidents, vandalism... Detectives' cars lasted longer, but they were beat up on too. The Crown Vics would all be gone soon.

"I couldn't come out earlier," he explained. "We had a shooting suspect in the box."

"How'd it go?" I asked.

"Good—the victim started cooperating and IDed him out of a lineup. So we had that going in to the interview. Once we got him to give up his partner, he couldn't stop talking. Started singing like a bird, trying to lay it all on *him*."

"That sounds nice," I replied distractedly.

Espinoza laughed. "Yeah, nice. You okay?"

I was thinking about the plastic bag intel Espinoza had just let me in on. It made what McCall and Harris believed a lot more plausible. "We should've looked harder earlier."

"If he *was* carrying, and he hasn't gone back to get it yet, you're with the right guy. I worked crime for eight years in the seven-five before going to the squad. Got to the point I could smell a gun from a mile away."

259

"Someone didn't have a hook." Eight years in crime was a long time before getting into a Detective Squad.

"Yeah," he laughed. "No hook. But I could've gotten to the squad sooner. I liked crime. Got my workouts in, then always running and gunning when we were on the streets. I miss it."

I directed him to the building where they'd first seen Deon Jenkins. We got out of the car, me in my uniform with a full gun belt on and Espinoza with just a suit jacket covering his gun and a pair of handcuffs. Espinoza said, as we were walking over, "One of Deon's girlfriends lives here. Probably wasn't expecting him."

Jesus. This guy was in and out of jail his whole life and had girlfriends, plural. I guess that's why there never seems to be any available single women. They're all involved with these winners.

The street and alcove leading up to the front door were well-lit. Espinoza pushed the door, as I had. Solidly locked. Then his eyes went over to the garbage cans seated on the curb. "We checked them already," I said, "but they had a good view of him and they're positive he couldn't have ditched it on this block."

Espinoza nodded. "So if he ditched anything, it was after they lost sight of him. We need to narrow the area down."

I agreed. This wasn't a canvass for a homicide or a shooting; in fact, no confirmed crime had been committed. We were just two guys with nothing better to do than play on a hunch that probably wouldn't pan out even if he had been armed. Because even if he had ditched a gun, the chances of us finding it in the dark in a heavily commercial/residential area were next to nothing.

I nodded, then called Jamel. "Hey, me and Detective Espinoza are just re-tracing your pursuit. Can you run me through it again?" I knew I was asking a lot. I'd been in dozens and dozens of foot pursuits over the years, too many to remember. They always happen so quickly.

Your adrenaline spikes, you're out of breath, and you have tunnel vision. That's good when you can see the perp; you'll see his hands with a clarity you never would in a normal state. The hands are what get you, unless you're so close he can knee or head-butt you. But other things, like time, street names, locations…these tend to blur.

Jamel was still adamant that he had a good view of Jenkins, and would've seen anything he threw or dropped, till he turned the corner at the next street, going from residential to mostly commercial, the south side a school and the north side attached businesses stretching out for a whole block. Nowhere to really duck into. We got back into the car.

Deon had made a relatively hard right, which meant that he was still running either on the sidewalk or just into the north side of the street at that point. Jamel estimated he was a few seconds behind him—the apartment building Deon had been trying to get into wasn't that far in from the corner. Espinoza drove slowly, scanning the street as I kept Jamel on speaker. A few seconds meant that he could have had time to duck into a little divot between the buildings half a block up, very small. But Jamel was adamant.

"No, I had sight of him from then till he made the left."

So Espinoza made a slow, looping turn when we got to the next street, the darkness reappearing as soon as the headlights brushed by. I could see how Jamel had totally lost him at that point, even after he turned.

There were no open spots, so Espinoza double-parked and we got out. He left his light board on so the car would be visible on the dark street.

We got out and walked back to the corner where Jamel had first lost him. I still had him on the line. We shone our flashlights over the street, into the front yards, but didn't see anything.

We got to the first fence Smith and McCall jumped, the cars parked behind it single file in the narrow alley. I could see that Espinoza, like me, didn't want to climb it if he didn't have to. I held the phone up to him, still on speaker.

"You two checked the first alley good?"

Jamel hesitated. "We were mostly just looking for the perp the first time. We checked the second alley better once we realized we lost him. Then we did go back to the first one, checked under the cars and on top of the tires. The trash cans too."

Espinoza again. "You checked the yard behind it good?"

Jamel hesitated. "Not as good as we could've, probably. We were thinking that he probably took the second alley, so we checked that one a lot better. Then before we could look again, the calls started coming out."

"He could've thrown it up on one of the roofs," Espinoza commented, almost to himself. He walked back to the street and looked for a sewer grate. It was very close to the intersection where Jenkins turned, though. He would've had to slow down to toss it in.

We checked the garbage bins as we walked to the next alley.

Espinoza shone his light and went up on the stoops of the houses we passed. He even checked inside a flowerpot that I think we'd also checked earlier. Nothing.

I still had Harris on speaker. I held the phone out so Espinoza could hear. "You went down the first alley?"

"Yeah, the one with the SUV parked behind the fence. But once we didn't see him, we came back out and checked the second alley."

Espinoza spoke near my phone. "So you were looking for *him* when you went down the first alley. Then you checked the second?"

"Yeah, we checked that one really good."

"So you were looking for the perp when you checked the first alley. Once you realized he was gone, you checked the second alley better for anything he might've dropped."

Jamel agreed with this assessment.

We got to the second alley. The first fence was waist-high, easy to jump. But the second fence that led behind the houses was high. Climbing while holding a bag with a gun could be challenging, especially when you're going as fast as you can and running from two in-shape, aggressive young cops.

We looked at each other, both thinking the same thing. The fence was high, and they'd searched the area already, looking for something he might have thrown. They didn't check the rear yards behind the first alley as well since they were still initially in pursuit mode, then thinking that he fled down the other alley.

We went back to that first alley. This fence was high too, wrought iron instead of cross pattern.

Espinoza looked at me like he was expecting this. "Gonna have to jump it, Josh. You wanna go first?"

Honestly, I'd thought he would just ask me to jump it while he stayed on the other side, as I was about a decade younger. He was a good sport.

I hoisted myself up onto the middle bar and scuttled over the top without much trouble, dropping eight feet down to the cement with bent knees. Espinoza came after me, surprisingly agile in his suit and jacket, his worn but nice shoes kicking up dust as he landed.

He shook his head. "Shit, first fence I've climbed in three years had to be a bitch."

We took out our flashlights and squeezed past the SUV. We checked under it again, just to be sure. We passed a second car and checked that too, including on top of all the wheels. Then we walked into the backyard area of the line of attached houses. Ahead of us, there was another fence and then the backyards of the houses on the next street, a small tree line in between. It was a relatively big area, as the street was wide.

Espinoza went left and I went right. I shone my flashlight over the short grass and dirt, not seeing anything that caught my attention. I spotted some brush on my right and combed through that with the light, but didn't see anything. I'd been on dozens of searches like this, going through the motions, no real reason to believe I'd find anything, pushing on just because there was a possibility that I might. These searches almost never ended well.

I double-clicked my light and got the wide beam. I saw grass and dirt and some bushes. No trash, no black plastic bags. Nothing that looked like the shape of a gun. As my boots kicked up dirt and I stalked toward the brush by the fence separating the properties, I had the same feeling I'd had on all those other occasions when I'd been chasing rainbows. Flat, utter failure.

I glanced behind and to my left, where Espinoza was arcing his light, doing a search of his assigned area. This wasn't like one of those calls when one of us had seen a perp throw something, or when we were searching for a gun or a knife that we knew was most likely around. This was a big nothing, a hope that the two of us were clinging to.

I heard him cussing; I was probably doing the same. I was almost at a clump of bushes lining the fence, behind which the opposite homes' backyards started, when I saw a crumpled heap lying on the ground in the shadows. I shone my light, trotted over to the fence-line and saw a black plastic bodega bag lying in the grass, with the first half-inch of a black semi-automatic handgun sticking out. Hal-Ay-Fucking-Loo-Yah!

I shouted, and Espinoza trotted over. He knelt down beside the bag and shone his flashlight. Using a pen, he lifted the top of the bag up so he could see the markings on the slide. He nodded. "Nine millimeter."

Nine millimeter was probably the most common caliber gun we dealt with. But it at least meant we were looking at the same caliber gun that had been used in the homicide. So, there was still hope that this might pan out.

Espinoza said, "Don't touch it—we'll call the Evidence Collection Team out."

I realized I was sweating—not due to the weather, which was chilly at almost 1:00 in the morning. Probably from the exertion of climbing the big fence and the excitement of finding the gun, something we'd both known was a long shot, to say the least. That and the fact that the vest and gun belt make your body sweat even in the freezing cold. The longer shift you work, the worse it gets.

I took a step back, not wanting the sweat on my forehead to drip down on the exposed part of the gun or Espinoza's shoe. He got up and whistled. "Shit, that was some fine-ass police work we just did, Rothchild! You need to put in for the squad, bro." He meant the Detective Squad.

I let the compliment stand, even though I never would have come back here tonight if it weren't for Espinoza. Not only because he was so knowledgeable about the perps that he knew Jenkins' preferred carrying method. It was more than that: He had seen something in me that I hadn't known was there. That I was capable of caring about a guy almost no one else did. That I wanted to give him and his survivors a degree of justice that way too often slips through the cracks. Espinoza taught me that I could think like a detective.

I took a deep breath, letting the cool night air deep into my lungs. This is the kind of moment I'd craved for the last ten years. Even before, back when I'd been dreaming of becoming a cop someday. I couldn't leave now, with my awareness of what the job really meant just starting to dawn on me. For better or worse, I was a cop. Better, a sergeant, leader of cops. I couldn't just throw that all away for a better paycheck and guaranteed hours.

"Hey—can I help you?!"

I turned around and saw a man, whom I assumed was the homeowner, standing just outside his back door. It was dark and I couldn't see him that well, but I judged him to be in his fifties.

"Sorry—" I shouted back. He could see us well enough to see that I was in uniform. "We had a guy run through here earlier, dumped something."

"Did you find it?" He asked this question a little less confrontationally, his tone still letting us know he didn't appreciate us being on his property. I didn't blame him.

"Yes, sir," Espinoza piped in. "Good thing too. Guy dumped a gun. We're gonna be here for a little bit so we can process it safely."

The man shook his head. "I've lived in Bed-Stuy my whole life. But this is the first time anyone left a gun in my yard…. Good thing it wasn't back when the kids were growing up."

He shook his head again. "You need anything?"

"No, sir," Espinoza replied. "We'll be out of here as soon as we can."

"Have a good night, Officers," the man said before going back in his house. Nice guy. I felt bad for disturbing him.

It was a busy weekend night, and I didn't want to bother the patrol shift covering the precinct with watching the gun till the Evidence Collection Team got here. "I'll stay with the gun," I told Espinoza. "You mind asking your boss to tell ECT to make it a priority?"

Like many units in this gigantic department, the Evidence Collection Team ran at their own pace. Basically, they were the junior crime scene people. Folks that didn't want to do confrontational, hands-on police or detective work. They wouldn't arrive till way after everything had settled down. Then they'd dust for prints and swab for DNA. Or they'd do this kind of thing—patrol or Anti-Crime or the detectives would get a gun off someone. Unless we knew it had been used in a homicide or something else extremely serious, Crime Scene Unit wouldn't come out. So ECT would come out. Back then we would wear gloves, unload the gun, and leave it in a secure place in the precinct for them to process.

A few years later it became standard that we had to leave the gun where we'd found it, if feasible, and ECT would come out to it. But since Espinoza and I were hoping this gun might be tied to a homicide, another leap of faith we were both obsessed enough to even entertain, we didn't want to move it. I just hoped the call Espinoza made to the Detective Squad sergeant would speed things along. Otherwise, I was in for a long night.

After he got off the phone with his boss, Espinoza put his hand on my shoulder. "They'll swab it and steam it and hopefully they'll get useable DNA. After that we'll send it out to be fired so we can see if the shell casings match anything prior—hopefully our homicide. Then we'll still need to get a comparison DNA sample from Jenkins. We can't tie him to this gun off a foot pursuit in the dark where neither cop saw a gun or got a good look at the bag."

I sighed. Nothing can ever be easy. Jenkins wasn't even wanted on any warrants. And we couldn't tie him to this gun without his DNA.

Espinoza saw my exasperated look. "This is detective shit, kid. You kill yourself chasing your tail half the time, running down any lead, no matter how small. And then you...*wait*. And *hope*. And prepare to be disappointed."

"That's why I never became a detective," I told him.

He shrugged. "It sucks sometimes, yeah. But when you're right—

when you know something, and no one else believes you, and you crack a case that no one even gives a shit about except for you and the family—there's no feeling like it in the world. And it's worth all the dead ends and bullshit."

Jesus. He should have been a recruiter. He smiled. "Either way, we got a gun off the streets. Not a bad way to spend an hour, right?"

I couldn't argue with that.

Before he left, Espinoza used his phone to take some photos of the bag with the gun and the backyard. I shone my flashlight to make it easier for him. "Every little bit helps," he explained. "Still have to get Jenkins into the station, and this isn't gonna do it. But when he gets collared again, if we manage to get an abandonment DNA sample and it matches..."

* * * * *

After Espinoza left, I waited. Then I waited some more. I couldn't leave the yard—I had no car to wait in anyway. I wasn't wearing my jacket, only a long-sleeve shirt, and the sweat under my vest made me feel the cool night air even more. I started to shiver.

The ECT guy got there about two hours later. He wasn't happy—I could tell by the pissed-off way he raised me over the radio, asking my exact location. I wasn't happy either, as I'd heard Espinoza relay all of that information before he left. I could hear his radio crackling from the street, so I just trotted to the fence and yelled for him. He looked to be in his early thirties. By the smug way he carried himself, I could tell he'd done very little patrol time. The gun was to my back but safe, as there was no one else in the yard. "We had to jump the fence," I informed him.

He took a look at the tall fence and shook his head. "I don't get paid enough to jump fences like that, Sarge. They said it was in a bag?"

"Yeah," I responded curtly.

He took out a pair of latex gloves and held them out to me through the parallel bars of the wrought-iron fence. Even though it was dark, there was enough light from the buildings that he could see the look on my face.

I didn't take the gloves. "The detectives want the gun processed where it's lying. We think it might have been used in a homicide."

He shook his head. "Every gun 'might have been used in a homicide.' You don't even have a perp in custody, Sarge. It's no different than someone finding a gun in their backyard or in the sewer. Low priority. I'll put the bag in my car and bring it back to the station. We'll call ESU if there's any trouble unloading it, then I'll swab it and steam it."

I still hadn't reached out for the gloves. He shrugged. "Look, Sarge, you got an iPhone? Take a couple of pictures of it on the ground, then the backs of the homes. You can even take a picture of the fronts of the houses when you get back over. That'll be enough."

Espinoza had already taken the pictures, so I took his gloves, put them on, and went to get the bag. Holding the bag by the plastic straps at the top, I carefully handed the bag to him through one of the gaps in the fence. He carefully took it, our hands touching as he grabbed the top also, both of us making sure the gun was on the bottom and undisturbed. You never know if a gun has a hair trigger or some other malfunction that will make it go off if you don't handle it carefully.

He turned and walked back to his vehicle, holding the bag gingerly. I hoisted myself back up to the bar that ran down the middle, then hoisted myself over the top, swinging my leg till I caught the bar on the other side. I wished he'd seen how quickly I did it.

Ironically, a few years later, ECT issued an order that all guns had to be processed where they were found, not brought back to the precinct, because of all the gun cases the department was losing.

***

The ECT guy processed the gun in the roll call room. It was a 9mm Taurus, with a magazine that held ten rounds. There was one round in the chamber and only four rounds in the magazine. Not uncommon—New York has strict gun laws, especially in the city, where it's hard to even get a permit. So a lot of the guns we take off the streets are not the best. I've had revolvers where the cylinder is taped or secured with a rubber band because otherwise it'll pop open—maybe get one shot out of it at most before you have to reset. Loaded pistols that looked okay but when the time for court came, it turned out that they'd been determined not to be workable. Plus a lot of shit like this—a decent gun, not on the level of a Glock but fine, that didn't have all the rounds it could hold because the person couldn't get ammunition to replace what they'd already shot. I'd seen guns loaded with different caliber rounds—9mm loaded with nines and .45s. So the fact that it wasn't fully loaded didn't surprise me much.

The shooter in the homicide had fired six rounds, though. This gun could hold ten in the mag and one in the chamber, so the fact that it had only the five rounds was looking promising.

I hung out just outside the roll call room as the Evidence Collection cop processed the gun. First he swabbed the outside and the accessible inside parts for DNA. Then he swabbed the bullets—I made sure he did every one. Afterward, he set up a bag and steamed it for prints. This was routine but usually didn't yield much—DNA was much easier to get. A print was obviously better, as it could yield a match quickly. But guns aren't the best surfaces for prints. Sometimes the bullets, especially the top one, will yield a thumb print or partial, but in a big department like this, with people who were just trying to stay off patrol doing the processing, DNA was what we usually had to rely on.

The ECT guy bagged up everything and I stepped behind the desk to log the stuff into the property room, giving the midnight desk sergeant a break. Then I walked upstairs, changed, and drove home, dropping an overtime slip at the desk before I left. I didn't even undress before I passed out, face-first on my bed.

***

The sun was bright and hit my right eye around seven in the morning. I rolled over, feeling like I'd just gotten off a night of heavy drinking, and laid on my back for a while, trying to get back to sleep. But the room was too bright, and I couldn't.

I sat on my bed and took my socks off. Peeled, more aptly. I stripped, put all my nasty clothing in the hamper, then changed into my gym clothes.

I was doing a dumbbell shoulder workout when my phone started buzzing. I finished my set, fished my phone out of my pocket, and answered without seeing who it was. I regretted it instantly.

"Why are you stealing overtime, Rothchild?"

It was the commanding officer. I had no idea what she was talking about. "What?"

"You put in for three hours cash last night. Evidence Collection? What the hell is that?!"

Holy shit. Was she really worried about three hours? The precinct literally doled out hundreds of hours in overtime every weekend, forcing a lot of it on cops and supervisors to cover all of the operations, even on those who didn't want it. How did she even know I'd put in an overtime slip? It was Saturday morning. She never came in on the weekends. Even on weekdays, she never got in before eleven. I walked away from the bench I was using.

"Ma'am, we found a gun—"

"That gun from last night that you can't even pin to a body? That's *found property*, Rothchild, nothing more. You should've assigned one of the midnight cops to take care of it."

"Ma'am, we think the gun might've been used in a homicide."

"Who the fuck is 'we,' Rothchild?" I didn't answer, not wanting to get Espinoza on her radar. "That's a found firearm. For you to take three hours to voucher it—"

"No, first we had to look for it, then I had to wait with it for Evidence Collection to come, then—"

"So there's no good excuse. That's what I figured." She clicked off.

I completely forgot about the weights I'd left on the mat by the bench. My hands were shaking as I called the precinct front desk. Eddie Kozlov, the "White Russian," answered.

"How's it going, Josh?" He sounded chipper.

"How did the CO know I put in an overtime slip for this morning?"

He hesitated before responding shakily. "She…asked if any supervisors put in OT last night."

There's no reason she would've called and asked that. "So she called the precinct and asked?"

"N-no. She told me to text her if any supervisors put in for unscheduled overtime over the weekends."

I almost threw my phone. "You could've just yanked my slip and I would've changed it to time, or just torn it up, asshole! You think I care that much about three hours?!"

He didn't respond.

"Yank the slip."

"Uhhh, I can't. I already signed it and put it in the box. I wrote it in the command log too."

This was definitely a set-up. He could've called me first; he could've put the slip in my mailbox and I'd figure it out later. But now it was documented. Technically, a supervisor has to either let someone know they're going to be working overtime or have a good excuse like a crime scene, shooting, or missing person. But in practice, sergeants and lieutenants rarely notified anyone. They'd use their best judgement whether to take the overtime in cash or not. Nobody cared if you took it in time, since it didn't affect the precinct budget, which is why I would've just changed it if this shithead had given me a heads-up. He knew that too. He was still rattling on about something, but I clicked off.

I stepped out onto Queens Boulevard. It was raining, but I didn't care. I ran home, trying to exhaust myself enough that I wouldn't punch the White Russian in the face when I saw him later. I'd been ready to call Bill and tell him that I was no longer considering the job offer. Now I didn't bother, wanting to at least leave my options open.

CHAPTER 32

ROTHCHILD: MORE TROUBLE

I was so pissed I lost track of time at some point. I arrived at the precinct and signed into the Command Log just in time—the White Russian probably would've notified his girlfriend if I was late.

"Hey, Josh. Tried to leave things nice and neat for you." Like we were buddies.

I ignored him and picked up the paper roll call from the desk. It was only a few pages, since it was a weekend and there were fewer personnel in—the house mice usually didn't work on the weekends. Not that it mattered, since you couldn't use them to do police work anyway. I was going to be the patrol supervisor tonight, so I'd be adjusting the roll call to account for our actual manpower, along with my personal preferences. My lieutenant was the only other supervisor in, and he worked the desk when it was just him and a sergeant.

Scanning the sector assignments, looking at crossed-out names (meaning they'd called in sick or had been given the day off after the roll call was printed), they all started to blur. I wheeled on the White Russian. "Don't talk to me, you stupid fucking commie." In fact, he hadn't said anything in at least two minutes.

Being guilty, he became defensive instead of angry at my admittedly immature insult. "Look, Josh, I didn't know she was going to get you in trouble!"

Who'd said anything about trouble? He just had. I looked down at him, seated in the swivel chair like he was a medieval landowner looking out on his fiefdom. My body and my brain both wanted to punch him in the face. Thankfully, I didn't. But I honestly don't know what stopped me.

* * * * *

"This is the biggest fuckin' bullshit, Josh, I agree. But she has you." Frank Cassella and I were in the sergeants' locker room, speaking low in case spies were hovering outside in the hallway. It was Wednesday, four days after the CO had called me about the overtime.

I wasn't mad at Frank. He was a pretty good union rep, and I considered him a friend. "Frank, this gun might have been used in a fucking homicide!" I realized I was shouting. Frank wasn't offended—he just motioned for me to bring it down, worried someone might overhear our conversation.

"Look, Josh, even if that's true, we're not gonna know for a while. And she isn't gonna give a shit anyway. She's gonna say that a sergeant took it upon himself to stay after his tour ended, not notifying anyone, including his lieutenant, then searched for a gun that may or may not have been thrown by a perp some of his cops were chasing. Then, instead of calling the command and getting a cop to sit with it, you wait for ECT like you're a fuckin' rookie. Then you come back and help voucher the shit, or whatever. I know your heart was in the right place—you were being stand-up, like always. You knew they were short on patrol, and it was a Saturday night. I've told all of this to her. She doesn't give a shit, any more than she gives a shit that you're a certified fucking hero who saved his partner's life and blew away a dangerous career criminal."

"Can't the union president make some calls?"

"He never does anything that won't get press coverage. Just like the PBA and LBA guys. They're all pricks, Josh. No better than that bitch we work for." He paused for a few moments, looking uncomfortable. "Plus, all of them—every single fucking one of these union and higher-ups—they're still pissed you collared that bigwig rabbi last year. If you weren't Jewish, you would've been transferred to Staten Island." So I was wrong, thinking it had been forgotten, or at least forgiven. I really wish Frank had told me this sooner.

"He wasn't a fucking rabbi, Frank. Not that it makes a difference—he's a *slumlord*. You know that disgusting building across from the PJs we're always having to escort HPD into?" Frank nodded. "That's his. Rats and peeling lead paint and shitty heat and caved-in ceilings."

"I know, Josh. He's a fucking savage. But you know how it is..."

He didn't come out and say it like he would have if I were a fellow gentile, but Orthodox and Hassidic Jews have a lot of power in New York City. In Williamsburg, their leaders can walk all around the precinct, including going behind the front desk, without being challenged. There was even a precinct in Brooklyn South that abandoned their station rather than being confronted by a group of Hasidics after one of their own had been arrested.

I rubbed my temple, my index finger brushing my Jewish nose. "I don't regret that collar, Frank. He had a seventeen-year-old black girl in the passenger seat—when do those guys give black people rides for free? She never copped to anything happening, but she already had two prostitution busts. I collared him for "endangering the welfare of a child" because she was drunk and high, and we found cocaine in the center console."

"You did the right thing. But seventeen is legal for sex, even though she's still technically a kid for the child endangerment, which is probably why it got dropped. And he shoved a dozen Captain's Endowment Association, LBA, SBA, PBA, and Chief's cards in your face. They can't get over that. Some of the ones who signed them are running this Patrol Borough."

"If he was some black guy, they'd all be calling him a savage."

"Yeah, true. Unless he had all those connections. Then they'd be the same way about it. Power talks in this city, even in Bed-Stuy."

"And they've been holding onto this for over a year?"

"First of all, our girl did that paper hit job on you only recently."

"That didn't go anywhere, Frank."

"But it got them to stop talking about the shooting that made you look like a hero."

He exhaled and continued. "Look, it's not like they're obsessing over it, Josh. But the way these people are—they get mad at you, feel like you're not respecting them or towing the line—they'll wait. Then when something pops up, they'll pounce. I mean, there was that homicide on New Year's when the photographer got into the crime scene. Even that wasn't enough—but it didn't help." He considered. "If the case against the rabbi hadn't gotten dropped…"

I took a deep breath and decided not to correct him again. "The girl he was with grew up in foster care, Frank. Abusive parents— everything going against her. She didn't have the—I'm using your word here, Frank—the power to push through on the charges. I wouldn't, if I were in her position."

To his credit, Frank didn't mention the New Year's debacle again. And he gave me everything. "They don't care that you stopped him— if you'd have written a ticket, whatever—but even after the collar, they're mad about the coke. They would've rather you parked the car or called someone to pick it up. Going through it, searching it…"

"It was a brand-new Honda Odyssey. He had a suspended license—rich fucker, all those properties he owns. He showed me a Benefit Card as his ID. Who am I gonna call to pick the car up? His wife, who can't drive and has six kids she's chasing after?"

Frank was seated in an old, worn but comfortable chair. He looked up at me, standing over him, pacing and angry and hostile to someone who was just trying to help.

"I love you, Josh. But you just don't get it. Right, wrong—some things are clear-cut, even to those assholes. But weak cases against their friends will always piss them off. And our—" He whispered this part. "—bitch commanding officer is well aware of that. She saw you as a target to help her ingratiate herself to the department leadership the day she stepped into this precinct. And she's been trying to fuck you ever since."

"You could've told me."

He looked up at me with those astute brown eyes. "Would you have listened?"

I didn't bother to respond. We both knew what the answer was. "What about my Jew card?"

"Your Jew card is written on very thin paper. And it's already worn through." He read the look on my face. "Your shooting was good, and it's gonna help you. But if you fight these fuckers, they'll tear through every case, every report you've ever done. Every interaction you've ever had—maybe you pissed some black cop off, and he thinks you're racist. It doesn't matter. They're gonna fuck you if you don't play along."

"Play along with what, Frank?"

"They wanna transfer you out of the borough. No discipline, unless you fight it. They'll let you pick a precinct."

On some level I'd probably known for a long time that my CO was trying to get rid of me. But it still hurt. I thought I'd just made the decision to stick with this career, for better or worse. Why did worse have to come so hard and quick? Despite the CO, I loved this precinct and most of the cops who worked it.

Since I didn't say anything, Frank continued. "It'll satisfy the rabbi. And the chiefs who signed all his police cards."

This was a lot bigger than I'd thought. "How long have you known about this, Frank?" My voice sounded weak, a little bit whiny. "Not that they wanted to get me, but this—?"

"The union called me Saturday afternoon. They're not your friends, Josh. You know me—I fought for you. But this is the best I could get. Nothing in your personnel folder. No discipline, just a change of where you work. It won't be logged as an administrative transfer, which would look bad on your record. They'll just move you, same as if you asked to be moved. And you'll be good." He considered. "Just pick a command with, you know—not too many…"

I had a week to decide. Why did this department have to be run by such vengeful people? If they treated the good cops and supervisors better, we'd stay on this job forever. But now what?

Frank had assured me that the "stealing overtime" charge wouldn't be initiated against me if I just shut up and accepted the transfer. But what assurances did I have that the higher-ups, especially my CO, would honor the deal? There was nothing in writing. If she decided to write me up on paper, I wouldn't even be able to get hired for the corporate security job. Two of the conditions were that I had to possess a license to carry and leave my current job in good standing. Neither of these things would happen if I left the department with pending disciplinary charges.

CHAPTER 33

ROTHCHILD: ONE LAST THING

I was in the process of deciding which precinct I'd like to go to. This wouldn't be that important if I decided to leave the job. But I was still waffling, so I needed to go somewhere that wouldn't drive my blood pressure through the roof every day. But I still had to come into work. And I still had a job to do.

I didn't want to risk coming in really early again—the White Russian was in the same days-off rotation as I was, and he usually worked the desk. I didn't want him to think I was trying to steal pre-shift overtime or anything. So I came in a little early the next day and tracked as many of my old day shift cops down as I could.

I was able to speak with most of the people who were working. Eric and Shayna were getting killed with calls, but they made it back to the precinct a little after their scheduled end of shift. They had reports to do, so they'd be here for a little while anyway. I asked them to speak with me in private, as I'd done with all the other cops.

As soon as I shut the door to the property room, Shayna smiled sadly. "We heard you're leaving us."

I laughed. "I'm not dying or anything, but yeah. More like I've been asked to leave. I just wanted to thank you both for all the hard work you've done, for always being there for me and everyone else."

Eric shrugged modestly. "Someone's gotta help you with these idiots."

Shayna shot him a look. "That's what I've been doing for ten years."

I laughed. "Look, remember the guy that bit me?"

They both nodded. "This isn't personal or anything—I'd be happy never to see him again. But he might have had something to do with that homicide on New Year's."

Eric smiled. "The one that made you and Chan famous, Sarge?"

"Yeah, that one," I replied tersely.

"Is there a warrant?" Shayna asked.

"No," I admitted. "But if you see him, and there's anything you can bring him in on—even petty shit; open container, smoking weed, whatever—I'd appreciate it if you did. Call for backup first, though. It seems like he doesn't usually fight when it's a minor arrest, but you never know what he could have on him. Also, if you do arrest him, call Espinoza in the squad. He's gonna get an abandonment sample from him since his DNA's not in the system."

An "abandonment sample" is used when cops don't have enough for a warrant to demand a suspect's DNA. You offer them a cigarette, can of soda, cup of water. You either do it when they're up in the Detective Squad and there's a clean trash bag that he can throw it into or take it from him when he's done and then secure it to send to the lab. It's much quicker than submitting a suspect's DNA to match against the database, even if it were in there, because you're just comparing the suspect's DNA to the sample you're looking at, in this case from the gun.

Eric asked, "How do they not have his DNA on file? He was upstate for five years."

Shayna gave him a look. "You've been doing this job for sixteen years, old man. *That* surprises you?"

Eric shook his head sadly. "I might just come with you, Sarge."

CHAPTER 34

ROTHCHILD: HARD GOODBYES

After this latest debacle, I was waffling again on taking the job. Jay was furious when I told him I wasn't going to. He knew Bill better than I did. He called him and got him to up the starting salary to a level I couldn't make as a sergeant even if I shattered the overtime cap every month. Plus, I could start within a month as an assistant and then take over in July when the vice president of security left, earning that salary the whole time. "Bill's company was really impressed at how you handled the shooting—unlike the NYPD. They're gonna treat you like a fucking celebrity, bro. Instead of shitting on you every day."

Imagine that! Still, I was unsure. I'd thought I made my mind up that night with Espinoza. But with finding out how much the higher-ups hated me, being transferred…it was really fucking me up. I had to let Bill know in the next few days. If there was ever a time to cut ties with this career, it was now. But there was just no certainty, no feeling that either way my life would start to make sense.

With the biggest decision of my life still weighing heavily on me, that last week in the precinct was hard. It's also very stressful doing this job when you're constantly looking over your shoulder, afraid someone who's got it in for you is going to second-guess your decisions out on the street. Also, I'd been busy calling around, asking people I knew to find out which of the precincts I was interested in had the best commanding officer, and if the cops there were all miserable or not. I'd finally picked a precinct and had let Frank know the day before.

I've always worked in busy areas—the cops are better in those places. The work environment is generally less petty as well. And since I was thinking Queens, there were only a few commands that fit that bill. Since Queens was overall a lot less busy and violent than northern Brooklyn commands, the cops in many of the slower Queens precincts were referred to as "Queens Marines." Not a compliment.

On my last day at the precinct I was covering patrol. I was so nervous about having to finally make the decision and the impending transfer that my hands were literally shaking the first few hours. But by 7 p.m. I started to get it together. Courtney was on a tour change, so of course I took him as my driver.

One of my units requested me to respond to a landlord/tenant dispute. Courtney glanced over at me as he drove. "You look a little more relaxed, Sarge. I was starting to worry."

"Yeah, I guess I've just finally accepted that there's things you can't change. Like the house mice—this department works the way it works."

"Still, that's some shit, man! We did the right thing pulling over that rabbi. And how are they gonna say you're antisemitic—you?!"

"He wasn't a—" I started and then just gave up. "They're not saying I'm antisemitic. They're pissed I didn't respect their authority, let the guy go because of who he knew. It's like when someone writes over a PBA card. But a thousand times worse."

"I've done that a few times," Courtney said proudly.

"Yeah, I have too when someone's a total asshole. A lot of those cards aren't legit anyway."

Courtney was silent for a moment. Then he brought up a conversation he'd had with the commanding officer that we hadn't spoken about in a long time. "Remember how I told you about how she called me into her office and started talking all that shit about Jews looking out for each other? And how black people don't?"

"Yeah, I thought of that. I didn't realize it back when you told me. But it's bullshit anyway. Everyone screws everyone over."

"The Hassidics *are* tight, though. I lived in Crown Heights not long after the riots. Those people are the second biggest gang in the city, right after the NYPD. But they stick together better."

I couldn't disagree. Courtney pulled up behind the cop car that was already at the location. It was dusk, but I could see one of the cops through the open door of a multi-family brownstone. I could tell by his body language that he was frustrated.

A white male in his early fifties was pacing back and forth outside the short gate in front of the house. He was holding a folder and appeared equally frustrated. We approached the male to get his side of the story.

"Are you the owner of the house, sir?"

"No, I'm the property manager. But I have a copy of the deed, a copy of my Power of Attorney, and anything else you need."

A prepared complainant. This was important. A lot of people—cops included—misunderstand "squatter's rights" law. This was especially bad in Brooklyn, where there were so many multi-family homes—you could have one side legally occupied, the other not—or a whole house of squatters. Since the housing crash in the late 2000s, there were more bank-owned and owner-absent properties. If there wasn't an owner to press charges, there was nothing you could do about squatters. Likewise, if a bank was the owner, a lot of times they wouldn't press charges or cooperate. They were content to leave the house to the squatters or decay until the prices went up and they were ready to unload it. Never mind the drug-dealing, prostitution, or dangerous parties and gatherings that turned what could be a quiet block into a problem one and caused the legal tenants and homeowners grief.

What people often misunderstand about "squatter" law is that there's really no such thing. It's landlord/tenant law, nothing else. If I tell my friend he can sleep on my couch, and he stays for thirty-one days, never paying rent—regardless of whether he gets mail there or not—he's established legal occupancy, and I'd have to legally evict him if he won't leave on his own. Likewise, if I'm a building owner, and I rent a room or an apartment to someone, they could never have paid me a dime. As long as they were initially there legally and stayed for over thirty days without interruption, they would have established residency.

However, I can't break into someone's house, stay for thirty-one days, then claim residency. The person might be on vacation or in the hospital—that wouldn't even make sense. Even if someone was rushed to the hospital, left their door unlocked and their house vacant, and someone went in through that open door without permission, they'd still be committing the crime of trespassing. So even if they stayed for thirty-one days, it wouldn't matter, because they never legally occupied the premises. It doesn't matter if they get mail there or what it says on their ID. If you can prove that they're lying about how they came to be in the house and that they've never actually established residency, meaning they are committing a crime, they can be arrested.

But a lot of times what happens is that cops get to one of these calls and the "tenants" have a bullshit lease—often notarized—showing they've been renting the place for several months. They may have backdated or even forged electric and utility bills as well as receipts for cash payments from their "landlord." A lot of times cops just see this and assume there's nothing they can do except refer the aggrieved party to court without looking into the matter further.

Before getting the property manager's story, I checked his ID, then went through the paperwork he showed me. I scrutinized his copy of the deed and the Power of Attorney that the building owner had signed, giving him the authority to manage the property. I then ran the address on a publicly available site called ACRIS, run by the City of New York, and verified that the person on the Power of Attorney was the actual owner of the house. So, I knew the copy of the deed wasn't fake.

"Okay, sir. So, what's the story?"

"I came here earlier—around 5:00 maybe—and the locks on the front door were changed."

I tapped Courtney and he took over. We'd been through enough of these together. "Front door only?"

"I don't know. I banged on the door, then one of 'em—a woman —she comes out screaming, waving what she says is a lease in her hand. Then two guys step into the doorway, also yelling. I backed off the property and called 911."

Courtney again: "When was the last time you were here and your keys worked in the door?"

"I think it's a little over two weeks," he stated, thumbing through his phone. "I check the place as much as I can—we're getting it ready to sell."

"You take pictures?" Courtney asked, indicating the phone.

"Not that day, no," he admitted.

I piped in. "Next time you have to take pictures every time you check the house. Just the front door and a few of the inside, showing it's vacant—no furniture or anything."

He shook his head. "So you can't do anything for me?"

"I didn't say that, sir. Can you give me the exact date you were here?"

Courtney piped in. "Look at texts and phone calls."

He thumbed through his phone and found a text he'd sent to the homeowner after checking the house. It was a little over two weeks prior.

"Okay, good," I stated. "And the house was vacant then?"

"Yeah, no furniture or anything."

I was almost done with him. But I'd learned from previous calls like this. "If we determine they are trespassing, are you and the homeowner going to press charges?"

"Definitely," he stated without hesitating.

Like I said, though, I'd been here a lot before too. "Okay, give this officer—" I indicated Courtney. "—your ID. If we arrest them, you can meet us at the station, and we'll make copies of all your paperwork, then you'll get your ID back."

If he protested, I'd know he wasn't serious about locking them up. The thing is, that's all we can potentially do in this situation. If we don't have a person to press charges for a crime, then it's a civil issue. Cops don't do evictions.

He didn't hesitate, though, immediately handing Courtney his ID. Courtney nodded and slipped it into his pocket. "Wait on the corner—things might get heated," Courtney advised him. He nodded and did as he was advised.

We walked through the small courtyard, up a set of concrete stairs, and entered a big but cramped living room. My two cops— Henry and Williams—were facing each other from across the room. In between them were four adults—one female who looked to be in her late twenties, and three males of around the same age. They weren't hostile, but they were arguing a lot as we stepped in. There was a couch in the middle of the room, but not much else. I looked back at the doorway we'd just entered through. An old doorknob and locks were lying on the floor just inside, along with the opened packaging for the new locks. I have no idea why, but scammers almost always leave the old locks on the floor after they change them. It's a big-time tell.

Like the property manager had said, the woman was still holding the lease, waving it in Henry's face. "I've seen it, ma'am," Henry said. "I believe you." One of the men started to say something, but I held up my hand.

"Is there anyone else in the house?"

Williams shook his head. "We checked, Sarge." He and Henry were good kids. Mid-twenties, black, a few years on the job each. They were both hard workers and eager to learn, which on this job is invaluable.

One of the males stated, in a loud voice, "We been here thirty-one days, yo! He don't have no right to be harassin' us."

"You all live here?"

They all affirmed that they did.

"And you moved in when?"

"Thirty-one days ago," the same male repeated. "March 1."

They all started talking again, acting aggrieved. I tapped Henry on the shoulder and indicated for him to follow me into the kitchen so we could speak in private while Courtney and Williams watched the occupants. As we passed the woman, I asked to see the lease. She looked at me suspiciously, clutching it tightly. I smiled. "Don't worry, ma'am. I'll keep it safe." She smiled back and handed it to me.

When we were out of the room and out of earshot, I glanced at the lease. It was notarized and dated December 1, 2013. Four months before. I looked up at Henry.

"We told 'em they just gotta go to court, Sarge. They have a lease, plus they had bills. The woman's ID even says this address."

"They're all saying they've been here thirty-one days, right?"

Henry shrugged. "Yeah, it's convenient. But they got the lease and the mail…"

I looked at the lease agreement. "They were paying $2,500 a month from December 1st through last month. So they were paying all that money for three months *not* to live in the house, apparently. Do they have receipts from the landlord?"

"Yeah," Henry said. "You wanna go back and see 'em?"

I said that I did. First, though, I asked him what the bedrooms looked like. Sometimes that's the best tell—no beds, no place to sleep. No one stays a month without a bed or a cot.

"Beds in all the bedrooms, Sarge."

I shrugged, and we walked back into the living room. One of the males provided me with several receipts for the supposed payments to the landlord. "I can't read the landlord's name," I stated.

"It's John," the woman piped in. "We don't know his last name. I got his cell, though."

"Okay," I stated. "Can you call him?"

"He's not answering now."

"Okay, where's his office at?"

One of the males now: "We did everything in person—here."

"Did you write checks?" I asked, already knowing the answer.

"No," the male responded. "He only wanted cash."

"Okay," I said. "You got an electric bill?"

One of the males conveniently did. It appeared to be legit, and was in his name, but was only dated two weeks prior.

"I just wanna get this straight. You guys have been here thirty-one days. But you've been paying rent since December 1st? And you lived the first two weeks without electricity?"

"We were moving in slowly," the woman stated.

"The property owner claims the house was vacant even two weeks ago," I commented. Before they could protest: "So you were paying $2,500 a month *not* to live here? You guys must be rich!"

Williams and Henry already had the occupants' identification information. I gave it to Courtney, and he ran them on the computer in our car, which was miraculously working. Two of the males had significant criminal histories. The female and the other male had histories, but nothing too crazy. However, none of them had active warrants.

I had Williams snap photos of the old locks on the floor inside the doorway. He and Henry were still stuck on the lease, though. "Isn't this just a court thing, Sarge?"

"Not necessarily—we see fake notarized leases all the time. We don't have quite enough yet, though. What I want you to do is knock on the neighbors' doors. See when they actually moved in."

Courtney and I stood inside with the occupants as Williams and Henry went outside to speak with the neighbors. When they got back, Henry quietly informed me that the next-door neighbor had seen them moving into the house in the middle of the night about two weeks before. He actually came outside and confronted the female. She stated that they were renting the place from the landlord, and this was the only time they could move in due to their work schedules. The neighbor didn't know what to believe, so he decided not to call the police. But he was adamant that, before that, there was no one living here.

"What about the other neighbors?" I asked, not only because I liked to be thorough but because I wanted to make sure that they had at least tried to speak with a few more.

"Other neighboring house didn't answer. But the people two houses down said the place was vacant for a long time, and they *definitely* haven't been here more than about two weeks. But they didn't see them move in."

I nodded, pleased that the cops weren't just going through the motions. "The first neighbor—does he know how they got in?" I asked Henry.

"No, but he thinks it might've been the back door."

I walked to the back of the house and found the rear door. Brand-new locks were on it as well, the old ones broken and lying on the floor just inside. I inspected the door—there was damage to the jamb, but I couldn't tell if they'd kicked it or pried it or whatever. At any rate, it didn't matter. We had the neighbor and the property manager to impeach their story. We had the old locks on the floor, the backdated lease, which made no sense, and, most importantly, their claiming they'd been here thirty-one days when their own lease and all of the other statements said otherwise. No real proof that anyone had rented them the place, so they weren't being scammed. They lied because they knew what they were doing.

I walked out past them and checked with the property owner again. He still wanted them arrested. I was being unusually cautious, not wanting to have any fuck-ups on my last day. Then I went back inside and broke the news to the squatters. They didn't take it too badly, and the arrests proceeded without incident.

Criminal Trespass is only a Misdemeanor, and they'd be out as soon as they saw the judge. But they'd all be issued Orders of Protection at their arraignment, barring them from coming back here and moving in again. So we'd actually solved the problem we'd been asked to instead of referring the property manager to a court that probably wouldn't be able to help him.

It was a Tuesday night, late, and not that busy. Courtney and I headed back to the station around 11:00. As we walked inside, I told him, "I know you've got a day tour tomorrow, but don't disappear on me. We'll need to go back out if something serious happens before 2330."

Courtney laughed. "I'm not worried about the day tour tomorrow, Sarge. I switched with Watson yesterday when I figured out this would be your last shift."

We stopped walking. I felt a wetness in my right eye. I quickly blinked it away and tried to keep my voice level. "Don't say last shift like I'm dying, bro. I'll be close by." I shook his hand, and we gave each other a quick bro-hug. Unfortunately, Doug Benson, one of the midnight sergeants, walked past just then. "Get a room, you two!" he shouted loud enough for people across the street to hear. Courtney and I laughed along with everyone else and went our separate ways. We didn't have to go back out again that night.

When the midnight shift got out of roll call and we were officially relieved of duty, I nodded to Courtney as I passed him by the front desk. It was odd that he hadn't rushed out yet, giving that he had to be back in another seven hours. Even on normal days, he'd be gone by now if he weren't stuck on something.

Courtney nodded back, and we bumped fists, afraid to do a bro-hug again with all the cops pouring out of the roll call room. "See you, bro," Courtney said.

"Yeah, man, see you."

Fifteen minutes later I was in my civilian clothes, standing in front of my open locker, looking at my uniform pants, shirts, and jackets. I had to report to my new command after two days off, and I didn't have the stomach to come back here. Especially not now, as my eyes were tearing up again.

I found a few big, sturdy black garbage bags in a hallway closet. I double-bagged the one I put my boots and helmet into. Then I placed all my uniforms into that and another bag, hoping they wouldn't break on me as I dragged them downstairs to my car.

Both bags held, and I just had to make one more trip up to get my patrol bag, gun belt, and baton. I put all the odds and ends I thought I might need into my patrol bag, leaving items I thought someone else might use behind, like an old raid jacket that I'd since updated. Then I went downstairs, snuck past the desk, and walked to the parking lot, hoping no one would see the wetness in my eyes. Luckily, there weren't as many cops on the midnight shift, and the station house was practically empty. I made it to my car unobserved.

I was turning the engine on when I heard a tapping on the passenger-side window. I jumped in my seat and looked up.

It was Henry. He'd lost the toss-up and had taken the trespass collars so Williams could go home.

I took a deep breath and rolled the window down.

"Sorry about that, Sarge."

"N-no, it's okay," I assured. My cabin light wasn't on, and I hoped he couldn't see that my eyes had been watering down my cheeks.

"I just wanted to thank you, Sarge. It's been a pleasure working with you these last few weeks."

"You too, Darren."

"Also, I'm sorry about tonight. Me and Williams haven't had too many of those fake squatter calls—we didn't know what to do. I'm really glad you were there to show us." He smiled and fished his phone out of his pocket. "Also, the property manager—he took pictures of the inside less than a month ago." He opened a text message and showed me some pictures. "Empty, like he said. They're definitely gonna be charged."

In the end, wasn't this what it was all about? Using my experience to teach the younger cops so that they'd go into situations more prepared? To make them better police officers and treat every job like it was as important to them as the person who called for help? I could do that in any busy precinct. And I'd chosen one of the busiest ones in Queens. This wasn't the end for me, only the start of a different chapter. And I was gonna stick it out with the NYPD, for better or worse. I just hoped Jay didn't yell at me too much when I broke the news.

I smiled, only a little conscious of my wet cheeks. "You almost done with the collars?"

It was a stupid question. Due to the time of the arrests, there was no chance that Darren had "made the book," meaning he would get to speak with someone from the DA's office tonight. He'd have to process all the arrests, then fax the paperwork downtown. After vouchering all of their property for safekeeping, plus the fake lease, he'd be lucky to get three hours of restless sleep on a locker room couch before he had to check in with the front desk in the morning. If he was lucky, he'd get to help out inside the precinct. But if they were short, he'd have to suit up and go out on patrol, then wait for the District Attorney's office to call. Only once he spoke with a paralegal or ADA and signed a supporting deposition attesting to the charges would the arrest process be complete.

Darren was a good kid, so he didn't respond sarcastically to the stupid question. "Nah, Sarge, I think this one's gonna be an all-nighter."

I wished him luck, as many a sergeant and fellow police officer had wished me when I'd been stuck on late collars. We said good night, and he walked back inside the precinct.

As I drove home, I resolved to try and be less angry all the time. To stop being bitter about the inside cowards and the assholes who ran the department—things I couldn't change even if I was three ranks higher. Every job has bad people and bad circumstances. But the NYPD also has a lot of the best people I've ever known. I had to concentrate more on that and try to actually *enjoy* a job that I truly loved. How fucking hard could that be?

I called Billy in the morning and officially took myself out of the running for the job. "Jay's gonna be even more disappointed than me, Josh," Billy said with a sigh. "I hope you're making the right decision." I hoped so too.

CHAPTER 35

DEON JENKINS:
IN THE FLESH

Shayna was driving today. It hadn't taken her long to get back into the swing of things after coming off childcare leave. Eric figured work was probably a break for her. His kids were in college now, but he remembered those days.

She turned down one of the main streets that crisscrossed north/south across the precinct more or less, then slowed down as they approached the next intersection. On the corner was a converted two-family house that was currently used as an inpatient drug rehab program. Eric didn't really understand it—the "clients" were allowed to come and go during the day; they just had to be back by a certain time. Just like the shitty men's shelter a few blocks down, which kicked the inhabitants out during the day so they could pretend to look for work. The rehab place wasn't unique. More and more halfway houses, mental health residences, sex offender residences, and transitional shelters were popping up in what used to be private residences. Eric was glad he'd moved out of Brooklyn. However, some of these places were now popping up near his house in South Jamaica, Queens. Fucking city, punishing black homeowners like always.

There was an alley behind the rehab house where folks, residents of the place or not, sometimes smoked up and drank. Shayna made a left, and Eric looked in the alley as they passed so she could keep her eyes on the road.

"All clear," he stated, chipper.

"Tell that to the White Russian. He keeps coming up to me, asking if we've written any C summonses here. Says it's on his to-do list from the CO."

"We can't make something happen if it ain't happening," Eric remarked.

"Yeah, I told him they usually do it after dark. But he's clueless."

"Tell him to stop hiding behind the desk and check it out for himself. He finds something, we'll write it."

Shayna sighed. "I miss Sergeant Rothchild."

Eric nodded. "I hear the White Russian's gonna go with the CO when she gets transferred. He was an admin bitch as a cop—she loves those people."

Shayna snorted. "Cause she was one of 'em. Good riddance—I can't wait till they're gone."

They drove in a comfortable silence for a bit. Eric was thinking about how he'd promised his older daughter he'd pick her up from Virginia on Friday and drive her to her mother's place in Connecticut, so she didn't have to take the bus up from college. Father of the Year, no doubt—as long as he didn't have to see his ex.

"Oh, shit!" Shayna shouted.

Eric jumped in his seat, reflexively looking around to see what was up.

"Up ahead, look who just came out the one building we know he doesn't live in," Shayna remarked as she kept the car at a steady pace.

The male turned his head to look at them, and Eric saw it was Deon Jenkins. His mind got right back in the game. "F-TAP location. Automatic trespass arrest, unless he can say who he was visiting—"

"Way ahead of you, grandpa," Shayna said as she hit the gas and sped toward Jenkins. His eyes got wide when he saw they were coming toward him. He turned around and started to walk away quickly.

Eric still needed to get surgery on his left knee from an old line-of-duty meniscus tear. And Shayna, though in good shape, was never gonna win any track meets. All he could think was, *Please don't run…*

Too late! Deon turned toward them and ran diagonally across the street, past their car, then made it to the next corner and turned sharply.

Shayna flicked on the lights and sirens and practically fishtailed the back wheels, making a U-turn. Eric keyed his radio.

"One-Charlie, pursuing a male—"

His window was open, and the siren was too loud. He wasn't sure if he was going over the air. Their car, going the wrong way, was almost up on Jenkins. Eric grabbed his door handle and was about to throw it open when Jenkins made a little loop and turned around, running the other way.

Shayna slammed on the brakes, and Eric got out of the car. He slammed the door, which was lucky because Shayna backed practically straight up and would've clipped him if he hadn't. He ran down the street, but he was losing ground on Jenkins. Shayna managed to turn the car around and was waiting at the next street when Eric got there. He got back in the car as Jenkins turned down another street about a quarter of a block up. Eric, already winded, keyed his mic again to transmit the suspect's description and direction of flight as Shayna turned down that street, going against traffic again.

But the patrol sergeant, Eddie Johnson, was already coming over the radio. "One-Sergeant, terminate pursuit! Have the unit acknowledge!"

Shit! Because of the sirens, he thought they were in a vehicle pursuit. Which would almost always be terminated during this time, a lot of schools in the area dismissing soon.

As soon as he could, Eric piped in, "Suspect is on foot! No vehicle pursuit!"

Shayna was busy driving. She slammed on her brakes for a jaywalker, then crept between a car coming down the street and a parked one. But she got caught up at the next car, an old man who couldn't figure out how to move over on the wide one-way street. Deon Jenkins made a right turn and disappeared at the next block.

Eddie Johnson was yelling over the radio for their location. Eric finally got Jenkins' description out and the corner they'd last seen him. "Heading southbound—Deon Jenkins," he said, then got out to help the old man move over so Shayna could get through.

* * * * *

McCall was driving so fast that Harris started putting on his seatbelt. But then he turned so sharply that Jamel was thrown against the door and lost his grip on the belt. "Fuckin' Jenkins, bro! He's probably carrying to be running like this!"

Jamel was about to agree when an Access-A-Ride van stopped in front of them, blocking the street so their car couldn't pass on either side. McCall started laying on the siren, but the driver was a fucking idiot, putting his hand out the driver's side window and waving them past.

"We can't fucking pass you, retard!" McCall screamed. Jamel threw open his door and ran over to the van. He saw the old lady whom the driver was picking up exit her apartment building. The poor lady was moving so slow that Jenkins would be in Queens by the time she got to the vehicle. He banged on the side of the van. "Move the fuck over or you're getting collared!" The driver gave him an annoyed look, but thought better of saying anything when he saw the look on Jamel's face. He pulled up and to the right, getting close enough to the parked cars that McCall could pass. Without missing a beat, McCall pulled past the van and stopped just long enough for Jamel to jump back in the car. McCall sped up again, taking the next turn as quickly as safety allowed, considering the time of day. They were about three blocks out from Jenkins' last known location, headed toward the direction he'd fled.

* * * * *

"Right. Go right!" Dominguez shouted, though Chan had heard him the first time. He slowed down to make sure he didn't clip the car parked near a stop sign on his right, then started the turn. As he did, Dominguez reached over to the board and turned off the lights and sirens.

Good call, Dominguez! Jenkins, who hadn't hit any alleys he could cut through, was running right toward them as they turned onto the street. Chan lurched to a stop, and Dominguez threw open his door, hoping Jenkins would run into it. But he was quick—he sidestepped, barely brushing the door as he ran past the car and then diagonally across the street so that Chan would have to turn the car around to give chase. He looked over at Dominguez to see what he wanted to do. To his shock, Dominguez bolted out of his door. "C'mon—leave the car!" he yelled, knowing it would take his partner forever to turn it around in this traffic. He ran past the trunk and across the street, nearly getting hit by a livery cab. Chan grabbed the keys out of the ignition and ran after his partner, broadcasting on the radio as he did so.

In less than half a block he was exhausted. Amazingly, though, Dominguez was a quarter of a block ahead of him, not losing much steam. Jenkins was still a good bit ahead of Dominguez, though. And gaining, by the looks of it. Chan gave an update on the street location and did his best to keep up.

His gun belt felt like an anchor around his waist, his vest like a giant crab squeezing the life out of him. He started to cough—*fuck,* he hadn't had an asthma attack since he was a kid, but… Up ahead of Jenkins, way up ahead of Chan, he could see two cop cars, lights but no sirens, coming quickly from opposite directions, both pulling onto the street. For a second, he thought they were gonna crash into each other. Instead, one of the cars stopped short so the other one could complete its turn and try to box Jenkins in.

Smith and McCall got out of the car that stopped to let the other one pass. They both ran toward Jenkins, who was now running toward them.

The other car angled and pulled up to the curb ahead of Jenkins. Eric and Shayna got out and ran toward him.

Digging deep, Chan found whatever reserves were left and pushed his legs as fast as they would go.

Dominguez stopped in his tracks as Jenkins turned around and ran right toward him. He crouched down, ready to tackle him, but Jenkins practically vaulted over a waist-high fence and ran across a small lot that ended at the corner. Chan cut to his right and arrived at the corner side of the lot just as Jenkins did. Jenkins cut away from him as Chan reached out and grabbed his T-shirt and some skin, forcing him to stop. But the T-shirt ripped, and Chan lost his grip on his sweaty skin. Before he could get away, Dominguez ran up and barreled into Jenkins' side. He didn't go down, though.

Dominguez had his arms wrapped around Jenkins' side like he was doing a football tackle that didn't work. Chan went for his legs. That's when Eric came, grabbed Jenkins around the back of the neck, and slammed him onto the pavement. Shayna got her cuffs out as Eric dropped his knee onto Jenkins' upper back. He was still flailing, though —he tried to kick out at Chan, but he sidestepped and then kicked his foot away. Knowing he was a spitter and a biter, Shayna put her foot on his shoulder as she bent down and slapped one of the cuffs on his left wrist. Eric and Dominguez were still holding his upper body down as Chan stood on his ankles so he couldn't kick anymore. McCall and Harris caught up and pried his other hand out from under him, then completed the cuffing with Shayna.

Eric looked back at Chan. "Nice grab!"

"Slow and steady wins the race," Chan said with a smile, getting the words out despite his heaving breaths.

In the half-second Chan waited for some kind of a laugh, a black livery cab pulled up to the corner and Courtney Jones, a.k.a. "Mr. Fixed Post," exited the front passenger seat.

Courtney's gaze shifted between Deon Jenkins, lying on his stomach, handcuffed, and Chan holding his sides, panting. He shouted, so they all could hear, "Y'all tryin' to give Chan a heart attack? Who's gonna carry his fat ass to the ambulance?!"

That they laughed at.

After the laughter died down, Eric looked back at Courtney. "Thanks for backing, Jones. You didn't point your gun at the livery guy, did you?"

Courtney smiled. "I *didn't* kidnap him—he didn't even have a fare. *And* I gave him a good tip." He held his right hand out, palm up. "You wanna reimburse me?"

Jenkins started to turn his head, mouth open like he was going to spit or bite. Eric shoved his head down into the pavement and looked up at Courtney. "I'll give you a dollar, which is more than your cheap ass gave the driver," he hissed. Courtney was about to protest. "You get here in time on the next one, I'll reconsider our arrangement," Eric assured him.

After a little more jaw-jacking, they rolled Jenkins onto his side and had him sit up. He didn't spit this time, which was good. They were all tired of his shit, and a couple of onlookers were already pointing their iPhone cameras at them. If he did spit in one of their faces and they reacted like a normal human being would, their careers would be over.

Deon struggled a bit, but they dragged him to the nearest police car and pushed him inside. Amazingly, he didn't rotate onto his back and start kicking the windows or start banging his head and throwing himself around like a toddler having a tantrum. He just stared straight ahead at the plastic partition separating the rear compartment from the front.

"That's a guilty man," Eric said softly to Shayna.

She patted his shoulder. "You're right about that, old man."

Even though the sun was in his eyes, Eric looked at his partner. Standing on this city street, pavement and buildings, and the occasional tree, he realized how much he needed her. Not in the way a man needs a woman, but in the way a male cop needs a female partner to ground him.

He had to say something, though. "Not so old, according to your sister."

Shayna shot him a laser look. She'd always suspected something had happened between him and her sister after her wedding.

"Just kidding," Eric said after a few seconds. It *wasn't* technically a lie—Shayna's sister, Tameeka, hadn't said anything about his age. But they *had* hooked up. The wedding night and a few times after. "I wouldn't do that to you, partner."

Shayna eyed him distrustfully. "Yeah, okay."

CHAPTER 36

ABANDONMENT SAMPLE

Eric and Shayna transported Jenkins to the precinct in their car; Harris and McCall followed. Shayna pulled into the precinct lot, and McCall pulled up right behind. He and Harris quickly got out and walked over to the rear passenger side of Eric and Shayna's car. McCall pulled the door open and said, "Let's go." Jenkins got out of the car, McCall holding his elbow as he did. He didn't even protest as Harris poked his head inside, scanning the back seat and floor to make sure he hadn't stashed anything.

They walked him into the precinct through the back door. Fortunately, the desk sergeant was expecting them. Even better, it was Reggie Braggs, who was one of the coolest supervisors around. He eyed Jenkins as they walked him up to the desk, looking down on him with guarded caution. "You gonna give us a hard time, Deon?"

Deon shook his head. "No, sir. Long as I get a couple cigarettes 'n' some food."

"We'll see what we can do," Sergeant Braggs said, friendly. Jamel's eyes met his—he knew they needed Jenkins' DNA. Braggs almost immediately broke eye contact, not wanting Jenkins to sense anything funny going on.

"I must be the biggest fuckin' gangsta in this precinct, way y'all always harassin' me," Deon complained as McCall searched him again and completed the pedigree card with his information. When McCall asked his current address, he scoffed. "I been arrested four times this year, bitch. Y'all should have that already." McCall let it drop, as he was eager to keep him calm until they placed him in the cell and then got what they wanted. After that, McCall didn't ask any more questions, and Deon didn't speak again.

Sergeant Braggs looked at the small monitor beside him on the desk, showing a black-and-white image of the main cells. There were only two, then the bench across from them where they sometimes put handcuffed perps, mostly females. Both of the cells had multiple people in them.

"Tell you what, Deon," Sergeant Braggs said like he actually cared what Deon thought. "We'll put you in a cell by yourself if you promise not to act up."

Deon nodded.

Harris took his and McCall's guns and secured them both in a locker behind the front desk. Then they walked Jenkins to the rear cell area. Technically, the rear cells weren't supposed to be used without a notification to Central Bookings. Also, a cop had to be present in the rear cell area to watch the prisoner at all times—like with the regular cells, but in practice they were actually watched through the monitors on the front desk and through intermittent checks. Additionally, some of the rear cells were being used to store excess property that was confiscated by the department. Jamel always wondered why the rear cell area was so much better for actually holding perps than the front cells, given that only one prisoner was allowed per cell, whereas the front cells could have fourteen prisoners in one of them, nothing but a bench or wall and floor to support them when they wanted to sit down or sleep.

They found a clean cell and put Deon in. He didn't protest. "Can I get a smoke?" he asked as Jamel slid it shut.

"We don't smoke, but we'll get you one," McCall promised, casually.

Harris ran out to buy a fresh pack of cigarettes so they'd be clean of DNA. They wound up sending Chan and Dominguez in to get the sample. Those guys were nonthreatening and could sell ice to an Eskimo.

Chan walked into the cell area first. He'd already opened the cigarettes with gloves on and thrown out eight of them so it wouldn't look fishy. He held the pack through the bars, and Deon took one out. He leaned forward, sticking it out through the bars so Chan could light it.

After a couple of seconds, he looked at Chan. "You gonna watch me smoke?"

"I have to—there's no smoking allowed in the precinct, so we do it on the down-low."

"Wachoo talkin' about? Cops give me smokes all the time."

"Yeah, when we're walking out to the transport van, but not in the cells—especially *these* cells. There's cameras all over the place," he lied.

Deon appeared satisfied with that answer. On cue, Dominguez came in. "CO is coming in. We gotta get ridda the cigarette till she leaves."

Deon looked at them suspiciously. "I can't smoke no more?"

"Not for like a half hour, till she leaves," Dominguez said. He held out an open bag. "Put it in here so I can throw it away before she comes in."

Deon stubbed the cigarette out against the wall and dropped it into the bag. "We'll let you smoke once she leaves, bro."

He nodded, and the two salesmen walked out, casual as always.

* * * * *

Eric and Shayna didn't want the collar, so McCall wound up processing it. His kids' mom was off work, so childcare wasn't an issue. He went up to the front desk and put the handwritten arrest report on it, same place they put all the perps' drugs and belongings while they were being searched.

Sergeant Braggs was still behind the desk. He picked up the report and looked at the narrative—very simple, a few lines. *"At T/P/O (time, place of occurrence), Defendant was observed exiting an FTAP building. Def't does not live there, and had no permission or authority to be inside said building. Defendant fled on foot from officers and struggled, kicked, and flailed his arms, refusing to be handcuffed."*

Sergeant Braggs perused the report like it was twenty lines long instead of three. He looked up at McCall. "I know you write more on your reports than a lot of cops (which was true). But this is kind of a weak trespass. He wasn't observed in the stairwell, the roof, even the hallway—just exiting the building."

McCall started to protest, but Sergeant Braggs held his hand up. "I'm gonna sign it. But you have to write a little more. If it turns out Rothchild's boner is pointed at the right chick, the circumstances of the arrest could be brought up in an evidence hearing. Then the DNA sample is thrown out and we're back to dealing with this shithead."

So what the fuck do you want me to write?! McCall thought but did not say. After three years of working together, Jamel's patience was finally starting to rub off on him. Besides, Sergeant Braggs was one of the good guys.

Sergeant Braggs read the confusion on his face. "Do some digging, bro. We know he doesn't live there. But he likes to hang out there, maybe scores weed from one of the apartments. Run him again—see if he's been collared there before."

"What if he hasn't?"

"Then we'll have to do some creative writing."

* * * * *

Chan and Dominguez had already given the cigarette to Espinoza, who handled the rest of the collection process before sending it to the lab. McCall went to check on Jenkins in the rear cell, since Sergeant Braggs couldn't let Harris get any more overtime watching him. In accordance with procedures, they'd removed his belt and shoelaces—ironically, the perps got these things back when they were transported to the bookings, where they were watched more closely. But perps had hung themselves with clothing before—one of McCall's first arrests had tied his undershirt to the bars and around his neck in a cell full of perps. A few of them ratted him out, luckily, screaming for the desk officer to come in. That had worked out okay, but since then, he'd always checked on his perps regularly, knowing a lot of times there weren't enough personnel to do so.

Jenkins wasn't as Zen as he'd been earlier. As soon as McCall walked into the cell area, he came up to the bars. "What they did with that cigarette, nigga?"

McCall mock-looked around, like he thought Jenkins was talking to someone else. "I don't see any 'niggas' here, *sir*."

Jenkins smiled. It was a mixture of cunning, potential violence, sarcasm, and a *slight* bit of mental illness. "Oh, you tryin' to front like you ain't a street nigga. You what—two, three years younger'n me? I *seen* you around, back in the day. Always by yo'self, even when you was little. Nasty-ass clothes, straight out the charity bin. You ain't even got people, yo! Don't try an' be actin' like you some uppity nigga. All you is is street trash, wearin' a badge that don't mean shit to Obama an' all them high-class negroes."

Even six months ago, McCall would have gotten inches away from the bars, daring this shithead to spit or keep talking shit. He wouldn't have, not the way he was back then. But he was changing. He'd never

308

ANOTHER BODY IN BROOKLYN

admit this, but it was because of Jamel. The way that brother looked up to him—*him*—from nothing and nobody. All his life he'd attacked at the slightest provocation—it almost got him kicked out of the application process for the job. Always walking so straight and cocky, angry eyes letting all the other males in the room know who the Alpha was. Dismissive of any type of weakness (which encompassed almost everything, from reading song lyrics—even rap—to discussing feelings or showing empathy toward cowardly people and deadbeats). Pretty much everything back then. Now, he was mellowing. Truth be told, though, Jamel making googly eyes at the sunset was still kind of gayish.

But that boy was his bro. Family. Jamel grew up in a not-so-great area, but he had loving parents and a middle-class upbringing. It made him a good man. A man who saw his jaded partner's faults as potential strengths and his strengths as much more than they really were. A good man, a brave man. Most of all, though, a decent man.

"I'm going to finish your paperwork so you can get outta here and see the judge, first thing in the morning. I'll get you a few cigs after that."

"Don't bother. I know y'all be tryin' to get my DNA." He spat on the floor of his cell. "Ain't gettin' none of that from one bullshit cigarette! I wiped that shit before I gave it to that Chink fuckin' cop."

McCall smiled. It was genuine, since he knew quickly wiping it wouldn't make much difference, even if it were true. "Guess you showed us, brother Jenkins."

He was walking back to the computer he was using when Sergeant Braggs called him up to the desk. He was looking at something on the computer as McCall approached. "I'm printing this out for you, Shawn. Jenkins got collared in that building two years ago—trespass. They were part of the FTAP program back then, and he was notified. Cite this arrest in the report, and I think we've got it. Clearly, he knew he wasn't allowed in there."

"Thank you, Sarge. I appreciate it."

Sergeant Braggs smiled. "I think that's the first time I've ever heard you say 'thank you,' Shawn. Did the words hurt coming out?"

McCall laughed. "Not too much."

CHAPTER 37

ROTHCHILD: A NEW START

Going into a new command is nerve-wracking. Especially when you've basically been kicked out of your old one, informally or not. Luckily, this precinct had a bigger lot than my old one did, and I found a spot close to the rear door. Not wanting to walk in like a mess, I just took out my patrol bag, in which I had my gun belt, and walked inside. I went up to the desk, behind which a beefy, white, middle-aged lieutenant sat. He looked down at me as I approached.

"You a rookie?"

I actually felt a little flattered that he thought that. "No, sir, I'm Sergeant Rothchild. I just got transferred here."

He didn't give any indication that he'd heard anything about my situation. "You just got promoted?"

"No, I've got two years in rank. I put in to transfer here—it's close to home." This wasn't actually a lie.

"Okay, great. Welcome. You live on the island? A lot of guys here do."

"No, Queens—Kew Gardens." I looked around. There were a few cops mulling about—one by the customer service window, one by the computers, two more in the lobby. All white. I'd just come from a precinct where the population was ninety-something percent black.

311

This precinct had a similar racial makeup. But the cops here, including myself, didn't look as much like the community they policed as my old precinct did. I knew this would be an adjustment.

The lieutenant nodded. "Kew Gardens is a nice area. I was a cop over there. This place is a lot more violent. You'll be busy."

"That's fine with me."

He looked down at me from his perch on the desk, like he was appraising a car or a house. "Long as you're willing to work, you'll be fine here. The CO is in—I'll let him know you're here."

I was on my second day off, not scheduled to start until tomorrow. But the lieutenant seemed like he'd already made up his mind. He picked up the phone and called the CO.

I was wearing nice jeans, a button-down shirt, and casual shoes. Nicer than I usually dressed for manual labor type of shit. But I was glad now that I'd shaved the day before and didn't reek of a guy who'd already given up. I knew that I sometimes did these days.

As soon as I walked into the CO's office, he stood up from his desk and smiled, reaching out his hand to shake mine.

He was an Asian American guy in his late thirties who'd grown up in Brooklyn and still had the accent. "Nice to get to meet the first Jewish sergeant to ever get kicked outta Brooklyn."

I could tell by the smile and friendly way he said it that he was just busting my balls and didn't mean anything by it. I smiled and shook his hand, then he motioned to a chair facing his desk.

"Have a seat, Josh."

Even before my ass hit the chair, he was talking again. "Sorry you had to go through that shit with the brass."

I nodded cautiously.

"You okay from that shooting?"

"Yes, sir. I'm good. Cop I was with is coming back to work soon too."

"Okay, great." He picked up a notepad and glanced at it, then put it back down.

"Never mind the shooting—you're gonna get a Medal of Valor for that, by the way. You had a great arrest record as a cop, nothing but good reviews. I talked to a lot of people about you. I know you got fucked with just for doing your job."

I almost cried. "Thank you, sir."

"Look, I know you wanted to stay in Brooklyn. I worked most of my career in Brooklyn North too. But I'm glad to have a hard-working sergeant to motivate all these fuckin' Queens Marines."

"I'll do my best."

He laughed. "Yeah, I know. Anyway, you're an extra sergeant right now. Least I can do is let you pick your tour."

After dreading what I'd be walking into with my baggage, this was a very welcome surprise. I figured I'd get stuck on midnights for at least a year.

"Is the 4-by shift open, sir?"

"Yeah, that'll be good." His phone rang and he answered it. After a few seconds, he covered the mouthpiece and spoke low. "I gotta take this. It was good meeting you, Josh."

I walked out of that office on cloud nine. What a great fucking guy, I thought. And I was right. Unfortunately, in three weeks he was transferred to Chinatown. But at least I was already settled in by then. You can't get too attached to bosses on this job. The good ones never stay long, while the bad ones stay forever.

CHAPTER 38

ROLL CALL:
WHAT IT WAS ALL FOR

There were ten cops standing roll call. Limited manpower as usual. Sergeant Johnson was standing behind a wooden podium, briefing them on their assignments. The cops were standing with their backs to the bathrooms, which were also used by the public. Sometimes there were bad smells.

Detective Espinoza stepped in from the lobby. Sergeant Johnson looked over at him. "You need anything, Marty?"

Espinoza shook his head. "Just wanted to say something, when you're done."

Sergeant Johnson nodded and continued with the roll call assignments. He read them off. No surprises—all the regular partners were in today. Then he looked at Courtney, the odd man out.

"As I'm sure you all know, Lieutenant Allen just went to the Inspections Unit. We've got a new platoon commander, and he doesn't see the need for a fixed post on Howard during the day shift when we're so short on cops all the time. The CO agreed, so the fixer is done. You're driving me today, Jones. Try not to fuck it up."

Courtney nodded and smiled, glad *that* chapter of his life was finally over.

Sergeant Johnson turned to Espinoza. "All yours, Marty." He stepped aside from the podium so Espinoza could talk to them.

"Thank you, Sarge. I just wanted to wait till everyone involved in this was working—" His gaze fell on Eric, Shayna, Harris, McCall, Chan, Dominguez, and Jones. "—to let you know that we're charging Deon Jenkins with murder. His DNA matched the gun he ditched when you guys chased him—" He looked at Harris and McCall. "— and the ballistics on that gun matched the shell casings found in the hallway on New Year's Day. Plus, he had a motive, being that…" He kept talking, but most of their heads were so swollen they didn't hear.

Patrol cops weren't used to being complimented like this. It was grunt work, handling the things no one else wanted to do day after day, year after year. Getting assaulted and bitten and spat at and cussed at and complained on—half the time by the very people who'd called 911. So to hear a respected member of the Detective Squad praise them felt good.

Espinoza paused and scanned the assembled cops. Reading the look of hunger on Jamel and his partner Shawn's faces, Espinoza let them know: "He's already in custody. Fugitive Unit tracked him down in Westchester County yesterday, squatting in the soot behind an old boiler like a little bitch."

That was just as well, Jamel figured. He was tired of dealing with that asshole anyway.

"So far Jenkins hasn't given up 'Big Boy,' the guy we think put him up to it—but he will, once he realizes how fucked he is. Big Boy's doing a year on a parole violation, so we have time. This murder was a warning for the victim's niece to stop cooperating with the DA's office on the domestic that landed Big Boy back in lockup."

Espinoza continued. "The victim's name was Lawrence Washington. Forty-seven years old. I told his younger sister last night that we caught his murderer. She's one of only a few surviving relatives, along with her children, including her daughter, who used to date Big Boy and was the real target of this murder that was meant to intimidate her. Do you know what his sister said?"

The room was as quiet as it ever got. "She said, 'Thank you and your officers for not giving up on my brother. The rest of the city did, but you didn't.'"

Espinoza took a deep breath, then fixed a steely gaze on the assembled cops. "That's what you did. You brought a little bit of peace to a good person—a home healthcare aide and her three children. You guys and gals gave them hope that they and the people they care about actually matter." He got a little choked up at this point, as did several of the assembled cops. "The way that we, as cops, honor murder victims is to give the family and society a sense of closure. And you guys went above and beyond to do that." He waved his hand in the air. "Unfortunately, Sergeant Rothchild isn't here to join us. But let's all take a moment." He bowed his head. Amazingly, the assembled cops did too. "You are the police. The dividing line between peace and anarchy, justice and atrocity. And you are appreciated."

Courtney piped up before anyone else even thought about speaking. "Can we get that in writing, Espinoza?"

Espinoza gave one of his tight, controlled smiles. He reminded Courtney of a couple of the officers and NCOs he'd worked for in the Army. "Anything you want, bro."

In the end, they all put in for departmental recognition. The special ops lieutenant wasn't as gung-ho about the endeavor as Espinoza was, and they all received the lowest level of recognition that the department gave out. But the speech was nice, and it meant something to all of them.

Jamel was already seated behind the wheel, the engine running. McCall walked up and placed his patrol bag in the back seat, then sat down beside his partner. Jamel turned to him.

"Congratulations, bro. I heard they picked you for the Crime team. When do you start?"

McCall looked confused. "Where'd you hear that?"

Jamel smiled. "C'mon, man, everybody knows."

McCall shook his head. "There's nothing to know. I'm staying on patrol."

Now it was Jamel's turn to look confused. McCall let the moment last, then finally smiled. "I told the lieutenant I wasn't going anywhere without my partner."

"Wait—you turned them down?!"

"Don't make a big deal out of it, Oprah. They said you need about six more months till you're ready for Crime. I told 'em I'll make sure you are, then we'll go together."

It had been McCall's dream to go to Crime ever since they'd started working together. Jamel tried not to tear up.

"Let's not start the waterworks, Jamel. Put the car in drive and let's see what we can get into."

Jamel smiled and did as his partner requested.

CHAPTER 39

ROTHCHILD: ONE LAST SHOT?

Turns out I'd missed my last pistol range qualifying date. The training officer, a nervous sergeant who was terrified of the streets, came up to me when I was seated at the front desk.

"Josh, you realize you haven't been to the shooting range in over a year?" He said it like I'd just fucked his kid. "This isn't good—the borough's gonna go nuts you haven't shot in so long."

I fixed him with a hard look. "I shot a real person a couple of months ago. That's gotta count for something."

He didn't respond, and I went back to updating my entries in the command log.

"You have to go tomorrow morning. We have an open spot on the day shift." I hadn't even realized he was still there.

"Nah, man, let me go on a 4-by. I don't want to have to get up at six tomorrow—the midnight relief is gonna be late. I'm not getting out of here till one."

"You gotta go tomorrow," he said as he walked away, placing a slip on the desk that told me I had to. Even worse, I couldn't go to the inside Brooklyn range anymore since it was only for cops who worked in Brooklyn. I hated the outside range up in the Bronx. You had to deal with the weather and literally hundreds of other cops shooting in

ANOTHER BODY IN BROOKLYN

different relays. It always reminded me of the Police Academy, which was a six-month experience I'd tried hard to put out of my head.

I got four hours of sleep and made it to the range a little late. I didn't mind the area—it was on the water and there was brush and marsh around—we used to go to nearby City Island when I was a kid, and it always brought back fond memories. But the day was usually a pain in the ass, hundreds of cops crammed into a military-style room, listening to safety and tactics lectures from guys who had almost no street experience. To make it worse, the police instructors would play their boot camp games, acting out drill instructor shit with each other.

The thing about a department as big as the NYPD is that you might go to the range and see people you went to the Academy with, worked with, knew socially…or you might not. I hadn't seen anyone familiar so far. Since I'd gotten here a little late, I was in the third and last shooting relay. So I had some time to wander around the place before my safety class.

It was a nice day, so I didn't really mind that there wasn't anything to see around there. We couldn't wander too far, so I just walked around the Quonset huts. I was about to head back into the cafeteria to get another coffee when I saw her. Her back was to me, but I knew that hair and body anywhere. She was walking toward the main classroom building, her head resting on the shoulder of a male beside her.

I watched them as they made their way into the building. When he turned to get the door for her, I saw it was my old coworker, Mark Sanchez.

That old heart-dropping feeling I'd grown so used to whenever the situation became seemingly hopeless again didn't come this time. Instead of lamenting that last night with her as something sad and final, I still felt it for what it was. A beautiful experience.

And that's the way I remember Melanie. Happy, close to someone who clearly cared about her. I didn't go to their wedding a year later, even though I was invited. I wanted my memories of her to be what they were.

I never saw either of them again, but I heard they've got three kids.

I was in such a reverie that I nearly bumped into Richie Willcox from the precinct I'd worked in before I got promoted. He was a big white guy in his late forties who got along with everyone. Twenty-five years on patrol, still manning a sector car as his contemporaries were promoted, went to other units, or retired. Great guy—he'd be there for you no matter what. We actually partnered up for about six months when I first got into a sector car. After about three months, I was making most of the decisions, other than where to eat. Richie's been accused of a lot of things—drinking too much, smoking too much, being an all-around fun guy. He's never been accused of being a genius, though.

"Shit, Josh, you okay?" Richie was paying attention, as usual. Guys like him never got into their own heads.

"Yeah, Richie. Sorry about that."

"No worries, bro. How you doin' after the shooting and everything?"

"I'm good." This was the answer I would automatically give, of course. I hadn't kept in touch with Richie enough to confide in him at this point. But then I smiled, and I realized it was true. "Yeah, man, I'm good. What relay you in?"

Turns out we were in the same relay. It can get a little confusing, as different groups are called at different times to do things like unload their guns on the firing line, go to classes, have their guns inspected, etc. Richie and I got coffee in the cafeteria and waited.

There was an announcement over the loudspeaker, but we were talking, catching up, and didn't hear what it said. But we saw a bunch of people stand up and head out the door. Since we were the last relay, I figured that was us too.

Richie looked at me quizzically. "We going now, Josh?"

I indicated the group of people heading out the doors. "Just blindly follow the crowd like you've been doing the last twenty-five years, Richie. It'll work out."

He laughed, knowing this was in many ways true.

EPILOGUE

The years have gone by. I finally found a great woman and got married. I've got two wonderful kids, and I'm still working as a patrol sergeant. When the new cops arrive in the precinct in big groups, I always give them an informal class. Sure, I cover tactics, "best practices," etc. But in the end, I tell them this: "This precinct has a high crime rate. But there's a population of over 120,000 people. Ninety-nine percent of them are good, law-abiding citizens. Honest, hardworking people. We have to aggressively go after the small group of criminals who are responsible for almost all of the serious crimes. If you arrest them for shoplifting, that's great. Catch them after they've just committed a serious crime, even better. But in the end, you have to care about the victims. ALL OF THEM. No matter where they're from, what they look like, where they work, who they know—they are what matters."

"As long as you're not a racist or a coward or a bully, you're willing to learn from your mistakes, and you care about people—even a little—you're going to be great cops. Despite everything that's happened these last ten years, this is still a great job. I've never once regretted taking it, and they're gonna have to carry me out."

If I'm lucky, a little less than half of the two dozen young cops get the message. Like most things in life, you have to take what you can get.

ACKNOWLEDGMENTS

I would like to thank my publishing team: David Aretha, an excellent editor who provided many great suggestions, Martha Bullen of Bullen Publishing Services, whose advice and guidance have been invaluable, the great people at Ebook Launch for their outstanding work, especially on the book cover, and Jeremy Avenarius for his website design. I would also like to thank my family and my advance readers.

About the Author

David Goldstein grew up in New York and attended Florida State University, where he earned a degree in Criminology.

After serving as an officer in the U.S. Marine Corps, David spent two and a half years as a patrol officer with the LAPD in Los Angeles. He then joined the NYPD and served in high-crime areas in northern Brooklyn before becoming a Lieutenant/Platoon Commander in South Jamaica, Queens. After retiring from the NYPD in 2020, he served for four years as a campus police officer in Boston.

Another Body in Brooklyn is David's debut crime novel. He decided to write this book because he has read too many unrealistic police procedurals where a cop or detective has all the time in the world to solve one murder, unburdened by other, unrelated crimes. However, in a busy patrol area, officers must deal with many other things that pop up before, after, and sometimes during the murder. While this book has aspects of a murder mystery, it is really a story of the workings of a busy police precinct and the men and women who are tasked with being society's first line between order and chaos.

He also wanted to showcase the tough work and even tougher decisions that patrol officers have to make with limited time and resources. While detectives investigating homicides are sometimes the only people who speak for the dead, they too are often burdened with new crimes and a lack of support after the initial phases of the investigation.

David is also the author of a book of short crime fiction, *Back Alleys and Unauthorized Donut Shops*. His upcoming science fiction book will be released in 2026.

David recently moved back to New York after five years in Massachusetts. In his spare time, he enjoys spending time with his family, exercising, and reading about politics and science. To learn more or to contact David, visit www.anotherbodyinbrooklyn.com.

www.ingramcontent.com/pod-product-compliance
Lightning Source LLC
Chambersburg PA
CBHW050008120726

47903CB00006B/1682